WHERE MAGICS MIX

BOOK 1

V. T. WREN

THE STORIES OF SCHEETZ

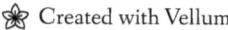

For Adam

*Remember that time you drove me out to
meet your parents? It was getting dark, out on
some country back road, and you looked at
me from the driver's seat and said...*

*"You barely know me and you just got in my car
and let me drive you out to the middle of nowhere.
How do you know I'm not a serial killer?"*

*That's when I knew my life with you
was never going to be boring.*

*(Thank goodness he wasn't, if he was,
you'd be reading something else.)*

CONTENTS

MAGICS MIX

LOST

TRAPPED

HIDING

ALONE

BOOKED

SPELLED

LIAR

HUNTED

RUNNING

SHATTERED

TAKEN

ALLIES

SHADOWS

STOLEN

BROKEN

SPILLED

AFTER

MAGICS MIX

SAM BREATHED MAGIC.

SHE BELIEVED IN IT SO DEEPLY, AT TIMES YOU
COULDN'T HELP BUT BELIEVE IN IT TOO.

BUT THEN SHE DIED...

AND JUST LIKE THAT, SO DID THE MAGIC.

LEAVING FOUR GIRLS BEHIND TO PICK UP THE PIECES OF
THEIR BROKEN HEARTS AND SHATTERED DREAMS...

UNLESS THEY CAN FIND THE MAGIC AGAIN.

LOST

1

Snow? I'd never seen snow before... had I?

My back on the ground, staring up at a cloudy, light-gray sky. Still spruce needles wore a thin white blanket, trying to block the snowflakes that slowly drifted down to meet me, and it all seemed unfamiliar... but not just the snow.

There was a heaviness in my bones, weighing me down. Half-lodged in the ice, numb to life itself as if I'd fallen asleep in a stream, waiting for it to freeze around me. The cold reached into my veins, holding me hostage. I pulled free of its hold, but it followed me up, sitting alongside me as I searched the empty forest. Layers of scattered trees blocked me inside, holding me captive in winter silence.

Numb. Physically, and mentally.

Nothing but questions, and I didn't know any of it. The confusion left an unsettling pit in my stomach. I couldn't recall a single memory prior to waking up.

Where did I come from? Where was I headed? Home? Family? I didn't even know my name. I'd been disconnected. Unplugged from my own mind.

I was lost.

I stood, as if a few feet in height would show me all the answers, but as I spun around, there was still nothing but the shadows of wooded secrets.

Two thin, off-white shoes barely reached my ankles, worn-out like I'd been living in them every day for a year, but I still didn't know them. The long cut in my jeans was clearly not a style choice, and paired with the bright red, short-sleeved shirt, they seemed as unprepared for the environment as I was.

Long scrapes lined my skin from hand to elbow, and the dried blood under my nails explained how, but not why.

I hugged my fingers under my arms at my sides, trying to thaw them, but mostly I was desperate to hide them from my view.

Not a single footprint marked the merciless, snow-brushed paths around me. I shivered as flakes continued to fall, forsaking me from any clues to my past.

A black bird soared above me, pointed the other way as something shifted through the trees ahead. My heart stopped, frozen in panic, watching, listening, waiting.

Snap.

I turned to run as the instinct to escape ignited within my chest, pumping through my blood. Ache pounded the pads of my feet with each step, as if I were on the last leg of a marathon. A marathon that I couldn't remember.

I chased after the crow, praying it knew the way out, when I hit a ledge. My arms hugged the branch of a tree as the ground crumbled, dropping off below my feet, watching as the bird's charcoal feathers carried on freely across the open sky without me.

The turning forest ran on forever, up and down across the mountain horizon ahead, showing off its autumn reds and golds. At the base was a small break in the tree line where man left his mark. Docks ran along a body of water as it rolled out through the mountains, small boats drifting across the tide. Chimney smoke lightly rose from the distant rooftops lining the roads, promising warmth and aid, and I desperately needed their help.

This had to be home, it was the only place here... so why didn't I know it?

I met up with a stream and followed it down, hoping it would lead me to a road before I had to cross over. The trickle of freezing water made me shiver, too cold to risk stepping through.

Silver fish scurried over the rocks, and the clear, clean water hid none of it. I stopped to watch them swim by one after another, when I realized what other wildlife might thrive through the woods around me. What predators crossed over the same trails I did?

My pace picked up again towards town. Whatever time it was, my desperation to get somewhere safe by nightfall hoped it was still early. Clouds or not, if I was that cold with the sun out, I wasn't going to make it through the night without warming up.

The town itself felt tiny. Old-fashioned shops lined the main, slushy road, and the forest consumed the world around it. Between two slopes of trees, the ocean waved in, promising another world out beyond the horizon.

"Where am I?" I muttered, lost somewhere between awe and frustration.

People walked up and down the road with purpose. Most probably didn't get pulled out into the cold without a destination. I searched their faces as I passed through, expecting to find someone familiar. Tourist stops and shops seemed to take over the street as men, women, and bundled-up kids went in and out.

One woman smiled toward me politely, but she didn't really look at me as she turned out of a store and went the other way. Three shirts hung up on the other side of the glass, each with the word *Swanoke* written across them in different colors.

I was at a loss. Who should I talk to? Where should I go? At the very least, I needed to get warm.

Stepping forward towards the souvenir shop, a low croak made me jump, and my ankle rolled against the curb. I barely noticed the black bird sitting on the street sign above me as I fell.

Someone caught me below my arms, helping me find my balance again. I turned to look up at the stranger, but his faint, crooked, closed-lipped smile didn't exactly seem pleased as his dark eyes glossed me over.

"Lost?" he asked, searching my face. The intensity in his eyes made my insides cower.

"That crow," I explained. "It made me jump."

"Raven," he corrected. "And I'm sure she didn't mean it." His eyes flashed up over my ear, lips closing firmly again as his teeth flexed behind them.

"Are you okay?" a more concerned voice called out. A woman darted down the walkway to join us. I couldn't help but feel jealous of the strawberry-blonde braid that hid behind the warmth of her half-zipped coat. Her rosy cheeks freckled and happy as she reached for my arm, hesitating only when she noticed the cuts, gently bracing closer to my wrist instead.

"Do I know you?" I asked her.

Her smile dropped. "I don't think so. Have we met?"

A new sense of panic woke up inside me.

"You're bleeding. It seems like you might need some stitching, or at least—" her voice went on as the man who caught me stepped around behind her. He continued to study my face so seriously as she rambled, like he was trying to figure something out.

"What happened to your head?" The woman hesitated, waiting for me to explain. "What's your name?" she added when I didn't answer.

"What?" I asked, barely registering her words. *My name?* I couldn't give her an answer. I didn't have an answer. "I don't know," I admitted, cheeks warming in embarrassment.

"You must be freezing. Come on, my dad's office is just down this way." She slid out of her coat and wrapped it over my shoulders.

"What?" I must have missed something.

"My father." She said it like I should already know. She paused, halfway through zipping up the coat in front of me to meet my eyes, clearly repeating the details I hadn't heard.

"He's a doctor. You hit your head. It's bleeding."

"I did?" I reflexively reached up to feel. The hair above my right ear was stiff with dried, frozen blood, and the tender spot beneath it made me wince.

"Oh. I guess I did."

"You don't remember?" she asked.

"No."

Her concern became antsy as she turned toward the man. "Help me, would you, Mylo?"

He didn't seem pleased to be volunteered, but she didn't give him much of a choice. She stepped around to support my right arm, and he stepped to my left.

"Do you think he'll know me?" I asked. "Your dad. Maybe he has my medical records."

"Oh, honey." Her teeth clenched together as her sympathetic light-blue eyes met mine. Then they flashed up at Mylo, who remained silent.

"What is it?" I asked.

She shook her head, obviously playing off her initial response. "Maybe you're right."

"You don't think he will."

"It's a small town," Mylo explained. "She thinks it's unlikely that you both grew up here and never met."

I looked from Mylo back to the woman. She gave him a quick glare for calling her out, then bit her lip with a guilty shrug. "I'm sorry, it's just, we get a lot of tourists."

"Maybe I just moved here this year," I argued defensively.

She patted my arm. "Maybe you did."

"By the way, where is here?" I asked as we started walking again.

"Swanoke," Mylo answered dryly. "Alaska."

My eyes went wide. "Alaska?" The word echoed through my head. It felt so far away. Too far. This couldn't be home.

Dr. Quinn's waiting room welcomed me with a calm warmth that soothed away my fears. I was with people again, I was safe. This doctor was going to help me get home. Everything was going to be okay.

"Emma!" The receptionist welcomed us in, and the woman at my side did all the talking.

Emma.

She fit right in, from her snug, knitted, pink hat, to the boots tucked beneath her jeans. The kind energy she wore was welcoming and contagious. Standing next to her almost made me feel like an imposter. This was her hometown. She belonged here, and I didn't.

"Hey Sue!" she answered. Emma let go of me and moved to the counter, folding her arms over the edge as she leaned into it. I glanced up at Mylo, who wordlessly let my arm remain linked with his, jaw flexing tighter again.

"We've got a new patient for ya," Emma announced.

The brunette behind the desk rolled her chair around to grab a blank form, spinning back toward us to set it on the counter with a pen on top. My eyes scanned over it, the blank lines requesting simple, basic info, and all the worry came tumbling back in.

NAME.
DATE OF BIRTH.
PHONE NUMBER.
ADDRESS.
MEDICAL HISTORY.

Blood pounded harder through my veins, my heart panicking. My eyes flashed up from the form, to Sue's, as a shallow breath caught in my throat. Pulling my arm free from Mylo's, I wiped both hands on my pants.

"Will you be using insurance?" Sue asked.

Emma grabbed the paper and slid it in front of herself. "Bit of a Jane Doe situation here, Sue," she explained for me.

"Aw," Sue answered more sympathetically. "So no insurance then." She winked at me, clearly trying to make a little joke. I forced a returning smile, but it was empty.

Mylo pressed a reassuring hand against my back as I let out a silent breath of relief. I looked up at him, and he gave a polite nod. Then his gaze shifted to the side of my head. The side that had dried blood smeared down it. His hand fell as he took a step back.

"I have an appointment," he commented.

"You're leaving?" My words sounded more disappointed than they should have.

"Thank you for helping," Emma answered over me. "We've got it from here," she added with committed enthusiasm as she wrapped an arm around me for a quick squeeze. He nodded at her over my shoulder, then dropped his gaze back to mine.

"Work calls," he explained, answering my question. He held up a buzzing phone just as the screen lit to answer it.

"Literally." I sighed. "Well. Thank you."

"Good luck," he finished, turning toward the door. "Jane."

2

JANE

"You really don't remember how you hit your head?" Dr. Quinn asked for the third time. The pale, middle-aged man studied my expression through his magnifying-glass-quality glasses. The rolled-up sleeves on his striped, blue, button-up flannel seemed out of place on a practicing doctor, but as he took notes on his clipboard, with the stethoscope around his neck, it balanced out.

"No. I don't remember anything."

He sighed, nodding his resignation. His content energy was easy to work with, not pushing any harder.

"Well, you're lucky. It looks bad based on the blood, but it's a small cut. It stopped bleeding well before you stepped into my office. Now that just leaves us with—"

"A thousand other questions." Lucky wasn't the word I would use.

He bounced his head back and forth. "Well," he gave in and nodded. "Yes, but I don't want you to worry about those right now."

"Not worry about them?" I studied his face, was he

mad? "Not worry about my life? Just pretend nothing before today happened?"

"Now, that's not what I said," he argued. "Stressing out over it isn't the answer. These things tend to come naturally. You never know what might trigger some memories back in."

"And I just wait around and hope that something does?"

Dr. Quinn stood, starting to reach toward my collar, but he paused.

"May I?" he asked. I looked into his eyes and nodded. He shifted the neckline of my shirt to one side, stepping out of my line of sight.

The reflection was alarming. I didn't know the girl in the mirror, sitting there staring back at me. She was a stranger. Why couldn't I remember her? I reached up to rub the sore spot hiding beneath a fading bruise. My eyes flashed back to Dr. Quinn, who gave a sympathetic half-smile, a sad hint of pity behind it.

Did he think I'd been abused? I looked back at the stranger again, adjusting against the thin paper lining beneath me, the scent of sterilizing products growing stronger as I stared into her eyes. *Was I losing it? Had I been abused?*

I fixed the shirt back over the bruise, grateful Dr. Quinn kept discreet with Emma staring at her phone in the corner behind us.

"Let's give it a few days," he suggested. "Seems you have a concussion, resulting in some amnesia. Give your mind time to rest and heal."

"I can't just do nothing. A few days? What if people are waiting on me? Worried about me?"

"I'll talk to the sheriff, see if he can do some digging. In the meantime, you rest!" His words were an order as he pointed at me. "No screens, nothing that strains your eyes. Limit socializing, and don't over-exert yourself. The point of this is to let your body rest. Maybe don't go out hiking by yourself anytime soon."

I rolled my eyes. As if I were planning on that. "I can't just sit around!"

"Too bad!" he argued. "If you have to do something, go talk to Dr. Marks. Maybe he can shed some light into that head of yours."

"I didn't even think of that!" Emma chimed in, tucking her phone back into her purse. She smiled at me. "He's a psychiatrist, but honestly, I think most people just go to him for a good therapy talk."

I ignored her quick testimonial. Therapy was the last thing I had on my mind.

"I don't even know where I live," I argued. My hands patted against my empty pockets. "No money, no nothing."

Dr. Quinn looked at Emma. "Set her up in the cottage. Maybe one of Jake's coats is still sitting around." I looked at Emma's coat, folded up on the empty chair next to her, wishing I had my own.

Emma nodded, still smiling. I knew she was just trying to be positive and support me, but she almost acted like everything was fine as my whole life crumbled.

"This is weird," I informed them both.

"It is," Dr. Quinn agreed. At least he wasn't trying to sugar-coat it. He reached a hand toward me, shaking mine as I accepted it. "But I don't want you stressing out. We're going to help you through this."

"Jane," Emma offered. She cocked her head, studying me over. "I like that. Has a nice ring to it."

"Mylo was onto something," I commented in a low

voice. My gaze fell to the floor. The nickname wasn't as amusing to me. I would have preferred a real name.

"Jane," Dr. Quinn repeated. I searched his face, wishing there were alternatives, but there weren't. Ready or not, I was amnesia Jane, stuck in Swanoke, Alaska.

With a list of things to avoid, sleep included, and explicit instructions to call Dr. Quinn if I got nauseated or felt worse, Emma was eager to escort me home.

The cottage was a little bunk house down the path behind their main home. The warm, tan stones and green accents fit right into the forest around it, with a neat stone pathway and front porch seating to match a doctor's budget.

Everything inside was happy and bright. Deep brown wooden furniture, decorated with a simple teal and yellow theme, complimented by a few coral touches to pull it all together. It made quite the guest house, though I was mostly interested in the large, quilt-covered, king-sized bed. It would sure beat waking up lost in the woods.

"So glad you stumbled into town on the weekend. Normally I'd be working."

"What do you do?"

"I teach third grade." She beamed as she said it. Of course she did, she totally passed the elementary teacher vibe check. "It's been a busy start to the school year."

"Is it Saturday?" I asked.

"Sunday. Dad's slow day. He's only in the office for a few morning hours unless he gets called."

"Got it." I awkwardly looked around the house, unsure what to do.

"Hopefully you remember some things soon. Maybe I can help you come up with stuff to do in the meantime. You might try the library. Maybe looking through some books could help jog your memories. And Dr. Marks! He really is amazing, even if you just need someone to talk to. He's really good at his job. Helped a lot of people here in town."

"I don't need a shrink."

She shrugged. "Whatever you say, Janey."

"I've known you barely two hours and you've nick-named my nickname."

"What if your name really is Jane," she mused.

"Then I'd be asking Mylo how he guessed it."

Emma stuck around all day, promising a shopping trip, delicious meals, and friendship, but I didn't want any of it. I didn't want to accept that I'd be stuck there long enough to need my own pair of boots, to take her up on future plans. They'd already done too much. Her dad instructed her to keep an eye on me, but I felt like a child.

Dr. Quinn stopped by that evening to check in, and since I'd made it through the day without getting sick or falling asleep, I had his okay to turn in for the night.

The cottage felt lonely when they left it. I'd been looking forward to some space, but as soon as I had it, fear replaced the company. What if I was stuck there forever? What if my real home never found me, the people I left behind? If I never matched up all the tiny puzzle pieces that made up my life, my childhood, and I never got to know the person that I was before? It felt like I'd be going forward as a fake.

I stared at the light-pink pajamas sitting on the bath-room counter, getting ready to shower off the day. I still felt frozen, unable to process everything that had happened. I looked at the bruise on my neck, studied the long scratches on my arms. I hadn't even been able to wake up my appetite as anxiety knotted my stomach tight, only managing a few scrambled bites to prove I was okay. To lie.

I watched the stranger in the mirror, her ratted, dirty-blonde hair. The tired, pale circles beneath her brown eyes as she stared back at me, until the steam blocked her out.

There couldn't have been a 'more alone' than that moment, that shower, as I cried into the wall, purging out the emotions I'd held back all day long. I was desperate for the hot water to wash away my bloody nightmare, this facade of a girl that no-one knew.

Uncertainty left me hiding in the blankets, waiting for my answers to come find me. Why was I lost in the woods? Why was I alone? It felt as if something watched me through the windows, and that urge to run away crept back in again... but what was I running from?

3

JANE

I t was like one of those dreams where you're falling into nothing, into darkness, and you don't really know it until you hit the shadows beneath you.

I startled up from the partially melted snow, ready to start running again. The winter breeze stung my back as Emma's damp, pink pajamas clung to my skin. My eyes bounced between trees, branch to branch in a still forest, isolating me under its silent watch as I fought against the need to escape... but there was nothing there.

I bent down, curling forward over my knees, squeezing the numb feet that cried against the cold, but my hands weren't any warmer. I couldn't last outside much longer.

What had happened? I'd gone to sleep in Dr. Quinn's guest house, so why was I lost in the middle of the woods again?

My face scrunched as I stood up, fighting the tears that begged to pool over as I took a sensitive step forward, unsure which direction to go.

I slowly spun, searching the trees, when a black bird

stopped me in my tracks. Was it the same black bird? It watched from its perch, meeting my eyes, before it dropped from the branch and blew past me. I turned after it as the raven glided into the distance, my gaze dropping to the snow. This time there were footprints to lead me back.

I studied the trail I'd left behind, directly below the raven's path. The steps were spaced out in a sprint, as if I'd run through my unconsciousness.

"What is wrong with me?" I whispered.

I followed the pathway back like a lifeline, until the footprints faded and my panic surged. The bird had gone too. Not that I trusted it to take me back to Dr. Quinn's, but at least it would have given me something.

I was alone again, consumed by nature, lost in the Alaskan wild. Harsh winters, and mountains full of wildlife. That's what Alaska was known for, right?

My eyes scanned the trees again, an active imagination seizing my thoughts. The echo of wheels on a wet road called me closer from down the hill, and I didn't wait to answer. I broke through the trees, not as far as I'd felt, straight into the road. The familiar little main street welcomed me back to safety again as I ditched the forest behind me.

Three men passed me by, dressed up to go fishing from what I could tell, too busy in their conversation to notice the girl with no shoes. I hurried past, avoiding anything more. Learning quickly that I'd started my day too early, I tried one locked shop door after another. All I wanted was to escape the cold!

A familiar, low croaking call sounded across the road. The raven watched me, perched atop a simple gray, brick building. What did it want from me? None of that mattered if it led me to an open door. I took the chance, and ran across. My fingers wrapped around the handle, starting to pull, when the name on the door caught my eye.

Dr. Marks. Psychiatrist.

"You're joking," I muttered. Warmth poured through the cracked door, demanding that I continue inside, and I pulled it open, too desperate to hide in its promise of comfort.

"Lost again?" The words made me jump, finding Mylo down a short hall. He didn't move, looking me over in question.

"Yeah," I answered awkwardly.

"You're bleeding," he commented. "*Again.*" His eyes darkened as they fell to my arms, and there was no hiding the long fresh cuts added to the old. "Does anybody know you're here?"

"Dr. Quinn suggested that I might try some therapy," I explained, trying to play it off.

"No luck with the memories, then?" He stood still, as if he were locked in place.

I shook my head, avoiding his eyes.

"Come take a seat then," he offered, eying my bare feet. His hand softly gestured to the open door at his side.

I pointed back at the entrance, knowing I was outside of the posted hours. "It doesn't look like he's in the office yet. I think I'll just find my way back to Emma's before they realize I'm gone."

"I'll give you a ride. Warm up a moment while I grab my things."

"Are you sure?" I asked. "I feel bad."

"Don't," he answered, finally breaking from his spot to lead inside the office. I gave in and followed.

A long gray couch sat in the middle, two similar chairs across from it. A small black table sat in the center, a matching black desk and chair below the large window across the room. A bookshelf stretched beneath the window, lined with strictly black, hardcover books. The sleek, neutral tones were the complete opposite of Dr. Quinn's warm, inviting guest house.

"Wow," I commented, taking a seat where he offered while he moved to a tall cabinet. "He has quite the office."

Mylo was quiet, shuffling through for a moment before he closed the door to answer. "You don't like it?"

"It's kind of dark," I admitted. The room lacked color, that was a simple fact.

"Just like this jacket, but that doesn't change its warmth." He handed a black, button-up jacket over my chair before sitting across from me.

"We need to find you some shoes," Mylo commented.

One foot tucked beneath the other as I tried to hide my embarrassment. "Not sure someone remembers to put on shoes before they sleepwalk into the forest."

"Then maybe someone should go to sleep with their shoes already on," he suggested without skipping a beat. "Maybe a warm black jacket too. Unseasonably cold out there this year, isn't it. Like we've skipped right past fall."

I fought back tears of humiliation, wishing I could walk away. "Is there a restroom?"

He met my eyes before looking across the room to a blank closed door. I moved toward it fast, desperate to have a moment alone.

The girl in the mirror stopped me again, eying me from

another dimension, and this time a part of me hated her. I wanted to grab her shoulders and shake her awake, to scream at her– *who are you!* The dry blood in my nails caught my eye, the long scratches down my arms. I'd done this to myself, ripped through my own skin.

I turned on the hot water and grabbed the soap, but the blood was like a rusty stain that wouldn't clear, no matter how hard I scrubbed.

"Come off!" I ordered, crying at my own skin. Mylo knocked, and the door I failed to latch swung open.

"Is everything okay in there?" he asked, hesitant to look around the corner.

"No!" I cried. "Nothing about this is okay!" I still scrubbed at my fingers, my arms, blind to whether the blood had actually washed off yet. I wanted to scrub my whole body, was it even my body? Everything felt wrong. I didn't recognize a single freckle on my skin, a strand of hair on my head. How could I look into those brown eyes in the mirror and even begin to claim them as my own? My brain was broken. I couldn't sleep right, I couldn't even breathe right as constant panic pumped through my chest.

Mylo moved fast, reaching into the steaming water to wrap his hands over mine. "You're going to make it bleed more," he warned. My eyes shut tight as I tried to force deeper breaths. This wasn't the time to lose it.

His unease was clear as one hand cautiously let go to turn off the water and grab the hand towel. He let go completely as he offered it to me. I turned toward him as I accepted it, when I realized my blood would ruin the pristine, white cloth.

"Sorry," I whispered.

He took a step backward, slowly letting out a breath as

he focused on my face again. "I'm sorry," he countered. "I wasn't very professional before. Mylo Marks. And I'd be happy to listen, regardless of the hours posted on my door."

"You?" I asked, taken by surprise. "You're the *amazing* therapist?" I wanted to smack my forehead. "I'm sorry, I should have realized."

"Well, I don't usually say it like that." He pressed an arm against the door to hold it while I walked through. I'd just had a full mental breakdown in front of the town therapist.

"I don't have money," I warned. "Insurance, nothing. I can't even tell you my name or age."

"Why don't you just tell me what you do know." He gestured back at the couch, and I gave in.

"What's the first thing you remember?" he asked as he sat across from me.

"The forest. The sky was white... snowing. I woke up on the ground. That black bird—"

"The raven," he offered.

"Yes, there was a raven. I was scared of something. My feet ached like I'd been running all night, but there was nothing there. I followed the—" *bird? No, that sounded crazy.* "The water. It led me here. Everything I saw was wrong. I didn't know any of it, all I knew was that it wasn't me. When I look in the mirror... it's not... me."

"You followed a stream here," he clarified, taking in the details one by one.

"Yes." His words put me back on track. "That's when I stumbled into you. Dr. Quinn says I must have gotten a concussion when I hit my head."

"You don't know what you were running from?" Mylo leaned forward, staring intently into my eyes. My head shook. I had no idea. What did he expect me to say? I stood up, ready to bolt, but he stood to mirror me across the table.

"I shouldn't have come here, I don't want therapy... I was just lost, and cold, and—"

"Do you still want that ride?" he asked. He pulled a key from his pocket to dangle between us. "Now that your feet have thawed a bit?" He remained so calm, giving me my space. I sighed, grateful he didn't try to talk me out of it, didn't try pushing me to open up.

"Can you keep this between us?" I asked. "I don't want Dr. Quinn or Emma to feel like they have to watch me any more than they already do."

"Waking up lost in the forest is definitely better than that," he mocked sarcastically. "Unfortunately, doctor-patient confidentiality only applies to patients."

"I sat on your couch, didn't I? Dr. Quinn just wants me to sit around and relax, but how can I relax when every single breath is stressing me out?"

Mylo took a step closer. He grabbed the untouched jacket from the seat behind me, holding it open so I could slide into it. I stared at the bloody rag in my hands, not wanting to stain his jacket too.

"My blood will ruin it," I argued.

He didn't move. "Then it's a good thing it's black."

I followed his lead, sliding both arms in, and he avoided my eyes as he did up the buttons.

"Maybe we can talk some more in the car," he offered.

I lifted the ruined hand towel. "What should I do with this?"

He stared evenly at the bloody cloth between us, a slight twitch beneath his eye as if he were really trying to decide.

"You'd better keep that," he suggested, but it almost

sounded like a warning. I rolled it up and stuffed it into the jacket pocket, deciding I'd have to find him a replacement.

I hesitated at the door, dreading the cold outside, even if I only had to face it to the parking lot. My feet were not ready to take on a second round with the frozen, morning cement.

"Come on," Mylo offered, hunching down with his arms out so I could climb on his back.

"What? Seriously?"

"Yeah, super serious." A hint of sarcasm laced his words. "It's not far." He didn't move, waiting for me to cave.

I jumped up, feeling silly wrapping my arms around the front of him, hugging his neck like a child. We were still strangers, but it was all I had. He kept things simple, and I was grateful for that. I kept my arms further down, worried that I would choke him, but it didn't actually seem like he was breathing at all. When we got to the car, he gently grabbed my wrists, pulling them slowly away as I sat inside.

The cold leather seats weren't as welcoming as the couch in his office, but they beat bare feet on the pavement outside. We rode in silence, my anxiety sweeping through me. Why couldn't I have woken up with answers? Something, anything, to help steer me back? I was still just as lost as I was the day before.

"What are you most worried about?" Mylo asked as he pulled into the long gravel driveway. I stared at him, less desperate to escape now that Dr. Quinn's house was right in front of me. His dark eyes were mesmerizing, staring into mine as if they could pull the words right out.

"Never getting my memories back," I started to blurt out. "Bothering Emma and Dr. Quinn. Waking up too lost to find my way back." I guess that had already happened though. I was permanently lost. He remained quiet, letting me purge my fears. "I have a life. It's out there some-where... but I'm missing it. I look at myself, and I'm a stranger."

I broke eye contact, turning toward the house. Through the window, everything looked just as calm and neat as the day before.

"You are going to need some warmer clothes."

"Accepting that is like accepting that I'm stuck here." The words spilled out before I could stop them. "Sorry. It's nothing against... I just–"

"Want your life back."

"Besides," I went on. "I have nothing, and Emma and Dr. Quinn are already doing too much. I won't let her spend her money on me."

"Fair enough," he answered, opening his door to get out.

I stepped into the rocks, deciding I could manage the short walk to the door, as Mylo moved back toward the trunk. He pulled out a pair of ankle-high, brown hiking boots by the shoe laces, carrying them at his side as he met me on the porch. He held them up for a moment to show me, his expression as casual and calm as always.

"You do need a pair of boots, though," he stated before dropping them back down to dangle at his side. "If you're going to keep waking up out there." He gestured up at the hills of trees as I shifted the last step toward the door, standing on the porch mat.

"They'll be big on you," he added.

"You own something that's not black?" I asked, pretending to be shocked as I turned toward him.

For a moment, Mylo stared deeper into my eyes. I got a little lightheaded when he set the boots down on the mat next to me.

"Not anymore," he answered as he turned to leave. "I've

got a few tricks up my sleeve. Let me know if you want to talk again," he called, halfway back to his car.

"I don't want a shrink!"

He opened his door, standing behind it as he paused to look at me. "Yeah, but you might want a friend. My door's open."

TRAPPED

4

HARPER

I'd always wanted to spend time in Maine. Ben made sure to post pictures of the trees and streams and anything else that might keep moving there on my radar until I did. To be honest, since ending things with Zack and losing Sam, moving away was the only thing left on my radar. Somewhere new, where I could sit to write, wrapped up in a cozy blanket on the inside of a rainy window. That was exactly where I needed to be.

I'd gotten so lost admiring the lightly-changing, deep-green wall of leaves that ran each road, I almost missed Ben's house entirely. It seemed early for signs of autumn to start popping through, but then again, I was from small-town Louisiana, where half of the time, fall colors didn't show up until November. Stepping out of my run-down, little red car, I took in a deep breath of the cool, humid air.

Was there a better place to snuggle up next to a fire and work?

It was weird to leave home. To pack my suitcase knowing that I wouldn't be coming back for a long time. Dad would never be ready for his little girl to go, but mom couldn't wait to hear about the adventures. I think they both knew I needed the change though.

I pulled out my phone, snapping a picture of the forest line behind Ben's house to send the girls.

I hadn't been as active on the group chat since Sam died, but I fought to keep it alive. I wasn't ready to lose our never-ending messages full of pictures from our adventures, long strings of late night gossip, funny stories, compliments, or over-all comfort. It was still too important. It couldn't die with her. But I also hoped they all felt some of the same fun and freedom approaching that I did. This was a fresh start, and I was taking it.

The messages were missing a piece, maybe even the main piece, but the rest of us still had to stay connected.

I hit send, just as Ben stepped out onto his porch. Throwing the car door shut, I cautiously ran up the wet path to hug him.

"Benny!" I called, letting his tall figure swing me around in a circle. "I missed you!"

Ben had always been my favorite cousin. Of course, he was my only cousin, but I couldn't imagine a better one. Our moms were best friends, therefore so were we. He was like an older brother that I got along with perfectly. He'd been one of the first people to learn sign language when we were kids, and he learned it all for me, opening the doorway to an early bond of friendship. Sometimes Benny would tell me that it was our secret language, anything to make me feel special. Between our close age, and matching dark hair, people mistook us for siblings all the time, and we felt so sneaky not correcting them.

"It took you long enough to graduate and come join me!"

"Forever!" I agreed. "What was your mom thinking? Having you three years early like that."

"Honestly, ridiculous," he answered. "And your mom so late? Why couldn't they have met in the middle? We should both be twenty, Harps." His smile held the warm comforts of home, confirming that I'd made the right choice going there.

"I can't wait to show you around town," he said. "It's so beautiful here. You're going to love it."

"This rainy weather is a vibe. Literally a perfect writing day, I hope it's always like this."

"Only you would choose it for the rain," he mocked.

"Well, I didn't choose it, you did! So no backing out now."

"You have to tell me what projects you've been working on." Ben turned toward the kitchen and began to stir up a glass of hot chocolate. His kitchen was so tidy. Classic Ben. He loved order and simplicity, just like his mom. His slightly tucked shirt and short gelled hair were a staple. I was just there to push him out of his comfort zone and make sure he still knew the word fun.

"Josh is excited to see you," he added. I rolled my eyes at the thought of Ben's best friend. I could just imagine him waltzing through the front door, leaving a trail of wet footprints and a pile of his things along the counter as he walked by. His loose t-shirts, messy hair, loud voice and bad habits were the opposite of Ben. I never understood how their friendship had lasted so long.

Every conversation I had with Josh turned from bickering to competition to fight. He wasn't a friend, he was a rival. Having him as a roommate was the one thing that made me second guess my choice moving up there.

"I'm sure," I joked. Ben laughed at my sarcasm. "You

know, just because some kid is willing to trade snacks with you on the first day of kindergarten, that doesn't mean you're bound by friendship until you die. I still haven't forgiven him for sticking that snake in my backpack." An event that would haunt me for life. Thank goodness for Ava, always first to act, jumping in to take care of it for me.

"Well, let's hope he's grown up a little bit then," Ben answered, handing me the mug.

"Doubtful," I countered. "He better not go locking me out of the house every time I step outside," I added demandingly, letting Ben know that I meant business.

"I'll put your key on a chain," he offered. "You can wear it around your neck, just to be safe."

Benny the mediator. I gave up the fight and turned my attention to the chocolate. I took a careful sip, the familiar flavor making me smile. "My favorite."

"I know," he answered with a laugh. "Filled that massive jar on the counter with grandpa John's recipe so you wouldn't run out... at least not anytime soon," he corrected in a mocking tone. "Let me get your bag."

"Can we label it something gross so Josh won't touch it?" I asked as he got up to leave. "I've been here five minutes and I already feel spoiled."

He stopped at the door to answer. "Mom said if you weren't, I wasn't doing my job." He always looked at me when he spoke, making sure I had a clear line of sight to his lips, even though my hearing aids did most of the work now. He barely got the words out before he threw on his hood and stepped back outside. I watched him dart across the grass, moving quickly through the rain outside his slightly-fogged window.

I tossed my bags in the spare room as the nightstand picture caught my eye. A framed four-by-six of a three-year-old boy holding his baby cousin for the first time. Leave it to Ben to stick something so sweet there to welcome me.

"I'll be sure to let her know you've been successful," I commented. "Now tell me everything. How are your classes? How is work? Your mom told my mom about your new girlfriend."

He looked down, hiding a slight blush. "It's nothing serious yet," he countered. "And it depends on the class. Work is good though, I can't complain about the pay."

"I don't think I can either," I agreed, making a point to admire the room I was sitting in once more. We both laughed then. Him and Josh had climbed a company ladder together, or as I imagined it, Ben climbed, and Josh hid in his shadow until the opportune moment. When work offered a promotion far from home, they decided to get a small house close to a campus where Ben could finish school and split the expenses. I'd really lucked out with the extra room.

That evening was perfect as I settled in and we caught up on life. I loved hearing about Maine through Benny's eyes. His favorite foods, spots, and people. We turned on a movie, but we were too excited to pay attention as the conversation between new roommates carried on well past midnight. Luckily we had a Sunday morning to sleep it off.

Ben promised me the whole day before life got busy. I would start classes, and really focus on my writing, while he would go back to work and school. We took a tour through his small town just outside of Portland, and every road was like stepping through a painting. Everything outside was healthy and green, flecks of gold and amber accents beginning to pop through. Fall seemed to race toward us, brushing its color through the world.

We passed by the library and a bunch of little local

shops. Ben showed me around the campus, and the building where he worked in case I ever needed to stop by. After a late lunch at a small, brick pizza place, my feet had had enough.

"Maybe it would be faster to go down that way." Ben pointed toward a less walked trail, a dirt road that led into the dense trees.

"Nothing will eat us?"

He laughed. "No, it connects straight through. There's an abandoned house down there through the trees, though. It's huge! Some of it burned in a fire, I'm not sure how long ago. Still really beautiful for a haunted house."

"Haunted, or abandoned?"

"Well, let's put it this way. If you were looking to write horror, it'd be a good place for some inspiration. Real quiet property. Nobody goes there."

"Sounds like a dream."

Ben gave me a knowing look. "It's not a destination," he countered.

"A quiet place where nobody else goes?" I started down the trail. "That will always be my destination."

Ben shook his head, no longer smiling as he followed. "Always the first one running away from caution."

"How can I write adventures if I don't live any of my own? How hypocritical to put my characters through such stories if I cannot share my own experiences."

"Shane Manor isn't a good place for you to hide out and write, Harper. I mean it. Nobody is allowed in there, and for good reason."

"Ghosts."

"More like it's hazardous. The place burnt. It's not like there's a desk waiting for you to pull up a chair. There's no electricity to charge your laptop."

"I've got a notebook." I stopped at the tall, metal gates, surprised by the view.

"If you want ghosts, we can go visit some lighthouses."

"Lighthouses!" Now that sounded like a destination.

"Along the coast," he confirmed. "They're so beautiful, and *those* we are actually allowed to visit! This place is off limits."

My fingers grabbed hold of the narrow bars. "Eerie," I commented. "But there is still something beautiful in it. How long did you say this house has been sitting here?"

"I'm not sure exactly. They make it sound like hundreds of years, though rumor isn't always the best source."

"Manor? More like a castle." The house was huge, even after burning down.

I shook the bars to freak out Ben, laughing as his widened eyes shifted to a glare. He had always been easy to creep out. The stubborn gate didn't budge, sticking to the spot it had been abandoned. The bars framed my face as it rested against them.

"So peaceful. I bet it's magical inside." I thought of Sam. She would have agreed. If only she could be there with me. "Who ever said hanging out with a ghost would be such a bad thing?"

"Come on, let's go home."

"Okay, fine," I gave in. "My feet honestly really do hurt." I turned toward him with a light laugh, we'd been walking all day. Ben went on, but I got the strangest feeling that I was being watched. Like a cold breeze, a chill brushed along my skin. I spun around to search the overgrown fields inside the gates. The sensation was still there, but there was no one.

I started walking again, my pace picking up to catch up

with Ben as if something chased my heels. In scaring him, I guess I'd managed to creep myself out too.

As soon as I stepped side by side with him, I peeked back once more. A tall black dog stood at the gate staring at me. My bones jumped, but I spun my face forward and carried on without a word.

This wasn't little red riding hood. The wolf wasn't watching me. There were no ghosts. There was no magic.

5

HARPER

Monday morning came too quickly. Ben was up and out early, leaving behind a silent house, and Josh got home so late I didn't even have to see him. It was the first day of a new chapter. I smiled at the thought from under my blanket. I had a plan. I'd been dreaming about this for years. With my part-time, two-class schedule, I was going to use my spare hours to chase that dream of becoming an author.

Still wrapped in my soft blue blanket, I grabbed a mug and mixed up some hot cocoa. A note sat on the counter, weighed down by a long chain that was linked through a key. I smiled as I picked it up, reading Ben's neat hand-writing.

Enjoy the rain, Harps. I'll see you tonight.

I put the necklace on, reminded once again how awesome my cousin was.

The list of story ideas fighting for my attention had been overwhelming, but I'd chosen one to focus on at the end of the summer and started plotting. Now I had my notes, a mostly figured-out storyline, and a blank document in front of me.

My fingers typed away, my mind fully absorbed in another time and life completely. I loved novels of contemporary romance. Fantasy was fun, but somehow realistic story settings made the normal world feel a little more special. The idea that a silly, cheesy love story wasn't that far out of reach.

That was the difference between my writing and Sam's. She was all about the magic, she wanted adventures that dove into new realms of thrill and danger. She wanted escapism, to live a life that didn't exist.

No fated mate would come to claim my heart, but I might bump into someone real cute at a cafe. I loved a daydream that connected to the real world. Bonus points if he owned a Christmas tree farm. *"Hot cowboy books,"* Ava always called them. The thought made me smirk.

It seemed silly, but there were still beautiful stories left to tell in our world. A place like Shane's Manor, so breathtakingly surreal, it had to have a hundred stories written through its walls. Something about it lurked in the back of my mind, an energy pulling me to explore further.

It was so grand, so tragically beautiful. As I closed my eyes, I could imagine my main character living in a home just like it. Sure, it was stained by heartbreak and smoke now, burned to the bones of the beauty it once knew, but oh, to see it in its prime. I didn't have to go inside to know its heart. There was an entire world just beyond its gated walls.

Neatly-kept green meadows that stretched around it, meeting the forest at its guarded bars. Light curtains draped down to frame each window, softly waving in the wind on a cool summer night. The candle that lit between them, shining bright as the stars above it.

The smoke that rose from its chimney through the falling winter snow, promising comfort and warmth from a long day's travel as one hurried home to the loved ones inside. A full moon chasing out the darkness as a distant wolf howled into the night.

My new story carried me away in a daydream. A home built of castle-gray stone. The wishing-well out back, inside a ring of silver-white rose bushes. It may have been a practical item that her house staff used on the daily, but to her, it was magic, as she tossed in a single coin, and prayed for love. The greenhouse, brought to flourishing life inside walls that looked simple from outside, all with an effort of passionate hard work.

The stable out back was lined with windows, as horses stepped outside, their hooves cutting through the frost and leaves on a crisp autumn morning.

Music softly played into the distance, elegant parties and masquerades, where guests danced the evenings away. The melody carried on through my imagination.

"If it is haunted, I get it," I told myself, standing up to stretch. "If that was my home, I'd want to stay there too." My eyes widened at the oven clock.

"One already?" I hadn't even stopped for lunch. It was so easy to get carried away when I was excited to work. Josh would probably be coming home to eat soon. I dropped the blanket and grabbed Ben's jacket off the couch instead. I wasn't ready to face him just yet.

"How about a little walk," I suggested to myself, tossing a few things into my backpack. Anything to avoid spending time with Josh. I smiled, knowing exactly where I'd go. Ben would tell me not to, but he wasn't there to stop me.

I stepped up to the gate, water seeping through the sides of my shoes from the pebbled puddle at my feet. The rainy night left one cold, muddy trail.

My eyes scanned over the house, through the soft fog stretching across its overgrown fields. A stone frame, hollow with ash and pain, heartache and neglect. A spot so forsaken. So lost. So forgotten from the world outside. That creeping sensation of being watched returned. I searched the trees behind me, but there was no one. Just me and the world in front of me. A world that had been locked away. Something inside me felt a connection to the view, as if some part of my soul knew it.

My hand hesitated to reach for the gate, almost afraid to touch it. I already knew it wouldn't give.

"Please let me in," I softly pleaded. "I know you still have a story left to tell inside this wall."

I leaned against it, my fingers wrapping around the bars, slipping as it swung open in front of me.

My clothes hit the mud, instantly soaking up water to exaggerate the chill that blew through against my skin. I got up fast, pushing away from the puddles that surrounded me, wiping away the muddy gravel as I turned to glare at the open gate.

"You were meant to be locked," I scolded, as if I hadn't just begged them to let me through. Ben made it sound so off-limits, like nobody had been able to get them open in years... but I did.

I spun around to face the walkway ahead of me. Sam always spoke of adventure, well this was mine. History and beauty that had stood the test of time, and it shared the same world as I did. I stepped forward, consumed by the awe, lost in the untouched acres that swallowed me into their real-life magic. How long had it been since anyone stepped along that path?

"Too long," I answered, decided in the truth of my words. "A place like this should be admired every day." I stepped up to the walls, my hand rising to feel the cold, ash-stained stone. How would it be to build the foundation of a home like this, setting the heavy, textured stones into place, one by one.

My palm gently ran along it as I paced the side, desperate to see how far its clear land rolled. The property line made a perfect ring, a circle spinning around its castle center. I continued around a corner, admiring the gardens that had long been left behind.

A small barn off to the side caught my eye from afar, a sense of life still carried through the fields around it as I turned another corner toward the back.

A stream rolled calmly by the path, without a care for the world above it. The current was too alive to fit such a silent corner, the only thing left with free passage to visit those forgotten grounds.

A shadow flickered along the stone wall behind me. I jumped, turning to face it, but the hedges kept their secrets.

"Hello?" I asked as my imagination kicked back on. What if a predator lingered, claiming this abandoned territory, and I'd stepped right into its grasp? With a cautious step back, I watched for movement, putting space between myself and any threat.

The trickling water dimmed from my ears, growing too quiet. I reached for my hearing aids, fidgeting with them against my ears. I'd just barely replaced the batteries in them, but they were already cutting out.

I cursed the timing of it, when the sound of running water came back. My shoulders sank with a sigh of relief.

"The spirit of this place is messing with me," I commented. It felt as if the mansion could hear me, as if it understood.

Another shadow flashed across my right, as I fell back against the untrimmed hedges. One hearing aid fell out, as the other went blank. Panic consumed me, the silence too loud, demanding that I know how helpless I could be. What little defense I had against whatever might dare to threaten me. I pushed up from the ground, searching my view.

A tall black dog stood knee deep in the grass. Its eyes held directly on mine, watching my every move. My breath caught. I'd seen that dog before. Something in its presence promised danger.

I got up slowly, watching for its reaction.

"Are you a friend or a foe?" I asked, hoping it would start to wag its tail and lie at my feet, but the sound was lost. I couldn't even hear my own voice. Had it betrayed my fear? The words had come out, but they were so disconnected. I searched for the fallen aid, barely noticing it through my tears as it sat with the rocks at the bottom of the stream. I used Ben's sleeve to wipe my eyes, mad at myself for dropping it.

"This isn't quite the story I was looking for."

The dog moved toward the house, its gaze still locked on mine. I was afraid to move, waiting to see where it would go, until it circled a round, stone well. I was so focused on the dog, it took a moment to realize how familiar the scene was.

"That well," I commented, trying to understand. I'd been daydreaming only an hour before about this property, and I'd imagined a well just like it. I reached into the cold water to save my hearing aid, rolling it into the bottom of Ben's jacket to dry it off. My gaze locked on the well, suddenly not so worried about the dog as I shifted closer. It remained calm, still watching me as we both circled the well on opposite sides. My gaze got lost in the dark water below, wondering how it was possible.

"A wishing well," I whispered, thinking of the character in my story. In the water where others saw work, she saw wishes.

I'd stopped spinning, and so had the dog. It felt as if it were waiting for me. As I met its gaze, it turned toward the mansion doors, trotting straight through beneath a half-burned wall. Once it crossed the threshold, it turned back toward me, as if it were waiting for me to follow.

I shook off my confusion, giving in to the moment, to the strange connection I felt to this lost story. I crept after the dog in silence as the thrill of trespassing suddenly made me nervous.

The dog continued through, running up a spiral staircase. Once again, it turned to make sure I followed, before vanishing into the shadows.

"This feels totally safe," I grumbled sarcastically with my first step up.

Vines grew through cracked stones up the staircase before it opened up into a large room. How grand it must have felt in a past life, as gray skies shone through unintentional windows where the stone broke down with age, painted in black soot. Random items sat on warped shelves, ragged fabrics, loose screws and change. A rusted pocket watch, its chain dangling over the edge above a cluttered crate. A collection of lost and found treasures.

A round table sat in the center, and once again, the dog circled around to the opposing side, watching me from across it. It seemed too strange to be for nothing. What was this dog trying to tell me? A white cloth draped over something on the table, blocking out the dust.

I stepped in closer, reaching for the edge of the fabric. With one tug, the small sheet slid off, uncovering a large hourglass with an intricate silver frame. Instead of sand, water filled the top half. One simple drop leaked through to the bottom, pooling into the base. I stared at the piece, finding it odd that the top half remained so full, while the bottom had such a slivering layer of water. Why hadn't the time run out yet?

I'd never seen one filled with water before.

"So strange that the water hasn't run straight through," I commented, reaching forward to grab it. As soon as my skin touched the glass, the water trembled, rippling off from the center as a distant footstep vibrated through it. I barely registered the dog bolting out the door behind me as the water in the top half began to spin, circling around into a whirlpool with a force that didn't make sense.

Drip... drip... drip.

Water started slipping through faster, as if I'd just woken it up or set it off. I pulled my hands away in a panic. *Did I break it?* I took a step back, wishing I could hear something, anything to help me understand.

Someone knocked me out of their way from behind. I tumbled to the floor, looking at the towering figure as he reached for the hourglass. He was furious, I didn't have to hear his voice to know he yelled. My hands braced fearfully over my ears, as if he were hurting them in the silence, tears of panic breaking loose.

6

ELIJAH

—THE WORDS SHE COULDN'T HEAR.

"What are you doing in here? You can't be here!" She didn't flinch, her back blocking the path in front of me. Then I saw it, the hourglass, just past her shoulder.

The curse.

I lunged forward, frustrated when she didn't move out of my way.

"What have you done!" The water already spun around, brought to life once more. It was too late. I'd been living on frozen time, but now the timer ticked down again, promising more pain. More of the fate I could never accept, but never escape.

"The hourglass tide."

I turned to glare at her, whimpering in the corner. She cowered back against the wall in fear. If only she knew how stuck she was now. How much each breath drew her closer to her own doom.

What was she crying for?

"You have no idea what you've just done!" I stared into the hourglass current, ignited by her touch. Why had the curse brought her here? What was the purpose of this eternal torment?

She was silent, terror reflecting in her eyes, waiting to see what I'd do next. I didn't know how, or why her fate crossed paths with mine. Why her life had been tangled into my mess. I knew one thing though, like the pit in my heart.

"Now you're as stuck here as I am."

The words stung. They would never not hurt. The countdown had begun, and she couldn't run from it. Nobody ever could. I'd tried.

She stared at me, frozen, and inside I was breaking. How could fate be so cruel?

"What?" She shook her head, studying my face so intently until her tears blurred over.

How could I even explain?

The girl jumped up, wiping her sleeve across her face as she made a run for it. The echo of her footsteps faded away. If only they could take her far from this nightmare, but they wouldn't even get past the gate.

I grabbed the backpack she'd dropped on the cold floor and followed. She ran to the gates, shaking them with everything she had. It was no use.

"No!" she begged, but it muffled into a soft sob. "No, no, no."

I wished I had the key. I wished I could break it down, swing that gate open wide and let her out, let her free, but it wasn't the gate that held its ground. It was the curse.

"Why?" she asked, searching desperately for help. "Please." There was nobody. The path beyond was empty.

It was always empty. I admired her footprints in the muddy road. The first mark of something new in years. My heart sank with her as she fell to her knees, reaching for her ear.

Then she looked back at me, startled, curling nervously into herself like she hadn't heard me coming. Like she was embarrassed. What was I supposed to say? I stepped closer, dropping the bag at her side. A raindrop hit my hand, then my forehead, the weather picking up on our gloomy situation, mocking us from above. My eyes shut for a moment of irritation, sensing the impending storm.

"You shouldn't be here."

"The gate won't budge." Her last word slurred a bit, like she was too nervous to get it out, like she was forcing it.

I turned toward the house, pointing up at its half-crumbled walls. "I'm sorry I can't offer you a more comfortable stay," I started. I looked down at her, but she just stared.

"What?" She stumbled over the word.

My irritation grew again. All this time alone, I wasn't used to conversation. I didn't want to get used to it. Nobody should be inside with me. I couldn't grow close to someone as our time together dripped away. It just made it harder. This wasn't a world of pleasantries, its cruelty wouldn't allow for those. I pointed at the house again.

"Look, I'm sorry you're stuck here, I have no idea why. Why you even stepped through that gate!"

I looked down at her again as tears pooled from her eyes. *Crap.* I was making it worse.

"I can't hear you." Her expression softly winced.

"What?" My brows drew together as I scrutinized her face.

"I can't hear you," she repeated in a whisper, hesitantly opening her hand to show me a set of small mechanical pieces. Whatever they were, they wouldn't work here. She pointed at her ear.

My eyes widened in realization, looking into hers for the first real time. "You can't hear?" I'd never met anyone who couldn't hear before, but mom told us that sometimes people in her world couldn't.

Vulnerability shined in her eyes, self-conscious about something she had no control of. The rain fell harder, framing her face in tears. The dark strands of hair around her forehead curled out as if the water set them free.

I shifted my gaze away, another layer of frustration pushing at my patience. Maybe this was a good thing, us not being able to talk. An excuse not to get as close to her over our short time together.

She shook her head, pointing from her lips to mine. "Look at me when you talk."

My eyes shut tight, wrestling against my anger. I rolled my shoulders back, and let out a long breath. Everyday I hoped my time alone would end, but not like this. Not by dooming another soul to this curse.

"I just want to go home," she explained. She pointed up at the gate behind her. "Can you help me?"

I didn't answer at first, staring into her eyes for a long time. I couldn't bring myself to say the words. My head shook, sadness replacing the frustration.

"I can't. We're both prisoners to these gates now."

I turned my back on her, heading toward the house. Her shallow breaths picked up faster, like she couldn't find enough oxygen, but there was nothing I could do to save her. There was nothing I could say to help.

"What?" she called behind me. "What does that mean?"

I stopped, wishing there was some way I could change

the truth. She was fighting it, her mind racing through excuses, searching for logic. I'd seen it before. I'd done it myself in what felt like another lifetime, but my hope for freedom had died long before.

"It's a curse," I explained, though her mortal mind wouldn't grasp it. Then I caught myself. She couldn't see my lips. I turned around, forcing myself to make eye contact.

"What's your name?"

"My name?" she asked, making sure she read my lips right.

I nodded. This was going to take some getting used to.

"I'm Harper."

"Harper," I said, looking her over again. My fingers rose to press against my chest. "Elijah."

"Elijah," she repeated.

I nodded. It was a small victory, but neither of us were smiling.

"I'll make up a room for you," I told her. "Whenever you..." I hesitated, searching for the right word. "Process."

I didn't stay for an answer, turning back toward my castle of ash. For all my years of waiting, I wasn't feeling very patient. Why sit there talking about something neither of us could control? There was no point in tossing her over my shoulder to carry out of the rain. She'd just run right back out again. There was no use in standing there pretending to be friends either. But still, I had to do something.

I thought of the few things left in the stables after the fire. It wasn't much, but a small piece of care was all I could offer before the curse took her from me.

"From me?" I asked, questioning my own thoughts. As if she'd been given... as if she was mine at all.

How did she get in? Mortals weren't meant to know about us, but there was no hiding it now. There was nowhere for her to run, nobody for her to talk to. All she had left now was the dripping time, the silence, and me. The magics mixed inside my home, and the ones who stepped through those gates to find it never stepped back out again.

We were stuck together now. I knew this reality all too well. I'd already lived it for more lifetimes than I cared to keep track of. She would come find me when she was ready. All I could do was what I'd been doing all along. Wait.

HIDING

7

WILLOW

The campus was everything Sam said it would be. Students walked paths through their university buildings as a city horizon lined my view. Surrounded by so many people, yet I stood there completely alone. Everything around me seemed to be brimming with hope and opportunity, but it was one building off in the distance that sent a different message my way, directly for me.

The hospital.

While most new adults moved there to chase after freedom and possibilities, my future weighed me down.

I'd never missed the walls of trees back home so much, the way it felt like I could hide inside them.

Sam had been so excited to move out, to step into her college dorm and start her future. She was excited about the school, the classes, and the road ahead, while I was sick. I came to get answers. To get treatment. To be poked and prodded until the inevitable day came to claim me.

So why was I the one admiring the view from her window, while she laid six feet underground? It wasn't right. None of this was. My twin was the kind of person everybody was drawn to. Her enthusiasm was contagious, and she was passionate about chasing her dreams, writing to be exact. She was going to write poetry, novels, short stories, all of it, and all of it would have been made of pure magic on paper. Her story wasn't supposed to end like this.

I, on the other hand, had no idea what my future looked like. Did I even have one? It didn't feel like I was meant to. Sam would have studied the campus in front of me, ready to take on the world. When I stared at it, I didn't know what to think at all.

The crash was an accident. The deer startled me. I didn't mean to swerve so hard. I didn't mean to hit that ditch... but I did. I wrecked everything that night. It was my fault she was gone.

Sam was meant to fly, and she would have soared. I was already dying. I'd made my peace with that.

Sam's purple computer dinged on top of its bag. The mostly-tangled cord barely made it to the outlet behind the bed. It wasn't the first time I'd ignored the sound. I couldn't let it die, I had to keep the battery alive, but I also couldn't stand to open the screen and look inside it.

That laptop held her whole life. Her writing projects, her pictures. Even messages synced from her phone. It was like a piece of her soul. She'd always been so against anybody reading her writing until it was done. Nobody was allowed to look over her shoulder while she worked. It would ruin the magic. I was afraid to offend her, as if she were still there waiting for the words to be completed. Still guarding her vulnerable heart until she got her writing right.

A worn page sat on top of Sam's computer. Her class schedule. I'd watched her pick up the freshly printed page, excited to start her next chapter in life. Her fingers had warped and bent it from the amount of times she'd picked it up to study since then. The spot where her thumb sat, wearing away the ink. The crinkle she'd made, picking it up in a hurry when my drink spilled across the table, barely splattering the edge.

When I looked at it now, all I saw was her hands. It felt strange to touch it, her fear of ruining it passed on to me. One single page had meant so much to her, held so much value. I had to protect it.

Creative writing. Ten to twelve, Monday through Thursday with Professor Nazurin. The class was under-lined in purple pen.

Sam had gone on and on about that class. She was so sure it would launch her dreams, change the course of her life forever. I wish I'd never scoffed at her excitement. She was allowed to feel that way, and I should have let her feel it as long as she had it. I was just jealous. I wanted to trade. Now she would miss everything she'd worked toward, while I lived on.

The phone buzzed in my pocket. My wrist twisted up, the watch displaying a familiar hospital number. Mom thought getting me a smart watch would put an end to the "missed" calls. It didn't change my lack of motivation to answer though.

I let the call ring on without me, to inevitably end and pile into the list of voicemails I was avoiding. I scrolled through my notifications. Dr. Murphy was a persistent caller. He was really trying, I'd give him that. I wasn't tech-nically due in his office for another week. We'd planned on getting me settled in early with Sam. I was just there to wait.

"He's just checking in," mom swore. Choosing a doctor

close to mom at home or Sam at school had been a strange choice. Wasn't a mom meant to hold your hand at the doctor? But the facility near Sam's school was too good to pass up. She'd promised to be by my side every step of the way, just like when we were eight and I broke my leg. That surgery to fix it ruined our plans for the summer, but Sam never seemed to mind. She just cared about my getting better.

Sam never broke. When the rest of my life shattered, she was there for me, and she made sure I never questioned that.

Besides, I didn't want to stay home. I didn't want to feel more stuck than I already was. I wanted a taste of the future Sam chased, even if I just lived it through her eyes. So we found the doctor, arranged the insurance around it, and made our plan. No turning back now.

I still had a week before I had to give in to Dr. Murphy's treatment plan. It was more of a research plan with all the tests I had coming. Sam should have been there studying for exams. Instead I was due for blood draws.

One week. Until then, my time was my own.

How is the apartment?

The preview of a new text from Sage scrolled by.

"Empty," I mumbled, tossing the phone on the bed. "Oh, Sam." I sighed, picking up her schedule. "If only we could trade." My eyes scanned the campus again.

"I would lie in my grave to give you this."

8

WILLOW

What was one lonely weekend spent in a room of packed boxes and silence? The barely-touched take-out box of fried rice mocked me from the table. A new set of apartment keys that were meant to be split between sisters sat stuck on the same ring.

It was nothing more than a retreat from mom's constant nagging. She couldn't reach me there. Though, if I didn't answer her soon, she'd probably show up at the door.

With a new motivation to avoid that, I picked up my phone.

"So many missed calls." I shook my head as I counted them up, choosing one to click on. The phone rang twice before her manic voice picked up the other line.

"Willow, are you trying to make me insane? I know you've been ignoring me!"

"Mom, I was resting."

"For three straight days?" she countered. "You didn't even let me know when you made it there! I had to call the office to see if you picked up your key!"

"I'm fine!"

"You're not fine," she reflexively argued, then cut herself off. Hesitation lingered between us. "I'm just worried about you, honey."

"I know." It's all she'd done for months. Between my getting sick, and Sam dying, her happy life had been torn up too. "It's going to be okay. Right now it just hurts a little extra."

"I know. It does for me too. You'll call me anytime, right? And answer more of my calls, would you?"

"Yes, I will."

"Promise?"

My eyes rolled. Sam had been a full believer in promises. She'd always insisted on them when she meant business. It didn't matter if it was mom or me, her friends, a high school teacher, or some bagger at the grocery store who swore they'd have her favorite soda back in stock by Thursday. She acted as if a promise was a legal contract, binding you to your word. Sam was a believer in all things magic, and somehow, she could make a simple word like 'promise' just that. Magic.

"I promise."

Mom seemed to be giving in. "Okay. But are you sure you want to be there all by yourself? It just seems so wrong. I could drive up next week." It was probably just as much about her being alone as me, but she had a life to keep living back home.

"It's a change of scenery. I can take care of myself for a while." I was supposed to be an adult now, right? All I really wanted was to be by myself.

"Okay."

I counted the silent seconds, waiting to see if she had more.

"I love you, honey. Call me soon. I want to hear about your first appointment the moment it's over."

"I will, mom, stop worrying about me! Try to have a good week."

I tossed the phone across the blanket, dreading what would come. I'd gone through so many tests since getting sick. They'd worked so hard to figure out what was wrong with me, but they couldn't pinpoint it. Part of me found comfort in the unknown. If I was being honest with myself, I was scared to learn the truth. I was scared of the treatment plan, the life expectancy, the term I would use to tell people what was wrong with me. I wasn't ready to know it yet, and I was afraid this new doctor was going to be the one to figure it out. I was sick, and it wasn't going to be some quick and easy fix. It wasn't something that just went away.

A new notification dinged through the air. It wasn't my ding though. It was Sam's. It dinged again, pulling me in with its echo, like it was calling to me.

I sat down to pull her computer into my lap as the third ding begged me to open it. A photo of four friends lit up the screen. My hand swung it shut again, alarmed by the pain it invited back in. The picture was gone, but the cut had already been re-opened.

Ava, Harper, Sage and Sam. *Not Willow. Not me.*

They'd always been her friends. I just tagged along. An automatic invite out of kindness. Part of the club based on my association with Sam. Before she was gone, they would mistake me for her, calling her name down the sidewalk only to catch up with me. It used to annoy me, but now I missed it. Now there was no mistaking the live sister for the dead one. Now when they saw me, I was just a reminder.

They'd really pushed to keep me in their loop after Sam died, even if they only saw her when they looked at me.

They tried to include me, but it was pity friendship. I could never replace my sister, no matter how much I looked the part. Among her friends, I was just an imposter. The piece that didn't fit.

I opened the computer back up, making my shoulders relax before typing in Sam's elementary lunch number, laughing as the obvious code unlocked her life. *Classic Sam.* The home screen wallpaper was a picture of the two of us from the year before. We were all bundled up for the colder day. She'd insisted on taking a picture in front of the pretty red leaves behind us, a yearly occurrence.

I clicked open a new screen quickly to block it out, not surprised by all the open tabs. Everything exactly how she left it. It was like a new world of applications and notifications opened up to me, all of them bookmarking where her life cut off... everything put on pause. 8 active internet tabs. 971 unopened text messages. Thousands of emails.

Emails seemed less invasive than the personal messages sent her way when everyone heard the tragic news, or texts on a group chat that I hadn't been added to yet. She never could keep up with her notifications, but most of her unread messages were sent after she died. Words of love and mourning that were meant only for her.

The emails were a never-ending list of scams, deals, author newsletters, and campus information. I clicked on the student welcome email, wondering if I should inform the school that they were welcoming a ghost. Mom had sworn she would call them soon, but she was putting it off.

I rolled my eyes after reading the bolded headline.

AN OVERVIEW OF OUR SCHOOL YEAR.

"How optimistic." I closed the page, finding the large

picture of two sisters again, our arms hugged around each other as we smiled at the camera. Our matching green eyes and warm auburn hair waving over our shoulders. How could two people who looked the exact same be so extremely different? I'm glad my realistic, downer attitude never dulled her fun, dreaming optimism.

Ding. A text preview ran along the top of the screen from someone named N.

> I can't wait to read more of your work.

How Vague. My brows drew tighter. "Who is N?" Everybody knew Sam was gone, but it sure seemed like this mysterious N person didn't. Was this some college writing buddy she was excited to meet? It felt awkward reading her messages. If she'd wanted to tell me about N, she would have.

"Imposter," I commented, staring at the two sisters in the picture. Just like I'd stolen her concert t-shirt that day in the photo, it felt I'd stolen everything else too.

I grabbed the well-loved yellow quilt from behind me, wrapping it up over my shoulders. I'd had it since I was a baby, and it showed. I always explained that its age made it softer, worn out for comfort. From camping trips to stomach bugs, the poor thing had endured more than its share of rips and tears.

It went missing for a few days when we first found out I was sick. Sam took it, spent hours secretly patching it back up for me. She wrapped it around me tight when she gave it back. *"In case you ever need a hug."* Sam had always hated sewing. I'd never felt so loved.

"If only I could give you back to the world I took you from. Everybody would be happier. If only you could have lived this dream of yours, experienced a piece of it, even just for a week." I stared into Sam's eyes in the photo, a jade green reflection of my own. It wasn't her face, her skin, her hair that I saw when I looked into her eyes. It was her soul. It was so much deeper than appearances. We saw each other for what we were beneath all that.

"What if I could? Just for one week." I said it as if her spirit was right there listening, waiting to give me an answer. "Trade places, pretend that I'm not just here because I'm sick. Give the world one last taste of Sam. Live a life that goes beyond myself." I could almost hear her telling me to start writing.

"There are entire worlds left to discover," Sam swore time and time again. *"Adventures still wait for you, Willow, and you can still find them from a hospital room."*

"I could use one last real adventure, Sam. A little bit of fun, before I give in. And then I will," I promised the thin air around me. I meant it too. The doctors, tests, and medicine could all wait just a few more days. A few more days, and then I'd be ready. A few more days, and I would try for real.

"For mom."

I lifted up the schedule, looking back and forth between the classes and Sam's eyes on the laptop screen.

"One week," I said, nodding my head with the decision. My teeth pressed over my bottom lip with a new rush of excitement. It had been too long since I'd dared a hint of mischief. I needed a little bit of fun.

9

WILLOW

Monday morning made for a busy campus as I tucked away the ignored calls in my pocket and set off into the traffic of students on their first day.

It took a while to find the class since I hadn't pre-memorized the layout like Sam had. Trying to wiggle out the nervous tension in my hands, I stood outside the classroom door and took a few deep breaths to push away the nausea. I wasn't sick, not today. Today we were going to blame first-day jitters.

I walked into her first class a few minutes past the bell, giving the teacher an awkward nod as he leaned back on his desk at the front of the room.

"Sam," he greeted, catching me off guard. Nobody knew Sam here. I should have blended into the sea of other students. I ignored him and his endearing smile as I found an open seat. This was the class and teacher that Sam had been most excited about. I never quite understood the big deal, but I remembered the look on her face when she'd read it on her schedule.

A unique mural ran along the walls, wrapping all four corners of the room as it brought the space to life. For a creative writing class, there wasn't much to complain about. I slowly spun in my seat to admire the piece, wondering how much he'd spent on an artist or whether he did it himself. The forest painting transitioned between seasons in each corner, a blossoming spring at the front, to a bright warm summer in the next. A narrow creek ran around the back from a forest of autumn leaves to the hooves of a wintery, snow-covered doe. The impressively detailed scene of four seasons beat the list of famous quotes that you'd expect to find on a classroom wall.

Mr. Nazurin started talking about how our words have the power of magic. He sounded just like Sam. As he went on, enchanting our minds with inspiration, it became clear why she'd wanted to take this class so badly. He scanned the room as he lectured, but every time his gaze landed on mine, it felt as if it was just us there, something so personal in his tone.

"Write me a poem about this world," he announced, gesturing at the walls around his class. "Tell me, as you sit within this forest, what do you see in it? What do you feel?"

I studied the walls again, this time feeling less of the magic as my eyes bounced from tree to tree, then to the faces of students around me. They each got busy writing their initial thoughts as I opened up a blank page in front of me.

I couldn't write. It was Sam who I made write for me. I never planned to turn anything in. I was there for the lecture, to feel a touch of my sister that had been lost. My gaze followed the teacher, shifting down when he caught me staring.

The little voice of panic in the back of my head mocked me. *Imposter.*

What was I doing? I was impersonating someone else, someone dead! They were all going to find out. I couldn't believe mom hadn't called the school. I was right there though, I could tell them for her. That was my reason for sitting in her class, the excuse I would use when the truth came out.

I avoided Mr. Nazurin as he got up and paced toward me. How would I tell him? Spitting it out in front of the entire class felt less respectful to Sam. Her death wasn't going to ruin the one experience in this world she was so eager to live.

"You know, as soon as I saw your poem, I had to make sure you were in my class," he commented as he crouched lower in front of my desk. "It's good to officially meet you."

I thought over Sam's poem. I knew exactly which one he was referring to. Her poem about a magic world, and how that magic world is ours. The lines where magics mix together. It made sense. He wasn't wrong. Nobody could argue her talent. Writing came so easily to her. The problem was, if he knew Sam's writing, he would never be fooled by mine. I wanted to tell him the truth, but it caught in my throat. He acted as if he knew me on a personal level, but he knew nothing about me. The nausea swept back through as I sat under his study.

"Are you okay?" he asked. "You seem pale."

"I'll be right back," I answered, standing to leave. I grabbed Sam's backpack at my side, forgetting the notebook and pencil, barely glancing back as I pushed out through the door. He still stood at my desk, watching me in confusion. It could wait. I would face him another day.

Fear chased me down the hallway, mocking me with

feelings of insignificance. *This isn't your school. You're not a student here. You're a fraud.*

Random outbursts of feeling sick weren't new to me. They weren't unusual either. I curled up in an empty stall, relieved to be alone until a door slammed open in the hallway, and I realized another class just ended.

My eyes shut tight, knowing the privacy would be gone too soon. I wiped at my watery eyes with my jacket sleeve, ready to get out of there for good after the pass-through students had all gone. Girls coming in to wash-up and fix their make-up before escaping to college freedom.

I rushed out the first door I saw before realizing I exited a different spot than I'd entered. The unfamiliar buildings didn't tell me which way to go, but then I noticed the library. The part of campus Sam had been most excited to explore. If I was going to do anything in her name, walking down the shelves of books would have been her number one request. Sam loved reading. Of course, the magic she felt in written stories was what inspired her to create her own.

I couldn't count how many times we'd gone to the one up the street growing up. As little girls, we would squish into one chair, and she would turn through the picture books, pretending she could read, even though we both knew she was making the words up. Her stories were always better anyways.

If there was one place I could escape to feel Sam's energy, the library was it.

I stepped inside, embracing the peaceful warmth within its walls. Students were scattered throughout the tables, ready to take their new set of classes seriously.

I turned into the rows of literature, admiring the stacks of titles and names. My finger skimmed over the spines, thinking of Ava. She was obsessed with books, always looking for the next one to add to her collection. She had a list of books she would one day own, insisting that the library was just her way of testing them out. She didn't exactly have the funds to build her own personal library just yet. Sam and Harper would insist that they both get a shelf reserved for their works. *"Signed copies, to be exact,"* is how Ava corrected them. She was their biggest fan, and they hadn't even finished writing anything yet.

I was never a huge reader, not a part of their book club, but between Sam and her friends, I was always hearing about the latest books.

My hand fell, and so did my smile as the nostalgia turned to ache. I was surrounded by adventures in that library, but all I really wanted was a nap. I admired a comfy corner nook, deciding to enjoy the perfect, peaceful ambiance a library offered.

10

WILLOW

A stack of books slammed against the table a few feet away. My head jerked up from the armrest, finding a girl fixing her pile of heavy textbook-worthy editions while complaining to the boy across from her. I watched her in a daze, until she noticed me sitting there and stared back. My eyes shifted away awkwardly, up through the once brightly-lit sun windows to the dark night outside. How long had I been asleep?

I stood up too fast, bracing myself against the couch with a lightheaded daze. It really sucked being sick. A year before that, I had no issues. Now the single act of standing up could be too much. Now I could nap away an entire day in a library without even noticing.

I stepped out into the quiet night, noting how few students roamed the sidewalks compared to before. Most college kids probably had a full plan of socializing to get back to by sundown. I'll admit, it would have been more fun with Harper, Ava and Sage around. Sam chose a school so far from her friends, the people she'd spent every weekend with since we were children. What would she have done without them?

She would have made more friends already. Socializing came so easily to her.

Turning down a road that I was sure led back home, one particular building stole the evening spotlight, or more like it demanded it. The start of a new semester was being celebrated enthusiastically as students crammed into one small house. I stopped to stare at it from the road, admiring the scene for what it was. A carefree fun that I didn't know.

"You going in?" I moved aside as a more mature looking boy stepped around me. Based on his toned build and brand name outfit, he was one of the jocks that usually didn't notice me. His smile was sincere though. He didn't know me. He didn't realize he was inviting the sick girl to the party. That didn't change the facts though.

"Oh, I don't—" Mom's number buzzed onto my phone screen.

"Everyone's invited," he cut off. "Aren't you just dying to join the party?" He smiled again, continuing up the sidewalk, still half-turned toward me. "Free drinks!"

I didn't even know how to fight off the blush. I wasn't used to cute boys like him inviting me to hang out. If Ava were with me, she'd be freaking out. Nobody had ever offered me a drink before. I wasn't supposed to consume alcohol in my condition. That, and I wasn't old enough. He didn't know that though. None of them did.

I slid the phone back into my pocket and stared up at the house with a fresh perspective. If there was ever a time to get away with some fun, this was my chance. What would Sam have done? *This is your week,* I reminded myself.

I returned the boy's smile, nodding to accept the invitation before I followed him up the steps inside. I wished Sam was there with me, giggling about college boys, telling me not to worry so much, reminding me that I was allowed to be happy.

All signs of maturity seemed forgotten behind an enabled group of high school kids no longer restrained by parental authority. I felt lost between the wild lines of people crossing through, bouncing to the sound with cheerful voices and cups held high. I weaved across to the kitchen, between a table of emptied, greasy pizza boxes and a counter of knocked-over, mismatched cup stacks, and beer.

Everybody was lost in the moment. Nobody cared. Nobody watched as I looked at the options. Nobody told me this was a bad idea… but it was. I smiled, grabbing a cup and filling it full of tap water.

This was my week, and as I studied the room around me, I realized I'd managed to find the fun. I wiggled back through the students, noticing the pool table and target on the wall as a dart flew toward it. It hit the center, a group cheering louder over the shot. The holes in the wall that surrounded it told me that didn't happen often.

I continued through, hitting the room of students most involved in the music. One boy slipped in front of me, his girlfriend barely catching his arm. They laughed, and I did too, before hiding my face behind the cup as I drank. I was already tired, but I didn't want to leave yet. After sleeping all day, I wanted to enjoy the night. I climbed the stairs and found a seat along the hallway railing, letting my legs fall between the bars toward the room below me as the party went on.

My eyes shut as I let my head rest against a bannister bar, the music filling my soul. I could have comfortably let the night pass me by, a light daze fogging my mind. I was nodding off, when my head fell, and I straightened back up. Falling asleep in a stranger's hallway probably wasn't so brilliant.

I grabbed the bars and pulled myself to stand. Maybe it would be better to find my way home before it got any later.

Someone pushed past behind me, making me stumble harder against the railing. I stared down at the lingering party as I braced myself, fighting a rolling surge of nausea, before spinning back on whoever it was that bumped me.

"Watch where you're walking," I growled before I could catch myself. My eyes widened at Mr. Nazurin, suddenly nervous to be found at some random party.

He locked eyes with mine, seeing the recognition. Suddenly it waved away with a blur, and his face was something different. I stared at him, then down to my drink, trying to regain my mind. Why was he fuzzy? I only drank water. I shook it off, my mind was playing tricks on me.

"I thought you were someone else," I explained in a softer tone, though I still meant what I'd said.

He stepped in closer, his interest piqued. "Who might that be?"

"Nobody." I turned away to cut off the conversation. His taller, sharper features didn't look anything like Mr. Nazurin. The professor had a warmer blond hair, but this man's medium shag haircut was pure white, like his genetics forgot to add any color. How had I mixed them up?

The night air was a breath of freedom after stepping out of the crowded house. I sat on the porch step to catch my sanity, enjoying the fact that almost everyone else had moved inside. My palm wiped over my face, trying to wake back up enough to find my way home as regret swept through me. Who was I fooling? I didn't belong there, I wasn't supposed to party. I stood up, bracing against the wall to avoid falling.

Someone caught my arm, helping me stand. I turned to find him, the stranger that bumped me inside.

"What, you're following me now?"

"Just checking that you're alright, you seemed..." His words trailed off.

"Seemed what? Sick? Drunk? Clumsy?"

"Confused. Upset. Frustrated."

I waved him off. "All of the things. I was all of the things." I went down the steps, eager to put an end to the conversation. "I'm fine."

"Have we met?" he asked. I turned to meet his gaze, confused by the question. He pointed back over his shoulder at the door. "It's just, you said that you thought I was someone else, maybe I was familiar."

"You're not who I thought," I corrected. "We've never met. I'm confident."

"Well," his words caught me again, stopping me from running off. "We have now. I'm Zager."

"Zager?" I echoed half-mockingly, before realizing how insensitive it was. My expression went flat, staring at his outstretched hand. Was he trying to shake out our awkward introduction? I hesitated, before slowly reaching my hand out to accept.

"Willow," I answered, instantly regretting it. "Sam," I corrected. "I'm Sam." He ignored the strange revision as he embraced my hand. His fingers squeezed mine, and his eyes refocused in sudden surprise, as if he were looking at me through a new light. I fought my lingering daze. His gray-blue scrutiny felt so personal. Had I done something stupid?

"Dead blood," he commented, just above a whisper. I waited for him to explain, but he didn't. A wave of stranger danger swept through me as I moved back to pull my hand free, but it didn't break away.

"Excuse me?" Somehow his words felt offensive. Why did it seem like he saw right through the illness I'd spent all day hiding?

There was no stopping it then, as if I'd crossed the line of what my body could handle. I leaned over our embracing arms and purged my stomach into the side hedge. Zager let go of my hand only to catch above my stomach, supporting me as my muscles collapsed.

As it stopped, he pulled me against him for support.

"I don't usually drink," I lied, blaming it on something normal. Something that didn't initiate questions like being sick did.

"Are you done now?"

I straightened back up, nodding my head. "Yeah. I'm good."

"Let's get you home," he suggested.

"I can handle it." I pushed out of his support, ready to make the journey home alone. With a wobble, Zager grabbed my arm and pulled me back, not letting go as he crouched down to swing my legs up and cradle me.

"Put me down!" I ordered. "How dare you, I don't even know you!" I tried to push out of it as three boys came walking outside.

"Help me!" I called back at them. "Hey, get me down from here!"

Zager started walking down the sidewalk, and not a single eye lifted to acknowledge us.

"Hello!" I demanded. Why couldn't they hear me? Didn't they see the random man carrying a girl off in the night?

"Put me down right now," I ordered again. "I'll throw

up on you—" The force behind my words was lost as the world went fuzzy around us, my head hanging limp over his arm.

"There's a reason I didn't throw you over my shoulder," he answered calmly.

Instead of fighting it, my body swayed with each step, rocking my mind to sleep.

"Where do you live, Willow?"

"Angus dorms. Building C. Room 312." The words felt distant, pulled out of a dream as my consciousness slept on.

"Good girl," his low voice lulled in the back of my mind as darkness swept through.

ALONE

11

SAGE

"I know you guys are excited, but this is the worst!" I made a pity pout, glaring at my three friends.

Willow watched from her lonely end of the couch as Harper pulled me into the spot between her and Ava.

"I'll come back to visit," Harper swore. "I just hate that I'll miss your actual birthday!"

"I'll still be around," Ava reminded her through a bragging smile.

"With the group chat it'll feel just like normal," Harper defended. She was trying so hard to reassure me.

"As long as you guys don't forget about me," I mocked. I tried to hide beneath sarcasm, but it still felt like the fear shined through.

"Willow, are you excited to go somewhere new?" I asked, pushing the attention away. It was hard to gauge how she was doing. We'd been trying so hard to keep her included since we lost Sam, but it didn't seem to help. I immediately regretted my question, what a stupid thing to ask. Excited?

For what? A new doctor? New hospital? Excited to start a journey alone that Sam promised to hold her hand through?

Willow forced a smile. "Maybe some change will do me good."

I nodded, my smile probably just as reassuring as Harper's promises to keep in contact. Willow was the one I worried about most. The one that didn't respond to the group chats. That stayed back when we went to do something fun, no matter how much we tried to invite her.

"I can't wait to see Ben's place," Harper commented, shifting the mood back.

"Even though Josh will be there?" Ava teased. I laughed, remembering how Josh always drove Harper insane.

"Ew," Harper shook her head. "I hope he works crazy long hours." She hadn't had to see her cousin's best friend very often since the two of them moved to Maine. She always said it was the one perk of Ben going so far away, him taking Josh with him.

"Let the bickering begin," I mocked.

"The peace was so nice while it lasted!" Harper grabbed the large bowl of popcorn from the floor, scooping out a handful to pick through.

"It's not going to be the same without—" Ava hesitated, avoiding the eyes around her. Sam. We all knew the word she left out.

"Without all of us together," I finished. We didn't have to get specific. This was about Harper and Willow leaving. We didn't have to bring up Sam. We didn't have to state how the one person most enthusiastic about planning our futures wasn't around anymore to live it.

"Yeah," Ava agreed. She bit her lip, looking at Willow, who leaned away from us against her arm, pretending to focus on the quiet movie.

Ava looked back at Harper and me, wishing she could make Willow feel better. The same thing we all wished. All she could offer was a button on the remote, letting the volume drown out our conversation. All any of us could do was get lost in our last evening. Pretending, for just a few hours, that tomorrow wouldn't come, each of us preparing to step into the next chapter.

Our last night together. The last glimpse at what was.

I shook off the memory, but it would be back. That Friday before had been replaying over and over on a loop through my mind all week.

No new notifications lit up my phone. Just the same as when I'd checked five minutes before. No calls. No messages. I knew my birthday was going to be different this year, I knew my friends were gone, but did they really all forget? Sam would have remembered. She would have found some way to bring magic into my heart no matter how many miles sat between us.

I didn't blame Willow for forgetting, but Harper and Ava? We'd been making big, embarrassing deals out of our birthdays since we were little girls! I felt stuck, left behind in the past, while they moved on to their futures and forgot me in their tracks. If only I'd been born a few weeks sooner, then I'd be graduated and moving on to the grown up world with them. My new reality just made me feel like a child.

Everything about our high-school was different now. I was alone walking down the hallways, no matter how many other students filed through. My locker seemed so empty without Ava's overdue library books piled on the top shelf, the random messy papers shoved in wherever they'd fit. Sam's math textbook sitting on some forgotten sweatshirt that fell from the hook, because my locker was closest to her class. There was no tangled-up phone charger, no shiny new lipgloss left for whoever needed it next. No messages written on the magnetized mirror about plans for after school.

The empty glass mocked me, displaying my pathetic, lonely reflection. I pulled the mirror off, along with the pink and purple markers, tossing them forcefully into the trash can. Who was I going to write to? The fun was gone this year, I couldn't find it. It was just me.

I sat on the bench outside of Carver's cafe and ice cream shop, bundled up in my favorite hoodie with my jean jacket layered on top. After pulling the soft purple fabric sleeves out from under the denim to wrap over my fingers, I folded my arms tighter, rocking on the seat.

It felt too lonely for the traditional slice of cheesecake or a scoop of rocky road. It felt too sad for a birthday.

I stared at my reflection in the long glass windows, wishing she could talk with me. It was like she'd been following me around all day, reminding me that it was just us two. Finally eighteen? I should have been excited.

The walkways around me were empty as everybody sought out the warmth inside.

I studied myself in the glass, and it studied me back. The neat brown french braid that ran from my forehead to my middle back. A purple ribbon wrapped through it at my neck, dangling down just longer than the actual braid. The unbuttoned jean jacket mostly hid the sweatshirt underneath, a shade lighter than my actual jeans. Even my cowgirl boots matched the purple, though nobody would know it because my jeans covered the violet accents.

But not even my favorite outfit could save the day.

Something slithered behind my legs. I could barely see it behind them in the glass reflection. A snake. I jumped forward off the bench as it got ready to lunge. My feet fought to stay off the ground as I bounced away, tumbling back on my pockets as I searched for the threat, but there was nothing.

I stood back up, looking around in paranoia as I wiped my palms together, knocking off the small rocks, but no creatures lurked around me. My eyes shifted toward the glass, studying the spot where I'd seen the snake, but it was gone there too.

My fingers brushed over my hair, checking that it still looked decent as I searched for lingering eyes, hoping nobody witnessed my embarrassing display, but it was only the face in the reflection that watched.

My eyes landed in hers, when I noticed a darkly-hooded figure standing behind a car across the street. Was he watching me? I spun around to see who it was, but like the snake, he was gone too.

"What is wrong with me today?" I muttered. My mind was playing tricks on me.

I grabbed my backpack, spinning the top handle to make sure nothing hid on it before tossing it over my shoulder. At least I still had a little bit of sunlight left to spend with my garden at home.

12

SAGE

Gardening had always been mine and my Grandma Nina's thing. Even as a toddler, I loved going out with her to soak up the sunshine and care for the plants. Although, at two years old, I was usually more invested in dancing in the sprinkler or making mud pies than the actual garden.

Nina practically raised me while my mom worked two jobs. With no father in the picture, it was just us girls working as a team. When Nina died, it broke both of our hearts. She took a huge piece of us with her, but left enough love in our memories together to carry forward with. Some days, when the warm sun hit my skin just right, I could still hear her singing, *"You are my sunshine,"* in the garden next to me.

"There's too much to smile about, child." I quoted her words to myself like an echo, kneeling down beside the soil with an overflowing, silver watering can.

The smile didn't last though, after watering the base of the first few plants. I set the can down and brushed my fingers through the large leaves, trying to understand why there still weren't any signs of pumpkins growing beneath them. No blossoms had appeared to mark my garden's success.

Nina and I grew pumpkins every single year, and they always did great, so what was I doing wrong? She'd always made it look so easy. Everything was changing. The life that I knew and loved was slipping further and further out of reach. I couldn't even keep the spirit of our simple garden alive. Now it had just become another reminder that she was gone.

I shoved the watering can, making it puddle into the grass as I reached for the forgotten hand shovel a few feet away and started to dig. I ripped at the leaves, angry at my plants for failing, angry at myself for not knowing how to fix it.

Dirt hit my face as the roots broke loose. I tossed the first plant aside, reaching for the next. The rough leaves broke apart as I crawled deeper into the garden, my knees getting caked in soft soil.

Something stung my leg, making me jump. I turned my anger on it, screaming madly as my reflexes swiped off the angry wasp. Two more joined in, circling me like their prey. *"The cold weather makes them grumpy,"* Nina used to explain. Well apparently so did destroying the garden they called home.

"Leave me alone!" I searched for their nest, wondering if I'd smashed it. A second one landed on my hand, stinging the base of my thumb. "Dang!" I swatted that one off too, ready to make a run for the house.

"You okay?"

"Just an angry wasp," I warned as a man jogged up the yard. "Better not come any closer." I reached down to save my backpack.

He softly grabbed my wrist as I stood, leading me ahead of him toward the porch. A dark pointed tattoo ran out along his forearm from under the sleeve, and a faded scar sat above his thumb.

"It sting you? You're not allergic or anything, are you?"

I looked back at his face, caught off guard by the gravelly note in his voice. The dark, hooded sweatshirt beneath his vest made me think of the reflection at Carver's, watching from across the road. Had he followed me home? I pulled my hand back.

"Twice. I'm not allergic, though. I actually get stung quite often."

"Really?" The monotone question didn't sound so much like a question.

"Guess that's what comes with gardening as a hobby."

He didn't answer, his eyes bouncing back and forth between mine. As if he'd caught himself, they fell to the ground, and with a quick nod, he leaned around to grab the door for me.

"Well, if you've got it from here."

I stepped through, glad the stranger didn't push to come in with me. He waited on the porch, giving a quick glance up and down the street behind him before he looked at me.

"Have a good night then..." he started to turn.

"Sage," I finished. "And thank you. For helping me." It was gentlemanly in its own semi-creepy way. Had it been that snake I'd imagined earlier, I would have appreciated his assistance more. How much of my freak out had he witnessed? *Embarrassing.*

He gave another quick nod, and I slowly closed the door between us. My bag dropped as I pressed my back against the door.

"Some birthday," I grumbled. "Not even mother nature

wants to be my friend." Where was Nina's optimism now? I climbed up to the attic, hoping I could feel some in her old things. Maybe I could find her little home-mixed jar of salve to put on the stings. I missed Nina and her home remedies. She always had some herb, or oil, or stone that she swore would help, and call it blind, childish trust, but I was always convinced it worked. If I was having nightmares and she handed me a feather to stick under my pillow, I didn't question it.

Mama could never get rid of Nina's stuff. She had to pack it all away for safekeeping. Now anytime one of us needed a touch of her warmth or wisdom, we were probably lost up there soaking up her good vibes.

I picked up the framed photo from her dresser, reminiscing in the past. Nina, mom and me, sitting on the porch swing out front. There was laughter in our smiles. There usually was.

I sat on the old wingback chair, draped in sweaters and a gold and brown granny-square blanket that Nina had since she was a little girl. I often poked my fingers through the crocheted yarn, wondering how on earth it had survived so long.

Something fell to the ground next to me. I leaned over the armrest and pushed the blanket aside to see. A small, palm-sized, silver locket sat on the floor. I reached down to it, refusing to get off the chair for even a second. My finger brushed over the engraved letters on top, wondering where it came from.

Unitus.

Unite?

"Random," I muttered. I'd never noticed it up there before. I clicked it open, expecting a watch, but finding my reflection instead. A mirror. It held the same lonely reflection I'd been seeing everywhere else. For a moment, I thought I saw trees. A dark shadow flashed in the glass behind me, making me jump. My fingers snapped it shut with a click as I stood up and spun around to see who was there.

"My mind is really playing tricks on me today," I commented, looking back down at the trinket in my hand. Where did it come from? "I'll have to ask mama about you later," I told it. "If only Nina was here to share your story herself."

I set it on the dresser, next to the familiar picture, running my finger down the frame once more in admiration before turning toward the stairs. At least I still had my birthday dinner with mom to look forward to. She always brought home the chicken pot pie soup that I loved, and it would go perfectly with the cooler weather.

13

SAGE

I dreaded the weekend that rolled closer with each passing day. Normally a simple weekend was exciting, but this was my first year without friends to hang out with. Ava was the only one left, and she would be busy working evenings for her dad's shop. All week long, it had been crickets. Not even she would bother to find the time for a quick text. I just wanted the entire school year over with so that I could start my next chapter and catch up with my friends, but time mocked me instead.

I stared at my empty phone screen again. Harper promised to send tons of pictures, but so far she'd only sent one. Willow was probably busy with doctor appointments. She said she'd share updates, but she's such an introvert that we weren't expecting a whole lot. Ava was working, but she couldn't have been on the clock the entire week, right? The three of them couldn't find a single window in their days to say hi?

I got hot chocolate at Carver's and sat on the bench. Our bench. Even if it felt lonely now, it was still our bench. There were too many afternoons spent with that bench to pretend like we weren't old friends. I'd been getting treats at Carver's with the girls since we were little. One day, they would come back to visit, and I would be able to tell them that I kept their spots warm.

I ignored the girl in my reflection. It seemed like she was out to get me. A man walked between me and the glass, and I stared at him instead.

I recognized him. The new student who chose a seat in the back of my art class that morning. I'd taken a second, third, maybe even fourth look because of how cute he was, wishing Ava was there to notice with me.

His cozy, hooded, light-gray sweater looked neat and expensive. He wore black jeans, and just like me, his own set of boots. They were more of a casual ankle boot, though. Worn, but still nice.

"I like your boots," I called out as he walked by.

He took two more steps before stopping, then turned to look at me, hesitant, as if he wasn't sure I spoke to him. I glanced down at his boots again before giving him a smile. His lips dimpled up, brows drawing together as he studied my face.

"I've seen you before," he commented.

"I believe we spent an hour together this morning, learning how to shade." I thought of the classic, beginner art lesson, showing light and shadows on cubes and cones. Art class was really the only class I enjoyed. There was such a free feeling in there as the teacher put on music and gave you space to create.

"That's right," he answered. "The girl with the blue ribbon in her hair."

I stopped myself from reaching up to check, remembering the long bow I'd tied over my ponytail, same way I'd been wearing them every day since I was five.

"Sage," I corrected, hoping he didn't see that I blushed about his noticing me.

"Sage," he repeated. "I'm Kett "

"It's nice to meet you."

He looked around. "It's so cold out here. Are you waiting for someone?"

"I wish." I looked down at my phone again, a little embarrassed by my quick answer.

"Can I see that?" he asked. I followed his gaze to my open, empty screen, wondering what he meant.

"My phone?" I asked, handing it up to him. "Sure."

He typed something in before giving it back.

"What's that?" he asked, nodding his head to gesture at my arm. When I'd reached up for the phone, my sleeve pulled back, exposing my wrist. My free hand covered the dark birthmark that crossed my inner arm.

"I was born with it," I answered, stretching my sleeve back down. I don't know why the mark bothered me so much, but I always felt the urge to hide it.

His phone dinged. He slid it out of his pocket for a quick text.

"It almost looked like a dragon," he commented. I thought about the birthmark, trying to make out a shape the way I would search for pictures in the clouds.

"Huh," I answered. "I never thought about it that way." My phone buzzed with a text from a new number.

Would you like to go inside with me?

A little spark of hope formed, and for the first time, I was glad I wasn't waiting on my friends. I nodded my head, my smile matching his. "I would love to."

He held out an arm for me to link mine through. We sat

in a booth towards the back and ordered sodas. I couldn't stop smiling, pleased by the way my luck was changing.

"What?" he asked, reaching up to make sure there wasn't something on his face. Maybe he'd caught me staring a moment too long.

"Nothing," I countered. "Sorry, I haven't had the best week, but this has helped turn it around."

He nodded his understanding, still wearing a warm smile. "Tell me about it."

I shook my head. "It's just... change. Lots of change, all at once." He didn't answer, waiting for me to go on. "I'll admit I wasn't exactly looking forward to the start of this school year. My friends all graduated last spring, and I guess I'm just the one that got left behind. It stinks, you know. Feeling forgotten."

"You seem hard to forget," he argued.

"Yeah? Well yesterday was my birthday, and not a single one of them even bothered to send a text."

His eyes widened a bit. "I'm sorry." He reached his hands across the table, only to pull them back as the waitress brought our drinks. She dropped two straws on the table and pulled out a small notepad.

"Ready to order anything else?"

"A slice of cake," he answered.

"Which one?" she asked.

Kett looked across the table, giving the choice to me.

I smiled, fighting another blush as I looked at her. "Strawberry cheesecake."

She nodded, silently taking her note as she grabbed our untouched menus.

"Thanks," I told him. "You didn't have to—"

"Who isn't looking for every excuse to eat cake?" he countered.

The conversation remained light and easy. I stared at the pair of forks she served with our single slice of cake, giddy about the fact that it felt like a date. And he was cute. So cute, I couldn't stop the way my eyes kept fighting to look.

He asked me about my favorite birthday memories. I told him about the year my friends all gave me stuffed animals, because I was obsessed with every creature under the sun, but mom wouldn't let me get a real pet. I'd always loved them.

"One day I'm going to rescue a couple of strays from a pound and give them the life every dog dreams of."

I laughed as I told Kett about my birthday the year before, when I made everybody go country dancing.

"I was always the more athletic one of the group. I've always loved sports and trying new things. The line dances were so fun, a couple of them felt impossible to keep up with, but there were a few easy ones." Even Ava got the hang of the easier ones, despite her naturally clumsy self. We'd spent the whole night laughing, Ava, Harper, myself and Sam.

My smile faded with the memory, gaze falling to the table. I swallowed back the heartache and reached for another bite, when I noticed a dark-hooded reflection standing behind me in the metal napkin box. I jumped, dropping a full fork of cake to the table as I spun up on my feet to see.

Ava's big brother walked the aisle toward us. "Noah?" He looked so raggedy, worn-down and sad. Not a black hood in sight.

"What's wrong?"

"Hey, Sage. I'm looking for Ava. You haven't seen her, have you?"

"Not for a few days."

He nodded, but it wasn't happy. "I thought maybe I'd find her here. If you see her, will you tell her to call me?"

"Sure, of course!" My heart was still pumping from the false jump scare.

"Thanks." He turned to leave, his shoulders slumped forward and resigned.

I studied the room around him as he stepped outside. There was nobody else, no creepy figure lurking in the background, nobody waiting outside the windows. I settled back down, pretending not to be afraid of the reflection as I reached for a napkin to help clean up my mess.

"That was weird."

"You okay?" Kett asked.

"Yeah, sorry. I thought I saw something."

"What did you see?" he asked.

I shook my head. "It was nothing."

"Hey." Kett reached his hand across to squeeze mine. "Are you sure? You looked scared."

I let out a breath and gave in. "You ever just feel like you're being watched? Or... followed?"

He leaned back, checking the room behind me too. "Maybe for a moment here and there."

"I keep thinking..." I didn't know how to say it. There's a stalker in my reflection? "I met this strange guy yesterday." Was he the same guy I kept seeing? Watching me from behind? "I just keep seeing him."

"He's here now?"

"No!" I sighed. "That's the thing. It's in my head or something. I'm just being paranoid."

His hand squeezed mine again. "Why don't I walk you home?"

I smiled at the single bite of cake left on the plate,

grateful for Kett's offer. I wasn't ready for our time together to end... maybe he wasn't either.

I should have sent a message to Ava, let her know that Noah was looking for her, but it wasn't my problem this time. They hadn't bothered talking to me all week, and for just a moment, I was busy sharing cake with the cute new guy. Harper and Ava were so excited for what was next, and maybe deep down I was jealous, but I just wanted to feel happy too.

14

SAGE

Kett's casual pace made the walk home feel safer, his calm energy assuring me that there wasn't some monster on our heels.

"Feel better?" he asked as I slowed in front of the house.

"You definitely made me feel better."

"Good."

I glanced back at the quiet house, not a single light on to welcome me home, and wished the night wasn't over quite yet.

"Is anybody else here?" he asked.

"My mom had to work late tonight," I answered.

"Do you want me to wait a while? I mean, if you're still worried."

"Oh, I—" a soft thud sounded from inside. I turned to look, questioning my senses. Was someone inside or was my imagination feeding off my nerves.

Kett grabbed my arm, stepping around me to study the house. "Let me help you check on things before I go."

He'd heard it too. The realization made my insides

shudder, unlocking a new fear. I hadn't thought of someone hiding inside my house, but now the worry would be stuck in my head if we didn't look.

"Yeah," I accepted, "that would be good."

I moved through the house quickly, leaving Kett at the entryway.

"I can check this way," he offered, moving before I could answer.

I looked through the bedrooms, closets, and kitchen. Every door and window on the first floor was locked up tight. That only left upstairs. The small little storage space, crowded with photo albums, baby clothes, holiday decorations and Nina's old things. I moved toward the stairs, wondering why it was taking Kett so long to finish looking.

I climbed the steps slowly, trying to see through the crack in the door as goosebumps crawled up my arms and neck. He stood facing the old dresser, his hand on the framed photo. I watched the large mirror on the dresser as I took the last step, pushing the door open just as he angled into view.

"Is this you?" he asked. He stepped aside so I could see the photo, turning to smile at me. "Sorry, I got curious."

"Yeah." I let out a breath of relief, going over to look at it with him. "With my mom and Grandma Nina."

"You look so happy," he commented. His hands dropped into his pockets as he turned away.

"We were," I agreed. "It was hard when we lost Nina. The three of us girls were really close."

"Sage?" My mom's voice made me jump as the front door closed behind her.

"Up here!" I called back, grateful to have her home. Now I wouldn't have to be alone.

"Looks clear," Kett decided, taking that as his cue. "I should go," he added, "but I'm glad I bumped into you today." He reached for my pony tail, running his finger down the blue ribbon over my shoulder.

"Yeah," I agreed. "Me too."

I followed him down the stairs, and he went straight for the door, stepping outside.

"See you later," I told him. He smiled, closing himself into the night. A moment later my phone buzzed.

> Let me know when I can walk you home again.

I laughed, giddy about the new friendship.

> Tomorrow.

I pressed send, and already couldn't wait. Friday. Suddenly the upcoming weekend days didn't feel so terrible. I turned for the kitchen and hugged my mom. While opening the fridge to find leftovers from the night before, my phone buzzed again.

> Tomorrow.

"What has you grinning like that?" my mom asked.

"I met the cutest boy today." All my worries about monsters and stalkers were buried by excitement as I scooped soup into a bowl.

"Cute, and he bought me a piece of cake."

"Aw, let your sweet tooth lead your heart," she mocked, but her smile was sincere. "I'm glad. Make more friends this year."

"I will," I promised, the same way I did every time she

said it, but this time I felt like I could actually follow through. This time it didn't seem so hopeless.

There was a knock on the door. Mom went for it while I watched from the kitchen, waiting on the microwave. Mr. Hillin's desperate blue eyes flashed from mom's to mine. Ava's dad. My heart sank. Something was really wrong.

"Have you seen Ava?" he asked. "We haven't seen or heard from her in days... she's just... gone."

Days? I glanced down at my phone, thinking of the days that passed by while I felt sorry for myself. My friend was missing, and I told myself she'd just forgotten about me. How selfish.

It felt like we talked to Ava's dad for an hour, though he only restlessly stood in our doorway for a few moments, refusing to come in. *"No,"* he'd say. *"I have to keep looking."* I told him I'd reached out a few times, but she never answered. Not since our movie night with Harper and Willow.

"I'll keep trying," I promised, ready to go hunt her down alongside him and Noah. It was hard to fall asleep, worry and guilt tugging back and forth at my thoughts. I tried calling Ava twice, but both times it went straight to voice-mail. The phone was dead. Where would Ava have gone? She'd taken the summer easy, leaning into their last free months before adulthood, but she was so ready to start working a full schedule and start saving up. She seemed so happy. Something must have happened to her.

I sat on our bench, waiting for someone to show up. Anyone. Harper, Ava, Sam or Willow. Maybe even Kett. The girl in my reflection mocked me, the same way she always did.

Someone passed behind my bench. I looked up, alarmed by the hooded man staring down at me. It was exactly who I imagined beneath the hood, the man that approached me in the garden.

"What do you want?" I asked him nervously.

He stepped around the bench, closer, taking the seat next to me.

"What do you want?" I repeated more demandingly, scooting away.

His face spun up to look at me as the hood fell down, but it was someone new.

"Nina?"

She smiled. "Hello, Sage."

I looked around, confused by the switch.

"What is it?" she asked, concern written in her face.

"Nina—" I sighed. "I've felt so lost these last few days. Everyone left, my friend is missing, and now my mind is playing tricks on me. It's mocking me."

"What kind of tricks?" Her brows drew together in instant concern.

"My reflection... just... silly."

She sat up straighter. "What do you see in your reflection?" she asked, keeping up with my worries.

"It just feels like I'm being followed. A man—"

"What does he look like?"

I shook my head. "There's something dark about him. Watching from far away." I thought of the moment he grabbed my hand. "He had a tattoo on his arm."

"The arrowhead," she commented. "It can't be." She stood up, a serious look on her face. I thought of the dark lines, his sleeve could have easily been hiding an arrow.

"I don't understand." I stood up too, searching her eyes.

"You've seen the hunter."

"The hunter? What does that mean?"

"The hunter," she said again. "He's back. And he's found you already. He'll bring the blood out of the shadows."

"The blood? Nina, stop."

"You have to go. He can't find you again!"

"Find me? How am I supposed to stop that?" She went silent, deep in thought. "Nina, he knows where I live."

"No," she whispered. "You have to get away. Leave. Take the broken mirror and go far from here."

"Go? What about mom? What about school! I can't just leave."

"Sage," her voice softened, reaching up to cup my cheek in her hand. "You have to." The comfort of her touch crumbled away, replaced by cold fear. "The hunter will come for you again. There's no time."

"Go—"

The word echoed through as I sat up in bed, the wind outside scraping a tree branch against my window. I stepped into the hallway slowly, afraid of every dark shadow through the house as much as I was afraid to turn on a light to notify any eyes watching from the outside.

"I don't understand," I cried to myself, wishing Nina were really there.

I opened my mom's slightly cracked door, and crept across the room to cuddle up with her the way I always did when I had a nightmare. Usually it made her stir, and she would turn around to wrap me in a hug, but this time she didn't move.

I snuggled into her back, hiding from the world outside her walls. There was something wet beneath my arm. I turned on my phone flashlight, wondering if her water bottle was leaking. A dark red stain blurred into the fabric, puddling across her weight in the mattress.

"Mom!" I grabbed her shoulder and shook. "You're

bleeding!" She didn't react. I pulled at her side as my flashlight lit up her still face.

"Mom!" I urged again, this time begging. "Please, wake up!" I pulled away the blanket, shocked by the hole slashed into the center of her chest.

"Mama?" The cry was barely above a whisper. My finger pressed against her neck, my breath frozen as I searched for a pulse. Nothing.

"No."

I pulled out my phone and called an ambulance, desperate for her community at the hospital to save her life as everything started to blur. They drove her away, the police were taking notes, investigating the house, and I was just there. Alone.

I tried to call Ava, a distressed attempt to reach the only friend close by, but she didn't answer. Straight to voicemail again.

No mom. No Nina. No Sam. No Ava. Harper was far away, and so was Willow. *"Tomorrow."*

I stared at the unopened promise of tomorrow that still ran across my screen. I'd been afraid to open it, to ruin the notification that told me someone still cared. I clicked the phone number, not even saved as a real contact yet.

"Hello?" he asked tiredly from the other end.

"Kett?"

"That's me."

The relief forced my tears out. My breaths shook as I wondered what to say.

"What is it?" His voice perked up. "What's wrong?"

"My mom..." I choked on the words. I knew the truth, there wasn't a pulse, but I couldn't say it. As if all of mom's years of diligence helping save people in the E.R. would pay forward a miracle. "She's hurt. They took her to the hospital."

I fought the panic, moving toward the back of the house to get some privacy.

I just turned eighteen, still had another year of high school left, I wasn't supposed to be alone. Everyone else was gone, the world couldn't claim my mother too. I had to hear the doctors say it. The people she worked with every day. The people who knew me... who knew her.

"We checked the house," I whispered to myself, shaking my head. It didn't make sense. "We looked."

"Where are you? I'm on my way."

"I'm at home—"

The phone ripped away from my ear. I looked up at the man towering above me, shadowed by a familiar dark hood. I twisted around, pushing off the back step, staring at his face as he held the call to his ear. His short-cut beard was as black as the shadow his dark hood cast over his eyes. Everything about him was cold as the inky tattoo pointing out of his sleeve. The arrow tattoo.

"He'll bring the blood out of the shadows," Nina warned inside my dream.

"What do you want from me!" I yelled. "Leave me alone!"

His gloved hand lowered the phone down, studying the screen before he hit a button. His eyes rose to meet mine, and I could have sworn they glowed against the darkness, two star-bright golden rings in the shadows of his face.

"You're not safe," he stated in low warning. "We have to go."

I stared at him, knowing I wasn't getting past him to my house. I bolted for the side yard instead, trying to catch him off guard. He dove into my back, rolling with me against the gravelly dirt. His hand covered my mouth as he held me tightly from behind. I fought against it, desperate to follow my grandmother's warning.

"He can't find you again. You have to go."

The words echoed in my mind as my energy blurred into sleepy darkness.

BOOKED

15

JANE

My head jerked up with a gasp, as if that single breath brought me back to life. I scrambled onto my knees, palms breaking through the thin layer of ice atop the snow, crawling desperately away from whatever reached for my ankles. My arms wrapped around the closest tree as if it would protect me from the monsters that chased me through my dreams.

Waiting for sleep felt like an invitation for the nightmares to creep back in. I'd stared at the ceiling the night before, afraid of what might possess me in the darkness.

What monster sent me running into that wintery labyrinth of trees? And would it come for me again?

The forest was empty, apart from the raven on its perch above me, watching in silence. Shaking out the fear, I stood, studying the warm black jacket and tightly tied boots I wore. Mylo's jacket and boots. I'd set them aside when I got into the house, but I couldn't remember putting them on before I left.

"Well, you haven't steered me wrong yet," I told my flying friend, eying me from a branch. "Which way today?"

As if on command, it dropped from its perch and veered left.

"That's not creepy at all," I commented, hoping the bird wouldn't take offense. What omen might a raven bring? Its coal feathers merging in and out of the shadows where only secrets lived. Darkness, death, and yet I followed, as if I were caught on a hook, rolling through the deepest waters where it tugged.

I studied each step ahead, reflexively anticipating the sharp rocks and twigs that scratched at my feet the day before. The sturdy boots reminded me they were there to protect me, supporting each step. The extra layer of defense took an edge off my fear. I would have to thank Mylo again for the donation.

My steps stopped short when I noticed the familiar brick office. I glared at the bird, wishing it would have led me back to Emma's instead.

"What, you think I need therapy too?" I sighed, knowing I couldn't find my way back to Emma's myself. At least I wouldn't have to explain my entire situation all over again if it was just Mylo helping me.

"He's going to get sick of giving me rides." I spoke to the bird like a companion, as if it could see into my soul and understood every concern.

As promised, Mylo's office was open and warm. I tip-toed inside, hoping to go unnoticed, when the raven glided through the crack above me.

"No! Shew!" I ordered, chasing it down the hall. It dove straight into Mylo's office, landing on the desk.

A gurgling croak vibrated through the quiet room as it called into the silence.

"No!" I said again, reaching to wave it off. I was not prepared to catch a wild bird.

"Back so soon?" Mylo commented. Once again, his voice came out of nowhere. My hand shot to my chest, covering the pounding heart inside it.

"I'm sorry! It snuck past me when I opened the door!"

"She's fine," he answered, moving around to his desk. He reached for the raven, which climbed calmly onto his arm.

"She?" I asked. "You have a pet raven?"

"I do not have her. She is not mine to keep. Just a friend." He smiled, brushing his finger along the back of her wings. I hadn't seen him smile before, not really. A purple undertone shimmered beneath her charcoal feathers.

"I call her Oculo. Oco. It never hurts to have an extra set of eyes."

"The secrets she must keep," I mocked. He didn't laugh, reaching for an open cage as she swooped smoothly through, but he did not latch the door.

"A true friend takes your secrets to the grave," he answered. My eyes scoped out the office again, taking more of it in. A thick gray blanket rested over the back of the couch this time, and I wondered if he'd been expecting me to show up barefoot again.

"Or a therapist with doctor-patient confidentiality, I hope."

His dark eyes flashed to mine, the right side of his lips quirking up into a dimpled cheek.

"And what is it you would prefer? A therapist? Or a friend?" The attention shifted back on me, making my stomach knot.

"My sanity," I answered. "Whichever can help me find it."

"The kind of sanity that keeps you from trying to claw free of your own skin in the night?"

"What?" I shook my head, remembering the scratches up my arms. My hands rubbed awkwardly over the jacket sleeves, glad for the layer of black fabric that hid them. I wanted to deny it, but he already knew the truth.

"Thank you for the jacket. And the boots. They really saved me today."

He gave a slight nod, with his always-casual expression. "No problem. There's a blanket on the couch if you want to stay and warm up a while."

"Thanks, but I already told you, I'm not looking for a therapist."

He sat and leaned back in the chair at his desk, giving me his full attention. "Okay, then. What can I help you with? A ride back to Emma's?"

I almost said yes, but second-guessed it. What would I do there all day? Nobody was home. Dr. Quinn had suggested walking around town, but I wasn't ready for more walking. Where would I go? I thought of Emma's idea to look through some books.

"Is the library close?" I asked.

Mylo stood, walking over to the window. He pointed down the road toward a small, tan building surrounded by a neatly groomed yard.

I stared at the library, hoping it held the answers I needed to find.

"They open in an hour," he said before cocking his head back at the couch.

"An hour?" I repeated. He let a moment pass, when his shoulders relaxed and he let out a long, resigned breath.

"Please, stay a while. Try to take a nap." He smiled, but it felt forced, waiting for me to accept the repeated offer.

"I'm afraid, if I fall asleep, there's no telling where I'll wake up next."

Mylo moved back to his desk and took his seat again. "I'll be right here. Why don't you let me worry about that this time."

I gave in and sat, grateful that his attention was busy typing away on the computer. I was too antsy to relax, willing time by faster. He seemed to sense it, closing the laptop not long after to look at me.

"What are you working on?"

"Just writing," he answered vaguely.

"Writing," I repeated thoughtfully. "That's nice."

"Jane?"

It took a moment for the name to connect. "Hmm?"

"You're tired."

"I'm sorry, I didn't sleep very well. I'm tired." My brows furrowed, thinking over what I'd said.

"Why don't you rest."

"I think I will," I agreed. He walked around the back of the couch to help me with the blanket. I wrapped it around my back and pulled it tight, letting myself relax against the cushion.

"No," I fought, sitting back up. "I can't fall asleep."

"You're safe," Mylo said, moving to the chair across from me. He took a seat, staring into my eyes. "Why don't I do the talking for a while. You just close your eyes and listen."

I snuggled back into the blanket as my worries drifted away. "Tell me about you," I suggested in a tired voice.

"I grew up in a forest as wild as this one, with my two younger sisters, Nya, and Brie."

"That's nice," I commented. "Are you close with them?"

"I was," he answered, a somber note behind it. "As children, we would play in the twisted trees that surrounded our home. I can still see the bright leaves of fall as they consumed the horizon in scarlet, maple, and gold. My mother was a seamstress. It was humble, but we never knew want. A simple life. We had each other, and we had our home. She would sit on the porch for hours and hum songs as she worked, the perfect background melody while we danced along in our games."

Mylo's voice softly hummed, and I could picture everything he said so perfectly as the words lulled to the back of my mind.

I was in a forest, but this one was different. It was warm, and familiar, just the way he described it. Kids laughed, running back and forth over the paths of fallen leaves. A young woman sat in a rocking chair, humming along with the breeze as she stitched a thread through a hooded, brown cloak.

I followed a little boy as he chased two girls through the woods, tossing rocks and hiding behind trees. Laughter echoed around me with a magical sense of nostalgic euphoria. No worries or cares followed us into those trees around their home.

One of the little girls had bright emerald eyes that glowed against her freely waving, long, red hair. As I closed in closer, and caught her gaze, she smiled. The stick she held waved up in front of her face, before she leaned back behind the tree, out of sight.

My body leaned forward to find her again, when something dark lunged toward me in her place, swallowing me into the shadows.

I shot up with a gasp, falling to the ground. Something was chasing me and I had to get away. I bumped into the table and fell against the armchair towards my escape, but it grabbed me.

"No!" I screamed, fighting out of it.

"It's only me," Mylo insisted, but I kept thrashing. His arms wrapped around me from behind, holding my wrists to cross across my chest.

"Let me go!" I ordered. "I have to get away! I have to go!"

"There's nothing here," he promised. "You're safe."

"I'm safe?" I asked, my heartbeat pounding through. His grip held firm as I slowly calmed down. I relaxed my scrunched eyes, opening them to study the familiar office.

"I'm safe."

"You're safe," he repeated. "It was a bad dream."

"I was dreaming."

He cautiously let go of me. My hands covered my face, trying to wipe away the panic. I thought over his words. It was a dream... but I didn't remember the dream, only his story. His words seemed so real, like I remembered them myself.

"I fell asleep," I realized. That hadn't been my plan.

"I'm sorry, Jane, but I don't think I can help you."

My eyes shot to his, wondering if I'd heard him right. The sudden denial caught me off guard, trying to understand what changed.

"Can't... help?" He hadn't even given it a try yet. Had I freaked out that bad? I panicked, the sudden embarrassed urge to leave surging through me.

"How long was I asleep?" I asked. "I need to go." I didn't bother waiting for an answer before sliding out the door, and this time, he didn't stop me.

16

JANE

I spent hours searching the library for something, anything, that would clue me into my past. Book after book piled into my arms. I sat at a table to skim through them, images of dogs, maps, cars, houses. I even read through a bunch of children's books, trying to feel a touch of sentimentality.

People came and went, but none of them skipped the opportunity to stare at me, the odd one out, the girl that didn't belong, with a stack of books that I wasn't even really reading. If only I could take my pile of stories and hide away.

For the tenth time, my gaze got caught outside the window, staring at the brick office across the street. I couldn't get over the strange nap... the dream, the bird. But mostly, I just couldn't figure out Mylo. I couldn't tell if he wanted me there, or hoped I'd find my real home and leave for good.

His words stung. Did he think he couldn't help me? Or did he just not want to deal with my mess? He'd remained so neutral, it didn't seem like he cared either way. I thought he'd wanted to help, but maybe he was just trying to be polite. At the end of the day, he still had a quiet office, and he'd offered me a sense of friendship that I desperately needed.

He might not want to be my therapist, but did the offer for friendship still stand?

"I wonder if my new friend has a library card."

I stood up. "I'll be back for these," I told the librarian across the room, pointing at my stack of random books. Her brows drew together, but she nodded from behind her tall counter. She must have thought me crazy by that point.

With a brisk walk across the street, I pushed Mylo's door open and walked straight in. He didn't even look fazed, still seated comfortably in his chair as he leaned back to listen.

"Okay," I decided out loud. "Let's be friends."

"Friends," he repeated. "Okay."

"We don't even have to talk, but you did say your door was open."

He seemed cautious as he watched me start my rant. "—Okay."

"Okay. So, now, how would you feel about your friend bringing a stack of books over here to read through without a bunch of strangers watching?"

"You want to use my office... to read."

"Read in peace, yes." My eyes flickered towards the shelf of books behind him. Was that so strange a request? He had to have done the same at some point, right?

He lightly nodded, and gestured at the couch. "Go right ahead."

"Also, do you have Emma's phone number? I don't want her to worry about me when she gets off work."

"I'll let her know you'll be back this evening."

"Okay, cool." I gave an approving nod, when I remembered there was one more favor. He seemed to sense it too as I lingered in the doorway.

"Yes?"

"I'm wondering, as your friend, can I borrow your library card?" I gave him a wide smile, showing off my teeth. "That is, if you have one." Surely if he knew what time they opened, he went there himself on occasion.

He laughed, and the tension broke, standing up to get the wallet from his pant pocket as he walked closer. He handed it over with no reservations.

"Anything else, Jane?" I scanned the card, running my thumb over his name, somewhat surprised that it was real, that he actually had one.

"I wish you wouldn't call me that," I commented. "I mean, I wish I could tell you my real name. I almost wish it really was just Jane."

"Maybe I should call you by different names until one clicks."

My face scrunched. "I don't know about that."

"It might be fun. Victoria?"

I slid the card into my jacket pocket and turned back through the door. Two could play at that game. "See you later, John."

"Yep. I'll just be here." His muttering made me smile as the door closed between us.

The librarian gave me a funny look as she scanned through my chaotic assortment of books, and then again when I handed her Mylo's card. By that point, I didn't even care. I had a plan, and I was sticking to it.

I let the stack of books neatly fan out of my hands across Mylo's table.

"You're in a better mood," he commented.

"I feel like I'm on a big treasure hunt or something. One of these books has to hold some answers."

"Don't you need to eat something?" he asked. "Breakfast... lunch."

"I already—" *ate*. I stopped myself in the lie, knowing he would see right through it. I'd practically spent the day with him, and he knew I didn't have a wad of cash hidden in his jacket pockets. Honestly, I hadn't even thought about food. My appetite hated this amnesia life as much as I did.

"I'm not hungry."

He let it go. "Well, let me know when you're ready to drive back to Emma's." He moved to the chair across from me to pick up one of the spare books.

"Oh." I hadn't thought about his schedule. "Do you have other appointments? I don't mean to— Don't let me keep you. What time do you normally head home?"

"My schedule is clear, and my apartment is upstairs. I'm in no rush." He gave an amused look. "You can *keep me* as long as you'd like."

I thought of the stairs going up from the hallway when you first walk in, looking up at the ceiling as if I'd been shown a glimpse into his personal life.

As I closed one book after another, my heart sank. Why wasn't I finding anything helpful? Dr. Quinn seemed so sure that something would trigger my memories. I stared at the one remaining book, trying to make it last longer, even though my gut knew it wasn't going to be the one.

"Why don't we call it a night?" Mylo offered. He was watching me from his chair, hand holding the page in a novel.

I nodded, trying to ignore the defeat. Digging through an empty brain was impossible.

"Same time tomorrow?" I joked as Mylo parked in

Emma's driveway. He twisted to reach into the backseat for a large, brown paper bag, then casually handed it to me, as if it were expected.

"I didn't spend any money," he assured me as I hesitated to take it.

"Thanks?" I answered before climbing out.

"See you tomorrow," he agreed, his polite smile fading as I shut the door between us.

I stirred through my bowl of the chicken noodle soup that Emma had thrown into a slow cooker that morning. She'd been busy talking since I came in, making sure I'd been comfortable in the guest house, telling me about the kids in her class. Then she got caught up hyping some upcoming country dancing night.

"Come on, Jane! I don't have anyone to go do this stuff with!" she pleaded. "I just want to find a cute cowboy, and I really don't think that's too much to ask. Plus, we eat there all the time. My dad has a running tab! Food is on him."

"What is the population of this town again? Haven't you met all the fish in this puddle?"

She shrugged. "You popped up out of nowhere, right? Maybe my future husband will too. Besides, we get so many tourists, you just never know who you'll meet."

"Well, good luck then. I hope someone sweeps you off your feet."

Her smile beamed. "Now that's the spirit."

I took a big bite as an excuse to answer with a smile instead of words. I actually found myself hanging onto my evening with Emma, afraid to let it end. Afraid of the night that inevitably crept closer. Afraid to be alone.

"What's in the bag?" Emma asked. I looked where I left it by the front door.

"I'm not sure," I admitted, getting up to grab it. I set it

on the table, pulling out the first of four, simple shirts. Two long-sleeved, two short, solid grays and black. I didn't bother pulling out the neatly rolled pair of sweats at the bottom, much thicker than the cutesy pink pajamas Emma lent me.

"He bought you clothes?" Emma asked. "That was nice." She turned to take the dishes to the sink. I drew my arms closer, instinctively taking a breath of the first black shirt.

I wanted to tell her he didn't buy them for me, that they were his, but my mind got lost in it.

"You could invite him, you know," she called from the sink, waking me from my thoughts. I put the shirt down, tucking them all back into the bag.

"Oh no," I shut down. "I've already taken up so much of his time."

"Did it help?" she asked.

I stared at her, unsure what she meant.

"Talking to him... did it help?"

"Oh, right." The therapist that denied any hope in helping me? How could I ever admit that to her? "We didn't really talk much. I spent most of the day reading through library books like you suggested."

"Nice! Find anything useful?" The subject change made a welcome relief.

"Nothing yet."

"Well, I still think you should give therapy an honest try. It couldn't hurt! Mylo isn't so bad to look at either."

"I'm surprised you don't try to date him," I commented, immediately wishing I could take it back.

She seemed confused. "Mylo?"

"Yeah, didn't you like, grow up with him here?"

"Well, yeah. He's been practicing here ever since I can remember."

"Ever since you can remem—" I stared at her. What did she mean? "What, he can't be more than a few years older than we are."

She shrugged. "I'm not sure. Never thought about it."

My jaw dropped behind her as she got back to cleaning dishes. "Okay, then."

"I'm sure he'd be able to help. He's really good at his job. Helped a lot of people here in town."

Her words felt familiar. It seemed like I'd heard them before. "Yeah," I commented, pushing the clothes deeper into the bag. I might have listened if Mylo hadn't already turned me down. I still wasn't sure what I'd done to make him reject me as a patient, just another reminder that this wasn't my home.

"It would be nice to figure out where I belong."

Emma turned to face me, concern spread through her expression. "You're welcome here as long as it takes," she reassured me.

"I know," I answered. "Thank you. I think I'm just tired. I'm going to shower and get ready for bed."

She gave a soft smile. "Okay. Goodnight, Jane. See you tomorrow."

Jane. The sound of it made me tense up inside. Like a lie. I grabbed the bag and reached for the door.

"Tomorrow," I agreed.

Tomorrow. The promise of it echoed through me. Promising another day of this nightmare. Promising to keep me lost there forever.

17

JANE

The days were falling into a pattern, but not in a good way. Waking up lost in the woods. Wasting hours flipping through books, while Mylo typed away on his computer. Dinners with Emma and check-ins with Dr. Quinn. Going to bed dreading the continuing loop.

Hope was hard to hold when I didn't know what to hope for. What did the life that I longed to return to look like?

I didn't bother knocking before stepping through Mylo's door. I'd gotten there extra early that morning, and the lack of sleep was really wearing on my mind... my heart.

I ignored the books from the day before, falling into the couch.

"Good morning, Emily," Mylo commented in his consistently casual tone. I never understood why he was always up so early, but I also never asked.

"Nothing's working," I complained into the pillow, completely ignoring his name game. My face peeked out to look at him across the room. An actual professional, sitting right in front of me. I got up, moving to the neat shelf of black, hardcover books behind him. My finger skimmed longingly over the line of titles, realizing for the first time that they were all tragedies. I sent Mylo a curious glance, with an unexpected new perspective, not sure what to think of it.

"Remember when you said you had a few tricks up your sleeve?" I asked. His fingers softly swung the cover of his book closed on the desk, his eyes flickering to mine, but they were dark as he slowly shook his head.

"I told you, I can't help you."

The denial still hurt. Why did it feel so personal? My gaze kept busy admiring the different fonts and styles along the spines, the only thing setting the books apart from each other. How had he even acquired such strictly plain bound copies?

"I wish I knew which book was my favorite," I commented.

"Why's that?"

"So I could read it again for the first time."

"A common wish," Mylo agreed. He smiled thoughtfully. "I wonder if one feels the same magic the second time around."

"Which book is your favorite?"

Mylo seemed to consider it, a spark of light shining in his eyes as he reflected in silence. His crooked smile stretched up higher before his chair rolled back and he turned to pull open the top desk drawer. He unwrapped an off-white cloth, uncovering a worn, brown leather book. The spine felt its age despite the years it had clearly been handled with the utmost care. Like a one of a kind copy of something special. A treasure.

"It's beautiful," I commented.

"It was my mother's," he answered. I'm not sure why the words surprised me so much. Maybe because I really knew nothing about Mylo. He didn't go out of his way to talk about himself.

"May I?"

He handed me the heavy book. I opened it slowly, as if it might tear with the slightest wrong movement. The pages looked just as old, filled with delicate calligraphy and intricate sketches of creatures and life. A water well, a hillside of flowers, a castle made up of stone.

I flipped through another few pages, past marks of hunters and dragons, to a detailed map of a world that didn't exist. A land cut into three main pieces, The Dark Woods, The Marked Kingdom, and The Token Wood, but it was three smaller words that caught my attention. The Wild Thost.

"Thost," I read to myself, my finger tracing a line over it. It almost rang a bell, but I shook my head. As whimsical as each page was, this hand-drawn world wasn't real. It couldn't be the book that would unlock my past. Mylo watched me quietly.

"Amazing," I told him. "I've never seen anything quite like it." Not that I would remember.

"It's very old," he answered. I let the pages fall until it landed at the front, the title page. A Hundred Tales of Magic. I smiled, because something about it did feel like magic. I closed it to hand back, and couldn't keep from staring, trying to understand this strange man that fate stuck me with. Some moments it felt like I got a glimpse of the person hiding behind his indifference, but then he kept proving that I didn't know him at all. My shoulders sank.

"You won't just try?" I asked, desperate for someone to help me through. This was his office right? His job? "It's not like your days are all booked out." My eyes widened as I realized how harsh that sounded.

He didn't react, his gaze holding mine, all sorts of tension written inside it.

"I'm sorry, that was—"

"It's not that simple..."

I took a step back. "Simple? None of this is simple. That's not what I asked for." I shook my head, and turned for the door.

"Jane, I can'—"

"I need a break... some fresh air. A whole week sitting around staring at dusty books and it's gotten me nowhere!"

"Where are you going?"

"Nowhere!" I spun around at the door, frustrated beyond reason. "I have nowhere to go."

"Jane, stop."

"My name's not Jane!"

I turned down the sidewalk, letting the cool air calm down my boiling blood. I couldn't even convince the one person that I thought might be able to help, a person I thought cared enough to help, to try. So instead, I walked. My feet went on, without a care where they led. Where was I going? Anywhere but here. Maybe I could stumble into someone who would actually be determined enough to do something about a missing person.

The path ended, turning to water. I stared down a dock, noting the few boats that drifted in and out. It was beautiful. I wanted to be swept away in the tide, carried somewhere new. Somewhere closer to home, but I'd gone as far as the path would take me.

I sat on a bench, letting my emotions wash away in the slow, constant echo of waves.

"Jane?" Emma's concerned voice rang through the air.

She called at me from her parking spot, hesitant to come closer until she knew for sure. I stood to face her.

"How did you find me here?"

"Mylo told me you were upset... that you headed this way."

I searched the world behind her, wondering how he knew, when a black bird floated into the distant trees. *Oco.*

"He also told me you've been having nightmares," she added as she came closer. "That you've been waking up in the woods every morning."

I fought back a rush of new emotions. Betrayal? What was all that talk about a true friend taking your secrets to the grave? *Some friend.*

"I didn't want you to worry. I know I should have told you."

"Are you okay?" she asked.

"I will be." I stared at the water. "I just wanted to try out something different." She took an open spot on the bench, and I sat back down too, accepting it for what it was.

"I used to sit here with my mom," she told me. "She loved the ocean."

"Hard not to with a view like this."

"Yeah," Emma agreed. "She loved watching the boats going in and out. Whale watching. All of it." She sighed. "I sure miss her."

I looked at Emma. It was the first time any raw emotion had crept through her enthusiastic exterior.

"Cancer," Emma explained, gaze falling to her knees as she answered the question before I could bring myself to say the words. "Something my dad couldn't fix. I was just ten years old. It all happened so fast."

"That must have been so hard. I'm sorry."

She nodded, accepting my sympathy. "Bad things

happen. Things we can't control. But good things happen too. Sometimes, right along with the bad. We just have to open our eyes to see them."

In a way, she was calling me out, and it didn't feel fair. She didn't know what it was like not to know your own face in the mirror. To wonder what loved ones might be crying over the loss of you each night. There was nothing good to go alongside that.

"I just want to understand what happened."

"I know." She didn't push it further, letting the sound of waves consume our thoughts for a few moments longer before patting my knee.

"Why don't we pick up some pizza and go have a movie night. I can even sleep in the cottage with you tonight so you're not alone."

Company, and a distraction. The thought of it invited in a new sense of hope. Maybe changing things up could break the cycle.

"That actually sounds really nice."

She stood, reaching a hand down to pull me up with her. "Come on, then. Girl's night it is."

SPELLED

18

HARPER

My arm braced against the ground as I fell from the gate, another failed attempt at reaching the top, pounding my fist against the gravel in defeat.

Where was that dumb dog? I was going to make it regret leading me through that gate. The wishing well? The hourglass? I didn't want any of it, not anymore. It felt as if I'd been swallowed up in one of Sam's books. This wasn't my story! This wasn't real!

Going against everything in my soul, I gave up and gave in. The gate would not give, and the promise in Elijah's words rang clear. I was stuck there. I moved back toward the house at a reluctant pace, afraid of the fate that waited inside its walls, but left with no other option.

Elijah didn't smile when I walked in. A gray shirt clung to his broad frame, spots still damp from following me out into the rain, his waving brown hair dripping lightly at his shoulders. I wondered how my mascara held up against both the weather and my tears, likely smeared out into the skin around my eyes. At least I'd kept it light.

"How do I get out of here?" I asked as directly as I could. "Is there no ladder? No shovel? No saw to cut through the bars?" Some kind of tool to free us both? Somehow I knew it was bigger than that. It wasn't that simple. "How do I go back to my life?" And why did I feel so disconnected from it?

"You don't," he answered. He said nothing else, as if he were waiting for me to accept it.

"I don't understand any of this," I admitted, though that much was already clear. He still wasn't helping me though. His expression remained empty, waiting for me to go on. I waved my hands out at the room around me, then dropped them in surrender. It looked like I was there to stay.

"Is there somewhere I can spend the night then?"

Elijah nodded, and stood up. He didn't say much as he escorted me through the house, though maybe that's because he knew I wouldn't hear. Instinct told me it was wrong following a stranger into his home, but what other choice did I have? Was it even his home? Had it just become mine too?

What would Ben think when I didn't make it back to the house? When he called me and I didn't pick up? What would anyone think? He would go looking for me. He would look here. I had to make sure he found me, and then he could help me get out. My face dropped, staring at the stones ahead of each step. Ben warned me not to mess with this place. I should have listened to him.

Elijah stopped in an open doorway, stepping to the side to let me through. I walked inside, admiring a room that was so clearly appreciated in a past life. The furniture was warped and worn, stained by ashen nightmares, a grave of the duty they once knew. A rug-like blanket sat folded on a table, a statement against the dust around it, as if it had just been shaken out. It reminded me of the fabric set on a horse beneath a saddle. The only warmth he had to offer.

I stood at the window, noting the familiar gate down below. I could sit there and watch for Ben, pretending as if that broken home wouldn't share the same cold air as the night outside. A chill swept through me just thinking of it. I pulled out my phone, but the dark screen didn't change. I wouldn't even be able to use it for a flashlight.

"No heat," I started, listing off my problems. "No light. No phone. No ears."

All I could do was sit there and wait. Ben could get me blankets, or a lighter, or better yet, call the fire department to come cut through those bars. There was another building off in the distance, on the pathway that wrapped around the side I hadn't walked. I didn't notice it before, and yet it was familiar.

A hand grabbed my shoulder, making me jump as I spun around. Elijah's bright blue eyes pierced through my own. Fear trickled up through the hair on my skin. Would he hurt me? Caught up in anticipation, my gaze met his until his lips spoke.

"Let me know if you need anything."

For a moment, I was dumbfounded. How was he going to help me? I almost argued with him like I would have argued with Josh, but stopped myself. He was trying.

"Thanks," I hesitantly answered before bluntness took over. "No offense, but it doesn't exactly seem like you've got a closet of hygiene supplies or a pantry full of food to offer up."

The truth in his eyes answered for him. I was right.

"Not even a simple nightlight," I grumbled.

"You won't be harmed," he said. My eyes shifted away from his, blocking out anything else he might say. How could he tell me that? As if I was meant to feel safe? Locked in a haunted house with a stranger?

I stared down at the out-building again.

"Hey," I said, turning to find him already halfway out the door. He stopped to look at me as I pointed outside.

"That building out there." My hand dangled through the open window frame. There was some mesmerizing pull that drew me toward it. "I feel like I know it," I commented, just above a whisper. I closed my eyes, imagining the green-house from my vision.

"To bring a touch of color year round," I said, imagining the budding blossoms despite the winter outside the frosted glass. Vegetable plants lined narrow rows, while a mischie-vous rabbit crossed through, one that someone didn't welcome in, but could never bring themself to kick out.

"Was it a greenhouse?" I asked, opening my eyes again as if I'd just woken up. My gaze shifted to Elijah, who looked lost for words.

He nodded. "Yes. It was my mother's."

My brows drew together. "What?" I stared back at the greenhouse. I had to have misunderstood. "Benny made it sound as if this place was..." *ancient.*

"Now you're as stuck here as I am."

Elijah's sentiments from before took on a different meaning. Frozen time wasn't any more impossible than the force that locked me inside those gates.

My eyes shot to his. "How long have you been stuck like this?"

His expression tensed. "Too long."

He left the room, his air-drying hair lightly curling up

from his neck. Whether it was to give me privacy, or to get some himself, I wasn't sure. He seemed so lost. So sad.

I turned back towards the open window, sitting on the cold, stone ledge as my head leaned against the wall. Benny would come find me sooner or later, and I would find a way out of this nightmare... maybe for both of us.

19

HARPER

I sat at the window, staring at the gates, determined not to miss it when Ben showed up. He had to show up.

Something shoved against my back, waking me in a panic. I reflexively caught the wall, bracing myself from the steep fall below. My gaze connected with the ground before shutting my eyes, forcing my breaths to settle. I pushed hard back into the room, spinning around to face the culprit.

The empty space shared nothing but a shudder. Who would shove me out a window? Had I dreamt it?

My hand reached over my shoulder, touching the spot where I'd been pushed. It felt so real.

I glanced back down through the window, noticing the dim, early-morning silhouette that stood at the gate. It reached up to shake the bars, but they didn't move.

"Benny!" I cried, rushing out of the room. I ran down the stairs, ignoring everything around me as I sped through. Frost-coated grass lined the path, my warm breath steaming against my face. I didn't care about the cold, the ache in my neck from leaning against a rock wall, or the mud that hadn't quite dried against my pants.

Ben was there, and I was going home.

"Benny!" I called again, desperate for him to hear me. "I'm here!"

He stared through the bars, but the closer I got, the more disconnected it felt. He looked so disappointed.

"Benny, I'm sorry! I should have listened to you."

He stood in silence, shaking his head at the house through the gate. Didn't he see me?

Josh walked the fence line to meet him. I was barely close enough to catch what he said on his lips. "I'm sorry, Ben, I don't think she's here." I glared at the more matured version of an enemy, wearing an old t-shirt I'd seen him in a hundred times, ready to prove him wrong.

"Ben, I'm right here!" I demanded, running the last few steps. I grabbed the bars between us, staring into his eyes. "Benny?"

"You joke about hiding, but you've taken it too far this time, Harps." I read his lips, trying to understand. Josh grabbed his shoulder from behind and squeezed.

"Maybe she's back at the house," he suggested.

"Benny, can't you see me? I'm right here!" I reached through, trying to touch him, but my fingers couldn't connect. "The gate is stuck!"

With one last longing look, Ben turned to walk away.

"Benny!" I begged. I paced the bars from the inside, trying to keep up with them. "Benny, I'm right here! Don't leave me here!" Josh walked alongside him, his head spinning back for one last look as the path parted ways from the fence. I stared at his troubled expression as it quickly scanned over the abandoned property, once again skipping right past me.

Why couldn't they see me?

Both of them turned with the wet gravel trail, sinking further away with each worried step. I was alone again. I sank to the ground, curling up in a ball. Why didn't Ben hear me? How could I break free of this terrible dream?

Something brushed up against my side, taking a seat next to me. I straightened back, looking at the same black dog that trapped me in there.

"What do you want?" I asked in a grumpy tone. "I'm still mad at you." The dog barely looked at me, calmly staring out over the grass. His fur pressed into my side, and it wasn't long before I gave in and reached my arm up to pat him.

"You know, you're about the closest thing to a warm blanket that this place has to offer," I grumbled, glaring at the house. "It's so cold."

The dog got up, just as I leaned into him. He took a few steps before pausing to look back at me.

"What, you think I want to follow you around again after what happened last time?"

He didn't answer, though I couldn't have expected him to. I got up to follow. How else was I going to spend my day?

"Not like I have anything else to lose."

The dog led straight for the greenhouse, which my curious side had already been eager to explore. He sat at the door, waiting for me to push it open. As I cracked it slowly forward, a subtle warmth swept through. I closed my eyes, picturing it in my mind before I peeked inside. Would it match?

The greenhouse was such a contrast from the main building, full of a life and energy that had long died within the burned stone home. My mind filled with questions as I took in the hidden green garden. I admired the long leaves and vines that had clearly received years of care, but it was the small section of tomatoes and berries that welcomed relief. Maybe I wouldn't starve.

"So beautiful," I commented, wondering how everything had survived. I tried to imagine Elijah out there working to keep it neat and healthy, but it wasn't an image I would have guessed.

"Why does it feel like I've been here before?" I wondered out loud.

I picked a few deep red berries, studying them in my palm as I stepped further. Something fell from above, skimming the back of my head as it dropped. I fell forward with a startled jump, turning to see the soil spilling through a shattered pot when my foot caught. Something stabbed my hand as it braced my fall, making me cry out.

The door swung open as Elijah stormed in. He watched me yank my hand back from the rake that cut it.

His glare shifted from my braced hand to the broken pot. "Do you have to be so clumsy?" His expression was angry enough, I didn't need to hear the words.

Tears collected in my eyes as I fought back my fear. I opened my hand, seeing the blood that pooled through the cut.

"I don't know what happened." I stared at the shelf above him, knowing there was no way I'd bumped it. "It fell from that shelf up there, I didn't even touch it! Had I not stepped out of the way, it..."

He crouched in front of me, softly opening my fingers all the way to examine. I thought he was checking the cut, but he held up a berry between our faces and stared into my soul. "Did you eat one?"

I shook my head.

He kept staring, as if he were trying to gauge if I was telling the truth, before settling with a serious nod. "Don't," he finished, picking up the other two that I'd dropped, before he turned to the broken pot.

It almost seemed like the pot had been aimed at my head. I looked back down at the floor, the rake, the spilled soil. A faint path of tiny dirt tracks ran along the ground. I studied the pattern, knowing exactly what left them.

"A rabbit," I commented, shaking my head. Just like in my daydream. I looked up at Elijah, who knelt with his back to me, cleaning up the mess.

"I know it doesn't make sense... but sometimes it feels like I know this place."

His face kept low, but his hands hesitated.

"A world from my dreams," I went on, admiring the room some more.

Elijah put aside cleaning the dirt, and sat a few feet down the same wooden garden box as me. He seemed to be absorbing the same energy that I was as he looked around the room. I waited for him to talk, watching his face, but he was lost in the silence... or the sounds I couldn't hear.

He waited a while before his gaze connected with mine and he spoke. I was grateful that he made such a calm effort to communicate with me.

"I've always loved sitting in here."

I nodded, understanding what he meant. "It's not hard to see why. It's so peaceful." It was naturally quite a bit warmer than the house too. "You know, some people say this place is haunted."

He looked me dead in the eyes, his expression serious. "Who ever said it wasn't?"

A chill swept across my skin, making me antsy as my

gaze fell to the half-swept, shattered pot between us. Elijah stood, holding a hand down to pull me up with him.

"Come on. We should clean that." He gestured toward the still-braced hand in my lap. I nodded, letting him grab my elbow to pull me to my feet.

20

ELIJAH

— THE LIFE HE LIVED BEFORE HER.

She was sad again. She'd been sad since she stepped into my world. I couldn't stand it, the echo of her cries at the gates, begging to get out. I just couldn't face it. I couldn't face her. I knew that ache too well, and it never went away. In all my time there, nobody ever came to help me. Only a few stepped in. Nobody ever stepped out.

Why did it have to happen now? Why her? Who was she?

I pulled her to her feet, surprised that I cared at all, cared about some little cut... but it wasn't about the cut. Not truly. It was the look in her eyes. A small slice in her palm was the least of our worries, but the fear I saw when she looked at me would haunt me forever.

I never let anybody sit in mom's greenhouse. Usually I kept it locked tight. Initially, I wanted to toss her out, threaten her for breaking a piece of something so sacred. It had to stay exactly as it was, keeping mom's warm spirit alive. My heart couldn't risk losing it. Yet, somehow this strange girl that couldn't even hear my voice had already been welcomed in. From the moment she'd pointed at it out her window, it was hers too.

She said she knew it, knew my home, and it didn't make sense. Nobody ever had. But the moment she stepped inside those gates, everything belonged to her. From the ash mixed through the soil, to the cursed moon above us, she saw right through it.

"I'm sorry for overreacting before." I led her out of mom's greenhouse, holding the door as she stepped through. She didn't respond. She hadn't heard me speak. Nobody ever heard me speak. But still, it was nice to have someone to talk to. She didn't have to listen, her company was enough, for what little time I had with it.

"It was mom's special place," I went on, walking behind Harper as she headed for the house. "I'm so glad the fire didn't take it. The greenhouse, the barn, all of that was for her. She grew up on a farm. Her dad had fields of cattle, and she spent most of her childhood horseback. At least, that's how she always put it." I laughed, thinking fondly of the nights mom spent telling stories of her past life to me and my brother Beau.

I would never trade the extra time tagged onto her mortal life for stepping into our world. Our time ticked by differently than her world's. Faster, though you'd never know it. But she still continued to age on her mortal-born clock. The hours felt the same, she simply got to live more of them. A single year in her world was multiple in mine. She was with us lifetimes longer than she was born with, but not as many as she could have lived without that fire.

"She wasn't from our world. She married into it." I studied Harper's dirty pants. "I guess she stumbled into this place, same as you." The thought tugged on my heart again.

Who was this girl? Why was I even telling her all this? Maybe the raw silence is what it took for me to open up.

Harper looked at me, her brows drawing together. She must have realized I'd gone on talking behind her back. I tried to smile, but it felt awkward. I pointed at the barn.

"That way."

It was strange to meet someone who couldn't hear. I had the opposite ability, my hearing was stronger than a mortal. Stronger than the other creatures in my world even, when I focused on it. I almost wished I could give her a piece of it, share it with her, sacrifice my extra hearing for her to hear at all.

We stepped into the hall of stables, same as I did every morning. It seemed odd bringing someone else in there, as if I'd walked her into a time capsule of my family. Another small corner that wasn't destroyed by tragedy. Four horses poked their heads through the open windows. The first horses to step foot across the lines between our worlds. Mom said she couldn't live anywhere that didn't have a horse to ride.

Harper's expression brightened, going straight for them. She reached up to greet each one, smiling back at me often to make sure it was okay. I nodded, letting her have her moment of relief. Her spirit connected with them so quickly. Did their souls recognize that they belonged to the same world? A world that felt so far away from this one?

"Hey, Shadow," I said, reaching up to pet the first horse. He belonged to my dad. I still couldn't explain how they'd survived so many years. They aged on their mortal-born clock too, but by now they still should have passed. Then again, I should have too. They were as frozen in time as I was. Normally I let them out to graze on the grass, but that morning had been especially cold. That, or maybe I was just more distracted.

"Do you ride them?" she asked, her eyes shifting back and forth from the horses to my face.

"Not anymore." I studied the beautiful deep brown horse as she rubbed between his eyes.

"That's Aria," I told her, though I wasn't sure she caught it. "He was my horse." The words drifted off, spoken only to myself. "Another life I suppose."

I shook off the wave of longing emotions, turning toward the back corner of the room.

Luckily for Harper, mom always kept some first aid supplies tucked away on a shelf in case somebody fell off a horse. Not that anyone in our family ever did, but she was all about staying prepared. My body healed differently than a human, good thing too with how Beau and I got along growing up, but I had watched mom clean a few of her own cuts over the years.

I smiled, but my heart hurt. Every thought of mom and the family I once had was bitter-sweet. It felt like all I had left of them was some plants and those four horses.

I grabbed out a bandage and an old bottle of sterilizing alcohol, noting that there was only a small line of it left at the bottom. I'd have to make sure she didn't get hurt anymore.

My shoulders sank with hopelessness. Maybe it didn't matter. It was all borrowed time. Still, the need to help while I could was there.

Harper winced as I cleaned the cut, turning her head far to the side so she wouldn't see. I tried to be gentle, but the alcohol didn't care. I covered it with the bandage, hoping she would forgive me. Maybe she just needed a distraction.

"You write?" I asked when she finally looked up at me.

Her surprise shifted to confusion as she tried to read my face.

"You dropped your notebook," I explained. It was probably a journal. Would she be mad? "I didn't read it or anything. It's in the house."

"Oh," she answered. Her gaze dropped to her hand, pulling it into her chest. "Thank you." Her eyes met mine again.

"You're welcome."

"It's just a story," she answered. Her voice was soft and hesitant, her arms hugging tighter around herself.

Her answer surprised me. "You write stories?" Suddenly I wished she could have seen our home before it was destroyed.

"What?" she asked. "Is that so hard to believe?"

"There were a lot of books here before this house burned down. My family, they loved them." Maybe not myself so much. I laughed at the thought. Everyone else got so absorbed in a good book, but I never quite understood that. I wanted to go out and do things for real, not read about them. Now I would kill for that room full of books, all of those characters to keep me company throughout the years of wasted time. All I had left was an empty journal, a place to record the one story I would never escape.

We stepped inside the house, and I held out the notebook. She claimed it quickly, folding it into her arms. It made sense that the simple object was so important to her. It was one of the few things she had left to keep from the world outside. It was a piece of her.

"Thank you," she said again. I opened my mouth to answer, but she left before I could get a word out.

LIAR

21

WILLOW

"*Dead blood,*" the low voice echoed in my mind.

I sat up to stare at the room around me. I was in my bed, covered by my worn-out, yellow, childhood quilt, but I had no memory of how I got there. I should have woken up sick, with a mild headache at least, but I felt completely normal. Strangely normal. Obviously someone had tampered with my glass of water for it to knock me out, but shouldn't I have felt some sort of hangover waking up from it?

What a strange night. What a strange man.

Maybe he'd been a figment of my imagination as I walked myself home, though I still saw glimpses of the night around me, swaying with each stride. His questions were direct, he wasn't there for small talk.

What had he meant when he said, "*Dead blood?*"

I couldn't let go of those two simple words. They felt like a weight on my chest, some truth I didn't understand, but deep down, I couldn't argue with either.

I could have sworn he was that writing teacher Mr. Nazurin. For a moment, it looked just like him. I shook that off, climbing out of bed. While I was on the topic of Sam's creative writing professor, it was probably a good time to get up and get ready for his class.

My one-week decision felt silly after attending the day before. What was I trying to do posing as one of the students? Was I really about to write a poem in my sister's name instead of fessing up? The school needed to know, and I got the feeling Mr. Nazurin did too.

There was such sincerity in his voice when he spoke to me... to Sam. As if he knew her, and was genuinely excited to have her in his class. I needed to inform him that he would never get that chance. I could have called or sent an email, but I'd already crossed a line. I'd already shown my face as hers. I needed to go give an explanation in person.

I hated telling people about Sam. About how her future was wasted. I hated the tragic pity in their eyes, the way their entire tone and attitude towards me shifted. The way they spoke to me with caution, being delicate with my pain. Trying not to offend me, as if it wasn't my own fault. As if I wasn't the one who crashed the car. As if I wasn't the reason Sam was dead.

I didn't bother counting up the missed messages and calls as I slid my phone in my pocket for one more day of ignorance. My notifications were starting to look like Sam's, collecting words that were meant for a ghost. Mom could wait. The doctors could wait. There was one message from Sage to the group chat.

Where did you all go?

She had a point. It was as if that slumber party was a big goodbye. Ava and Harper had promised to stay close, promised to keep talking every day like they did before. I knew I'd only been added into the group chat because of Sam. I never participated in it, but I did enjoy watching the conversation roll on down my screen. It made me feel less alone. There was still a spark of Sam kept alive within the spirit of their group. Being able to watch their friendship from what felt like the outside was something I still needed.

"Where did we all go?" I echoed Sage's sentiments. I should have answered her. I should have responded to the text with one simple little word.

Here. I'm right here.

She probably felt as lonely as I did after everybody left. The one friend that got ditched behind while everyone else stepped into new chapters. I couldn't answer. I wasn't the friend she called out to. Not really.

There was nothing like crisp, morning air, as the sun broke through, mocking me with its optimism, promising to cut out the cold with its warm light. I didn't want it. It didn't match the frozen winter in my heart.

As if I'd summoned it, a chill followed me along the campus paths. It felt as if someone were watching my every move, and the creepy suspicion only grew stronger. I stepped into a campus shop, pretending to skim the line of sweatshirts as I scanned the world outside the window. Nobody lingered outside. Nobody was following me.

I turned around, my eyes caught by the cases of student supplies with university logos printed across them. Folders, paper, pencil cases, markers, erasers. I'd been avoiding the office section at every store for months. I could hardly bring myself to step into a store to begin with.

I used to roll my eyes every time Sam went missing at the store. We never could make a simple grocery trip without a walk down the notebook aisle, or past the pens.

"*Don't you have like twenty packs of those at home?*" I would ask.

"*What if they stop making these though, this kind is my favorite!*"

"*I know,*" I'd mock. "*I've seen your desk.*"

After she died, I'd stared at her collection of pens, the color-coded sticky notes on her wall, the messy notebooks full of late night ideas, the jar of bookmarks. Every single thing on that desk was important to her. It was worthy of precious space. She had plans for every drop of ink, and I couldn't bring myself to touch any of it. Not a thing. Suddenly it was a time capsule, and mom and I weren't ready to open it. It had to be tucked away for safe keeping.

Now the same pack of pens I'd watched her obsess over dangled from a hook in front of me, mocking me. She was worried about pens, but she got discontinued instead.

I pushed out the door, moving fast down the walkway, desperate to be as far away as I could get from those memories. The other students and teachers were on their own schedules, moving around me in a hundred different rhythms. Despite the sixth sense begging me to hurry faster, still no stalker trailed my shadow.

My eyes followed the ground, carefully calculating every step ahead to miss the sidewalk cracks like I did as a child, until I looked up and realized I'd passed my building. I pulled out my phone, knowing I would be late. My conversation with Mr. Nazurin would have to wait until after class.

I circled back around the block, and stepped into the English building, letting the warmth ease my nerves. I made it. I was safe.

I could already hear Mr. Nazurin giving his lecture from the hallway. My back pressed against the wall to wait.

I was already late, my heart rate could calm down before interrupting him. He was talking about pacing like it was a song. As if each word you chose to write was a note, each sentence one single thread in a symphony. He made it sound so beautiful, it was hard not to see it playing out in my mind.

I let out one last sigh before turning into the doorframe.

22

WILLOW

Mr. Nazurin faced his board, continuing his speech as I made my way to the empty chair up front. I sat down before pulling off Sam's backpack and setting it on the floor. Why did I even carry her backpack around when I wasn't a real student? This life wasn't mine to live.

Mr. Nazurin turned around as I slid my legs forward, noticing me instantly. He smiled as his eyes caught mine, a pause in his lecture. Then his line of sight flickered to the back of the room and the happy light in it dulled. His entire demeanor shifted, and my curiosity rose. Everything seemed normal when I walked in.

My gaze followed his as someone new stepped in through the door, making my whole body tense. Zager's casual steps seemed unconcerned with timing. He smugly smiled at Mr. Nazurin, the very man I'd mixed him up with, before Zager's eyes flashed to mine. He lowered his head in a small nodding bow, and his smile widened, as if he'd just won a game. My heart stopped beating, what did he want?

The last time I'd encountered him, I passed out as he carried me off into the night.

"So sorry," he told Mr. Nazurin. "Please, do go on." He pulled out the empty chair next to mine and took a seat, waiting for the lecture to continue. I looked back and forth between the two, trying to understand the sudden strain.

Had my subconscious been right about a stalker? Had he followed me there? I sank back in my seat, wishing I hadn't been so late. I should have pulled Mr. Nazurin into the hallway on the spot and explained everything. Maybe I should have just sent that email. The urge to bolt from the room consumed me. Did I stay after to talk to the teacher, or make a run for it now?

Mr. Nazurin collected himself, and continued his lesson, though the enthusiasm felt somehow drained from every word. As he went on, my mind twisted into knots. All the good vibes I'd felt that morning slipped away, replaced by vertigo and nausea.

"Oh no," I mumbled to myself, lying my face into my arm. *Not now.* Mr. Nazurin continued, as a hand braced my back. I startled up straighter, shifting my chair ever so slightly away. Zager stared at me from the side in concern.

"Are you okay?" he asked.

"Why are you here?" I countered in a hushed voice, ignoring his question.

"I'm just asking if you're okay."

So he did follow me. He wasn't denying it. The nausea thickened.

"Why, because of my dead blood?" I whispered it out like an insult. I didn't know what he'd meant when he said it, but it was like he knew everything. As if he were calling me out on the illness my denial tried to hide.

"I'll be fine," I finished. I held out against the battle inside me. I'd already interrupted the class once, I could sit through the remainder of it. Zager also seemed to be waiting for the minutes to tick by. He clearly didn't care about the material, twisting a pen through his fingers. I thought he was checking a watch, when I realized he held a small round mirror in his hand. The strangely vivid scene of a bright green forest lit up in the reflection. I would have played it off as the mural on the walls, had it not been for the sunlight that bounced into my eyes through the weaving branches.

He swung the silver lid back down, snapping it into place, and once more it looked like a simple pocket mirror. My mind was wide awake with curiosity, tensed in my chair as I studied the trinket. I tried to read the word etched across the top, shifting when he looked my way, pretending not to notice.

Whatever it was, it made a welcome distraction against the clock. The bell rang, and I was ready to run.

I grabbed the backpack and stood up, my legs shoving away the chair. I had to get out of there and find a restroom to hide in.

"Sam," Mr. Nazurin called as he moved to his desk. "I wondered if you had a moment." I froze, wanting it to be a different Sam, any other student than me, but I knew. There went my opportunity to escape. It cut my heart to hear him call my sister's name. I had to tell him. I nodded to myself with the decision to do just that, when I noticed Zager still calmly sitting in his chair. There was amusement in his eyes as he stared straight at me, patiently standing by to watch the show. I'd hoped for the conversation about my dead sister to be more private.

I moved to Mr. Nazurin's desk, desperate to put space between myself and this stranger. Was Zager really going to sit there and wait for me to leave? I didn't know anything about him. For all I knew, he'd drugged me the night before when I passed out. Then he followed me to class for what? Mr. Nazurin stood at his desk, rearranging papers.

"You can dismiss yourself," Mr. Nazurin told Zager before his attention shifted to me.

"Hey," he started. His tone felt a little more personal, like he was ready to express some concern. I looked back toward Zager, stubbornly ignoring Nazurin's instructions. What did he want from me? Mr. Nazurin opened his mouth to go on, but I spoke first to cut him off. Safety had to be the priority.

"Can we talk alone?" My arms wrapped nervously in front of me as I leaned closer. "I think that guy might be following me." His gaze flickered past mine to Zager, his jaw clenching tighter.

He sighed, muttering something under his breath. Mr. Nazurin stepped around the desk and cut into the line between Zager and me.

"I'm going to have to ask you to leave," he said in a cold tone. "What are you even doing here? I don't believe you're signed up for this class." His demanding shift surprised me, somehow lacking the professional manners of a teacher.

"What are *you* doing here?" Zager countered. He stood too, an unworried expression on his face. He smiled again, stepping in closer.

"You followed her here?" Mr. Nazurin accused. "How did you even know?"

An odd energy was building between the two of them, and it felt like my fault. I didn't want a stalker any more than I wanted to tell this man that his student was dead. I also didn't want them arguing over me. I took a deep calming breath, searching for the right words to say.

"I have a job to do. I'm not leaving here without you."

"Then you'll take a cold corpse," Nazurin snapped.

Wow, that had nothing to do with me.

"Wait... you two know each other?" The dizziness sank in deeper. I almost fell, catching myself on the edge of the table. I grabbed the small trash can next to the desk and dry heaved, but there was no food in my system to purge.

Zager's attention shifted, making Mr. Nazurin turn to see too.

"Sam," Mr. Nazurin said, reaching to support me. "What is it?"

"She's—"

"You stay away from her," Nazurin growled.

Zager's eyes widened, and Mr. Nazurin seemed to catch himself and correct his own statement.

"This is between you and me, leave my students out of it. No more of your tricks."

"I have to go." I shook off his hand before he could help. The trash can wobbled where I lowered it, dropping the last inch before I desperately half-ran to the door.

"Sam!" Mr. Nazurin called, but the other voice stopped him.

The sound of it broke me inside, the way he said my sister's name. Nobody said it like that anymore, like she was still there, still important... but she was gone, and she was never coming back. Maybe I wouldn't either.

HUNTED

23

SAGE

Morning sunlight filtered through the white drapes in rays across the ceiling, but neither my room nor my mom's had an east facing window. This wasn't my house. I sat up slowly, remembering the way an ambulance rushed off with my mother, leaving me alone on our porch in the middle of the night. But I wasn't alone.

I slowly stepped to the hardwood floor of a bare room. No pictures on the walls. No junk sitting around claiming it as home. A thin layer of dust on the empty dresser, suggesting that this wasn't home at all. Just a passing point.

"The hunter will come for you again," I whispered, afraid of a warning that I didn't understand.

The wood creaked beneath my next step. My heart stopped, listening for any hint of movement outside. Was this hunter guy close by? Someone ran up the staircase outside my door, making me panic. I took two quick steps to stand behind the door with nowhere else to go.

The door swung open, giving me a glimpse through the crack before he stepped inside. This time it was just a black shirt, no hood to cover up his head, but I knew his face. It was him. He stopped inside the doorframe, studying the empty room. Silent. Waiting.

Hunter.

Some wild animal, sniffing out my scent.

I couldn't hold my breath any longer.

I shoved the door into him, trying to push him back as I jumped over his leg. He was up fast, his footsteps pounding down the steps behind me. I grabbed the door handle straight ahead, desperate to reach the sunlight outside its window, but as I pulled it toward me, his weight slammed it shut.

I was stuck, pinned against the door with him at my back.

"What do you want from me?" My voice trembled. I wasn't getting out without a fight.

"I'm trying to help you," he answered in that same coarse voice. "If you'd just let me." I was stuck in a cage, blocked in by some towering nightmare.

"Help me? By kidnapping me?"

"I was hoping it wouldn't come to this." He leaned away, and I slowly turned to face him. There was a deadly darkness in his eyes, his hard, threatening expression, but he hadn't hurt me yet.

"Did you kill my mom?"

"No." He took a step back. "Someone was there before me."

My head shook. "The house was empty, I checked it myself. Everything was locked up." I took a deep breath, looking him over more slowly. The long arrow tattoo was just as Nina described. The arrowhead point sat at his wrist, while the full arrow ran up to his elbow, even lined feathering at the top.

"I don't believe you. My grandmother warned me about you. She said you would come."

He shook his head, looking up at me from a head hung low. "It's not me you should be worried about. We need to stay together."

"I don't even know your name."

"Rogue."

"Rogue?" I scoffed. "Really? You expect me to put my life in your hands and you won't even offer your real name in return? You don't know anything about me."

"Sage Thost, daughter of May Thost, granddaughter of Sila Thost, I could go on. Father not in the picture. Eighteen years old as of two days ago. Spent your entire life here, same house, same friends, same town, until now, of course. You can't stay here. Not anymore."

I scoffed again, my denial front and center between us. His words hurt. Who was he to decide my future?

"And my real name is Grim."

Why that part shut me up, I wasn't sure. Grim? Who would have thought Rogue could be an improvement. I wasn't sure what to say next, staring at the scar on the side of his forehead, running from higher above his brow into his hairline.

"I have to go see my mom."

"She's dead."

I glared at him, the lack of sympathy in his raspy tone as he crushed what little hope I had left.

"I have to see her!"

He stared straight into my eyes. Every move he made with intention, so calculated.

"Then I'll take you." His words caught me off guard, his quickly giving in to what I wanted. He was saying what I wanted to hear, playing nice, but I wasn't going to be fooled by it. My eyes flickered once more over the bold black tattoo. I had to get away.

Hunter.

I nodded, my gaze shifting to the floor as I pretended to accept. "Thank you."

He stepped around me, pulling a key from his pocket.

"I'm going to use the restroom," I lied. "I'll meet you out there."

With one low nod he let me close the door behind him as he stepped through.

24

SAGE

I ran toward the back of the house, searching for a different way out. The back door flew open as I raced through, sprinting across the grass toward the cinderblock wall. I lunged up the side of it, my fingers gripping the top as I pulled my weight up. One leg swung over, scraping against the rough corner edge until I sat on the top. I paused to study the view, sending back one last glance at the house. It looked completely normal, matching the neighborhood of houses that lined the curving roads around it.

I dropped down the other side of the fence, and started running. I had to put space between us, had to hide, but first I had to see my mom. I had to know for sure, to hear it from the professionals, to see proof that, for whatever reason, she was gone. What else could I do? Where would I go from here?

I stepped through the hospital doors, straight for the front desk. The red emergency signs were a normal sight, I saw them often, stopping by as mom worked. I was never the one there for the emergency though.

I knew the young, blonde woman at the front desk.

Sidney. The recognition reflected in her eyes too as her expression shifted to concern.

"Is she…"

Sidney shook her head, and a tear broke free. I could see the sad news weighing on each of the staff faces behind her as they turned to look at me, locked in place. "The police have some questions," she told me, picking up a phone to make a call before waving her hand down the waiting room hall. "There's also a boy looking for you."

"What?" Rogue couldn't have beat me there. Did he realize I was gone that fast? I wanted to kick myself, I'd literally told him exactly where I would go next.

Hunter.

I looked around the corner, terrified of who I would see.

"Sage?" Kett stood from a chair and rushed over to wrap his arms around me. How long had he been sitting there waiting?

"What happened to you? I got to your house as fast as I could, but nobody was there!"

I let his warmth wrap around me with the promise of comfort. If only for a moment, I didn't have to be alone. Not completely.

"My mom's gone," I cried into his chest.

"I'm so sorry," he whispered into my hair. "What can I do?"

A motorcycle pulled up at the curb. Something about the sound of it felt out of place. I looked out from Kett's shirt just as Rogue swung the helmet off his head and turned for the door, a determined, livid look on his face.

"Get me out of here," I begged. "Quick!"

"What—"

"Now!"

"Okay," he agreed. He hugged me in at his side,

ushering me straight for the door. Rogue walked right past us, a black leather vest over the top of his sweatshirt. I eyed his tense expression as we stepped by, but he didn't notice me at all.

I peeked back, watching how he angrily leaned against Sidney's counter like he was ready for battle.

"Where do you want to go?" Kett asked, pulling my mind forward again.

I thought back on Nina's warning, ordering me to run. Ordering me to leave. *He's a hunter. Get away.*

Mom was gone. Maybe there was nothing left for me there anymore.

"It doesn't matter, I just have to get out of here."

"Okay," he agreed, no questions asked. "Let's go."

25

SAGE

"That's yours?" Most high school kids didn't drive around in shiny new trucks.

"It's my dad's," Kett answered with a shrug. "It seemed so urgent earlier."

"Yeah," I agreed, feeling a little guilty that he'd sat there waiting for me all morning. It had been urgent, and this boy I'd only just met so quickly came running to be there for me.

The clean, spacious cab made the truck feel brand new. "Your dad must love his truck to keep it this nice," I commented, thinking of the car mom and I shared. Worn seats, a floor covered in take-out garbage, and a check engine light that would stay on permanently until the light bulb itself went out. I guess it was my car now.

My head fell against the window, hands covering my face as if they could hide my pain, tears spilling free. Why was this happening?

"Hey," Kett reached to pat the back of my shoulder.

"I need to check in with the police," I commented, unwilling to breakdown completely in front of this boy I'd just met. "My house is basically a crime scene. They're going to want my story." At least I'd turned eighteen before becoming an orphan.

"Why don't you give yourself a minute to process first?" he asked. "That will all be waiting when you're ready to face it."

"Tomorrow's problem," I commented. Now that did sound like something mom would say, outside of work at least. We were always big fans of procrastination. It didn't feel appropriate this time though. I studied him for a moment, finding his suggestion odd. It didn't fit the situation. My mom just died. The police had questions, and I'd fallen off the map. It probably looked like I was running away... like I might be guilty. This was urgent.

"No, I need to check in. This is too important."

"Okay," he agreed, returning both hands to the steering wheel as he refocused on the road.

"Maybe I should report that creep—" I hadn't told Kett about Rogue yet. Not completely. I'd been avoiding the side mirrors, my reflection in the glass, terrified he would be there the way he always showed up, watching me from under his dark hood.

"You still feel like someone is following you?" he asked.

"Yeah," I commented. "Can't shake it."

He fixed the rear-view mirror, studying the road behind us. "Well, it looks all clear to me."

"Great," I answered, forcing a smile. "I think the station is that way," I added, pointing toward the left.

"Got it," he answered, hitting on the blinker.

I closed my eyes, resting my head against the seat until he stopped the car. I sat up to scan the parking lot, but we were on the side of a backroad No police station, no anything.

"Flat tire," he explained.

"Really? It didn't even feel bumpy."

"I'm not sure, it just popped up on the dash."

"Okay," I said, following his lead to unbuckle and check.

Sure enough, the back right tire sank low. Too flat to drive on. I paused to stare at it as he circled around to join me.

"Dang. Is your dad going to be mad?"

Kett shrugged. "Probably."

"Such a pain," I commented. I wondered if his dad was strict. Mom had always been so calm and cool. We were more like teammates when it came to this stuff. "I'm sorry, what rotten luck."

"You're sorry? I got a flat tire. Your mom died. Don't worry about this." He let out a sigh. "I'd better call him." He slid the phone from his pocket, turning toward the wall of trees behind us to get a little space.

I waited for him to come back, staring at the tire. If Ava were there, she would have already been halfway through changing it. I loved that about Ava, she was never afraid of work, and she always worked hard. She would probably hurt herself in the process, but that never stopped her. From what I could tell, we weren't that far from her house either.

The urge to text her made me pull out my phone, but the empty screen still hurt. What happened to her? I was sick of trying to reach out if nobody was going to answer. I opened up the list of one-sided messages, none of which had even been acknowledged.

"He's on his way," Kett announced behind me. I spun around. "It's probably going to take him a bit to get here from work though."

"Okay, that's fine."

"I think there's a path right there." He pointed at the trees. "It looks like a pretty area, want to go explore it with me for a few minutes?"

I looked around, wondering if the property belonged to anyone. Probably a hunting trail. "I mean, I guess if we have to sit here for a while we might as well."

"Maybe it can help clear your head. Fresh air is good for the soul."

He smiled, holding a hand toward me. For just a glimpse, the troubles felt further away. He was the cute boy, and his attention was on me. I paced through the un-cut grass, my heartbeat picking up as I accepted it. How could something as simple as holding hands with a new boy be so tempting? But I couldn't fully reach the giddiness behind my pain. For now, he was just the cute boy who'd shown up for me when I needed someone most.

"Random spot for a hike," I commented as we stepped into the wall of trees.

"I mean, aren't they all?" he countered. "Every popular spot was found by someone trying something new."

"Good point," I answered, all humor lost, confident this was just a good area to hunt in. It probably even connected with the same paths Ava's dad and brother used every fall behind their property, which made it feel closer to home. We used to play in spots like that as kids.

"Let's go discover something cool."

Kett made a good distraction. It was strange to process the fact that mom was gone. It didn't seem real. Maybe if I was being honest, part of me was avoiding it. I'd just lost my friends, I wasn't ready to be alone yet. With Kett, it felt more like the start of something than the end of everything else.

I was so caught up in that feeling, I didn't realize the

time passing until the sky got dimmer. Already? That's not right. I hadn't even eaten lunch, could have sworn it was still morning.

"Kett? It's getting late."

He looked up, noticing it too, brows drawing together.

"Is your dad going to be mad that you're not waiting by the truck?"

"I think it's okay," he answered.

"Well let's go back, okay? I've avoided real life long enough." I turned around, but he grabbed my arm.

"It's fine!" he answered. "We're just hiking, what's wrong with that?"

"What?" Was he stopping me? *What's wrong with it?* "Are you serious?" The wave of fun evaporated. "What's wrong with you! My mom died this morning."

"I know that," he answered. "It's just, I feel like we're so close to the end of the trail."

"Yeah, maybe, but I'm hungry. We don't even have water and the sun is already sinking. I don't want to be stuck out here for the night if we get lost."

Kett reached for my hand and squeezed it, looking into my eyes with a warm smile. "We're not lost. I won't let anything happen to you."

I didn't feel the same giddy energy as before. Something was off. I looked down at his hand, holding mine just a bit too tight. Under his sleeve two dark lines peeked out, pointing at his wrist. Just like the tattoo I noticed on Rogue.

Hunter.

My eyes flashed to his, trying to remain calm. He couldn't know I knew.

"Okay, just a little bit farther," I agreed, pretending to be swept up in our date as I let him pull me back toward the path. We took a few more steps, when he let go to reach for his pocket.

I spun around fast, making a sprint for the road we left behind. It was hard to watch the path beneath the shadows of fading light, desperately trying not to trip.

Something screeched up ahead before I noticed a large, deer-like creature racing toward me. Its antlers whipped forward to charge through, when Kett smashed into my back and we tumbled to the earth.

He rolled us into the brush, wrapping me tight so I had to go with. What was with these hunters and tackling?

"Let go of me!" I cried, trying to break free. He wrapped his fingers over my mouth, pulling my head against his chest so tight the ponytail dug into my scalp. Another sharp screech hit my ears. I sank into his hold, afraid of the monster lurking through the trees around us. The world grew quiet again as I got ready to bite his hand.

"I wouldn't do that if I were you," his low voice warned in my ear. "Your cursed blood calls to these wild woods, and I'm the only thing keeping you alive."

My cursed blood? I looked around the trees, realizing they were different from the path we first followed. There was a strange humid mist in the air, a nearly full moon lighting the sky above us. The creature through the trees ahead was on all fours, sniffing out the ground. The silhouette of an elk with a ghostly gray coat. It looked sick.

A branch snapped, and its gaze whipped up past us into the trees at our side. There was a greenish tint reflecting in its eyes, it didn't seem real, a monster from a movie, and we were waiting for it to give up the hunt.

I remained frozen until Kett's hold softened, and he dropped his hand. Half of my hair dragged with it, caught in his sleeve. I reached to feel it, only a few strands still left in place, rubbing the sore spot on the back of my head where the ponytail originally sat, the ribbon long gone.

"What was that?" I asked, my heart still pounding. He started talking, but the words faded out as I noticed the small mirror sitting in the dirt in front of me. Nina's mirror. But I wasn't the one that dropped it. I couldn't be. I never took it from the attic. *He did.*

He must have grabbed it when he helped me search the house... but why? My heart sank. He was in my house, helping me check if it was secure... or maybe he was doing the very opposite. The last person inside before mom died. What did he want with Nina's old mirror? Kett swiped it from the dirt, sliding it back into his pocket. In my dream, Nina mentioned something about a broken mirror. Something in my gut told me that was it.

"Time to go," Kett said, his friendly tone forgotten. My hand fell from my hair as he stood next to me and pulled out a knife, his smile stretching wide. "Let's move," he instructed, nudging me forward.

I stumbled the first step, staring at the overgrown path ahead. That's when I knew I wasn't home anymore, and I wasn't going to make it back anytime soon. Nina's warning repeated over and over in my mind as I thought of my hooded stalker. The hunter. The one called Rogue. Maybe it was more like the rogue hunter.

He said he was trying to help me. Maybe he was telling the truth. Maybe he was on my side all along, and I'd chosen not to trust him.

Either way, in all the confusion, only one thing was clear I'd made a big mistake.

RUNNING

26

JANE

My eyes opened slowly, taking in the heavy gray clouds that packed the sky above. A burst of wind dared me to stand up, challenging the air in each breath. A storm was coming.

Last I knew, I was still comfortably wrapped up in a blanket next to Emma, a projector movie playing on the wall. Not even a rom-com slumber party could ward off the nightmares.

I sat up to take in the forest. Straight ahead, a branch broke out from the base of a tree, arching over the path in front of me. From the ground, it almost looked like a doorway. Until I stood, and it felt more like an obstacle to block my path.

Something about the spot seemed familiar, like I'd been there before.

I cautiously stepped in closer, as if something might lunge through the arch from the other side. My fingers ran along the top of it, trying to remember how I knew it. I knelt down, searching the opening like some window to my answers.

A light breeze brushed leaves down the path inside it, blurring the seconds, drawing me in, when the sound of hooves smashed against the ground. I spun around fast, desperate to run and hide.

I hit him hard, trying to shove through, but he'd caught me.

"Something's out there!" I reached across, trying to claw free of him, free of myself, scratching my arm like I could rip it all away. He grabbed my hands, caging his fingers over mine. "When will I ever wake up from this nightmare!"

"You shouldn't be here," Mylo said, squeezing me to his chest when I stopped resisting. For a moment, I let him, until all of the emotions rushed back in. I shoved him back.

"I didn't come here by choice," I fought. "What are you doing here? You can't help, remember?"

I stubbornly turned to pace away.

"Emma woke up and you were gone. She didn't know who else to call."

"Great." I nodded, throwing out my arms, ignoring the sting of new cuts over old. "Well, here I am." I searched the tangled woods around me, standing in the middle of nowhere... so how did he find me? A shiver in the breeze swept over my skin.

"Did you follow me?" I asked.

He hesitated, clearly holding something back. *Secrets.*

"Oco," he answered. I couldn't even fight it. Somehow that bird had found me every single morning. She repeatedly led me back to safety, though I didn't know how or why.

"Come on," he said. "Let's tell Emma you're okay."

"I asked you not to tell her about me." She was only worried because of him.

"I'm sorry. I thought she could help you. She deserved to know."

"It was mine to tell her!" My head shook. "You just pushed my problems to her so that you could keep staying out of them without feeling bad about it."

"Jane—"

"What way do I go!" I demanded. "I want to get out of this storm."

He stopped fighting it, raising a resigned finger to point me back.

I stomped through the trees, pretending like I didn't notice Mylo shadowing my every step. At least I wasn't alone in the woods this time, though I wasn't going to admit any relief at that moment.

When I broke out of the forest, Emma was already there waiting. "Jane!" She ran up to me with a blanket ready to wrap over my shoulders. "I thought it was a little silly when you put on the coat and boots before climbing into bed, but now I get it."

I thought back to the night before, but couldn't remember any of that. That first morning I'd woken up barefoot and gone to Mylo's. He'd made a comment about finding shoes. I'd told him something about my unconscious self not stopping for shoes before it ran outside.

"Then maybe someone should go to sleep with their shoes already on."

Since then I'd woken up with shoes every morning, but I never remembered putting them on. My gaze snapped back to Mylo's, searching for answers in his mask of indifference. *More secrets.*

"Let's get you home," Emma said, pushing me to keep going. "I'll take the day off."

"No, you don't have to do that."

"I just spent half the night searching for you."

Her worry caught me off guard. Emma really cared. She was genuinely invested in being my friend, and it was interrupting her life. A new pressure weighed on my shoulders, reminding me that I had a life outside of this. I still didn't belong here. All of these friendships were temporary, and I felt guilty for it.

"I'm sorry," I told her, letting her pull me to the car. Mylo watched from across the grass. I stared into his eyes, taking my spot in the passenger seat, holding his gaze until Emma's car inched forward to break my view.

"Don't apologize. I can't believe what a heavy sleeper I am!"

"Same."

She sighed, unable to argue.

We practically spent the morning on the couch, and I was kind of relieved when Emma fell asleep. I got up to put away the breakfast mess she'd created out of her stress cooking, drying dishes and wiping bacon grease off the counter.

If I was going to be stuck there, I needed to find a way to pull my weight. Dr. Quinn was so patient, insisting that I still try to relax. He'd been working with the sheriff to find answers, but there was nothing even remotely close to match me to. I tried to reassure him, thank him, tell him it's okay, but we both knew it wasn't. I just hated seeing the pity in his eyes each time he brought me more nothing.

"How long did I sleep?" Emma asked, searching the window behind her. Storm clouds continued crowding in all day, building thicker with the promise of a long night ahead. I tried to hide my anxiety, knowing where I would probably find myself in the middle of the upcoming blizzard.

"We don't have to go tonight." Emma told me as she sat on the stool next to mine.

"Yes we do," I argued. She'd spent the week catering to my needs, and after days of hearing her talk about this one night, I couldn't take it from her.

"Really?" she asked, biting her lip.

"Yeah, let's go. I think we could use a bit of fun."

"Okay," she agreed excitedly. "But let's go shopping first."

I half-rolled my eyes, but she was quick to defend it. "One outfit!" she insisted. "I've already taken the day off, and I haven't gone shopping for clothes in so long. We still have an entire afternoon!"

"Fine," I agreed, "but nothing crazy."

"Never," she insisted, but the enthusiasm in her voice didn't match.

"Tonight is about fun," Emma reminded me as she stepped out of the bathroom in her new shirt. She had a curling iron heating up, ready to give me my makeover. Based on my internal cringe, I was guessing makeup hadn't been my thing in my past life either.

"We are going to dance the night away!" she announced excitedly.

"Stumble the night away," I countered with a laugh. I'd tripped enough that week just walking to know that dancing skills were a leap.

I'd grown to appreciate Emma and her relentless optimism more over our days together. Once we got past the awkward first evenings, it felt more like a normal friendship. Spending time with her had gotten easier. I'd successfully dodged her curiosity about Mylo, and she didn't put any pressure on my remembering the details of the person I used to be... but there was still a pressure. Time was still ticking away from the life I was meant to be living.

My mind continued to remind me that this friendship was fleeting. She was babysitting me, making sure I didn't run off and get lost again. I still had to figure out where I really belonged.

27

JANE

Trying to follow Emma's steps turned out to be quite fun as we laughed together through each song. It felt good to do something so carefree, to be active. It was the first time I'd really laughed, the first time my smile stretched into my cheeks so much they hurt. I stepped to the side as Emma hurried to grab a water, but as soon as the song changed, she came running back.

"Jane!" Emma called. I followed her excited voice through the crowd. She met me in the middle, grabbing my hand to pull me along.

"Come on!" she insisted. "This is the best one! It's super simple."

I started to copy her steps, surprised by how easily they came. We got halfway through the song, when Emma noticed too.

"See, it's a good one, right?"

"Yeah, I like it!" I wasn't even watching her steps by that point, dancing on my own.

"You got it down fast too!" she commented. "I told you it would be fun!"

Shoes shuffled to the beat around me, and I knew the steps perfectly. I'd already known them before the music came on. I'd danced to this song before.

The music continued, and I almost sang along, mouthing the words as I heard them. My eyes scanned the room around me giddily, checking if anybody had noticed, but nobody else would know just how big of a deal it was.

I was out of breath when the song ended, my heart still pouncing as I followed Emma to the wall, both of us laughing like childhood friends. It was the first touch I'd felt of my past, a new rush of hope pounding through me. For the first time, it felt like I had something. One small glimpse into before. I was about to tell Emma, when someone tapped my shoulder from behind.

"I don't think I've seen you around here before." I turned around to a tall, dark-haired man with a charming smile. His trimmed beard and button-up flannel basically screamed lumberjack tough-guy.

Emma looked between the two of us with a wide grin. I wondered if she knew him, but couldn't tell by her giddy shrug.

"I'm just visiting," I explained.

His hand reached toward me. "Joel."

I stared at him for a moment, when Emma answered for me. "Jane!"

Shaking off my hesitation, I accepted his hand. "Jane," I agreed with a smile, but it felt like a lie. I wasn't Jane, I was an imposter. I hadn't planned on that. I wasn't there to make more temporary friends.

"Jane," he repeated. "Would you like to dance with me?"

I looked back at Emma, who seemed thrilled to watch it unfold as she nodded her approval.

"Sure." I let him pull me forward, hoping he knew the steps well enough to dance for both of us. It was a slower song, full of undesired opportunity to stand close and talk. I immediately regretted accepting his hand, wishing I'd pushed Emma in my place. This was her home, not mine. She was the one looking for a date, not me.

"How long are you in town for?" he asked.

"Oh, I uh, haven't quite figured that out yet." The question stung in ways he would never know. He had no idea how badly I wished I had an answer to give.

"Well you have to let me take you on a date before you leave," he commented.

I have to? That was quick.

"Well, who said I'm—"

"Where are you from?"

Single. The music was loud, but it wasn't the thing that drowned out my question.

My heart pounded, the blood pulsing through my skull. Would he notice that the hand he held was starting to sweat? My other hand discretely left his back for a split second to wipe against my pants. It should have just been one short dance, but it felt like an interrogation.

"Colorado," I lied, listing off one of the random places I'd checked out a book on.

"No way, what part?" he asked. "I lived in Colorado for five years! Still have an uncle there that I visit." I didn't anticipate the returned enthusiasm. Of course he had a connection to the one place I chose off the top of my head.

Joel was trying to create simple conversation, but it terrified me. I didn't have the answers, and I didn't want to explain why. This was meant to be a night off from my problems.

"My parents live further south," I answered. My

parents? The words spilled out, but they broke my heart. How could I not even remember my own parents? Were they out there somewhere looking for me? Wondering where their daughter went? A pit of nausea dropped in my stomach.

"I lived in Denver," he said. "I did really love it there."

"What brought you here?" I asked, hoping he would take up the rest of our time talking about himself.

"I guess I was looking for some adventure. I took a summer job up here a couple years back and I don't think I'll ever leave."

"It is beautiful here," I admitted. There really was something breathtaking about the mountains of changing leaves, the ice in the sea. It was like a painting. I just preferred not to get lost in it.

Joel readjusted his arm more snugly on my back. I looked over his shoulder, noticing the heavy snow falling under the street light outside the glass entrance door. A shiver ran through me, refusing the way I would inevitably wake up lost in it.

"It really is," he agreed. The way his eyes bore into me as he said it made me antsy.

I tried to conjure up any other questions that couldn't be turned back on me, but nothing came. He spun me around a couple of times.

"What do you do, Jane? Are you a student?"

I stared at him like a deer in the headlights. The questions felt like weights on my chest, and he just kept adding more.

"Yeah, I'm just on a break right now," I lied.

"What are you studying?"

"Therapy."

"You needed a break from therapy?" he mocked. "That almost sounds contradicting."

"A break from school," I corrected. Something about him irritated me. We definitely weren't a match, not that I was looking for one.

"What do you like to do in your spare time?" he asked. "What made you choose Alaska for your break?"

I stared up at him, but I couldn't find an answer. *I don't know, I don't know, I don't know!* I wanted to yell it, but my voice was caught.

"My friend," I lied. "Emma."

"That girl you were with?" he asked, looking over at her standing by the wall. So the two of them didn't know each other either.

"How did you meet?" he asked.

How did we meet? I'd known her less than a week after crossing paths with her on the street. Instant roommates. The song ended, and I accepted its cue to pull free.

"Thanks for the dance," I told him, ready to put all the space between us. "It was nice to meet you."

"You too, Jane. Let me know when—"

I turned to walk away before he could ask, pretending not to hear over the speakers. I skipped finding Emma and went straight to hiding. There had to be a spot where I could sit alone unnoticed for a few minutes.

"Can I get a drink?" I spontaneously asked a passing waitress. Maybe if I drank enough, my body would pass out too heavily for my nightly hiking adventures. The thought of waking up with a hangover seemed better than becoming a corpse buried beneath a fresh foot of snow. My finger ticked against my leg as fear and anxiety pushed at my nerves.

"I.D.?" She patiently stopped in front of me, scanning

me over, like she doubted I was old enough. I couldn't have even told her if I was. Embarrassment burned at my face.

"Nevermind," I countered, turning to walk away. I scooted into a booth, ready to hide from everything until the night was over. My face fell into my shaky hands, Joel's questions running over and over through my head. My night had been so perfect before I met him, yet suddenly I was second guessing everything. Suddenly I was fighting for composure.

"You know, we could have that date right now," Joel's voice slyly commented. I looked up just in time to see him sliding into the booth next to me. He held two shot glasses, offering one to me.

I shook my head, nervous to take a drink from a stranger. He shrugged, pulling the glass in front of himself. If he was so willing to drink it then it was probably fine, right?

"Now where did we leave off?" he asked.

More questions.

I grabbed the glass, leaning my head back for one quick drink. I was going to need help to get through this. I coughed into my elbow before looking back at him.

He seemed surprised, but smiled. "Did you want another?" he asked as I recovered my breath. He moved to wave down the waitress when I took the second glass and drank his shot too.

As soon as I set the glass down, I froze. Would he be mad? I studied his expression, but he just looked amused. Maybe he thought this little date would be more entertaining if I was drunk. My stomach soured at the idea.

"Gonna be real fun watching you try to learn the steps now," he commented. Had he been watching me long enough to know I was a beginner? The idea made me cringe, wishing Emma would notice I was gone and come rescue me. Joel leaned in, closing me deeper into the booth.

"Oh yeah? How about we go do some dancing now," I suggested, running along with his comment.

He was too close, cornering me against the wall with his face between my ear and my neck. I could have sworn I heard a smile in his breath. He gave in, scooting back out, but not without grabbing my hand, pulling me towards the dance floor with him. Who did this guy think he was?

I started to pull away, but my ankle rolled. My arm shot out for balance, hitting the waitress behind me as she cleared a table of dishes. Two drinks rolled off of her tray, soaking the front of my shirt. Left over alcohol dripped down my arms, seeping between the cracks of my scabbed-over cuts with a searing promise of pain.

My eyes filled with tears. I had to get out of there. My hand yanked free, apologizing to the waitress as I hurried toward the restroom.

The soaked, ice-cold fabric stuck to my skin as I unbuttoned the front of my new shirt. Emma's new shirt. All I could claim was the black bra beneath it. I stared at myself in the mirror, grateful nobody else lingered in there with me. My hand reached up to cover the exposed, faded bruise on my neck, another mystery from the life I lived a week before. What if something truly bad had happened. Maybe I really was trying to run away.

How many times had I felt the urge to run? What if someone was coming for me and my subconscious was just trying to help me get out? What if my amnesia was just trying to cut off the past and save me from myself?

My heart started pounding. I was cold, a nervous sweat on my forehead. I shook my hands out, regretting those drinks as I grew dizzier, hoping Joel hadn't put anything extra in them. I moved to the largest stall, wiping the moisture from my hands to my pants as my back pressed to the wall and I sank down it. My face fell into my knees as I forced each breath in and out, but I couldn't fight the trembling that ran through me.

"Jane?" Emma's concern rang through the door. "I saw you come in here, are you okay?" The words came out cautiously. She slowly pushed the stall door open before falling to the floor in front of me.

"What happened?"

I was shaking as short, shallow breaths fought their way in and out. My body couldn't work past the panic enough to answer.

"Are you hurt?"

I shook my head, ignoring the sting in my arms, still trembling into myself as I fought for air.

"Come on," she offered. "Let's just go home." *Home? This wasn't my home!* My mind was losing it, but my body was numb.

I shook my head again. "I can't go out there."

"I'm going to call my dad, okay?" Emma didn't wait for my approval, acting out of her own nerves. She dialed twice, doing an antsy little walk back and forth in front of me.

"He's probably gone to bed," she admitted. She scrolled through her contacts in what felt like a desperate search for help Emma reached down, trying to pull my arm, but I didn't move. All I could think of was Joel, and the drinks, and the questions, and the snow, and I couldn't face any of it.

"Come on," she encouraged, grabbing my wrist to tug harder.

"No!" I cried, scooting further away. "No."

"Have you been drinking?" Her brows drew together,

scrutinizing my face. She pulled up her phone again, and the other line answered immediately.

"Hey, sorry it's late—" she started. Her voice paused to hear the other end. "I don't know what to do, I think she's having a panic attack— My dad didn't answer, I didn't know who else to—" Pause. "Okay." Pause. "Yeah, here."

28

JANE

"Jane?" Mylo's voice echoed from the speaker on Emma's phone as she lowered it. I sniffled. Why did she have to call him? Why every time I got into trouble it fell back to him?

"What's wrong? What's happened?"

The night was such a mess, I didn't even know how to start. "The song," I tried to explain, but couldn't finish. My evening had been on such a high note, I knew the song! I wanted to rejoice in that small victory, I finally had some kind of progress to share, but I couldn't get the words out.

"His questions," I cried. "I couldn't answer his questions I don't know my own name!"

"Listen to me, okay?" Mylo asked. "Let's focus on what we do know. What color is your shirt?"

My eyes shut tighter, refusing to look at it. "It's all wet," I cried, readjusting my knees in front of me as I realized again how exposed I was. His words caught, but he made a quick recovery.

"What color is Emma's shirt?" I forced myself to look up at my friend.

"Red and white."

"Her shoes?"

My eyes moved to her cowgirl boots. "Brown."

"What color is my car?"

"Black," I answered. "The same color as everything else you own." The playful comment gave me a tiny bit of my sanity back.

I sniffled again, but each breath grew calmer. It was so simple, but he'd known how to help me. I cried about questions I couldn't answer, so he gave me questions I could. Some moments it felt like Mylo knew me better than I knew myself. Knew where to find me when I was lost. I didn't know myself at all. Maybe that's what made me feel so drawn to him. But every minute he gave me worked towards finding my real home again, and home wasn't here. It wasn't with him.

Emma's relief turned to concern again as the emotions shifted back in through the silence.

"What is it?" she pleaded, desperately trying to get through.

"Hey you can't go in th—" someone started to say from the hallway.

"Try me," Mylo practically growled. The door slid open behind Emma as he stepped inside. He knelt down, putting a gentle hand on my arm. I winced, hugging my knees in tighter, hiding my face in them.

"I can't make friends here." I barely got the words out. "I can't spend a lifetime pretending to be someone I'm not. I'm a whole other person that I don't even know. One day that person is going to find me." The words squeaked. "What if my parents think I'm dead? What if I'm married, or have a little baby waiting for me at home?" The hushed worries became sobs, and they were all real possibilities. They were too valid to argue.

Mylo didn't answer, grabbing my hands to pull me to my feet, and I let him. I fell into him, unable to hold myself up.

"Something out there doesn't want me to remember," I whispered. I felt it in the forest. Mylo was there, he had to have sensed it too, some force outside of my control.

"Please, you have to help me," I begged. "Try everything, whatever it takes, just, don't leave me alone in this!"

"I won't," he swore, still holding me tight. I grabbed his arms for support as I leaned back to search his eyes.

"You won't? You promise me?" I asked, ignoring the tears streaming down my cheeks. "You'll help me find myself? Whatever it takes?"

He hesitated, letting the words sink in. His eyes quickly scanned down my unbuttoned shirt, my shoulders nervously rolling in against the wet bra straps beneath it, when his gaze landed on the bruise at my neck. His teeth clenched tight, his black eyes meeting back with mine.

"I promise you."

His gaze was so intense, I started to get lost in it, but it didn't take away from everything I'd said before. The people that might be out there waiting on me. My hands pulled back, wrapping the loose, cold fabric over my chest.

"I can't fall in love with you." The words spilled out. I shook my head. There was no future here. There couldn't be. "I can only promise you right now." I wanted so badly to hide my pain, wavering a half-step to the side. Mylo reached out to steady me.

"I know," he agreed. He looked back at Emma. "Where's her jacket?"

"She left your jacket in the car."

He stepped between me and her, reaching for the open collar of my ruined shirt, sliding it down off my arms. I ignored the cold air as it hit my skin, the burn as he exposed my scrapes.

He slid off his own solid black sweater, ignoring the way the shirt underneath rose with it. A long scar wrapped around the side of his ribs. He caught me eying it, fixing his shirt back down, before opening the bottom of his sweater for me to slide my arms in, pulling it up over my head. I hugged my arms in front of myself, relieved by the extra layer of protection and warmth.

"Who even served you alcohol?" he grumbled.

I knew I shouldn't have accepted it, but I'd panicked. "He had so many questions." I shook my head. "And then it was snowing!"

"Who is *he*?"

"The guy looking for a quick date," I grumbled.

"It must have been this guy named Joel," Emma softly clarified behind him.

Mylo turned for the door, but I squeezed his arm tight. "No, don't. Please. I just thought... it was snowing so hard outside the windows." I hesitated. "I thought maybe if I had a few drinks—"

Realization shined in his eyes. "You thought your body might skip getting lost in the woods for a night." I nodded, a bit embarrassed about how I'd gone about it.

Mylo didn't speak as he helped me to Emma's car, his body shielding mine from the still dancing crowd, though nothing could shield the crowd from his glare. The car ride with Emma was awkward. Neither of us knew what to say as she slowly made her way down the snow-coated roads. When she parked in her driveway, I couldn't take the silence any longer.

"I'm sorry I ruined the night."

She shook her head like she didn't agree.

"He was asking me so many questions, I just panicked."

"Don't apologize to me for panicking," she countered. "For being scared... for feeling. Don't apologize for having amnesia, or borrowing clothes, or taking up our guest house! That's not what ruined the night."

I watched her short rant, trying to understand.

"Don't sit here and pretend to be my friend if you don't want to be. I don't care where you came from. If you never remember your life before this, I'm here for that!" She hesitated, finally meeting my eyes. "But if tomorrow you wake up and you remember it all... some happy life that I never would have originally been a part of... if you buy a plane ticket and leave within the hour, and I never get to see you again .. I'm here for that too. I don't care how long it lasts, but right now, right here in this moment, you're here. I don't regret getting to know you. I'd never change being your friend, no matter what comes after. Not after, there's not an after. Not to me. There's just a next."

New tears pooled in my eyes. I nodded, finally accepting a piece of this life that I'd found. She cocked her head toward the back of the car as another set of headlights pulled in from the road behind us.

"And just for the record, I think he's here for it too."

We both stepped out of the car when Emma immediately turned in.

'Goodnight, Mylo," she commented as she passed him, before turning to me. She hugged her arms around me tight. "You'll let me know if you need me, right?"

I nodded. "Thank you. For everything."

"I'll see you tomorrow," she promised in my ear.

As she stepped away, Mylo stood a few feet behind her,

his black eyes focused on mine. We stayed where we were, silent, until Emma closed the door behind her and we were alone.

"Thank you for helping me. For letting me be insane without making me feel like it." My heartbeat picked up again as the words spilled out. "I got so scared... I'm terrified—"

"What are you so afraid of?" he asked. He slowly walked closer, his gaze never breaking.

My mind dazed as a nervous energy tingled on my skin. "I lost everything," I whispered against the cold night air. "The more I have here, the more I have to lose again. I can't grow to love this life... the more I love it, the more my heart might break the day I tell it goodbye. I don't want to build anything else that might be torn away. I don't want to lose everything all over again, I don't want to lose—" *you*. The realization surprised me, maybe even scared me on a deep level. Where was this confession coming from?

I could feel the panic rushing back in, pushing me towards the edge as my breaths caught in my chest.

"You don't want to risk growing new roots for a tree that will only be cut down." He was right in front of me. He leaned down, the side of his nose barely brushing down my hair until it reached my neck. I was frozen. My breath caught, waiting for him to go on as the snow pelted my face.

"Why did you come? Before... you said you couldn't help me," I whispered.

"You want me to go?"

I swallowed hard, ignoring the way he was right there at my neck. "I don't want to be alone," I admitted in a whimper. "Not tonight. I don't want to wake up lost in a snowstorm." My voice became a cry. "I don't want to die." Full panic surged back through like the dam broke loose.

"You said you would help me! You said you would do everything you can!"

"I did," he agreed. There was something off in his tone. It sounded distant.

"What is it?"

"I will help you, I gave you my word. But I have to warn you that you might not like it." His cologne was like a drug, his breath softly sweeping over my neck. A snowflake hit my eyelash, making my eyes flutter.

"Can't be worse than waking up buried in the snow," I countered.

"Not tonight." He straightened back up again.

"Please," I pleaded. "Don't go."

"I'm right here," he assured me, brushing a hand over my hair before it drew beneath my jaw, slightly lifting my chin to look in my eyes. "I'm not going anywhere."

"I need you to try... I need you."

His jaw flexed, dropping his hand. "There will be no turning back," he warned. "You have to understand that."

"Okay," I agreed.

He straightened taller, head leaning back, leaving the words to process between us as he continued staring into my eyes. Then he gave one single nod. "Okay."

I grabbed a blanket, offering it to Mylo before I sat on the couch. He sat too, taking in the room around us as he set a bag on the table. It was nothing like his cold, colorless office. The walls held warmth from the stone fireplace to the paintings and hardwood floor. I'd grown to love the balanced mix of wood and color. Not for the first time did I admire the set of miniature rocking chairs and the wooden cradle full of folded quilts and a fabric doll that waited for a child to visit.

"Sure is lucky I bumped into someone who had a

guest house," I commented. "And a doctor for a dad. I don't know what I would have done if I didn't find Emma." Dr. Quinn had given me an opinion to trust. Something to hold onto, to rely on, when everything else fell flat. I didn't mention the fact that technically, I'd found Mylo first.

"You don't need to worry about that now," Mylo commented. He pushed the bag toward me.

"What's this?" I asked, opening the end to find a neatly wrapped sub sandwich. "Oh, thanks. I'm not—"

"Eat, Jane," he said. I rolled my eyes, but pulled out the sandwich, taking a big bite of one end.

"What, no more name game?" I joked. The first bite of turkey and cheese actually made me want more. I took two more bites before talking again, grateful that my stomach didn't complain.

"All I do is worry. What else can I do?"

"You can rest... *Sam*," he added randomly for my benefit.

Sam.

My brows drew together, staring at him as I chewed, trying to find the connection. It wasn't me, but it was someone.

"Rest," I echoed with a hint of sarcasm. His serious expression didn't waver. I didn't say another word, trying to swallow the bite of food in my mouth. What had I expected him to do? Start a late night therapy session? He'd promised to help me, I had to trust that he would keep his word.

"The only thing I want you worried about tonight is sleep."

I scoffed. "As if it's that simple." I set the remaining half of the sandwich down on its wrapper, my stomach already feeling full.

"Sleep. I'll still be here when you wake up." I stared into his eyes, desperately wanting to believe it was true.

"Sleep," I repeated. The daze came back, blurring my vision, consciousness waving in and out. "You'll still be here," I added, echoing his words further.

My eyes rolled back, my head nodding forward, falling into his arm. It wrapped around me, hugging me tight.

"And so will you."

29

JANE

I bounced up off the snow as if I'd only just sat down and didn't want to give the cold a chance to seep in.

Trees. Everywhere. I spun around, searching the forest. One large branch ahead broke out from its trunk and arched back down over the snow like a rainbow. It caught my eye, because I'd seen it before.

I studied the path behind it, and I knew. This was where I woke up the first time. This was the spot where my nightmares began, but why was I back? I spun around, searching for that raven. Where was that dang bird!

"You said you would keep this from happening again!" I cried into the thin, cold air.

"I'm here," Mylo answered. He stood behind me, the familiar, casual expression on his face.

"Why are we out here?" I asked.

"You know this place," he commented.

I glanced around. "I know this place. I woke up here."

"With no explanation," he added.

I searched his face. Was he questioning my honesty? "None."

"You were scared of something."

My brows drew together. I'd been scared of something. A twig snapped at my side. I turned to examine the woods tucked behind that arching tree. Suddenly, it felt as if the shadows were playing games with me, a monster lurking within them. My feet ran into the thick of the forest, desperate to flee.

"What are you so afraid of?" Mylo's voice rang closely through my mind, but as I looked side to side in my panicked sprint there was no one.

I faced ahead again as a wall of darkness swallowed me whole. The ground dropped below my feet as I tumbled back into nothing but more shadows.

"Mylo!" I cried, begging him to wake me up from this nightmare.

"You're somewhere safe," he answered. I sat up in the snow again. It no longer fell around me, replaced by a deep, still nightfall that consumed the woods. My arms wrapped into a tight hug across my chest, my breath steaming against the cold.

"Mylo?" I asked, more quietly this time. Nervously.

"You're somewhere safe," he repeated. "Among people you know and love. People that would never hurt you."

I searched the world around me, who did he mean? Emma's cottage sat between the trees, warm light shining through each window. I let out a sigh of relief.

"I don't want to play anymore. Can't I just go inside?"

"That's not up to me." The echo of his words rolled through the background of my thoughts as I slowly paced toward the cabin. My head cocked to one side in a daze as I looked through the window. Four girls sat at a table, laughing as they played their game. I couldn't see their faces, but I knew the sound of their joy.

I knocked on the window, certain they would come for me. Nobody moved. I pounded harder.

"Hey!" I called, yelling against the glass. "Hey, let me in!"

Nothing. I studied them, curiously stepping over to the next window.

"I'm supposed to be in there!" I told them, my fist hitting the glass. It didn't make sense. One of the girls winced, leaning back from their table. Her blurry face turned its attention to me as she stood to come closer.

"Yes!" I cried, finally being heard. "I'm here! Please, let me in!"

The face cleared as she approached the window, her familiar brown eyes meeting mine through the glass, but it didn't make sense.

"You already are, Ava." My name whispered through me like a breeze, a secret unfolding.

"What?" I asked, shocked to find my own face staring back at me. In a blink, the light was gone, leaving only myself and my empty reflection. I took a step back, this time from inside the glass window, alone in a dark, silent room.

"You just have to turn on the light," Mylo called through my thoughts.

My hands searched the wall, failing to find the switch. "There's nothing," I cried.

Weight shifted against the stairs behind me, something creaking down the steps, making the hair rise on the back of my neck. I turned toward the wall, my palm swiping over it more desperately for the switch. Stumbling into a corner, I barely hit the light as the footsteps reached me.

A large, brightly-lit ballroom ran across my view, made up of black, white and gold. Masked faces danced in their heavy gowns and solid dark suits. I searched their eyes, trying to find a face that I knew. Nobody bothered looking at me, as if I wasn't really there at all while they spun along the checkerboard tile.

The song ended, and the crowd parted just enough for a tall, slender man to walk through. He wore a long-sleeved, button-up, white shirt, tucked into coal black pants. His warm smile beamed as he reached a hand toward me. I stared into his light blue eyes, eyes that I'd known well in a previous life.

"Ava," he greeted.

"Noah," I answered. His name was Noah. His smile stretched wider, as if to reassure me that I was right. I placed my hand in his, letting him pull me into the crowd.

"Try not to trip," he mocked before we began circling around to the center of the room. So much was happening, but all I could see was his eyes.

When the song ended, he looked sad. He hugged me closer, and whispered into my ear.

"Where did you go, Ava?"

I closed my eyes, absorbing that moment as his words echoed through me.

Then I was alone again, standing in the dark woods as if it had all been in my head. No cottage, no music playing in the background, no laughing friends.

"Noah?" I called, searching the shadows.

Something shifted through the leaves, making me jump. The same familiar branch arched over the forest floor. The raven was there, perched calmly above it. Oco.

"What are you so afraid of?" Mylo asked from behind. I saw him in the corner of my eye, a few feet back with the trees. He was so calm, patiently watching for what came next.

"What are you so afraid of?" The words repeated, this

time like a whisper in my ear, though Mylo still stood five steps back.

The shadows stretched heavily beneath the night sky as something drew closer. Heavy hooves stomped against the ground as a horse came into the starlight, rearing up on its hind legs in front of me. Its rider wore a firm glare, warning me that I was not welcome.

"I shouldn't be back here!" I cried, falling away from the pressure of the horse. It stomped down, barely missing my legs, when the rider's wings stretched wide behind him.

"No." I shook my head as the memories came crashing back in. I'd only gone for a walk, I was sad! I'd gotten lost! I was just trying to avoid reality for a few hours, but I took a wrong turn!

Home. I'd been so close to home.

I'd stepped off the path of my world and tumbled into a new one.

The silhouette of a distant dragon ran across the clouds like a dream. It wasn't real. It was something out of Sam's stories, out of her poem. Then I was lost in it, wrapped up in the chaos of a different world, and I couldn't get out.

Somehow I knew I wasn't supposed to be there. I hid at the base of a wide tree trunk. The men, they weren't... men. They were different. They spoke of mirrors, broken mirrors and gates, their voices angry and hushed. The confrontation was private, I wasn't meant to hear it.

One man sliced the other straight through the heart. The memories all flashed before me, a nightmare come to life. I fought my cries, desperate to stay hidden, when the assassin's gaze flickered my way, standing to scan the darkness between us.

"He heard me."

A twig snapped around the tree I stared up at the mythical face, a face that belonged in my world no more than I belonged in his. He grabbed my neck, pulling me up to pin me against the tree. I reached my fingers over his wrists, trying to push them off. I shocked him, or maybe burned him? I wasn't sure. Whatever it was, it caught him off guard. His hands jerked away, rubbing together in front of his gut.

Another voice called from the distance, a woman's voice, demanding, and dangerous. A strange dark energy weaved through her chant, a curse in the air. I lunged the other way, sprinting against the tall hedges and uneven ground.

The assassin muttered under his breath as he chased my tail, until he'd chased me out of it. Out of the nightmare. Out of that world.

"That voice in the air made me forget."

The vision dispersed around me like a fog, the nightmare leaving me be, but I could still hear the echo of her spell in the darkness.

"Her words made me forget," I repeated on the brink of consciousness. I didn't know how, but it was the truth.

I sat up with a sharp intake of air, my fists clenching the blankets tightly as I studied the familiar room around me. "I'm still here."

I looked up at Mylo, standing behind the couch, staring at the hardwood floor. I stretched my neck, sore from the angle I slept at.

"You are," he agreed.

"I had the strangest dream. It went on and on, I just couldn't escape it."

"Yeah," he agreed.

"And then— Hold on, I remembered!" *Wait.* He agreed with me? "What?"

"What have you gotten yourself into, Ava?" He shook

his head disapprovingly, his voice laced with a strange sense of concern.

"Didn't you hear me? I remember everything! I figured out who I am! I—" *Ava.* I hadn't told him what my name was.

"But, how—" I started to ask. "What happened? What did you do?" He talked about having some trick to help trigger my memories, but it was all a dream, wasn't it? A subconscious hunt for myself.

"You're not safe... the woods?"

"I'll never step foot in them again! I can go home now! I know where I belong, this nightmare can finally be over!" It felt as if I'd broken a curse, like the mess could finally be cleaned up.

"A guard chased you out of that world, that doesn't just go away—"

"Guard? No!" I stood up, the couch sitting between us. "That man in the trees?" How did he know about that?

"Your ring. It burned him. He knew you didn't belong."

"Burned? That wasn't real!"

"It wasn't part of your world," he argued.

"Well this is the world I'm sticking to." What was his deal? This was something to celebrate! *Your* world.

His lips drew a thin line, chin lifting stubbornly as he straightened up taller. I matched his energy, my fingers grabbing my sleeves, stretching them over my hands as I folded my arms across my chest. My wrists hit together with the sting of a cut.

"Ouch," I commented, pulling up the sleeve again to see. Teeth marks circled around the side of my wrist. "What?" My finger brushed along the small cuts, studying the bite, eyes shifting up to his with a newfound fear.

"You bit me?"

"I would never hurt you, Ava." He took a step closer.

"I never told you my real name."

He reached forward.

"Don't touch me! You bit me! You literally drew blood." *Your world*. I repeated the words in my head, wondering what that meant. "What are you, a vampire?" I thought back on everything and scoffed in disgust. The way he stared at the cut on my head when we first met. *"You're bleeding."* It was always the first thing he seemed to notice. And the strange mind tricks, the way I would go into a daze. The way he could say anything, and I just went along with it... believed it! The way I put boots and a jacket on every night before I went to sleep without remembering.

Ava. He knew my name.

"You got inside my head. What is this, a game to you?"

"I told you I would do whatever it took. I swore it!"

"You're not a psychiatrist, you're a fraud!"

"I help people. Someone comes into my office that wants to quit smoking, I tell them to stop smoking. Problem solved. Someone complains about their fear of heights, I tell them not to be afraid anymore. I give people what they want. You wanted to remember, right? Now you do."

"And we pay with blood." I held my wrist up, shaking my head. My hand fell as I turned away from him, trying to remain calm. "This is impossible," I told myself. "This isn't real."

"So what! A few drops of blood, I'm not dead, I'm cursed." This time he scoffed. "I couldn't die if I wanted it." His words turned somber, spoken out of longing pain.

"You drank my blood."

"I warned you, you might not like my tactics. I was never meant to find peace in your world. A curse made me a monster. It made me live for one thing, the death of the humans, but even stronger, the death of my own. After years of getting it under control, you have no idea how hard I fought! If I get close to anyone, anything that has touched the magic of my world, the craving becomes too much—" His lips pursed together angrily, muscles tensed, but he stopped himself, rolling back his shoulders.

"They wanted me to suffer," he continued evenly. "And they wanted me to do it alone. I've kept so discreet, survived here so long! And then you walked through, and you'd touched the magic—"

"How many times?"

He stared at me, waiting to understand the question.

"How many times did you stop yourself from killing me?"

He took a careful step around the couch, eying me from the side, his lips in a firm line as his teeth slid into place behind them. "I've wanted to kill you since the moment I met you."

My blood iced, standing at the edge of a cliff, and if I made one wrong move, I'd fall, trying not to stumble as I matched his steps the opposite way around the couch.

"You were standing there all alone in the street with that cut on your head. All that blood staring back at me? You showed up at my office the next day. I told myself Quinn would know where you went, he was already looking into missing people. He'd know if I did something. All that blood in my sink. That towel." He shook his head in disgust.

"You're lucky I don't have to breathe very often. I told myself my clothes would mask your scent, hide it somehow, make it easier, but the smell of me on you only makes me want you more. The fact that you're still standing there, alive, should mean something."

"I'm sorry, should I be thanking you?" I shook my head in denial, but I was staring into the eyes of an animal.

"You said you wouldn't hurt me. Get out," I ordered. "Leave now! None of this matters anymore, I have my memories, I'm going home."

"Just like that?"

"Just like that!" I glared at him, wishing he'd disappear. What did he expect? He should have warned me that he was different. I held firm, standing strong. "I promised you the night, and I gave you that. It's over."

His eyes darkened with threat. "You've crossed the lines where magics mix. Be careful, Ava, another world knows your name."

"Another world?" He was ridiculous! "What, your world?"

He didn't answer, and my rant stopped as it hit me. "That is your world."

"If you'd just give me a day—"

"Give you a day to what? Wipe my memories again? Keep me hostage in this tiny town? Use your compulsion to guarantee that I won't spoil your perfect therapist reputation? Kill me?"

"Ava—"

"No, Mylo. Thank you, you fulfilled your promise." He'd given me exactly what I'd wanted. The job was done. I didn't want to hear another word. "Now go back to your world, or wherever the hell you came from. Just stay out of mine."

That stopped him. A hint of something flashed through his eyes. Hurt? It didn't matter. The cold calm expression was back as quickly as it had gone. The fight was over.

"Have a good life," he said, turning out the door and into the night.

SHATTERED

30

HARPER

I sat at the window of burned castle stone, my eyes closed as I focused on each breath. I had to be in tune with something, to remain connected to my own skin. The silence had gone on too long. It felt I'd never get my hearing back, lost in this impossible void on earth. This strange realm between life and nothing. Emptiness. I looked down on the fields that wrapped the mansion, an opening off in the distance.

"It's open!" I said with a jolt, straining my eyes to make sure. I threw myself from the wall and ran. Ran through the house, ran out the door. Ran like my life depended on it, because it felt very much like it did.

As I got closer, I couldn't find the opening. I stepped up to the metal bars, searching for my way out until I saw it, the open gate down the field. My hand brushed against the bars as I ran on, feet pounding with each step, eyes fixated on my escape. I never stopped moving, but no matter how hard I pushed, how fast I ran, the opening never came.

"No," I whispered, realizing the trick. "I have to get out of here." I ran faster, pushing my limits in a desperate plea.

The opening inched closer as I pulled along the bars to reach it, some force holding me back. I fought through to the end, grasping the last bar between myself and my freedom, fighting with every muscle to just hold on.

The constraint let go, dropping me to my knees. I stood free again, shifting toward the center of the open gate, standing on the boundary between what was. What was my life, and what was his.

I stared through the opening, a doorway into the thick dark forest. I was finally there, I'd fought to get that far, so why did I hesitate? Something other than freedom seemed to lurk within the shadows ahead, daring me to cross the line in front of me. Would it let me through? I stepped forward slowly across the gated boundary, pushing for the world I desperately wanted to return to. My foot pressed against the fallen leaves with a soft crunch.

A gray wolf lunged forward from the darkness, snapping at my leg. I fell back, scrambling to scoot away from its jaws. Three more wolves joined in at its sides, slithering out from the forest behind. The leader of their pack waited on the line, blocking my only way out, promising pain if I returned to try again.

Something snapped behind me, the click of teeth biting tight. I turned as the black dog lunged for my face, jaws wide in attack.

I sat up as the air broke through my lungs, frozen in the dark room around me. The stars outside shared little light with our world. Benny was right about horror stories, they hid in the air around me. I'd snuck into the greenhouse, desperate for its warmth, but the nightmares ripped away my peace.

Something grabbed me. I fought against it, pushing it away. I couldn't hear the growls, but their jaws still bit at my subconscious. An arm squeezed around my stomach. I defensively kicked back, making contact with the body restraining me from behind as I fought between a dream and reality.

Someone. The only 'anyone' that was locked in there with me. He barely loosened his hold to recover, readjusting to the side.

I forced myself to relax as his warm arms hugged mine in front of me. My head fell back against him, with nowhere else to go, making myself breathe. There was no wolf. They weren't really there. Elijah's fingers slowly softened, but still held me as he turned me around to face him.

A hug, that's all it took for me to break. I collapsed into him, crying out fears weaved into my very soul. I had nobody else, but I did have him. He reached up slowly, brushing the soil from my cheek. I almost felt embarrassed for sleeping on the ground, but it was the warmest option I had.

"A nightmare," I explained, knowing I would read no answer from his lips within the darkness. "I hate the dark."

Elijah let go, but grabbed one hand. He pulled me along, and I followed without a second thought. I didn't really care where he led, I had nowhere else to go. I just didn't want to be alone.

Elijah led me outside the back of the house, past the wishing well, toward a patch of lined old orchard trees. I could see a little bit more outside, the scattered starlight more distinct as it lit our world below. Their light always shined so brightly in the darkest corners of the world. Elijah pulled me to a small bench, offering a seat. I took it and waited as he carried on.

He stacked chopped wood in the pit at my feet, and quickly had it smoking. The fire was welcome and needed. As soon as I saw the flame, I fell from the bench and scooted in closer, reaching my hands out to absorb its heat.

Elijah watched me from across the pit, making me feel a bit ridiculous.

"I didn't realize I needed to pack for a campout," I muttered. For a moment I was annoyed, but it humbled quickly. This guy was just as stuck there as I was. He'd let me into his home, and shared what little it had to offer. He'd just come to find me in the night and built me a fire to help chase away my fears. I let out a big sigh.

He held up a line, a dead fish dangling at the bottom.

"You caught that?" I asked, searching his eyes. He nodded before pulling a knife out to start preparing it. I moved back to my spot on the bench.

"You aren't cold?" I asked him, still standing a few feet back from the flames. That time he shook his head, pausing with the fish as his eyes got lost in the fire.

"I swear something here has it out for me."

Elijah didn't answer, but I was sure he heard me. He was always so serious, and maybe a little bit broken. That was okay though. He was allowed to be him, just as I was allowed to be me. As long as he didn't go anywhere, that's all that mattered. Not without taking me with him. Broken or not, he was all I had.

"Will you sit by me?" I asked. "I just... don't want to be alone."

He studied my expression before giving a soft nod. I tried to straighten as he lowered to the bench next to me.

"Thank you," I told him with a shiver. He cut through the fish on his knee, reminding me of campouts with dad growing up. "All these cold nights. I don't know how you've done it by yourself."

"Tell me about your life. Before this." I read the words on his lips.

"My life?" I shook my head, wondering what he wanted to hear. "I guess if you have to be stuck with me, you might as well know who you're stuck with. Honestly I just moved up here to my cousin's a few days ago. I thought I could hide out and focus on my writing."

I pulled the phone from my pocket out of habit, just as I'd done a hundred other times since it went blank, wondering how many failed phone calls Ben had tried to make.

"What is that?" Elijah asked.

I held up the phone. "This?" It seemed like a silly question, but his curiosity was sincere.

"It's my phone. I guess it doesn't work here, but out there we use them for almost everything."

"What's everything?"

"I don't know, to look stuff up, order food, do math, take pictures, send messages. Call for help when you get stuck somewhere." I guess this world missed the memo. I'd never missed my friends so much. "A simple flashlight."

"You really don't like the dark."

"It terrifies me," I admitted. "The fire helps, though." I gave him a grateful smile. "I miss my friends. It's so lonely here."

He looked sad, but didn't argue. How could I complain when he'd been trapped by himself for so much longer?

"Tell me about them."

"My friends?" I asked. "Well if I was home... home home, before I came to Maine, we would probably all be together right now. It was Sage's birthday this week. We would have stopped for a treat after school, and stayed up late laughing and dreaming about the future."

"What are their names?"

"Sage, Ava, Willow and—" I stopped myself. There was no *and* not anymore. "Me," I finished.

"Do you have a boyfriend there?"

"No. I mean, I used to."

"Hence the hiding out?"

It caught me off guard. "Maybe he was part of it," I admitted. "Why I wanted to get away." I shook my head, wishing I could go back and rewrite a chapter. "Zack wasn't bad, he just wasn't right." Leaving home was more than that though.

"My other friend, Sam, she loved writing too. She used to talk about going on these big adventures. We were going to travel, explore, live a life full of inspiration to flood our stories with... but she's gone now. This wasn't exactly the writing retreat I had imagined." I stared out into the dark world around us.

"She would have loved it here, though," I commented after a moment. I'd thought those words over and over since stepping through those gates. "I almost feel closer to her here."

I looked up at him, watching me intently from the side as I rambled on. I pushed a tear from the corner of my eye. "I guess I just couldn't let her go."

Maybe that's really what pushed me so hard to leave, to give in and join Benny up in Maine. I couldn't stand our broken friend group, pretending like things could still be the same without my favorite person. Like a thousand of my dreams didn't go to her grave with her. She was the glue that stuck us all together, and I stepped in to replace her, to hold everything tight, but I just wasn't as strong. Not without her.

Elijah set aside the fish to reach around my back, and I

let him pull me closer, relaxing into his heat. I sniffed back the emotions, letting my thoughts get lost in the fire again as I soaked up his comfort.

"I wish I could hear you," I whispered. "I wish you could tell me about your world."

I closed my eyes, letting the flames chase away the shadows until I drifted off.

31

HARPER

The longer I sat there, the more my previous dream played tricks on me, telling me monsters watched me from the shadows. My eyes opened to stare at the wall of trees beyond the fence, wishing I could turn off my imagination.

"There aren't wolves out here, are there?"

He didn't move, and part of me felt nervous about the answer. I sat up, looking at his face.

"Are there?"

He shook his head. "They won't come through the gate. This isn't their territory."

Just like in my dream. How could my subconscious have guessed that? I thought over the nightmare, the way they waited on the fence line like they couldn't cross through. All of them except one.

"What about that black wolf?" I asked. Elijah went still. "He's the one that got me stuck in here to begin with. The one that attacked me in my dream."

Elijah pushed up off the bench, staring into my face. "What black wolf?"

"The... black wolf?" I wasn't sure how else to say it. "You haven't seen him? When the gate opened, when I found that room with the hourglass... there was a black wolf."

Elijah shook his head. "It can't be."

"It can't be what? I don't understand."

It was like I'd lost Elijah's attention entirely, his mind wrapped up somewhere else.

"Elijah? What is it?"

"It's Beau. It's my brother."

"Your brother? What do you mean? The... wolf?"

"Wait." Elijah shook his head, his brows drawn together. "So he's the reason you're stuck here?"

"The wolf," I asked again to confirm.

"Yes, the wolf."

"Well, it led me right to that hourglass if that's what you mean." My head flinched back slightly as I searched his eyes. "You're telling me that wolf is your brother?"

"A piece of him."

"What does that mean? A piece of him... a wolf?"

"He was a shifter."

"Was."

"Beau died. Before the fire."

Of course he did, everyone Elijah knew was dead. "A shifter," I repeated. Now I was definitely stuck in one of Sam's books. "A werewolf," I whispered, thinking of the pack of beasts in my dream. A dizzy wave floated through my head as I leaned into the back of the bench for balance.

"He shouldn't be here," Elijah warned. "You need to stay away from him." I thought of the wolf, knowing that it was him that continued to find me. How was I to stop a wolf, dead or not?

"But if he's a wolf, then you're a..." All of my fear

shifted. "You can't be a..." I fought it, but the answer was obvious in Elijah's face.

"You're a shifter too." I took a step back, my mind wrestling with reality. "And this curse? It's trapped you here? That hourglass?"

"The hourglass tide. It counts down to the full moon. The night I'm forced to shift... the night I kill you."

I stared at his lips. They couldn't have said what I thought they'd said. *Kill me?*

"No," I denied. "That's not— You told me I wouldn't be harmed!"

"I'm sorry. I didn't want any of this."

I searched his eyes, wishing there was some glimmer of hope within them. They flickered past me, darkening on something else. I spun around, expecting the wolf.

Josh dropped a bag to the grass before hopping down from the distant fence. He looked both ways, as if he might get caught, before sliding the backpack back onto his shoulders and jogging toward the house.

"Josh? What is he doing here?" He could save me. I ran toward him, desperate for his help. Desperate for any piece of the world outside those gates.

"Josh!" I yelled. "You have to help me!" He didn't react to my voice. He still couldn't hear me. He slowed as he approached the stone wall, nervously pressing his back against it. My jog became a walk as I stepped in front of him, trying to understand.

He looked like he was on a mission. Was he there looking for me?

'Josh, I'm right here!" I reached out to touch his arm. "Please."

He pulled a flashlight from the side pocket of his pack and turned down the wall, starting his hunt. I followed him through the property, shining his light in and out of rooms, but I wasn't there for him to find.

Josh stopped at the well, dropping his bag to take a break. The flashlight still shined off the stone where he set it, pointed at just enough of an angle for me to see his face. He stared into the dark well hole, lost in far away thoughts.

"Where did you go, Harper?" he asked the silence around him. He opened his bag, digging his hand past a stash of first aid supplies to his wallet. He pulled out the gold dollar that was tucked inside. He'd been carrying that coin in there for years, claiming it was lucky. He slid the wallet back into his pocket, dropping the unzipped bag back to the rocks.

"I don't know what I thought I'd find here. I was so sure..." He shook his head, fighting his thoughts. "I didn't even get to fight with you one time, Harps."

He waited for a long time, as if the silence would offer an answer. "Ben is so worried about you."

"I'm right here," I cried, wishing so badly that he could see me.

"Just come back," he wished. He dropped the coin over the well, and wiped a single tear from his eye. "Find a way."

I'd never felt more broken, sitting at the well as Josh disappeared into the night. I couldn't watch him leave again. I couldn't say goodbye as the last piece of my life walked away. I would never go home. I would never see Ben again. My mom. Sage, Ava, or Willow. And they would never know why.

If only I could talk to Sam. What would she tell me to do?

I sensed him in the shadows around me before I saw Elijah's face cross the dim path. He took a slow step forward, letting the moon reveal his face.

"Was that your boyfriend?" he asked.

I would have gotten defensive. Before that, I never would have claimed Josh as anything more than an enemy, but then he'd come looking for me. Suddenly I'd claim him as anything, just because for that brief moment, he was all I had. Maybe we were friends after all, in our own twisted way. When I was lost, he came to rescue me. He hadn't given up.

"What does it matter?" I shot back. "Anything I had in that world died when I stepped through your gates."

I didn't look at him, I didn't care what he had to say. He took another step toward me, but I held up a hand to stop him.

"No," I ordered. I stood up and took a step back. Too many secrets. He told me nothing would harm me, but it was all a lie. He was just putting off the inevitable, letting me suffer, leaving me in the dark. This was just the first act to his game, and I never had a chance. We were not friends.

"You stay away from me." I turned my back on him and ran for the only thing in that direction. The stables.

One by one the horses looked me over. Did they know my fate? Did they sense the clock ticking down toward my impending doom? I went straight for the back corner, curling up in a ball to hide. To cower. To cry.

32

ELIJAH

— The broken heart she didn't see.

What could I do? There was nothing. That was the problem. She was cursed to die, and I was cursed to live with it. I would rip her apart. I'd done it to others.

But what was it about her that I couldn't let go of?

I told myself I wouldn't fight it anymore. It wasn't up to me, I couldn't change fate. The fight made losing so much harder. The wolf would come whether I was ready or not. I told her nothing would harm her, the words just spilled out, but I couldn't save her from myself. How could I tell her that? But how could I not?

This was not my destiny. This wasn't the life I was born into. What happened to the world I was raised to love?

I stared at the filling moon, knowing there were only a few days left... but I wanted more. I wanted Harper. I wanted to know her, to be with her. I didn't just want to prevent her death, I wanted to see her live. It wasn't fair.

I flipped through the blank pages of a journal I never finished. A story left unwritten. It was the only thing left to greet me into this cold void. An empty book for an empty life.

I gave it one single entry, one single notice of the doom that consumed me. The first day of a forsaken forever. I didn't care about my story, it was the story of a monster, the story of the victims that fell in my path. The innocent faces locked in my trap. They were the ones who deserved to live on these open pages, not me.

I looked across the field at the stables. The place she ran to hide... hide from me. Hide from a monster.

Her story was the one that needed to be told. In a few days, the chance would be gone. I didn't deserve it, but I desperately wanted a piece of her to stay. To live. To keep with me through my imprisoned eternity. Maybe if she left a small piece of her to keep me company, I wouldn't have to feel so alone.

I stepped into the barn slowly, afraid to scare the beautifully lonely soul inside it. She would hate me forever, and she had every right. I was starting to think I'd hate myself forever too.

She was sitting on the floor in the corner, hiding in the very darkness that terrified her with a soft sniffle. I grabbed a candle from the shelf and struck a match to light it. One of the many things that had been left behind by my victims. Humans came up with the most curious things.

Harper noticed the light, turning to face me.

"I told you to stay away from me."

I ignored her orders, continuing closer. "You also said you hate the dark." I sat on the old bench, placing the candle between us so she could see me. So she knew that, for now, I wasn't a threat. Not yet. I never wanted to be her monster.

My fingers fidgeted with the match box, remembering the boy that brought them in and taught me how to use them. He was so young, he'd gotten lost exploring, coming through the gates for help. It was the last place he'd find it. I'd tried to be his friend, tried to enjoy each day I had with him. Tried to ignore his impending pain, and the fact that I'd be the demon behind it. He was so worried about his mother, trying anything he could think of to get past the gated walls. I went along with it, maybe even encouraged it. I wanted him to escape. I wanted him to hope. If he was going to die, did that mean he had to spend all week waiting around afraid?

Over those days together, he became a dear friend... and the look on his face as I hunted him down, as I tore him apart? That would haunt me for eternity. I wanted to be numb. I never wanted to care again.

"I'm sorry this happened to you." I made sure to face her as I said it, then turned my head back down in shame. How could I show her just how deeply I meant each word?

She slowly got up, cautious as she sat opposite the candle.

"I'm sorry this happened to you," she echoed. The words surprised me. I met her eyes, and they were just as sincere. My thumbs rubbed over the journal, and again my gut knew it belonged to her.

"I found this. My first day in this cursed life. There wasn't much for me to tell. I'd just lost everything, everyone. I was trapped in this prison with nothing left. Somehow, I knew in my heart that my life was over."

She watched me silently, allowing me the space to talk.

"You have to understand, I never got a choice. This is

my forever. This is all I'll ever be. But *you* still have a 'something' to say." I held the closed book up to show her. "A story to tell."

She looked between the book and my lips.

"The world should have gotten to know it... but it's just me here. That's all I can offer you. Me. But if it makes any difference, I really want to know your story."

She opened her mouth to answer, but words didn't come out. I set the book on the bench in my place as I got up to leave. I had to tell her that before she was gone, but I would give her her space, just as she asked. She owed me nothing.

I stared up at the night sky as I stepped outside. "Why have you done this to me?" I asked the moon. We were meant to have this beautiful bond, the shifters and the moon, but I couldn't find the beauty anymore.

"Why do you make me kill?"

I thought of the dripping hourglass tide, and all I could see was the blood I'd spilled. It wasn't the moon, it was this curse tied between us. Her light hurt reflecting on my pain, as my heart cried looking up at her.

"Help me," I begged. "I won't give in without a fight. Not now." My voice strained with the rage of denial. "I won't kill that girl." My words softened. "She's too good for this."

I stalked across the grass, to the room of things left behind. Remnants of my victims, doomed friendships that I'd buried over the years. A treasure trove of guilt, and pain. Her story wasn't going to be another piece in my collection.

I threw down a broken crate, full of dusty trinkets from the casualties of this curse, random technology and jewelry clattering to the floor. My hand swiped over the worn-down table where a wallet and dirty hat flew to the wall behind me. Things that were not of my world, things that had been carried into it from across the line. Then I spun around, meeting that cursed hourglass with a glare. The timer of my suffering, dripping down with the promise of blood.

"No," I demanded, refusing to listen. "No more death. You won't take her from me!" I lunged forward, grabbing its silver frame from the table. I tossed it across the room, watching the glass shatter against the wall, drops of magic pooling to the stone floor.

Lightning struck the ground outside as a crack whipped through the air. Wind burst in all around me through the open gaps. I ran to the window, staring up at the new clouds that blew across my clear night sky.

"No," I muttered, searching for the moon. "What have I done?" I waited, watching for what would come. The moon peeked through with the sudden heavy rain, the same waxing moon it was before.

The breath I held swept out with relief as I braced my weight with a hand on the wall.

I still had time.

My heart squeezed with a painful gasp, my skin tingling with the promise of the shift.

"No," I cried, trying to find the moon again as I dropped to the broken glass below me. "It's not time yet!" My back cracked back as my body fell against the stone completely, unable to take back one single breath.

I'd pushed back. I'd fought for my freedom. I'd fought for her. Maybe I could finally find peace with the shattered glass beneath me. Or maybe the wolf would claim me forever. Whatever was going to happen next, I would have to kill her first.

33

HARPER

I opened up the large journal, wondering why it was so important to him, until the tragic words stole my breath.

The fire took my home. I'm trapped behind these broken walls of terror, and I cannot break free. The moon watches me from her sky above, but even her light cannot brighten the darkness inside me. I fear the forever that lurks ahead, as nightmares of ash consume my every breath, and I suffocate to their demands.

I turned the page, a heavy pit dropping in my stomach, twisting it into a knot of sympathy as I scanned the long list of names. My finger trembled, drawing a line down his page of victims, a reoccurring nightmare. And I was next.

How could I follow that? There was nothing I could do to help carry the pain in his words. All I had was me. I took the lid off my pen, staring at the next blank page, but what should I say? It all started as a simple story... a strange illusion.

I stepped into a dream. I had to know the world inside these gates.

I rambled on in a daydream, stopping myself to read over the entry. What was I supposed to say? What did he want to hear? This wasn't the type of story I ever thought I'd write.

"Oh Sam. Why did you have to go?" I asked. "What am I supposed to do? This was your story, not mine. Curses? Shifters? Other worlds? Magic?"

I scribbled a few more notes down.

There was a flash of light through the cracked door. The ground shook with a sharp static vibration. Was it thunder? The sky had been so clear before. I hated not being able to hear.

I forced myself to focus, to write the story that I wanted to hear... that I needed to hear.

I wish I could go back to where it all started. For this nightmare to be a distant dream. I'll step through those gates again and be reunited with the family that's waiting on me. My soul will always be tethered to my home. Even when I'm gone. Even after I'm free.

Another flash of lightning lit the crack beneath the door. I got up slowly to approach it, waiting for another rumble of thunder to vibrate through my feet. I pushed at the door, and it swung open with a windy force, smacking back into the barn wall. The beautiful starry night had shifted into the same storm I felt deep inside my heart.

A wolf howled, breaking sharply through my ears. I fell into the door frame, trying to block it out, but it rolled through my mind. And then it ceased, and the emptiness drowned me in silent terror. A flash of lightning lit the silhouette of the wolf at the doors across the field.

Elijah.

I reached desperately for the door swinging outside in the wind, using my body to pull it shut as the wolf lunged into a sprint. I had to block him out, I had to save myself. He swept across the field, coming straight for me as I forced the door between us. I slammed it shut hard, reaching to grab the lock.

THE METAL BARS wouldn't budge, my fingers wrapping tightly around them. Just as I'd predicted.

My hands fell. Heavy rainfall echoed through my ears, soaking my face and hair as I looked up to study the familiar gates. The world suddenly seemed so loud as I reached to adjust my hearing aids.

The dark forest behind me was empty. Lightning flashed across the sky, lighting up Shane Manor. Thunder echoed through my rising goosebumps, demanding my mind's attention with its crackling fury, but the view remained empty, just as it was the last time I'd walked past its property wall. No shadows standing in the doorways. No wolves waiting to pounce.

I took a step back, trying to remember what I was doing there, but no answers came. It was the strangest sensation, as if I'd stepped out of a dream.

I picked up the backpack that had fallen in the mud, going to zip it shut, when I noticed the unfamiliar book inside it. I reached in, pulling it up just enough to get a peek, but it wasn't worth the rain getting inside my pack. I let it go, zipping it all the way shut before I threw it over my shoulders and ran back to Benny's.

TAKEN

34

WILLOW

Wednesday passed me by from my bed, wasting away in a fog of depression. I wanted to hide there forever, under the comfort of my worn, old blanket. To hide from Sam's friends, from her school, from a worried mom, from the insistent doctor, from a world without my sister.

I ignored the knocks on the door. They knocked for Sam. Sam was gone. I was numb. Stuck staring at a blank ceiling from across the room, unable to break free. The knocks came again, and they came again, but all I could do was wait for the echo of the hand to leave my door.

"Sam," the voice called from the other side.

I wrapped myself in tighter, hiding my head as I rolled deeper into the bed.

Sam would have never let me rot away like that, but she wasn't there to stop me anymore. It was my day. Tomorrow could be for her.

One last stop. This time there was no knock. Each step seemed lighter. Calmer. Almost apologetic after the last visit. Something softly slid against the door. There was a moment of silence. Darkness. Then the footsteps left me alone.

Midnight. I picked up the already lit screen. It spent the day sitting on a box next to my bed. The screen never stayed dark long enough. There was always somebody trying to reach me, trying to pull me back into reality, but I wasn't ready yet. I was pushing the pause button. Comatose. Numb. The hours were gone in a blink as the clock lit up my screen to remind me that it had already been five minutes since the last ignored message.

"Oh, mom," I said, my finger rolling over the list of things I'd avoided that day. Halfway to the bottom, I chose a missed call, my thumb tapping it to call back.

"Willow, you are so grounded," mom's angry voice trembled on the other end.

"Mom, I'm literally an adult. I moved out. I'm fine. Seriously."

"You're not fine!" The words spilled out of her before she could stop them. It wasn't the first time she'd lost it reminding me, and it wouldn't be the last. She hesitated, as if realizing just how harsh her words were, then resigned, finishing her small rant. "That's the problem."

"I'm eighteen. You have to let me live whatever life I've got left."

"Are you though? Living it?" She knew me too well to hide it. Sometimes I think she had counted on Sam to walk through my illness with me. Sam was supposed to be there, to make sure I went to the doctors, to support me in my treatment. To give me a little taste of normal along the way. Now it was just mom and me, and she didn't know what to do. Her plate was already so full with work. She'd already lost one daughter and a husband. Now she was afraid she'd lose me too.

"Just try, please."

"Tomorrow. Right after I meet with Sam's teacher."

"Willow—"

"I just had to see this world that Sam was so excited about. Besides, you're the one that didn't notify the school yet." Wasn't she the one just pestering me about living? Her guilt filled the silence on the other end of the line.

"This teacher was really excited about Sam's work. I need to tell him, mom. To his face."

"Then straight to Dr. Murphy's office, right? He wants to get started with some tests. No more of this game, Willow, or I'm coming out there."

"Straight to Dr. Murphy's, cross my heart."

"You'll call me right after?"

"First thing, I promise."

"Okay," she agreed, giving me one last inch of trust. "I love you my Willow."

I fell back on the bed with a heavy sigh, pulling Sam's computer over from the box. My fingers brushed along the front edge, opening the top to stare at the background image. I clicked one of the two random icons she had saved, sitting in the top right corner. A video pulled up that she'd taken with Harper.

"You're looking at two future best-selling authors," Sam started. "The world just doesn't know it yet." Giggles filled the background as Sam walked alongside her writing buddy, one arm over Harper's shoulder, while the other held her phone at selfie angle.

"And I'll be the one with a collection of their exclusive, signed, first editions!" Ava's voice rang through from behind the phone camera.

"Maybe I'll be the cover model," Sage commented. Sam's laugh was contagious as she flipped the phone around on her friend, watching as Sage pretended to pose. "Then I can be on the shelf too!"

"Instant seller," Ava joked. The video cut off, taking back its laughter and leaving me with silence. I craved the sound of Sam's laugh. My heart would never stop missing it. I clicked the second icon, pulling up exactly what I expected. Sam's poem. The one that seemed to bring her magic to life. The one that Mr. Nazurin would have read in her applications. Part of me felt he saw that same magic in her too.

Her computer dinged. The count of unopened texts still going up. It almost made me feel better that I wasn't the only one holding on. The only one having trouble in a world where she didn't exist. It almost made it feel even more the opposite. Like she'd left a mark in our world that kept her alive.

I opened up the messages, wondering who was missing my sister with me. Who was up sharing late-night thoughts with a ghost. N. Who was this person? I clicked open the messages.

Monday.

> Meet me tonight!

Tuesday.

> Did I do something?

Today.

> Where did you go?

> I'm sorry. My offer still stands. It will always stand.

What offer? Meet me tonight? Where did you go? This person didn't know.

Sam's dead...

I typed out the words, then stared at them. Why couldn't I just say it? All I could think of was the pain I'd felt when I lost her. When I looked at the passenger seat across from me, and her empty gaze stared back. I did that. And this person was about to lose her too, all because of my mistake.

"I'm sorry," I whispered.

I closed her computer as tears consumed my sight, pulling air back from each crying breath.

"I'm so sorry," I repeated, begging her to forgive me. "I'm so sorry, Sam."

35

WILLOW

I got to the English building far too early, fighting the nervous energy that consumed my soul, begging me to walk around the block another lap or two before going in. I pushed past all that, determined to get this done. Whether it was nature, fate, or just straight fear, some force out there did not want me telling Mr. Nazurin the truth, but that ended now.

I was a disaster. Eyes dry from crying so hard, the skin circling them slightly swollen. Would it be obvious? I had to get through one more day, to finish what I'd started, to clean up my mess.

I held a thin box tight in my hand, not sure what to do with the gift. I'd nearly stepped on it on my way out, but the deep olive box was too much of a contrast against the pale carpet to miss.

The lid slid off easily, uncovering a single, thin square of light-toned wood that fit just right into the center of my hand. The edges were smooth, and even... but what was it for? A simple note sat beneath it.

I'm sorry.

Why was someone giving Sam a wooden block? Who was sorry? It had to be N. The mysterious stranger. He was the one person with some deeper personal connection to my sister. The one that didn't know she was gone.

I shoved the box in Sam's backpack and went on my way.

The door was propped open wide, but the classroom was empty. I stepped inside, searching for Mr. Nazurin, but nobody was there. I sat in a chair and pulled out the computer. Today was about business, I needed to go through Sam's emails and make sure nobody else was waiting on her ghost.

A familiar argument grew from down the hall, identical to the bickering voices I'd run from two days earlier. *Again?* What was their deal? At least it seemed Zager's problem was with Mr. Nazurin instead of me.

"I'm not going anywhere with you!" Mr. Nazurin announced in a scoffing tone. He stopped just outside the doorway, as if he were hoping to ditch their disagreements there. "I don't care what happens to those gates, I found the world I want to be a part of!"

"So you'd rather be cut off forever," Zager countered disapprovingly. "I'm not going back without you." His tone was stern and final. He wasn't there to negotiate. He was on a mission.

"Go ahead, take me back. I'll just disappear again."

"No you won't," Zager argued, as if he were calling a bluff. Zager's silhouette passed the door frame, making me jump. Had he caught me eavesdropping? I pulled up the laptop screen and clicked open the emails.

"There's something that ties you here," Zager went on. "You care too much, or you would have vanished the moment you saw me."

I clicked a random email, pretending to skim through it. A secret string of conversation lined my screen. Messages between Sam and N... and then just N.

> Only a few months left!

> And then a lifetime of magic.

N's answer felt like a promise. An entire future, ready to be unlocked.

"What?" I muttered quietly, trying to understand.

> The waiting is over. Tomorrow is ours.

The message was sent Sunday. I remembered the ding, seeing the name flash across my screen.

"Who were you talking to, Sam?" I clicked on the contact, recognizing the name in the email address. My hand shot up to cover my mouth. Nazurin.

"No... no, no, no." My hushed whisper grew urgent with the desperation to disappear. My eyes flashed back toward the fight that I'd tried to tune out.

"You never were one for routine," Zager commented, wearing an expression of deep contemplation as he slowly circled Nazurin. "But it sure seems like you refuse to miss this class." His eyes flashed to mine over the professor's shoulder, a spark of realization inside them. I spun around to face the computer, slamming it shut. Why hadn't Sam told me about this secret relationship?

"Don't act like this is about poetry and art," Zager went

on. "You didn't spend all day stewing yesterday just because I'm here."

"Yes, I did. You're terrible company."

Zager smiled victoriously, shaking his head. "It wasn't about who was here. It was about who wasn't." Nazurin followed Zager's gaze, catching me inside his class.

"You leave her out of this," he ordered, turning from Zager straight down the aisle toward me.

"What happened to you yesterday? I was worried."

My mouth dropped to speak, but the words caught. Who was this guy? What was going on between him and my sister? I didn't know if I was more annoyed with him, hurt that Sam never told me, or just plain sad that he didn't know. He truly thought I was her. A normal teacher marked you absent and moved on.

"I'm fine, I took a day—" My arm held the laptop down tight, hiding a secret, afraid he would realize I wasn't really her, and now I knew the truth. I looked back at Zager, who gave a small acknowledging nod.

"You were sick," he offered, the perfect excuse after how I'd left them, running out of the room to throw up.

"Don't speak for her," Nazurin grumbled. He side-stepped, trying to block Zager behind his back. Zager ignored him, taking the closest seat to wait it out.

"That's one way to put it," I answered. This was no stomach bug, I was permanently sick. Students started filing in, and I was actually grateful for the break in the awkward tension, a moment to process, but I couldn't sit through another one of his lectures, not now.

"I'm so sorry, I shouldn't have come." From the very first day.

"Sam—" he started to argue. "Don't go." His tone was

pleading, his concern genuine and clear. I still had to tell him.

"Can we talk?" I asked, turning to face him from halfway up the aisle. "After class." Chairs were filling quickly, students getting ready for another one of his magical lectures. Heartbreak could wait until after. A spark of hope lit in his eyes, knowing I wouldn't disappear completely... but it was a trick. The girl he wanted to talk to had already disappeared.

He nodded.

"I'm sorry," I mouthed again, turning to leave. I kept to the right of the walkway, trying to stay clear of the path of students coming through, hoping to avoid Zager on the left. He stood as soon as I passed, giving one last look toward the front of the class before shadowing me out.

"I want to be alone," I demanded without stopping, making myself clear as I turned down the hallway. My pace picked up, trying to put space between us.

"And I want my brother to listen to me for once," he countered, keeping up easily behind me.

"Your brother?" I turned around to face him, partially out of surprise, when I realized he wasn't dropping it.

"Yes." His answer was simple as he pulled the strange round mirror from his pocket.

"Zager!" Mr. Nazurin called from down the hall, stumbling out of his room. He watched in alarm, silently begging Zager to stop.

"I won't lose you," Zager said, grabbing my arm too tightly to pull out of. "He already has the witch. I'm sorry, brother, but if you won't come, then I'm taking her instead."

36

WILLOW

Zager snapped open the mirror, still holding my arm as he pushed us forward. In one step, we stood outside, shaded in the thick cover of trees, as if I'd landed inside the painting on Mr. Nazurin's wall.

"What is this?" I demanded, yanking my arm free of his hold. "Where are we?"

"Sorry to rope you into this, we're just going on a bit of an adventure, okay?"

I scoffed. "An adventure? It's not like you've given me any choice in the matter!"

"Look," his tone softened as he stepped in to face me. "I just need my brother to come home. It seems he's..."

Interested? Infatuated? In a relationship with a student he's never met? In love with my dead sister? It *seemed* difficult.

"Yeah," I agreed, not willing to say the words.

"He's stubborn. He'll come for you."

"No," I argued. "He won't. I just needed to talk to him! It would have only taken a few minutes! You have to take me back."

"Not until my brother returns. Naz cares about you. He won't let my taking you live on his conscience. You'll get your chance." He let go, looking down at the ground behind us. Dead grass stretched over the spot we'd just entered from, and for a moment he knelt down, pressing his palm to the dirt.

"No, it's not that," I argued, rubbing my hand down over my eyes. Was I about to admit my lies of impersonation to this man I barely knew? "It's not me he'll be coming for. He'll be chasing after a ghost."

Zager stood back up to face me. "He doesn't know you're sick?"

I stared into his eyes, trying to understand. I'd never told him about my illness, yet somehow he knew it. He saw the truth that I'd tried to keep tucked back in a dark corner. He saw past my lies.

"How is it that *you* know that? When we met, you said something. Dead blood. I'm already dead? Is that what you meant? There's no hope for me?"

He took a step back, running his hand over the back of his neck as his gaze shifting up toward the sky. "You're mortal. You all walk a thin line between life and death. You just stand on a... particularly fragile one. You're plagued by so much for such a young soul."

I closed my eyes tight, wishing I could shut out the pain. "Some days I feel like I'm waiting for the line to break."

"The line is stronger in my world," he said. I looked up at him, and his eyes met back with mine.

"Your world?" It sounded like something out of one of Sam's stories.

"What plagues you in your world, it can't hurt you the same way here."

My brows drew together, trying to process. "You mean, I'll feel better? I'll be... normal?"

He smiled, a small laugh playing on his lips. "I'm afraid normal is different in my world too."

"Great," I answered, not even wanting to know what he meant.

"What is it that you're hiding?" he asked. "I know you're sick, but I sense something else. A sadness. The energy that lives inside you. You're lost... confused. You're lonely... but it's more than that."

"I said it before. Your brother won't come for me. If he comes, it's for Sam." He searched my eyes, trying to understand. "I may be close to death, but Sam... she's my twin sister." I let out a shaky sigh. "And she's already dead."

He hesitated to answer, processing my words.

"So the one thing that has him so stuck there isn't even there at all." Silent understanding sat between us until he finally broke it with a whisper. "Willow."

Something shifted in the brush before I could answer, and he pushed me behind him as he spun around.

"I take it normal here is more dangerous than my world too?"

"Normally yes, but in your case, your world guarantees your death."

The words stung. I thought of mom. I'd promised to go to the doctor, to call her when I got done. She was not going to like how my day was playing out. I pulled out my phone, but the screen was black.

"Great," I muttered. The one time I actually wanted to check in. "So what do we do now?" Whatever potential threat moved through the bushes must have been a false alarm as Zager relaxed again.

"My brother still thinks you're Sam. He'll come." Zager

turned to face me again. He slid off his pack, pulling out a long gray cloak. Without asking, he slid it over my shoulders and hair.

"Keep this on. Humans aren't exactly welcome here. Someone might notice you." He grabbed my wrist, lifting my hand between us. "The ring. Take it off. It could give you away."

"What? Why?"

"The metal. We don't wear it in this part of my world. The magic doesn't like it. If you do, it'll make a statement."

"But I never take off my ring. It's our birthstone. My mom gave Sam and I matching ones when we turned sixteen."

"Off," he instructed. "You can't wear that here."

Whatever world this was, it made my heart pound. Humans? Mortals? It was as if the whole conversation had just caught up to me. I snatched the mirror still in his hand, opening it to see, to find my window back, but all it held was my reflection.

"This is metal, isn't it?" I asked, looking it over.

Zager slowly took it back, shutting it with a soft click before he dropped it in his pocket. "It's spelled."

"How did we get here?" I looked around. "This isn't possible. Spells? Other worlds? That's all make believe. Where did you take me?" I demanded. He didn't seem too worried about my denial.

"The less you know, the better. I brought you here, that's on me. I'll protect your life until you step back over the line."

"The line?" I quizzed.

"The line where magics mix."

I stared at him, surprised by the words. *The lines where magics mix.* Sam's poem. All of the magic. It wasn't a coincidence. She knew about this world. She was friends with Nazurin, and he was from this world too.

I reached out for balance against a dizzy spell, when Zager caught my hand. "I have to be dreaming."

"You're not." It was flat and simple. I studied his face, trying to decide if I could truly trust him when he said he'd protect me.

"Until Naz comes back," I clarified.

"Just stay close and you'll be fine."

"Careful, that almost sounds like a promise." Another word that made me think of Sam. It felt as if another entire side of her was being unlocked. Secrets uncovered.

He hesitated, turning to look me over before he started into the trees. "Maybe it was."

I gave in, tucking the ring into my backpack. I put it in the box with the wooden block, deciding it was less likely to get lost in there. I pulled out the block again, fidgeting with it in my fingers as I put my backpack back on under the cloak.

"I can't believe Sam never told me about Mr. Nazurin. Nazurin," I corrected. The formal title felt weird now.

"Naz. My baby brother."

"Someone kept knocking on my door yesterday. They left this. I think it was him. He'd been sending her messages all week. I should have told him right from the start." Guilt pushed everything out of its way to flood me with regret.

"I had no idea about him! I never would have pretended to be her! I didn't think it would hurt anyone! This isn't mine, it wasn't meant for me! I have to give it back!"

"Not everything has to be about Sam."

"It does though." I shook my head. "You don't get it. I'm the one who was meant to die, not her. I'm the sick one. She was the one with a list of dreams to chase."

"And you don't have dreams?"

My voice caught. Dreams. My dreams had all slipped away long before. All I saw for the future was my illness. "Dead blood, remember? Kind of hard to dream." He glanced down at the block of wood in my hand.

"It's a cut of willow wood."

My eyes flashed down to it, once again surprised. "How did he—" Again, it was too much of a coincidence.

"Did you know that willow trees are said to inspire? In not just your world, but mine too. A symbol of endurance, through all the trials, through all the loss. Surviving the worst of days. In my world, they used to say that a cut of willow close to your heart could soften your troubles. It could hold your secrets, could tuck them away for safekeeping, could help you come out stronger on the other side."

He turned around, unwrapping a long, thin leathery rope from his wrist. He took the willow square and crossed the rope over each edge, before tying it off. It dangled down as he knotted the longer ends into a loop, before reaching both arms over my head.

The willow cut landed against my chest, but I couldn't break my gaze from the soft blue eyes captivating my attention, lost in some long-lost legend of his world.

"There," he stated before breaking contact. He turned back toward the path. "I cannot speak for the knocking, but it was I who left the cut... and I left it there for *you*."

37

WILLOW

"How far do we have to go? I mean, if you're just going to turn right around to take me back when Nazurin gets here, maybe we should stay close to that line or whatever."

"After Naz comes home, I'll take you wherever you want to go. Whenever you're ready... but tell me, Willow, how do you feel? Are you really in that much of a hurry?"

We'd been trekking through the trees all day. Apart from being a little out of breath I was fine. *I was fine?* He told me I would feel different here.

"I don't feel sick," I answered. The words didn't even sound real. They didn't quite connect. "That's impossible."

"It's the magic," he explained. "The magic in my world is different than the magic in yours."

"There's magic in mine?" I countered doubtfully.

"That's what Naz believes. He'd fight for it to his death, too. He prefers it. Says the trees are calmer there, the air is more simple... more peaceful or something." Zager shook his head like he didn't agree.

"Why are you so eager to force him back, then?"

Zager seemed hesitant to answer. "It's just, the lines might not be drawn much longer."

"What do you mean? Like the line we crossed to get here?" I stumbled a step back, all of my trust in him suddenly faltering. "What happened to humans not being welcome? I can't be stuck here forever! My mom!"

"You won't," he assured me. "Naz will come for you, I'll fly you back myself if I have to."

"Fly me back?" I scoffed. "And you can guarantee it? You swear?"

He hesitated again.

"That's it! You can't, can you! You're so desperate to get Nazurin here, but you can't promise me you'll get me home in time!"

"Would it be the worst thing?" he fought. "It's not like your world is doing you any favors."

Ouch. I stared into his eyes. "I can't believe you said that."

Something rustled in the brush again, making me jump. This time it was bigger. Zager dropped the arm full of wood he'd started to collect and grabbed my hand, pulling me behind him. I peeked around him just in time to see Nazurin step out of the forest.

Zager relaxed, sending his brother an even look. "I told you he'd come."

"Let her go," Nazurin ordered. "What do you think you're doing? Look at yourself! Kidnapping? I told you to leave her out of this!"

"Stay awhile, brother. I was just going to set up camp."

Zager stepped to the side, grabbing the wood he'd dropped to build a fire. I stared at Nazurin, trying to process everything that had happened. What was I supposed to say? How was I meant to respond?

Nazurin stepped closer, lightly cupping my biceps with his hands. "I'm so sorry," he said. "I'll get you out of this mess." It felt like he was ready to sweep me off my feet and take me home, but I wasn't ready. We couldn't break off from Zager just yet. I wasn't sure how Nazurin would react to the truth. What if he figured it out before we got back, and didn't want anything to do with me? He was still waiting on a ghost.

"Tomorrow," I corrected. "I'm tired. You'll take me home tomorrow."

My eyes passed from Nazurin's to Zager's, the instructions meant more for him.

"First thing," Nazurin answered.

I let myself relax a bit, knowing that whatever happened with Nazruin, Zager had already promised to keep me safe until then.

Nazurin pulled out a bag of chocolate-covered cinnamon gummy bears and set it in my lap. I stared at the candy, one I'd never been too fond of. I'd never liked them much, but Sam, on the other hand, loved them. He'd stopped to get her favorite treat on the way. He knew her so well, but he didn't know.

I slid off the rock with a dizzy wave, falling into the dirt. I wanted to move, but suddenly I couldn't find the strength.

"Sam!" Nazurin said, jumping from his seat to follow me down.

"Zager," I wheezed, trying to catch my breath.

"No," Zager said in denial. He followed too, reaching under my neck to pull me back up. "No! You shouldn't be sick here, why isn't it working?"

"What?" Nazurin's confusion was obvious, but Zager ignored him.

"You took off your ring, you crossed the line," he was walking through our day. "Where did I go wrong?"

I could feel the magic rejecting me, telling me it didn't want me there. All of the symptoms it had taken away, it was shoving back at me full force. His world didn't want me any more than the one where I belonged.

The ring. *Metal. The magic doesn't like it.* That was it.

"There's metal in my leg," I told him.

"What?" He looked down at my jeans as if he'd be able to see.

"When I was little, I broke it. They put a little plate in to fix it. Screws."

"Metal? No," he argued.

"Your world is killing me," I pleaded. "I can feel it." All the sickness was hitting me at once.

"I'm sorry, Willow, I'll take you—"

"What?" Nazurin asked. He stood up and stumbled back, his hands held out in front of him. "What did you call her?"

Zager leaned away, and I stared past him to Nazurin. He studied my face as my tears began to brim over.

"You're not Sam?" He shook his head. "Class? The missed messages? The way you ran away? I should have seen it, you're..."

"Willow," I whispered. "I'm so sorry. I swear I wasn't trying to hurt you. I didn't even know—"

"Where is Sam?" he asked. "You used her sister to get to me!" His anger shifted back on his brother.

"We don't have time for this right now!" Zager argued, but there was no time left.

I couldn't stop the tears from pooling over, running down my cheeks. I shook my head. "She's gone."

"No! You—" He was searching for words. "You're a liar! Both of you! You—"

"Enough!" Zager ordered. Nazurin stumbled back further, then turned into the trees, leaving us alone.

"I'm such a fool," I cried. "I'll never be able to replace her."

"Nobody's asking you to," Zager argued. He propped me up against the rock, then turned to chase after his brother.

I could hear the fighting, the moment the bickering picked back up again where it left off. I couldn't sit there and listen, I couldn't pretend like it was okay. I climbed to my feet. Zager only brought me there as bait. I was nothing to either one of them. The fight turned physical, I heard the first punch.

I fought my cries, the strain for panicked air, bracing against the trees as I turned to run away. I didn't know where, but maybe it didn't really matter anymore. Either way, I was dying, it didn't make a difference which side of the line I was on. I just couldn't stay. I couldn't stand to see another heart break from losing Sam. I couldn't sit by and watch the pain in Nazurin's eyes as he realized he never got to meet the girl he loved.

I stepped around a branch into the shadows, when something wrapped over my head and everything went black.

SECRETS

MYLO

Mylo stood in the middle of the forest. The same spot he'd stood hundreds of times. It wasn't one of the three, it was different. There was never a line drawn there before, it had just shown up with no explanation. He closed his eyes, sensing the magic from the other side. It was calm. Quiet. Secret.

And for years, he'd taken advantage. For years, it was just him. Until *she* stumbled through and turned the peace he'd found upside down.

His second set of eyes dove out beneath the arch, her wings pulling up to rise to his arm. She stared into his eyes, a low croak vibrating through her chest. His gaze shifted to the small mirror in his hand, lined by its antique silver frame.

"Kia's blood still flows through, like a river across time. Things are changing, old friend."

His fingers snapped the mirror shut tight.

ALLIES

38

SAGE

I was livid with myself for falling for Kett's lies. How could I so quickly trust this stranger? Somehow he'd stepped into my school and passed as a student, and I'd given him a perfect, easy target. He showed up at the opportune moment, when I was so desperate to feel loved that I let a few minutes of smiles and cake break down any notion of caution. I'd walked right into his trap. I was a fool.

My friends were gone, now my mom was gone too. How long would it take before anyone noticed that I was missing as well?

No. That wasn't true. There was someone that would notice. That other hunter.

Rogue.

I didn't know anything about Kett, not anything real. The stranger in front of me was full of secrets, but Rogue, on the other hand, had been blunt and direct. He was mysterious, sure, but at the same time, he wasn't hiding anything. Not from me.

I'd seen the mark on Rogue's arm though. He was still a

hunter. They both were. But there was something different about Rogue. They weren't on the same side, him and Kett.

The rogue hunter. He'd been tracking me. All that time I'd spent scared of the man in my reflection, and now I desperately hoped to see him there each time I found myself shining back. Now I wished for the silhouette of his shadow standing behind me.

He would know I was taken, but was he still willing to help after the trouble I gave him? After I refused his attempts to warn me, to aid me? After I ran away? I sure hoped so, because he knew a lot more about what was going on than I did, and he was probably the only person who could hunt me down now.

I should have listened to him.

Kett set up camp as if we were out on some casual campout. It lacked the sense of adventure though, his silently preparing to spend the night in the middle of the woods.

Ava would have had a tent up already, and a plate of s'more stuff ready to go. Harper would have brought her dirt-stained, worn-out pack of playing cards, ready to stay up all night laughing. Willow would be staring into the fire, bundled up in her old, raggedy childhood quilt, with a cup of hot chocolate warming her hands. Sam would have already read through a new book of ghost stories to share over the campfire. I could hear her voice in my memories, pointing out the constellations, reminding us to watch for shooting stars... but she wasn't there. None of them were.

I stared at the empty flames, waiting for an opportunity to run, waiting for Kett to turn his back, but I was his prisoner and he wasn't letting me out of his sight. Not for the night, anyways. It had been a long day, and home felt so far away, but I feared it was only the start. What did he want from me?

A small stream ran past our camp where he quickly caught a fish to cook up. After handing me a drink, he sat down across the fire, making a point to let me know he was still watching. He was always watching.

Every move he made seemed so calculated. Every item he had on hand was simple, but efficient. His pack was light, nothing without a purpose. Who would have guessed his school backpack was stocked for a wilderness hike. Keeping minimal made discretion easy, but it was clear now there was nothing spontaneous about his intentions. The hunter had caught his prey.

I fought a shudder as I drank. The clear liquid tasted strangely sweet for water. Maybe I shouldn't have been so quick to accept it, but I'd been too desperate for a drink to question the motives behind it.

The empty cup dropped to the dirt as my blurry gaze met his across the flames. His eyes darkened, watching me as he pulled out a sharp knife, slicing straight through the fish on his leg.

I fought to focus my vision on the knife in his hands, unable to move as I watched him clean his catch. Skin. Bones. Flesh. Why did his show of cutting through that helpless fish feel so personal? My body grew numb, swaying as a daze swept me into darkness.

We moved through my sleep. My stomach was sore, a dead weight hanging over something hard. I fought to wake up from the dizziness as the world rocked back and forth below me. I was upside down. A gravelly, dirt path ran below my half-fallen hair, the loosened pony tail only hanging on halfway, my blue ribbon long-lost. What was happening?

I stared at Kett's boots, trying to summon my memories, my alarm, my fight. I wasn't supposed to be there. He had me on his shoulder, carrying me further away from the life I knew, and I had to get away.

"Put me down," I groggily demanded. How long had we been moving? I couldn't remember falling asleep, only the imagine of him slicing through that fish. It had to be that strangely sweet drink. The moment my body went numb.

"You drugged me."

"Not my fault you don't know your fae drinks." He ignored my orders, continuing up the path.

Fae drinks? "Put me down," I repeated. This time he listened, setting me on my feet, but still bracing me as I found my balance.

"Woke up just in time," he commented.

"For what?" I grumbled, turning around to see. "Why are you doing this?"

Up ahead the forest walls opened up into a kingdom of color. Light broke the shadows as wildflowers warmed the hills, leading up to a border of homes grouped around a large, castling center. Harsh, bare mountains lined the right side, towering to what felt like the sky, before dropping from the clouds into a stretching world of light and river.

"It's beautiful," I commented, my anger lost in a moment of wonder and awe. It felt as if we'd stepped into a painting. "Where are we?"

"Center Sun," he answered. "Home."

I pulled my eyes away from the kingdom to look Kett over again. This was his home? He wasn't just some random kid, maybe he wasn't even human... but why bring me here? Why were they hunting me?

Nina told me to run. She knew about this world, and she warned me to stay out of it.

"It's amazing," I told him, going along with my initial awe. "Just like a world from a movie."

He huffed with a prideful scoff. "This world is real. Your movies of pretend don't compare."

His tone made me wince internally, but I fought to hold my composure, staring at the view ahead. Kett's charming side had long been forgotten. He wasn't pretending anymore. He was way past playing games.

"Show it to me?" I asked, looking into his eyes. I needed his guard down if I was ever going to get away.

39

SAGE

Walking up a long slope of wildflowers, I almost missed the tiny, winged fairies that fluttered between them. I had to catch myself from the magic that continued pulling me in, hard not to get lost in it, an energy that could have drawn me deeper forever and tucked away my soul to keep.

"Pixies," Kett explained when he caught me staring. "Pesky little things, really."

Water ran toward us as we passed, and I wished it could wash me away, to lead me back home. The warm light shone beautifully over the surface as it rolled by on its way. I knelt down to brush my fingers through it, when I noticed my reflection staring back. I looked into her eyes, my eyes, wishing she could give me help, offer me some way to break free.

Take me with you, I wished into the current. Where was that dark, hooded silhouette shadowing my trail now? Would he still come for me?

"The Light River," Kett said, interrupting thoughts he'd mistaken for admiration. "Even the sun rises with this river, puts our corner of the world first before echoing into the others." Kett raised his hand toward the sky. "It chooses our home for full light, the brightest part of the day, offered freely to the kingdom forged in stone."

His resolute tone tried to prove something, to justify some notion that his part of this world was superior. I avoided his eyes, looking back to the shadow at my side. *Help me,* I silently pleaded, but she was as stuck there as I was.

Kett led past the first line of homes and shops, where color and life consumed the streets. People brought their stands outside, sharing without walls to separate. But they weren't ordinary people. Horns, and wings, colorful auras, and strange tattoos, each had something that made them unique, different things to share. The street was more like a trading market than a business zone. It's energy was freeing, apart from the hunter at my side, reminding me that I wasn't.

Kids excitedly lined up along one counter, in awe as a woman showed off her magic tricks. Small silver charms lined a thin navy cloth draped diagonally across her tan face. She worked in silence, captivating their attention, her bright violet-brown eyes as mesmerizing as the show.

She picked up two boards and clicked them against each other. A spark of light flew out from between them, transforming into a blazing little bird. A magical firework, flapping higher as it looped around and dispersed into a shimmering circle of light. My stunned silence hid the way my excitement matched the cheering children, but she still seemed to sense it, her eyes meeting mine across the path, nodding a soft bow.

She grabbed a small pouch off the table next, pouring a thin pile of sand into her hand before blowing it straight up.

It sprinkled lightly through the air, landing against her sash as she began to spin around, the ruffled layers of her dress waving around her in blue and gold, when she disappeared.

My steps caught, slamming into Kett's back, trying not to fall. He pulled me forward with a glare as I searched for the missing woman. Had she shown me that trick on purpose?

Something settled in my palm. I stared at the leather pouch, wrapping my fingers around the sudden lifeline, when the woman snapped her fingers, standing in the exact same spot she'd vanished from behind her table.

Her eyes barely met mine before she moved on to her next trick. I studied the bag, a simple blue stone bead dangling from it, matching the ones tied through her long, partially-dreaded black hair. Could I disappear too? Fidgeting with the small trinket, I tucked the bag out of sight before Kett could notice, wondering when to use it.

I waited for the crowd to build around us, filing in closer through a narrowing corridor. My free arm rose with the small bag, I only had one shot. I shook some out, letting the tan sand sprinkle into my hair before ripping my arm free, spinning around to run.

Pushing back through the crowd, I hoped it was equally difficult for him to navigate behind me. Nobody could see me as I brushed past, making me bump against them more, but I refused to stop and give Kett the chance to catch up.

I sprinted across the cobblestone to press my back against a wall, hiding behind the path of moving strangers to check my trail. Kett was fuming, his angry back and forth shuffle disrupting the flow of traffic. He was searching, but he hadn't been able to spot me yet. The strange sand had worked. This was my chance.

I ran for the flowering hills, letting gravity pull my

speed down the sloping trail as I followed the river current beside me. The thick forest welcomed me in, only a few steps further, promising protection beneath its heavy cover. I reached for the first tree, ready to swing past, when I thumped against another stone wall. My steps stumbled back, staring up at the tower of rock that replaced the trees.

I studied the wall, placing my palm against the same spot where a heavy bark trunk stood only a moment before. An arched opening dared me to step through.

"What?" I asked, cautiously crossing the shaded boundary inside. Another busy street of color and creatures lined the sun-lit path ahead of me, a mirror of the one I'd just left behind. A new layer of city, challenging me to sift through it, caught in a maze that I couldn't control.

I'm going backwards.

I studied the crowd, then the path behind me, seeing the same tree line I'd raced toward before. It called me closer, promising that same protection under it's branching blanket if I just turned around. I moved back toward it slowly, listening to its call, when I heard the water running beside me.

I stood at the edge, watching the simple current flow by my feet, running along the trail. The same river I'd begged to take me home all along, racing toward the new layer of city behind me. Racing the way I'd originally run before the trick.

My brows drew together, it was telling me something. It was a lifeline, guiding me home.

I had to keep moving, keep fighting this terrible dream. I ran beneath the archway, straight into the crowd as I fought to keep standing, keep moving, keep pushing away from him. The bodies half-carried me along as I moved forward with the crowd, until the shuffling split to two sides, opening around the center of the uneven cobblestone path.

Kett stood in the center, blocking my way as the crowd filed around him. His low dark eyes focused on me, his jaw set, ready to make me suffer.

I whipped around, ready to push back through the chaos, but he blocked my path again as if I'd turned on a mirror my vision a dizzying kaleidoscope of the colorful patterns around me. Rainbows of fabric, shuttered windows and rock walls, faces of creatures I never could have dreamt up.

I fell to my knees, a frustrated fist thrown to the cold stone beneath me.

A familiar dark boot casually stepped next to my fingers, straight out of the illusion that consumed the air around us. Kett crouched down in front of me, and then we were back in the forest, the illusion gone.

"Found you."

There was no mercy in the fingers that grasped my arm, pinching the nerves tight enough to bruise. He shoved me forward, making me lead the way back up the hill into the real city.

He yanked me ahead of him, veering through a shadowed side door, forcing me to guide him down long, dim hallways accompanied only by a few posted guards and the small windows spread out between them. The air was cooler, blocked from the warmth outside by thick tunneling walls.

The last guard nodded a bow at Kett as he pushed open the door at his back. I stepped first into the bright, round room, only it wasn't so much a room, as we stood outside, circled in vine-covered, stone walls. The same vines twisted up the large tree rooted in the center, branching widely over us to create open windows to the sky above.

A man stood at the base of the tree, leaned over a table to study notes on a large worn map. All I could make of it were shapes of a land I'd never seen before.

The man calmly turned to face us, wearing a wide smile. "You made it!"

Kett shoved me closer so the man could study me, eying me curiously as he stepped around. My arms folded over my stomach, awkwardly waiting for some explanation as to why they'd gone through such trouble to get me there.

My gaze shifted from him to the woman standing watch behind him. Her pale white hair lacked any warmth, her aura an inky, cold void. She watched us, still and silent, on guard for whatever came next. Her dark eyes pierced my skin, giving me goosebumps from across the room in an amused, wicked way.

The man casually circled back around in wide, even steps, his ginger hair and bright mossy eyes the total contrast of hers as they met mine. Strong posture, and head held high, his status there was clearly powerful, his aura bold and firm.

"You don't know how long I've waited for you," he commented, gesturing a hand between us. He spoke with ease, in the most confident way, controlling the space around us. His voice sent a shiver down my spine.

Nina's warnings echoed through again. She knew the hunter would come. Somewhere along the way, she'd been mixed up in this mess too. Whatever *this* was, it ran so much deeper than myself. It was generational.

"What is this? Why am I here? What do you want from me?" The words started strong before my nerves spilled out with them. He squinted, still so focused as he studied my face.

"I sense a stubbornness," he commented, looking past me to Kett. "Good work, Hunter."

Kett took a small step forward and lowered his head. "Always up for a challenge. She's here now."

My nostrils flared, blood boiling beneath the pressure. They'd skipped right over my questions, acting like my voice didn't matter at all. I'd lost my friends, my mom. I'd been taken, kidnapped, and all the building stress was steaming at my skin, until the heat burst through.

"What do you want from me!" I yelled. "I'm sick of this! I've had it with your games."

The silence that followed felt loud, as the surprise wore off and the stranger's approaching smile grew wider, stopping only inches away.

"Sick of it?" he asked, letting the words soak deeper inside me. "But you've only just begun! I, on the other hand, have been playing this game for a very long time," he countered before leaning in closer, whispering just above my ear. "And my patience is up."

He took a step back, straightening as he gave me one last look, before nodding to Kett. He spun toward his table. "You'll see exactly what I want, Sage Thost. As soon as I get the third piece." Without another glance, he waved us off indifferently behind him.

40

HARPER

I'd just pulled up to Sage's house when an unknown number popped up on the screen. I rolled my eyes, fully expecting a scammer. "Hello?"

"Harper? Is that you?"

"Ava?"

"Yes!" She was instantly in tears on the other end. "Thank goodness you've kept the same number so long, I lost my phone! I need to reach Noah."

"Yeah, let me send you his number!" I hesitated, something was clearly wrong. "I wondered why you wouldn't answer. Are you okay?"

"It's been the worst week, I just want to go home."

"Tell me about it," I grumbled, emotions starting to sting my cheeks. "I never thought I'd be ready to visit home so soon."

"You're home?"

"Yep, drove back already. Wait, you're not? I haven't been able to get ahold of anyone! Your phone goes straight to voicemail, and Sage and Willow won't pick up! I'm glad you finally called! Whose phone is this again?"

"It's my friend Emma's. Long story. I got lost and she literally found me and took me in," she started, launching into a quick recap of her week.

"Seriously?"

"Seriously. I had nothing. Complete amnesia. I just walked until I found this little town, and you'll never believe where I am... Alaska."

"Alaska?" I repeated, trying to understand. "That's so far though, how did you even get there?"

Ava paused for a moment. "I have no idea, I'm just excited to go home."

My brows drew together. You don't accidentally travel 3,000 miles, especially not overnight. There had to be more to the story than she was ready to share. I decided to let it go, we could talk more when she was home. I needed an Ava hug as much as I needed a Sage one.

"Only you, Ava, are clumsy enough to stumble so hard you land across the country." It explained the random text I got from Noah, asking if I'd heard from her. When he sent it, he had no idea that I was missing too.

"Right," she laughed, accepting the joke.

"Well don't feel too bad. I mixed myself into some trouble this week too, and it wasn't for being clumsy."

"What, by moving into the same house as Josh?"

"No, it wasn't that. Actually, I didn't even fight with him one time. It was weird." I told her about my little trespassing adventure.

"Harper!"

"I couldn't help it, okay! This place was calling my name! I felt so drawn to it, I can't even explain it."

"Well, I can't explain half the things that happened to me this week," Ava admitted. "So I guess I'll let it slide."

I spilled every detail of my week, telling her about the

house, the gates, the trespassing, the dream, the curse... and Elijah.

"Wow."

"I know. It was a pretty wild dream."

"That does sound wild. Stuck in a curse with a werewolf? So... was he a hot werewolf, or—"

"Ava!"

"What! Just answer the question!"

"Stop it!" I couldn't help laughing. It was healing talking with a friend. "My hearing aids died, my phone wouldn't work, and we were on this strange supernatural timer! Like if I didn't escape by the full moon, he would turn into a wolf and kill me. It was actually so scary, and I just couldn't wake myself up."

"So what happened when it got to the full moon?"

"I don't know," I admitted. "I never actually got to that part. Luckily, I guess."

"That would make such a cool story though," she commented. "You should write a book. I'd read it."

"I think I'll stick to my lighthearted rom-coms," I countered. "I wouldn't survive in a fantasy world."

"So then what happened? After you woke up? What made you decide to come home?"

"That's the weird part... I woke up standing at the gates in the pouring rain, and found out I'd been missing all week. Benny was freaking out, even Josh was worried! He was being over the top nice, making sure I had everything I needed as I packed up to head home. I don't even think he wanted me to leave. Benny definitely didn't, but I don't know—"

"Enemies to lovers," she half-coughed from the other end.

"Stop!" I argued. "Absolutely not." She'd been trying to

paint that narrative between Josh and me forever.

"How long are you home for?"

"I'm not sure, maybe a week? Though I don't think my dad will ever be ready for me to go again."

"Oh, I bet," she laughed. Everybody knew how much of a daddy's girl I was. He'd driven up to Maine so fast, and I'd never felt such relief from that protective side of him.

"Benny said he'd never been so scared as the moment he told my dad I was missing."

"I don't blame him! Geez. No more trespassing in haunted houses, right?"

"Learned my lesson," I agreed, letting a deep breath loose. "Now hurry home so we can go to Carver's and talk more over some cake! I hate that I can't find Sage. She's got to be around here somewhere."

I looked back at the house through my window, still dark and empty. Where could she be?

"That sounds like the perfect way to end the week," she agreed. "Have you tried her house?"

"Just pulled up," I answered. "It feels so quiet, I don't even think she's home."

"Well, if she's not in the garden, you're probably right."

"I feel bad I missed her birthday. Apparently you missed it too! She kept trying to text us, but nobody answered. I had so many missed calls! We should have given her a puppy before we left to keep her company."

"She would have loved that."

"Her mom wouldn't have. I feel terrible, she probably hates us now."

"Especially after how worried she was about us forgetting her."

Guilt knotted my stomach, I hadn't intended on dropping off the map on day one. I stepped out of the car and started up the sidewalk. "We will make it up to her," I said, climbing the porch steps. "I'm going to—"

My hand was halfway to the doorknob when I froze.

"What is it?" Ava asked.

"The door," I whispered, staring at the sliver of darkness beyond. "It's just weird... it was already cracked open."

"Can you hear any—"

"I don't know," I cut off, my voice still hushed. "I'm getting a weird feeling."

"Maybe that's a sign you shouldn't go inside."

I hesitated a moment before pushing the feeling away.

"Of course not, I'm talking to the person who admitted to trespassing five minutes ago. Harper, be careful."

I scoffed, smiling at the voice in my ear as I pressed an arm against the door to swing it wider, stepping across the threshold.

"I thought you learned your lesson about trespass—" Her voice faded as I lowered my hand, keeping her on the other end of the line as a precaution.

I flipped on the dim entry light, barely catching the silhouette in the doorframe at the top of the stairs. The door to a cluttered-up storage room of dust, spiders, and boxes that I used to choose during hide and seek because it was so creepy up there nobody dared come looking.

Other than that, or a holiday to decorate for, nobody really had reason to go up there. The man could have been a shadow, blending into the air around him.

"Who are you?"

"Who are you?" he countered, his voice low and raspy, unashamed of being caught.

"A friend of the girl who lives here." The girl I couldn't find.

Did he have something to do with that?

He stepped down the stairs slowly, looking me up and down as if he were trying to decide if I were telling the truth.

"The girl who lived here. Do you know where she went?" *Lived.* I hated the way he said it in past tense.

"Why would I tell you? Some strange man in my best friend's house? Somehow I get the feeling you weren't exactly invited in."

"She's in danger. I'm looking for her."

Danger? The blunt response caught me off guard, his expression cold and serious. Sage was in danger? My shoulders sank.

"I haven't been able to get ahold of her," I admitted. "I came here looking for her too."

"You won't find Sage here." He pointed at the phone clutched tightly by my thigh. "Who's that?"

"Not Sage," I answered, lifting the phone back up to my ear. "Ava?"

"Still here. You should leave." I probably should have listened, but I couldn't turn away. What if he was telling the truth?

"He said she's in danger."

"He sounds like the danger." Under the scrutiny of his sharp, cold features, I couldn't argue her.

"Looks it too," I muttered, giving him a side-eye. From his dark hair and short beard to his black clothes, he didn't just blend into the shadows, he was the shadow. His build was intimidatingly athletic, his golden eyes demanding, but he wasn't trying to hurt me. He meant what he was saying... and I had to listen.

"I'll call you right back."

"Harper no—" I barely heard her voice as I hit end.

"Who are you?" I asked for the second time.

"Rogue."

"No, but *who* are you? Why did you say Sage is in danger? Where's her mom?"

"Sage has been taken," he paused only a moment. "May is dead."

My mouth fell open, stumbling back a step to brace my hand against the wall. His tone was short and pressing, as if there was no time for sympathy. As if his grave message wouldn't send a static shock through my very soul. It was too urgent.

"She can't be." My voice trembled as I searched his eyes. The woman that had been like a second mother to me since we were little girls was dead? My head shook with denial. His scowl was impatient, teeth clenched tight. He reached for my arm, but I pulled away.

"Why should I believe you?"

"Don't. Don't believe anyone. Go home and stay out of it, I'm going to do my job."

"Your job? And what would that be?" He still hadn't really explained who he was.

"They sent me to find her. I was never going to—" He seemed genuinely frustrated, pacing two steps away and back as he raked a hand down the back of his hair, until he was square with me again.

"She had the mark. It was too late, I led that hunter right to her." The words were coming out fast when he caught himself. "It's my fault." He pointed up into his collar. "Now I'm going to find her and bring her back."

The promise shined dangerously in his golden eyes, threatening anything in his way as he stepped past me to leave. He'd admitted his part in it, his guilt, and it seemed sincere. So many details I didn't understand yet, but my gut trusted him. He would do everything he could... and this was about Sage, so I would too.

I spun around. "I'm coming with you." He stood halfway through the doorframe, pulling his hood over his head with a sideways glance.

"I work alone."

"Well it sounds like you're the one who lost her." My own defensive harshness made me cringe inside. I made myself relax, knowing that if I wanted to help, we had to work together.

"Look. You're here trying to find some clue to get her back, right?" I was guessing, but his glaring silence confirmed it. I let out a deep breath, trying to remain calm. I had to convince him to give me a chance.

"Sage is my best friend. I know her better than anyone. If she needs help, I'm helping."

He looked me over again, and this time it felt different. "She trusts you," he commented. His jaw set tighter as he considered it, before mumbling in a low voice, "More than she'll ever trust me."

I nodded slightly. "We've known each other our whole lives."

"Fine. Let's go."

"Wait." I pulled my phone back out. "I have to tell Ava."

He opened his mouth to argue.

"No!" I cut off, unwilling to negotiate it. My chin lifted stubbornly, looking him square in the eyes, daring him to challenge me. "I'm telling her. If she comes looking for me, the strange man in our missing friend's house will be suspect number one. No more disappearing without a trace."

"On the contrary," Rogue countered. "Disappearing is my specialty."

That explained the nickname, but that's not how we were doing this mission.

"Well that's a terrible habit," I answered sternly, feeling like a parental figure as I held up my phone so he could watch me press send.

> I'm fine. Text me the flight info, I'll be there to pick you up.

41

AVA

"Are you sure you don't want to say bye to Mylo?" Emma asked, handing me my backpack after I picked up my ticket. The short airport security line waited a few steps ahead of us.

Dr. Quinn got online and bought me a plane ticket the moment he'd heard the news, contacting my dad to help smother any fires waiting for me back home. It would take a couple of flights to reach it, but I could finally continue living my life instead of waiting for it to find me.

I shook my head, unwilling to put it off. "I'm sure." We'd already parted ways. Ordering him to stay away from me forever was goodbye enough for one lifetime.

Emma nodded, unwilling to spoil the moment. "Okay... Ava," she added, shaking her head. "I still can't believe it."

"Me neither," I admitted, when she handed me a bright pink gift bag. "What is this? You've already done too much!"

"It's just something to remember me by." She smiled, but it was a little sad. "I hope you'll call?"

"I will definitely call. And I don't think I could ever

forget you." I pulled out the souvenir shop shirt, SWANOKE, ALASKA, written in Emma-style, bold, pink letters. The same shirt I'd seen in the shop window the first time I'd stepped into their little town. The first day we met. The day I woke up with nothing and she took me in.

"One day I'll come visit you and find a Louisiana shirt to match," she said in her usual hopeful optimism, always looking for something happy. I don't know what I would have done without that side of her walking me through the week.

"We'll find you a cute boy there too so that you never leave," I joked, but I was overwhelmed by gratitude. "Thank you," I said, reaching forward to give her a hug. "Seriously, I can't thank you enough. I don't know what I would have done—"

"It was fun having a roommate for a few days, but I'm so happy for you." She sniffed over my shoulder, pulling back to look at the flight status screen. "You'd better get going so you don't miss your flight."

Emma's finger brushed under one eye, her cheeks a little redder than usual. I'd wanted so badly to avoid building friendships there, to prevent new roots, because I hated this part. The moment where we had to part ways.

"Right," I agreed, still determined to make it home. Antsy too, after my phone call with Harper. I'd tried calling her back multiple times, but all I got was a quick text.

The weight of worry grew heavier on my chest, crushing my heart. Mylo's warning played repeatedly through my mind with memories of being lost in the forest. *"Another world knows your name."* I wanted so badly to go back to normal, but the anxious pit in my stomach told me that my normal life wasn't back just yet. Not quite. Something was still wrong.

I turned toward airport security, pulling my backpack tighter before I sent Emma one last small wave. I cared so much for this girl I'd just met. Who knew one week could feel so long.

She sent a returning wave, her soft smile stretching wider as she waited for me to get through security.

I owed her so much for the brief space in time she'd devoted to me, to keeping me safe, to making me happy. She was my friend when I needed one, but she'd needed one too.

For those few short days she gave me, I would pay her back over a lifetime.

"I'll text you when I land," I promised.

42

AVA

I almost ran out the door when I saw Harper's car, but stopped myself to grab out one of Mylo's long sleeve shirts first. Despite the warm humid air waiting for me outside, I wasn't ready to explain the long scratches running down my arms just yet. Harper, Noah and dad could learn about my nightmares another day, I just wanted to be home.

I slid in my arms, hesitating to pull it over as the familiar scent of a stranger hit me. How many times had his clothes saved me now? I pushed out the thought, sliding it over my head and grabbing the half-zipped pack to run outside.

I'd kept my cool up until climbing into Harper's car, greeted by her smiling face. The familiar radio station, trees, and humidity a sentimental jab against my melting composure as a breakdown threatened to spill free. I was back where I belonged, back with a real friend, headed back down a route of houses, rivers, and street signs that I'd passed by hundreds of times.

I shoved the backpack down by my feet, ignoring the fact that it was full of hand-me-downs from my creep, vampire therapist. It felt ridiculous keeping them, but I couldn t bring myself to leave them at Emma's either. Not that other items were competing for space in my bag anyways, but deep down I still wanted the warm black sweaters, hoping they never lost that familiar scent. A small keepsake to remember those few days that we were friends, however twisted that friendship was.

I never wanted to see his face again, but I didn't want to forget it either. I never wanted to forget anything again. I was finally home, and now I could move on with my real life, but that other life? That other girl, Jane? She would always remain, like a scar across my soul. I would forever see a piece of her when I looked at those brown eyes in the mirror.

"I feel like you should have a suitcase or some-*thing*." Harper's words muffled into my shoulder as I leaned across the car to hug her.

"Right?" I sniffled a laugh. "I guess I forgot to pack for winter before getting lost in the woods."

"Nice backpack though," she commented. I rolled my eyes. Leave it to Emma to have some fancy, heavy-duty hiking backpack to donate.

"It was Emma's. Her dad is a doctor, and she really likes shopping."

"Ooh, your favorite!" she mocked. I'd always hated shopping, unless it was in a bookstore, though my budget always kept me as more of a browser.

"Can't wait to see what else she bought you."

"All that mattered was the plane ticket, I didn't really care about anything else. I'm so glad her dad could get me one so last minute. That would have been harder for my dad." I stared out the window, admiring how beautiful and green the trees were since they'd only barely started changing. "I can't wait to see Noah and dad. Thank you for picking me up!"

"I'm sure it goes both ways," she answered, but she was biting her lip. "Here." She held out my phone, charged and ready to go. "Noah found it when he was out looking for you."

I accepted it, staring at the list of notifications blocking my background picture. I sighed, trying to figure out what I would tell my family.

"What am I supposed to say? Hey dad, sorry I've been gone all week. I went for a walk and got lost in Alaska." Dr. Quinn had explained the best he could, but there were still some gaping holes in my story.

"That's hard," she admitted. "I get it though. I went missing too, remember? Hey Ben, decided to go explore the house you explicitly told me to leave be and woke up outside a few days later. Sorry to scare ya like that."

"How did he handle it?"

"It was just confusing. He didn't fight it, but obviously it didn't make sense either. My dad was there, you know how he is. Eager to bring me home where he can keep an eye on me." I laughed softly at the image.

"Dr. Quinn talked to my dad, assured him that I'm fine, but it just feels so obvious that *something* isn't fine. Something happened to me. It looks like I got kidnapped or ran away."

"That would be hard to argue," she agreed. "Are you though? Fine?"

It got quiet really fast. "I will be. I just want to be home."

She nodded, but bit her lip again like she was holding something back. She held her eyes forward, ignoring my stare.

"What is it? What aren't you saying?" She didn't answer, when it hit me. "Sage. Did you find her?"

"No..." Her guilty expression made my heart drop. "But I found us help, we're going to get her back!" She had been holding something back. I thought back on our last phone call, the one where she hung up on me.

"Help? What, you mean that weird guy in Sage's house? Harper, how do you even know she's really missing? You don't think that's the least bit sketchy?"

"She is. I know it. The house was empty. She won't answer. She's just... gone. I think he is really trying to help her."

"Or he kidnapped her, and we're next! Come on, Harper! We should stay away from that guy." She didn't answer, shifting in her seat as she swallowed back her words. I stared at her again, still pointing her face forward to avoid my eyes.

"Harper."

"So, about that," she said quickly, turning the car. A bike leaned around the corner closely behind us. I spun around, studying the black helmet through the back window.

"Is that him?" I asked in disbelief. "Harper! You went from being the trespasser to inviting the trespasser to follow you home!"

"Ava, he's not the bad guy!"

"You don't know that!" My eyes shut tight, my head pressing into the seat behind me. "So many red flags. Harper, you're color blind!"

"I can feel it! In my gut! I know it sounds crazy, but Sage is gone, and I think he's the only one that can help us find her." She pulled up to a red light and finally met my eyes.

"Seriously, Ava. Think about the weird stuff that happened to us this week. You woke up in Alaska overnight, while I was mentally stuck in a haunted castle with a were-wolf. None of that makes sense! I can't explain it, but I just know something happened to her too."

"This is dangerous." I wanted so badly to deny it, but I couldn't. "You should have called the cops."

"Ava—" she hesitated. "May's dead."

"What?" I thought of Sage's mom, the woman whose door was permanently open to us girls. The one who kept her freezer stocked with treats, who let us stay up all night giggling countless times on her couch, even when she had to wake up early for work. The one who had bandaged all of our injuries since we were five-year-olds crying over scraped knees.

Harper nodded, tears pooling in her eyes as she slowly pressed the gas again.

"She's really gone?"

"Yes. And now Sage is gone too... but she's still out there somewhere. We can't change what happened to May, but Sage? We can get her back. We have to."

I nodded, giving into her desperate pleas. I was so ready to go home, we were so close, but if Sage was really in trouble, she deserved to make it back home too.

"Okay," I agreed. "What do we do?"

43

AVA

Harper turned down a small dirt road, a hunting trail I'd seen a thousand times.

"What's this?" I asked.

"It's our way through," she answered.

"Through what?" I stared at the trail, trying to figure out where it would lead. "If you turn left you'll end up in my backyard, Harper. I've been all through these trees, all that's back here is lumber and deer."

She parked the car and turned to look at me. "Through where magics mix."

My body tensed, hand frozen on the door. "What?"

"Where magics mix," she repeated. "Like in Sam's poem."

A chill swept over my skin in a wave of goosebumps. I'd already gone where magics mixed and it didn't like me very much. *"Another world knows your name."* Mylo's warning ran through my mind, making me shiver.

"Come on," Harper said, climbing out of the car.

"No, Harper..." I got out too, but stood in the corner of the door as the motorcycle drove in to park beside us.

"Noah and my dad are waiting for me. I can't just not show up."

Her steps slowed only slightly as she turned back. "I know. I just need you to hear out our plan so you know where we are. Like you said, we're not far from your house. You can take my car back after we're done. I just don't want anyone else to disappear."

I tried not to stare at the man swinging from the bike behind me as I listened to her. His black boots hit the loose gravel as he slid off his helmet, his stern expression making my heart pound with intimidation.

I threw the door shut and half-ran to catch up to her, leaning closer to mutter in her ear. "You're not just following this guy because he's hot, are you?"

It felt like she'd just swept me right into a murderer's lap. Was he ridiculously strong or was that just my fear telling me I had no chance against him? I glanced back for another quick, nervous scan.

Nope, it wasn't the fear talking. Strong and dangerous.

"No!" she grumbled back, matching my hushed tone, but then she laughed. "He is though, isn't he?" It wasn't a question. I wanted to shove her arm, but cowered instead as he stepped in closer.

"Ava, this is Rogue. Rogue, Ava. Our save Sage alliance starts now." Rogue didn't stop for pleasantries, passing by us straight into the trees.

"Alliance? Do we get to pick code names before we start?" I mocked, relieved he didn't stop in front of us to pull out a knife.

Harper rolled her eyes, turning to follow his lead. "Very funny. Let's just focus on getting our friend back."

"And how's this guy gonna do that?"

"I'll track her," he answered, dismissing my complaint.

"If we hurry, we might be able to catch up. If we're lucky, she got away."

Within a few minutes of hiking through the forest, I knew exactly where we were. I'd spent a lot of time lost in those trees. We'd played in them all the time growing up, watching out for snakes, crossing rocks over rivers, but one specific instance came to mind.

I stared at a familiar fallen log, one I'd seen only a week before. We were headed straight toward the very spot that got me lost the first time. The place that launched me into a nightmare. This line where magics mixed was practically in my backyard.

My heart rate picked up, desperate to prevent that from happening again. I'd gone into that world, and the monsters chased me out. Studying Rogue up ahead, it felt like I followed a monster blindly back into it, and I didn't trust him.

He slowed down, holding a few fingers over his shoulder to stop us before crouching to study the leaf-covered dirt ahead. His hand brushed over the side of a hedge before straightening back up.

"They were here." Rogue's gravelly voice was quiet and firm, blending into the forest around us as much as one could, cautiously continuing forward. He remained so calmly focused on one single goal, moving so quietly that my own movements felt loud.

"How well do you know the other side of the line?" I asked.

"The other world is my home," he answered without so much as a glance, leaving it at that. I nodded, wishing it had been more reassuring. He stopped walking, when I recognized a circle of spaced out stones and stumbled back.

"I don't think I can—"

Rogue spun around to study my face. He was silent, intently searching my eyes, listening to each nervous breath. "You already know it."

"Not fondly," I admitted.

I fought the urge to run, cowering slightly as Rogue stepped in closer, reaching toward my neck. His palm pressed against the skin at my collar, closing his eyes to focus on something I couldn't see.

His golden eyes shot open to meet mine. "Interesting," he commented, breaking the silence. Had he just looked into my soul? Seen all of my secrets?

I glanced past him to Harper, her forehead wrinkling with a shrug.

"Another world knows my name," I whispered between us two, wondering if that meant anything to him. He didn't seem to question it.

"Stay," he ordered, turning back towards the stones. His voice was as intimidating as the rest of him. "There's no need for you to go any further. You know the line where we cross, now go home. I don't need anyone else to keep alive."

Harper sent me a nervous look, but his instructions filled me with relief. This time I was the one shrugging at her.

"It's okay. I'll wait here for a little while. It's not far, I can keep an eye out. Just go get Sage, don't worry about me."

"You'll wait here?" she asked. "Are you sure?"

"For now. Go. I'll be like your tether to this side," I said as she stepped in for one more hug. It was close enough that I could find the line again and check in... but check in for what? What would I be looking for from my spot on our side of two worlds?

"I'll see you soon," she promised.

I nodded, looking up at Rogue over her shoulder. I think we all knew that soon wasn't the right word for it. It wasn't that easy. The trouble wasn't over yet. My gut was right before. We were still searching for normal, and I wasn't so sure whether we could find it again.

"You keep her safe," I instructed, raising my brows at Rogue. "Bring both of my friends back, you hear me?"

He gave a soft bowing nod, waiting for Harper to join him inside the circle.

"Ava?" he called before I could turn away. The sound of it caught me off guard, my name from the raspy voice of a stranger. "The trees won't haunt you forever." His low gaze met mine one last time before reaching behind Harper's back to usher her forward.

Why did it feel like he could see right through me? And why did it leave me so empty after they were gone?

I sat on a log with a sigh, checking the time on my phone. I may have been home, but there was a lot to process. It looked like the haunting forest and I would be spending more time together. Maybe I needed that silence to get my story straight before facing Noah and dad. A little more time to decide how much *impossible* I could admit to.

"*Another world knows your name.*"

I just hoped Harper had a better experience in their world than I did.

44

AVA

It was weird sitting in the trees, like a step backwards, stuck in the same spot I was a few days before when I woke up lost. Minus the snow of course, the warmth was a welcome change.

I kept reflexively scanning the trees, paranoid, sure Oco would be watching me from one of them. Maybe sitting there alone, letting my building imagination consume my thoughts, was a mistake.

I grabbed my bag and stood, ready to ditch. I wasn't lost this time, I could find my way home, and Noah and dad were waiting. For all I knew, it would take days for Harper and Rogue to find Sage. Harper would call me when they got back.

"Stupid forest," someone grumbled. I spun around as a man stepped out over the stone circle.

He brushed his hand over his warm blond hair like he was wiping dirt out of it. A thin red cut ran across the top of his cheek, as if he'd just stepped out of a fight. I pointed a finger at him and he froze when he noticed me.

"Did you just—"

"No, what?" he defensively cut my question off, as if he'd been caught and quickly tried to divert.

"You just stepped across the line," I argued. "You did! You're from the other side!"

His hand fell from his hair, waving out between us to deflect. "I don't know what you're talking about." I ignored the gaslighting and continued to press.

"Did you see anyone crossing through? My friends... they just went in a few minutes ago."

He cut the act, his shoulders relaxing as he gave in. "I saw no one."

I nodded, accepting it for what it was. I didn't really know what I was expecting him to say, this man wasn't a part of the Harper-Rogue alliance. How often did people walk in and out?

"You're waiting for them?" he asked.

"I was— I am. Just, the forest makes me nervous."

"Sitting out here by yourself probably should make you nervous."

Quite the reassurance. "Yeah. Thanks."

He wouldn't look me in the eye long, keeping his head down as he moved to the log where I'd just been sitting. "Why don't I wait with you a while," he offered, his voice low, rubbing a hand down the side of his face.

"Oh—" I almost told him no, but his slumped posture, and the vacant look in his eyes as he stared off into nothing, made me think he needed a friend at that moment as much as I did. "Thanks."

"I'm Naz," he added, resting his elbows into his knees as his face dropped into his hands.

"Ava," I returned, hesitantly accepting the seat next to him. 'Are you okay?"

He let out a long, drawn-out sigh. "No. Not really."

"Well... do you want to talk about it?"

"I'll talk if you talk," he answered.

"Fine." My curiosity was too piqued to turn it down. He stared at the dirt for a moment before answering.

"This week I met the girl that I'm hopelessly in love with..."

"Well that's—"

"But it wasn't her." His hands dropped and he straightened back up. "It was her twin sister. I was too eager, I let myself believe, skipped right past the signs." He shook his head. "Apparently she died a few months ago."

My head jerked back, eyes wide. "Oh, wow... I'm so sorry." I cleared my throat, turning to look the other way. "I recently lost a good friend too."

It went silent for a moment, before he cashed in on his side of the deal.

"You knew about the line," he commented. "Few mortals do, and it's so much safer not to. Why didn't you go in with your friends?"

I hesitated, shifting in my seat as I pulled the sleeves of my shirt longer before folding my arms. *Few mortals* knew about his world, and I got the feeling his world preferred it that way. Us mortals weren't meant to know about the lines.

"Come on," he encouraged. "Your story can't be much worse than mine."

I swallowed my fear and gave in. "Last week I stepped across those stones and woke up in some forest in Alaska with no memory of who I was before."

His eyes widened. "Alaska, huh? That's quite the trip. Okay, maybe we can be tied."

"It was such a nightmare." The words started spilling out, venting to a stranger. "All I wanted was to know who I was. For days I searched for clues, but nothing would come."

"How did you remember?"

I hesitated again, picking at my finger nail. Would he believe me? He was from another world, the one where magic did exist. Maybe he could give me some real answers, some closure. Maybe I could ask him the questions that I couldn't ask Mylo.

"Are there vampires in your world?"

His brows drew together. "No. Not in my world."

My cheeks warmed. "I don't know then. I was so lost, and there was this man, but I don't think he was a normal guy."

"What makes you say that?"

"He got inside my head." How much more could I admit to without sounding insane? I stared at the backpack stuffed with Mylo's clothes, fighting some protective urge to keep them safe, but why? My forest was a lot warmer than his. I was never going to see him again.

He got inside my head. I was starting to wonder if he would ever get out.

Naz sank back a bit as he contemplated it. "I've never known of any vampires, but compulsion... he could have been fae."

"Well, whatever he was, he made me remember."

"A lot of us have tricks," Naz admitted. "Compulsion must have been his. It's fascinating really, I haven't heard of anyone with that gift in a long time. Not in my lifetime even. It's not common."

I wish the answer had helped more, but it left me feeling just as stuck. I turned away, my fingers picking at the edge of the fallen log next to me, getting swept away in childhood memories.

"We used to play in these woods as kids, me and my friends. Spend hours catching lizards and frogs. Most of the forest gets so thick, you can hardly walk through the brush and vines, but dad always kept our land clear for hunting. We used to use his hunting stand as our little clubhouse, our secret hideout base in the woods. Then our friend got lost and my mom freaked out." I shook my head, missing the sound of mom's voice calling through the trees to let us know it was time to come home. "We all made it home fine, but Mom never let us go explore very far after that."

"Hmm," he softly answered, listening as I rambled on.

"Feels so long ago now," I finished, a part of me wishing I could turn back time and go back. The flutter of wings mixed into the hushing echo of moving water as we sat in silence.

"So what's yours?" I asked. He looked up at me, a little distracted. "Your trick," I clarified.

"I'm that obvious, am I?"

I shrugged. "You did say a lot of *us* have tricks. Not to mention five minutes ago you walked across the line and called me a mortal." I stared at the stone circle where my friend disappeared. "You know a lot more about that world than I do."

"Didn't do well hiding it. My head's not right. I didn't exactly get any sleep, and I wasn't expecting—" His hand gestured at me again. "There's not usually someone sitting at the lines waiting around."

I nodded, remembering how caught off guard he'd been. "Sorry."

"My gift is a connection to the world itself," he explained. "The seasons, the stars. Your side has so much more if it, you know. Pieces shifting back and forth for their time, claiming their territories. One corner of your world experiencing winter, the other side basking in sunlight. It coexists in a way. There's something so beautiful in it, the way everything gets its turn. A simple balance." He gestured up at the branches above us, and a soft cool breeze followed as he waved his fingers through the air.

"My gift holds an outward expression, connected to the very air around me. How I feel displays itself through fog, or rain... a soft breeze, or a storm. My brother's gift is connected to the soul. He can sense what's going on inside. What you feel within your heart. What troubles you, your pain, your anger... the simple things that make you smile. All he has to do is focus."

I thought of Mylo, the way he could dig through my mind. The way he discovered the nightmares hidden underneath.

"I stumbled into it by accident. Your world. Right there." I pointed at the stone circle, giving up the full story. "Heard something I wasn't supposed to hear, and something in your world didn't like that. It spelled away my memories, chased me out through a different line." My fingers dug into my temples, staring at the stones.

"And to think I could have avoided the entire mess by walking a few steps to the right." It was the most honest I'd been since remembering. The first time I'd said the story out loud, spoke of the world I wanted to forget about. The one I hoped would forget about me.

He was waiting for more, his full attention on me. "What did you hear?"

"Just some talk about mirrors and gates." I shook my head. I'd told myself over and over again that it wasn't real. "Mylo told me to be careful. He told me another world knows my name."

"He's right. I'm surprised you weren't marked. If you heard anything to do with the prophecy then—"

"Marked? Prophecy?"

He stared ahead in thought, and I felt bad for cutting him off.

"I'm sorry. It's just that it sounds so fictional... but I want to know, please. Tell me about this prophecy."

"It's not so small a story," he answered. "Years of history written in blood, with a king willing to die over it."

"I've got nothing else to do." It was a lie, but I was too invested. Who knew if I'd ever get another chance to ask these questions, and I wanted to know everything. I needed to know why this happened to me, to understand what I'd gotten mixed up in. Home could wait a little while longer.

He looked me over, sharing a polite smile, but it fell with an agreeing nod. "I'm afraid I share the sentiment."

45

AVA

"Many creatures live within those woods," Naz started. "The main three are the witches, the shifters, and the fae. The territories of our world are divided between them, and for a long time all stuck to their corners. Years ago, there was a truce. A leader from each territory gathered under the full moon. Gifts were given, laws were created, and a new peace was born."

"And the prophecy?"

"Not quite. There was to be peace. The three leading bloodlines had to respect the truce. There had to be a balance between them. An equality. Respect. Nothing deeper."

"So no romance."

"*Forbidden love*," he countered, a poetic note in his tone "Some stories are born of heartbreak."

' So then who broke the rule?"

' The fae king fell in love with the witch," he answered. "The shifter alpha felt his position slipping. He refused to stand by. Two could not combine to outshine the one. But it was too late to stop it. When confronted, the fae king refused to give her up, nor she him. He was banished for breaking the new rule, for choosing her over the peace. The witch, brokenhearted, went into hiding... but not without making the shifter pay. She came back for him. To burn his home to the ground, turning his entire pack to ash."

"The truce broken."

"She felt that if power was all that mattered to him, the shifter would know none. And he would lose everything he loved for it. A whole rule gone, a prophecy written in its place. Cosimo, the new fae king, led our world in their absence. Now that he's gone, his son, Echo, stands in his place. Her prophecy still waits. A story of broken glass, a lost prince, and the blood of a witch."

"The lost prince?"

"They say he's the son of the shifter king." Naz shook his head. "I've been to those haunted grounds myself. There is nothing left but ash."

"And the witch?"

"Her name was Kia. Her bloodline is out there somewhere. Echo hunts for it, still searching the world after all these years."

He stopped there, allowing the silence to paint his ghostly legend in my thoughts.

"Tell me about the friend you lost," Naz said. The subject change squeezed my heart, the same way it did every time I thought of Sam. I'd avoided talking about her, and nobody ever really pressed.

"Her," I started, a little shaky. "Sam." He did a double take, going still in his spot as he studied me. I stared ahead at the stone circle, thinking of her poem, remembering all the magic that she so full-heartedly believed in.

"She was everything you could want in a friend. Fun, encouraging, loyal. She chased her dreams, and pushed us to do the same with this wild enthusiasm that no one could argue. She truly believed we were all going to make it. So much so, that for a moment, you believed it too."

A raindrop hit my forehead. I stared up at the clouds, watching a few more softly falling around us.

"What if one step, one stumble, one roll, you find a forest that consumes your soul." This time I did the double take, my head jerking back as I met his eyes. I'd read those words a hundred times, the first line of Sam's poem.

"How did you—" I stopped myself when it hit me. "The love of your life had a twin. You knew her too."

His soft nod was shaky as he turned his watering gaze away. The raw heartbreak reddening his cheeks confirmed everything I needed to know.

"Sam was the one you loved. The one that died. And Willow was the girl in your class." I reached for his hand, shielding it from another raindrop as I softly squeezed. "And you just found out about her?"

He nodded, and a tear fell. He moved his hand from mine to wipe it away, when I sat back to study the sky above us, matching his grief from the clouds. There was anguish in the air itself, radiating from his very soul.

"I'm so sorry."

"As am I," he answered with a deep breath, pausing a moment as the rain sprinkled lighter, his emotions settling. "You loved her too."

"Yeah," I agreed, my voice barely above a whisper.

"You got to know her a lot better than I did," he added, attempting to push his pain away like he wasn't entitled to it, but the wall broke again as the emotions strained his expression.

So many questions raced through my mind. Secrets Sam took to her grave. How long had she known about this other world? About him? I guess if us mortals knowing about it was so serious, it made sense that she didn't tell us, though in her own way, in her poem, she did. The only way she knew how.

"Tell me about her?" he softly asked.

I let out a shallow breath, my fingers fidgeting with my sleeves. "What do you want to know?"

He met my eyes for the first time since we brought up Sam, and he smiled. "Everything."

I told him about our summers as children, how Sam was always the leader of the group. The way we talked on a daily basis, shooting messages back and forth. She was always instigating fun, always pushing us closer to happiness. Closer to the magic.

"She saw it everywhere she looked."

He nodded, another tear breaking free. It seemed he already knew the story, I just offered a clearer picture. I bit back a smile as I imagined Willow sneaking into his class, pretending to be her sister.

"I know it was hard for you, finding out about Sam... but she would have been so proud of Willow for daring to do what she did. Sam would hate to see how Willow's been living, if you can even call it that. This depressed, lonely, hollow version of the girl Sam so adored."

He didn't respond, and I knew I wasn't helping. "I'm sorry."

"It's okay," he answered. "Really, thank you. I never got to be with her, but it's nice to see her through someone else's eyes." He swallowed hard. "How did she die?"

I nodded in silence. I knew the question was coming, but I hated answering it. I hated thinking about what my friends had gone through, imagining the pain and fear in those last seconds, the moment the world lost something so special

"It was late. Willow was driving them home, just the two of them. There was a deer in the road." I shrugged, unable to go any deeper. Willow only told us about it one time, said the deer looked like a ghost in the headlights, layered in fog. The disturbed look in her eyes still made me shudder.

"Willow walked away, and Sam didn't. She'll regret it the rest of her life. She's always going to wish it had been her. You can see it in her eyes. She's the sick one. She was supposed to die. Not Sam."

Naz watched me so intently, hanging onto every word.

"So you're waiting for Willow, then?" he asked.

"No, Harper."

He flinched slightly back, brows drawn together as he rubbed two fingers against his forehead.

"Why do you seem confused?" I asked.

His hand fell to the log as he shifted his legs away. "It's just—"

I studied his face, realizing the red slit no longer ran his cheek. Hadn't there been a fresh cut there? *Focus Ava. Why would I be waiting for Willow? Why does he look nervous?*

"You're hiding something."

He bit his lip, looking off in the other direction.

Wait... is Willow in there?"

His gaze fell to the dirt like he didn't want to say it. "My brother took her. He was trying to force me back into a world I wanted no part of. Worried about the gates closing me out. He just can't understand that I don't care! I want no part of that world, not without—" he stopped himself. *Sam.* I'd been filling the blanks with her name enough to know when she was the piece left out.

"I hope I never step foot in it again!" he rambled on.

I stood up fast, stepping away from him. "Hold on, he's got Willow in there too? Against her will? What do you mean the gates are closing? You mean the lines? And you just left her in there for him to keep hostage forever?"

My breaths shook rapidly in and out. It wasn't just three friends tangled up in this mess, it was all four! Five counting Sam! This guy knew her, *really* knew her. Had she started this?

"He won't hurt her—"

"How can you say that? The gates? She'll be trapped!"

"Because I have this!" he insisted, standing to face me, desperately pulling a silver trinket from his pocket. "They can't close the gates..." his tone softened, his eyes falling from mine to the dirt again, like he were admitting something. "Because I have this." He opened the mirror for me to see.

"Why?"

"It's part of the prophecy. The broken glass. There used to be one portal, it belonged to the fae king. He split it, his gift in the truce, a line drawn in each territory. The three pieces..." he stopped to clear his throat. "I have one. You have to have the blood of the witch, the ash of the shifter, and the king's *completed* mirror. Only then, under a full moon, in the spot where it began, can he close the gates."

"But why—"

"Echo thinks your world is a poison to ours. He doesn't see it the way I do, but I'll never let him close the gates!"

"My friends are all still stuck in there!" I half-yelled before pointing at the mirror. "And you're telling me that's all that's keeping those gates open?"

His shoulders sank. "My brother said they've found the

witch. The ash is scattered through the soil of the burned kingdom… and there's a full moon coming up."

He held the mirror out higher. "I'm afraid this might just be the only thing keeping those gates open."

"My friend is stuck in there because of you and your brother! Go back in there and get her out! She's sick! She can't be lost in another world!"

"I can't just—"

"You have to! Sam would agree with me!" The words blurted out before I could think them through.

His mouth shut in a firm line, the nerve I hit was raw.

"Please?" I begged more softly.

"Okay," he agreed. "Fine. I'll do what I can."

The buzz in my pocket made me jump. I'd gotten used to not having a phone on me. I turned around, taking a break from the conversation to scroll through my notifications.

"Oh, Sage," I sighed, seeing just how hard she'd tried to reach me. I wish I could have been there for her.

At the top sat two new texts from an unsaved number.

Hey, it's Emma!

Let me know when you make it home!

I'd saved my number in her phone the night before, insisting that she text me so we could keep in touch.

I made it back! Tell your dad thank you again for the plane ticket!

I slid the phone back in my pocket, turning to face Naz. "Thank you—" I started to say, cut off by the empty forest in front of me. "Naz?" Silence. "Wait!" I stumbled two panicked steps closer to the stone circle, but couldn't get all the way there. I couldn't cross that line again.

He was gone, and so was the one thing guaranteeing that those lines stayed open.

"Crap."

I sat back on the log, defeated. He had to find her now, had to get her out. All of them had to make it back! I should have gone with him, but I couldn't. I looked up at the trees as the empty air around me invited the discomfort back in.

I reached for my backpack, about to dig to the bottom, but the shirts stopped me. Mylo's shirts. Everything I'd learned was as impossible as he was. Every time I'd gotten lost in the trees, he'd been the one to save me, and maybe a part of me was still lost. Every time I thought I'd stepped out of this nightmare, something pulled me deeper inside it. Maybe part of me still needed to be saved.

I lifted the collar of my shirt, pressing it over my nose to breathe him in, wishing things had gone differently. There was still so much that I couldn't explain, that I didn't understand. Maybe I'd been too quick to shut him out. Maybe it was time to give him another chance, to let him explain.

I pulled free the half-crumbled pink sticky note that I'd secretly hidden in my pocket, his number written across it just in case.

Mylo. It was time to hear him out.

SHADOWS

46

ZAGER

I was going to kill Naz if I ever saw him again. Kill him, for not letting me save him. He was so stubborn, giving up everything. He would never stop resisting. Maybe it was time to give up the fight. The gates would shut, the magic would be cut off, and he would be cut off with it.

"Willow?" I scanned the small camp, but it was empty, and I couldn't sense her energy in the surrounding woods. She was too weak to have gotten far.

I never anticipated the metal in her leg, we didn't use metal like that on our side of the lines. Iron, and silver? Only a witch could wield them both, their strongest defense against the shifters and fae. They learned long before to spell metal and bring it across the line, but only their magic could. Enchanted metal was a valuable trade, among most things that a witch could create. A witch made a powerful ally, though they rarely chose it.

It couldn't be too late. I'd never seen the magic reject someone, but I'd also felt the weakness inside her. She would never survive on my side of the line, and her dead blood ran too deep. I had to find her and get her home.

What kind of monster blindsides their brother with heartache and dooms an innocent girl? I'd sensed her secrets, had seen pieces of the truth shining through, but I played along for my own benefit and hurt them both. My actions made her seem disposable and I'd give anything to take that back.

"Looking for something?" The careful voice stood deep through the trees, greeting from the border of my senses, and for a split second, I was grateful the human was gone. I turned to face Echo as he came closer, his witch in the shadows behind him. Clover.

Despite my loyal lifelong friendship with the king, I'd never cared much for his witch. She'd been his number two for years, a descendant of his father's witch, Ivy, but I could never get a clear read from her. She was guarded, a defensive perk to their coven blood. The witches had always been clever with their trinkets, spells, and herbs.

"I thought I sensed your brother," Echo said. "I came to welcome him home."

Of course. He'd been watching for Nazurin. Echo cared about his old friend just as I cared for my brother.

"May I?" he added, holding out a hand.

I looked down at the mirror, still sitting in my palm. A tool to help find Nazurin, to stay connected, but I'd given up hope. It still felt strange to hand it over, but he was my leader, and my loyalty had never been questioned. I set it in his hand.

'I'm sorry, Echo. I thought I could bring Naz back, but that was foolish." My eyes fell to the dirt, wishing I had better news to share. "He's gone."

"He's chosen his side, then. Pity." Echo spat the word out, dripping in judgment. "But he is here."

"Was," I admitted, feeling like a failure. Why did my brother have to be so stubborn? "You're still set on your plan then?"

"All set. Getting the last piece as we speak." Echo grinned victoriously, so close to winning, his confidence shining brightly inside him. He looked to two of his men, cocking his head toward the trees in silent order. He'd been looking forward to this day for years, splitting the two worlds as they were always meant to be, to protect our side of the lines, our magic. The full moon was fast approaching, and so much would change beneath its light.

"You tried your hardest." He reached for my shoulder and squeezed. "Let us cease our search, and leave him in peace." His hand fell, turning back towards the path, pausing at the first tree. "Won't you come home, *brother*?" A hint of empathy flickered through.

With one last longing look through the forest around me, I gave up on my brother, and turned toward the future.

"Right behind you," I answered. My loyalty couldn't be questioned. Not now.

"Good," he said before slipping back into the shadows toward the kingdom. Toward home.

My eyes shut tight, focusing on the trees around me. Nothing. Had I lost her for good? I thought bringing Willow into my world would lighten her burdens, but I'd only made them heavier. I promised to keep her safe, and I meant it. If she was alive, I had to find her and get her out in time.

47

HARPER

Rogue gently ushered me forward, when a new blanket of trees blocked out the sun. The shadows darkened to a bolder green, the sky a softer blue haze, the forest air like summer against my skin.

I stopped walking, and his hand dropped from behind me as I slowly spun, head tipped back to take in the consuming energy around us. Thick netting moss dangled over strong branches of low trees, shaded by the higher canopy of leaves above, layers and layers of hazels and green. Earthy beige and red mushrooms dotted a path across an uprooted trunk. A small, squirrel-tailed mouse with tiny horns froze in its path to gauge the sudden company, while two glowing, yellow lights floated unbothered in the distance.

"The Token Wood," Rogue announced. He seemed hesitant, turning his low gaze up on me.

"What?"

He paused to answer, giving a slight shrug. "Nothing."

"Not nothing... what?"

"I'm just not used to having a partner."

"Have you ever had a partner?"

Rogue looked down at his hands, one thumb rubbing over the other. "I've trained a few hunters over the years. I had one a few months ago, but he didn't last."

"What, like he died?"

"No." He turned toward a set of trees, retrieving a hidden pack from behind them. "Just chose a different path."

He acted so casual, swinging a pack of arrows over his shoulder, carrying the bag and a bow back over. "You kept a stash there ready to go?"

He rubbed his chin, brows slightly furrowing together. "I keep one at every line."

Of course he did. I stared at the simple circle of rocks, brown weeds taking over the dry dirt around it. "Everything here is so beautiful, until the spot that connects to the other side."

"It's a lie," Rogue muttered. He pulled his sweatshirt off, handing the black fabric to me. "Put this on," he instructed, sliding his vest back on without it.

The dark arrow tattoo that ran his forearm caught my eye as I slowly accepted. "Why?"

"It'll help you blend in," he explained, looking over my shirt. "Pink doesn't exactly do the trick. Anything metal, you should put in your pockets now."

"What?" My hands shot to my ears, ignoring the way he searched me for jewelry. It wasn't bracelets or rings that I cared about. "What if it's under the hood?"

He leaned closer as I shifted my head to expose the hearing aids.

Rogue shook his head indifferently. "As soon as we step away from the line, they'll die." It was honest, and blunt.

I let out a shaky breath, pushing to stay strong. "I won't

be able to hear." I looked him directly in the eyes. "You're going to have to look at me when you talk."

His head fell an inch, eyes shutting as he pinched the bridge of his nose in frustration. I was adding another complication to a mission he wanted to go on alone. His hand cropped with a nod of understanding, accepting the road forward. "Then I'll look at you when I talk."

I returned the nod, but sank in the discomfort of moving forward without one of my senses. I would be vulnerable, and he was the only thing I could count on. The one thing I could trust.

I looked back at the weeds behind us. "What did you mean. . it's a lie."

"That your world is draining our magic. Killing it. The king wants to close the gates, and he needs his kingdom to support the decision. It's his witch that killed this soil, it has nothing to do with the lines."

"Will he be able to close them?"

Rogue's expression darkened. "Not if I have anything to do about it." He started to turn away when I stopped him.

"Please don't let me get lost in here."

His head turned to meet my eyes more sincerely, pausing to take in my request. "I won't."

I took the hearing aids off, consumed by the immediate silence as I stared at them in my palm. I hated the quiet. It mocked me, told me I was helpless, but then there was Sage, and she needed my help. Giving in, I slid them into my pocket and jogged to catch up with Rogue.

We didn't talk, and I got the feeling Rogue preferred it that way. He would stop every once in a while, studying the trail ahead of him for signs, pointing out details in the world around us.

"Hold up," he said, side-stepping off the path. He shoved his gloves into his back pocket. Something blue was caught in the brush. He pulled the long ribbon free of the thorns.

"That belongs to Sage!" I insisted.

"Yeah. Looks like she fought back." His answer gave me hope.

"How can you tell?"

"The tracks." He pointed at the path behind me. "They were consistent up until here, then they fumble out." He pointed towards the brush, unevenly bent down in two heavy spots.

"Do you think she got hurt?"

He studied the ground before moving back toward the trail, searching for footsteps. "No. Not bad. I don't see any blood. She kept walking from here."

"So she didn't get away."

He didn't answer, wrapping the ribbon into a neat roll before sliding it into his pocket. He followed their tracks back on course, when he stopped to trace his finger over a subtle mark carved into a tree, two lines angled at a point.

"What is it?"

His hand fell, turning his head back to look at me. "It's my mark."

"It's like the tip of an arrow." My eyes flickered over his tattoo again, then the pack of arrows sticking out above his shoulder.

"I know the path they follow well."

We hiked on quietly, when Rogue crouched lower and went still, raising a hand at his side to stop me. He slowly reached for an arrow over his shoulder, raising the bow in front of him as he took two more careful low steps. My heart pumped nervously as he calmly angled into the trees, drawing the string back as he focused his aim, then let the arrow fly free.

The bow lowered to his side, and he stepped off the path to grab a copper-coated rabbit from the ground. He pulled the arrow out, briefly lifting his tanned, dirty arm just enough for me to get a glimpse of his catch.

"Dinner," he explained, ignoring my wide-eyed disgust. At least I knew he wouldn't let me go hungry.

He slid the arrow back over his shoulder, and added the catch to his pack. I admired the soft purple flowers blossoming into unique shapes in the tree above me. His finger drew a line from the blossoms to the base of the trunk.

"Safe place to rest."

I studied the words on his lips before I crossed my hands over my chest in fists, spinning them forward as my hands pulled apart. "Safe."

He repeated the sign, and I nodded. If we were going to be working together, he might as well know a few basic signs. I took one more look at the flowers before we moved on. Their sweet scent filtered through the air, but as I moved to keep up, I could have sworn one of the petals lifted up into a wing as two tiny lilac eyes peeked back out at me.

Rogue showed me which berries to eat, which to avoid. Blue ones that could make you more alert, could build up your energy, versus the bush of tart, deep red berries that would trigger hallucinogenic nightmares.

Our journey started in witch territory, where they didn't just let plants and nature run wild, they encouraged it.

'Don't be fooled by this world," he warned. "Don't trust

everything you see. The witches can make use of anything found in this marsh."

Vines crawled through the trees around us, hanging their large leaves along our path. I shuddered as Rogue brushed his fingers along them, so at one with this terrifying world.

We followed a mucky path that he called the Mella Marsh. Rogue explained how it skirted between the territories and led straight through to the fae kingdom. The place they would have taken Sage. Steep walls started to line the right of our path, wet with streaks of water running down them, puddling along the base to create the marsh. Rogue stopped to collect some in a canteen. It felt like we followed the muddy moat of a mountain, a ditch that couldn't quite drain all the way.

Every few steps became sloppier through the mud, cool water seeping in at the base of my shoes. Rogue didn't seem to notice at all, not a care for comfort, only focus for the path ahead.

We passed a line of darkened woods. The shadows felt heavier beneath its cover, a warning in the air itself, and honestly, I was grateful we weren't passing through.

"Those trees are kind of creepy," I admitted.

He turned to face me as he answered, a grim expression on his face. "They're haunted."

I nearly stumbled, hesitating to go on. I wanted to roll my eyes, to tell him that's not funny, but the words sank in, and I got the feeling he meant them. My mind got lost in the shadows, when I realized Rogue's pace hadn't wavered, running to catch back up with him.

"Where are we now?" I asked when the trees started thinning, the soil growing dry and rough as it rose into the rocky hills ahead.

He went a few steps further, stopping at the bouldering base of a mountain, his focus fixed on the uphill climb. "The Wild Rocks." He turned back just enough for me to see the answer, gripping his hands together in contemplation.

"What is it?"

He barely met my eyes, lips quirking into his cheek on one side, before concentrating back on the rocks.

"You're second guessing the route?"

"We could hike around, follow the path they took, or hike over and try to gain. One is faster. One is safer."

I pointed at the rock walls above us. "Faster?"

He nodded, and what he wanted to do was clear. He was second guessing it because of me.

"I can climb," I blurted out, trying to sway his doubts despite the high notes in my voice. For Sage, this could be life or death. I could face my discomfort with heights and hike the mountain.

He rubbed the back of his neck, apprehensive to accept. "We would be less likely to have a run in with Echo's guards," he commented. "Nobody climbs up."

"See," I added. "Sage needs us. I refuse to slow down her rescue."

"I don't kn—"

I stubbornly stepped past him. "Which way would you go if I wasn't here?" His empty expression answered for him. "Yeah, thought so. Come on."

He still seemed unsure, starting to lead the way again despite the disapproving shake of his head. Rogue studied the climb before picking our starting point, hesitating on one last chance to back out.

"No time to waste," I reminded him. He slid out the pair of black gloves hanging from his back pocket and handed them over.

"Here. For better grip," he explained.

The rocks built up together slowly, sloping up from the base. The majority of the cliffs above were steep and bare, but I was confident in the steady inclined path Rogue pointed out. As long as I stuck with him, I could make it.

Halfway up, the boulders grew less forgiving, with less to hold, and larger sections to climb. Rogue led through the corner of two slanted ledges, each step back and forth between each side. I lunged from the base to follow, leaning against one side as I searched for a spot to hold. The slick rock didn't offer much, when my foot slid, and gravity teased the weight hanging in my hand, fighting to rebalance.

I caught my grip between the two sides, shutting my eyes tight as I calmed my breath. "This was so not part of my plans," I muttered under my breath, pushing up the sleeves of his sweatshirt.

Rogue peeked back through, reaching a hand down for me to grab. "You good?"

I faked a smile, too stubborn to turn back now. I didn't dare the climb back down any more than I feared the rest of the way up.

"Great," I lied as he pulled me forward.

He took the rest of the climb slower, giving me tips on where to hold and lean. When the sun started to sink, I worried about the dark path waiting on the other side.

"Are we camping up there?" I asked.

He was slow to answer, pausing to take in the dimming sky. "We can. I'm not sure you'll want to."

He pulled me over the last ledge as a spiked set of turquoise wings spread out in front of me, a dragon defensively lifting onto its hind legs.

"Rogue!" The ground shook as the dragon landed back

onto its front feet, small rocks sliding around us from the pressure.

Rogue whipped around, holding a hand at the dragon as it backed into the cliffs behind it. Its snout flared with a forceful breath out, the hot air wafting around us, before it lifted more intently to smell. It took a deep breath, cautiously stepping forward to meet Rogue's eyes.

"Whose territory is this again?" I asked, wondering which of the three claimed the dragon cliffs. "The shifters?"

"Nobody claims it." For the first time, he smiled, cocking his head at the beast. "It's theirs." He held his palm higher as the dragon pressed its snout against it, bowing into the touch.

"The Wild Rocks," I repeated from before, looking at the cliffs around us in a new light.

"Technically it borders the fae line, but nobody messes with the world up here. It's wild." His fingers brushed over the scales beneath its bright gold eye to trail down its neck. "It's free." The creature's guard had fallen, relaxed at the touch.

"Does it know you?"

"She's a friend," he answered. "We're lucky she still lives, no other dragon has claimed this cliff."

"Can I?" I asked, reaching for her snout. The dragon huffed, as Rogue put up a hand to stop me, but it was too late. She took a step forward, studying my scent. I pressed my hand against the smooth warm scales between her watchful eyes.

"She's beautiful."

"She is," Rogue agreed, equally lost in admiration. "When you become a hunter, they take your wings. If you're lucky, a dragon will choose to replace them."

He crouched down to pick something up, flipping it over in his hand before sliding it into his pack.

"Why would they take—"

"It's the law."

I didn't press more, sensing the defensive wall he still had up between us.

48

HARPER

"Come on," Rogue said. "We gotta work our way back to the forest before sundown."

I followed closely, letting him help me over another set of rocks, when we reached a high slope.

"Here." He laced his fingers together for me to step on, and I grabbed the corner as he hoisted me up, swinging myself over the top. Staying on my stomach, I reached over the edge to help him too.

He had one knee over the edge, when his eyes opened wide. He reflexively grabbed my stomach and rolled forward, swinging me around with him. We rolled twice before he landed above me, blocking me in. Heat burned at my arm, him locking us both in place until the fire eased and he pulled me up, pushing me toward a more even path.

I looked back as he threw his finger toward the rocks ahead of me. "Run!" he mouthed, keeping in step behind me. With one last glance, a golden set of wings reared up higher, the air vibrating around us, when turquoise smashed into it.

I didn't look back again until Rogue pulled me behind a

wall, both of us searching for the threat. The turquoise dragon pinned the smaller gold one, growling in its eye. Two deep cuts ran along her shoulder, but she'd gained the upper hand.

Rogue tapped my bicep to get my attention, making me startle as I spun to face him. He held his hand toward my other arm, the one that had been exposed to the heat. I shifted around as he pulled it up to examine.

"I'm okay," I assured him. "Let's just keep moving."

He nodded, letting go of my arm to lead the way again.

From the dragon's ledge, Rogue shifted deeper through the rocks instead of hiking higher. We didn't travel far, when the path sloped back into the tree line on the other side.

My feet ached when Rogue finally stopped, though I got the feeling he would have gone on without me. I found a flat rock to sit on quickly, dreading the moment I had to stand back up. I tried to search the dark trees above me for those strange purple flowers, but I couldn't be sure.

"I hate the dark," I muttered, counting up the twinkling starlight beyond the leaves. "That sky is the one perk to nightfall."

On cue, he started prepping a campfire, moving through the motions like he'd done it a thousand times before. He pulled a knife from his waist, and the rabbit from his pack, starting to cut through it. I watched him work, unfazed by the job, dirt under his nails, hair greased with sweat. This was his world, his life, surviving on his own.

"How come the knife is okay? I thought you said no metal."

"A knife is different. A tool, a weapon. The witches have enchanted many over the centuries, they're not uncommon. Silver burns the shifters. Iron burns the Fae, but I am a hunter. The metal does not hurt me."

"You sure know a lot about survival," I commented.

"You have to in order to survive on your own." Another reminder that he was a lone wolf, like he had to make a point of it, but why? That was before, this was now. He finished preparing the rabbit, splitting the meat between the two of us. We ate quietly, when I tried to stretch out my arm, fighting the pain of the burn that ran down it.

Rogue grabbed a small jar and tan wrap from his bag, crouching next to me as he opened it.

"What are you—"

"Your burn. This will numb the pain... help it heal." He dipped his finger into the milky mixture, scooping some out to brush along my arm. The touch made me wince, but I tried to breathe through it.

I studied the faint scar above his thumb as he worked, then the one on the side of his forehead, wondering how he'd gotten them. "How come *you* didn't get burned?"

"I did. I just heal differently than you." He wrapped it gently, making sure it sat securely before he stood back up. "That should keep it clean."

He returned to his seat, picking his knife up to fidget with.

"You're not alone anymore," I told him.

He paused, his low eyes barely meeting mine.

"You're not. So get over it." I reached for my backpack, pulling out the deck of cards that I kept handy for impromptu moments like this.

' Come on," I said, scooting to the edge of my rock as the backpack fell back on the ground.

"I don't know—"

"I hiked a dragon cliff for you, buddy, you can learn a simple card game."

He didn't fight it further, watching as I dealt two piles.

We sat in the dirt and played four rounds of speed, a game I could play with my eyes instead of my ears, and I fought hard not to laugh as he tried to understand the basic rules. It wasn't long before he found his competitive side though, and I really put on my game face. It was a race, slapping down the cards one by one, until mine ran out. He laughed a little, setting down his remaining two, proof he had a fun side once he let his guard down.

"Almost," he commented.

"You only got close because my arm is half-numb," I mocked, softly shaking out the strange sensation from his first aid mixture. His smile stretched wider, eyes down in the dirt as he sat back against a log in silence.

I admired his smile, hoping one day Sage would get to see this side of him too. The side that wasn't busy fighting the battles of another world. He was doing all of this for her. She needed to see past the hunter to the person underneath.

I pulled a bag of grapes from my bag. "I don't suppose the survival expert packed any hot cocoa mix," I commented wishfully, when his eyes shifted defensively to the bushes behind me.

My shoulders went rigid, neck slowly creeping around to see the threat. Something shuffled through the brush, branches waving, when the fire reflected against two small eyes. It froze too, the light shining against the orange fur on its face.

"Is that a fox?" I asked, looking back at Rogue as he slumped over, face falling back from the false alarm.

"One of the few creatures that dare to sneak back and

forth over the lines." He looked annoyed, but I could feel my tone shifting higher.

"It's so little!"

"Probably lost," Rogue answered with a side-eye to the trees.

"Come here!" I could feel the baby voice reflexively shining through like it did with any cute animal. Its head lowered, studying me through the leaves. I bit a grape in half, tossing a small piece over.

Rogue leaned forward to pat my leg for my attention. "Leave it."

I rolled my eyes, fully ready to ignore the instructions.

"He's probably lost," I repeated mockingly. "You're lucky I'm not Sage. She wants to rescue every animal in the world."

"Then let's get her home so she can save a puppy." His answer made my heart squeeze. Sage would have loved to save a dog, and he would so quickly offer it.

"When this is over, and we can all be normal friends, we have to have a real game night."

His brows drew together. "A game night?"

"That was one game, Rogue. There are still so many you have to learn."

"You're so certain I'll stick around," he commented before his lips closed into a thin line. He stared into the flames.

Friends was clearly a new term for him. I'd have to teach him the basics of that too.

"Thank you," I told him, putting my fingers to my chin, then pulling them forward, teaching him another basic sign. My hands folded into my lap. "For today. For bringing me along, and teaching me about your world."

He remained silent, but the sentiment was there as he briefly met my eyes.

"Your tattoo. What does it mean?"

"It's a hunter's mark. We all have it."

"Part of the deal, huh... when they take your wings?"

He was quiet again, his expression fading.

"That dragon was beautiful," I went on. "I never imagined I would get to see one."

"They're not to be messed with," he commented. "Be glad she didn't snap your hand off. They're not kind creatures." My jaw fell half open. "I wouldn't have climbed that way with you if I wasn't sure it was only her at the top. And it wasn't."

"You could have warned me, you know!"

"You insisted we go my way, remember?" There was a hint of a smug smile, and my guard softened again. Somehow, deep down, I knew he wouldn't let me get hurt.

"She respected you, though," I went on. "Defended you even... was she..." He'd mentioned that hunters and dragons sometimes paired up.

"No," he answered before I could find the right words. "I had a dragon once. He was blue, and beautiful, like the deep rolling sea." There was a moment of silent appreciation before he went on. "That dragon we saw today... she was his mother."

It was the most personal thing he'd shared. There was pain behind his eyes, like a glimpse into his soul, a look at the man behind the wall. His face told a sad story, details left unsaid. I wondered how he'd lost his dragon companion, the one single partner to this lonely hunter's life.

"Well, it must have been a special bond you had, you and your dragon. She respected you like *you* were her son too."

Rogue's eyes flashed to mine, the muscles in his arms tensing. His lips parted slightly, but he didn't speak.

"What was his name?" I asked. "Your dragon." Darkness swallowed the world around us in shadows as we sat by the flickering flames.

"Aero."

49

HARPER

The night air cooled around us as we soaked in the quiet. Our day played over in my mind, the dragon encounters, and the question that had nagged me since.

"What was it you picked up? At the top of the cliff. You grabbed something off the ground."

He waited a moment before sliding a stone from his pack to show me. "A dragon scale."

My hand lowered under the weight as I accepted, rubbing my thumb over the smooth, translucent, turquoise scale. One small piece of what made up her large armor.

"So pretty," I commented, turning it over to study, then handing it back. "What will you do with it?"

He went quiet, like he didn't want to answer. "It's a gift," he simply explained, and I didn't push for more, seeing the sentiment in his eyes.

A gift for Sage.

"Tell me about you," Rogue said, initiating small talk for the first time since we'd met. He clearly preferred the silence as we traveled. Maybe the quiet kept us safer... or maybe he simply hadn't cared before.

"Me? I don't know, what do you want to know about me?" I watched him, waiting for an answer, but his teeth shut tight as he searched for what to say.

"Small talk isn't your strong suit, is it," I softly mocked.

"I don't have much to say," he admitted. "Usually I get everything I need with one touch."

I frowned, my head tilting. "How do you mean?" I had to have read his lips wrong.

He reached out a hand. I hesitated a moment, before placing mine inside it, no gloves to cut off the connection this time. He closed his eyes in concentration, focused on something I couldn't feel for a moment, just like he had with Ava. Then his hand yanked back from mine, eyes flying open wide.

"What is it, what did you see?"

His eyes searched mine silently before answering. "Wolves."

The word cut off the warmth of the fire, as the cool night air hugged my skin in goosebumps. "I hope you're not telling me my future, I've already spent enough time with wolves for one lifetime."

Rogue frowned, his gaze softening as it shifted to the moon. "The wolves no longer run these woods." He let out a long sigh. "But how I miss the sound of their howls in the night."

My arms folded nervously across my stomach, rubbing away the chill. Wolves were the last thing I needed feeding my imagination before bed.

"So you see memories then?" I asked, still unsure how one touch told him anything about me.

He admired the sky a moment longer before meeting my eyes again. "No. Not memories."

I shivered, wishing I'd missed his answer.

"It's why they sent me for her. For Sage. Why they bound me to her." He seemed lost in a daze. I wasn't sure if he spoke to me, or more himself. "I was the only one who could find her. All it took was a simple touch, and I would see a piece of her soul, I would know her blood."

"But you said you didn't want her to be taken... if you're the only one... did you tell them?" My heart started to pound.

"No. I tried to help at first, was willing to give my life to find Kia... I was Cosimo's soldier, the diligent hunter my king wanted me to be, and I almost succeeded. As a hunter, I can't ignore his orders. I used to care, and I worked so hard to follow."

"You said you *almost* succeeded? What happened?"

"I found her. Sila Thost."

"Sila? Sage's grandma? Wait. *you* killed her?" Alarm pumped through my veins as I thought of the years I'd known Sila. We all called her Nina, and she treated us girls all like kin.

"She killed me," he corrected. "Stabbed me straight through the heart."

"What?" I couldn't picture it.

"Kia's lineage has always been clever. They always knew how to hide, how to run. But Sila found her home, and she wasn't running anymore. That's when I truly caught up with them. That's when I learned about the blood bounty." Rogue shook his head.

"He wrote my fate in the blood of my wings. Tied me to their bloodline eternally. My gift is my curse. It's the only reason the new king wanted me, to become his puppet. Kia left him a prophesy, a promise, and he refused to lose the one hunter that could track her down to fix it. So he stuck me in this eternal loop. Everything was different after Sila, she made me see the truth, but ever since I found her, her bloodline draws me closer. I can't escape the pull of it." Rogue closed his eyes like he could shut out the past.

"I won't sit by and watch his son destroy the world I love, but he already sold my soul to one purpose... and I can't quit until the job is done. A constant battle with fate."

"The rogue hunter."

He nodded, his expression so haunted. "That's what they call me. I didn't care either way, at the beginning. It was the job. But then I met her. Sila. She was so strong, I felt it in her touch. She changed me. After a while, it wasn't about finding her so much as keeping her hidden. I became determined to leave her untouched by my world, only allowing myself to cross paths here and there. As long as she was still safe, I would leave her be. Then Sila was gone, and now May. She was left there all alone... Sage... and I just couldn't turn away."

"You found her," I whispered.

"I had to know for sure." He straightened. "One touch. I sensed all of that same strength that I felt in Sila. All it took was one touch. I saw how good she was. How warm. I wanted everything to stay exactly as it was... for her. Just like with Sila. It wasn't about finding her, it was about guarding her. Keeping her hidden. I wouldn't be the reason they found her, I refused to be the reason she died! She had to live."

"Then what happened?"

"There was another hunter. He was watching. He knew I found her... through me, he found her too."

' She wouldn't just go with—"

"I know him. We've crossed paths before. He played with her mind, turned me into the villain. Or maybe I did that myself, I'm not so sure. Either way, he got inside. He holds the gift of illusion. Tricks, really. He gave her exactly what she craved." Rogue shook his head, lip curling in disgust. "She was so lonely."

"We'd all left," I commented, knowing how worried she was about being forgotten. "She was so desperate for someone to come in and save her." My heart squeezed, realizing we all left her forsaken the week she needed us most.

"She just wanted a friend."

"This other hunter, he can make you see a lie." Rogue leaned into his knees, rubbing his forehead. "He'll lie her all the way to Echo's feet."

"What's the prophecy?" I asked. "The promise Kia left the new king?"

"A truce broken. Hunted, exiled, burned. Out of the shadows, a crown of blood and ash returned. A grave of secrets to be disturbed. The witch, the prince, the banished king, sealed by shattered glass, vengeance bring."

"The witch," I repeated.

"Sage," he confirmed.

"We'll get her back," I assured him, the roles switching between us. He was the strong one, the one with the plan. I'd known Sage my whole life, but he was the one that seemed to be breaking. Somehow it felt like he cared about her as much as I did.

"You found her before, you'll find her again! You're like her guardian angel."

He scoffed, hands falling as he sat back. "You mistake me for a hero."

"You can curse your gift all you want, but don't forget it led you to her. Without it, you would have never known

Sage Thost. And when we make this right, because we will, I'll make sure she knows you were the one tracking her down. Going against everything to save her. Your own blood. You are her guardian. Sila would be proud of you for fighting."

His head jerked back, his deep stare diving back into the fire. "You should get some rest," he said, cutting the conversation off there. "We have a long way to go tomorrow."

I gave in, seeing the pain he tried to hide shining brightly in his eyes. He pulled the blue ribbon from his pocket, rubbing his fingers over the smooth fabric.

"Okay," I agreed, moving to find a spot to sleep, when the large moon caught my eye. I paused, mind lost in its light. It wasn't the first time I'd stared. I watched it, my back on the ground, waiting for sleep. Something in my gut begged me to listen to it, like it expected something of me, like it was waiting... but for what?

50

HARPER

Something brushed against my arm, making me jolt. My head spun to find the red fox curling at my side. With a deep sigh, my head fell back to the ground, stifling a laugh so I wouldn't scare it off.

I looked across the lightly smoking fire from the night before, wondering how late Rogue stayed up to keep it burning after I fell asleep. My shoulder tingled, long before numbed against the rock beneath it. I gave in and sat up, grateful the fox remained calm beside me instead of racing back into the bushes.

A black dog watched me from the trees, dangling a notebook in its mouth. That strange journal that showed up in my pack. My teeth clenched with a glare.

"Hey!" I forcefully whispered, still trying to be quiet. I stepped over a large rock to reach for it, but it only triggered a game of keep away. The dog launched into the trees as I stumbled forward to catch myself instead of the book.

"Dang dog," I muttered, feeling the strangest sense of déjà vu as I braced against a tree to stand. He stopped a few feet ahead, mocking me with playful rivalry.

I looked around, wishing I had a treat to trade him. "Come here!" I called, trying to sound friendly. "Come on, buddy, come here!"

He set the book against the ground to adjust his grip. His head held low as I took a step forward, snatching it back up to bolt.

I ran after him angrily, swatting branches out of my way as I fought to keep up. I almost lost him in the shadows ahead when he stopped short, dropping the book for good. I knelt down, out of breath, gripping the spine tight so nothing would fall out if it hadn't already. Why did it seem like I'd been mad at this dog before? It was long gone now, leaving me alone with a large pond.

"Sage can save any dog she wants," I cursed under my breath as I stood, before yelling, "but she better not save you!"

I hugged the book to my chest, about to turn back, but something drew me in. The light ripple of water was soft and calm, a mesmerizing rhythm. I thought I caught the glimmer of something swimming closer beneath the pristine waves, a clear reflection of the starlight above, when the water shifted darker into a thickening stormy gray.

The waterline rose, slowly stretching toward me, calmly rising to meet my feet. I watched the dirtied tide roll over my shoe, hypnotized by the soft pull that carried my laces up against my shin. The water seeped in around my feet, warm and inviting as the shadows consumed it. I couldn't remember stepping in, and I wasn't worried about stepping out.

Two eyes shined darkly below the surface, watching me from beneath as the gray storm shifted to a charcoal ink. Something deep in my own reflection.

Something hit me from behind, scaring away the daze as

two arms wrapped around me to yank me back. The warm air dropped to ice. I fought to turn as Rogue tore me from the water, cold water puddling out of my shoes as he set me on my feet. He pulled me square in front of him, getting a close look inside my eyes. My focus bounced between his eyes and lips, trying to understand his questions under the pressure of his scrutiny.

"Did the water turn black?" he asked. "What were you thinking wandering off!" I barely caught the words on his lips in the chaos of it all.

"There was a dog," I answered, trying to catch my breath. "My notebook," I added, looking down in my hand, but instead of a book, I held a rock. The journal wasn't there. The fox paced back and forth, sniffing along the water's edge.

Rogue turned my jaw to face him, studying my eyes harder. "Something is playing tricks on you. You don't wander off anywhere without me, you hear me?"

Tricks? I gulped with a nervous nod. I didn't *hear* him, but I understood the threat. "I won't, I'm sorry."

"You're lucky that fox likes you," he said before stepping back. "Making such a fuss about you going in the water." His grip softened as he pulled my arm ahead of him to lead the way back.

I looked down at my new friend, surprised the fox cared at all. I'd have to give it another treat before we parted ways.

Rogue packed up camp quickly, ready to get moving again. I opened my backpack to make sure I had everything, when I noticed the same notebook, perfectly safe, right where I left it, and Rogue's warning sent a chill down my spine.

"Something is playing tricks on you."

I glanced through the trees, wondering what was out

there watching me. *Illusions. Tricks.* The dangers of this other world were feeling all too real.

"What happens if the water turns black?" I asked.

"Did it?" he asked, searching my face from across the cold fire pit.

"No," I lied a little too quickly. "You asked me before... if the water turned black."

He kicked away any trace we'd left in the dirt before he spoke, stopping to face me so I could read his lips more clearly.

"It's called the shadow pool. It's said to grant wishes. A long time ago, a king wished he could only give his best to his kingdom. Only the good. In doing that, he wished away his demons. His darkness. The pool claimed it all, stealing his shadow, leaving only what it deemed good." Rogue shook his head disapprovingly, a stern look in his eye.

"There is only good in the contrast of bad. After that, he just was. He is gone now, all of the good gone with him, but his demons remain, still living in that pool, waiting to collect more shadows."

I shuddered, grateful he hadn't told me this story before I'd gone to bed.

"Magically terrifying," I commented.

"There are many legends whispered over those dark waves. Beauty and terror, but nothing that is happy. A witch once believed that water could grant eternal life."

"What happened to her?"

"She disappeared. Was killed. There is great threat that lives in a rumor like that. The demons of that pool will never die. Her daughter was the only part of her left."

"Do you think there's any truth to it? Eternal life?" I imagined some fountain of youth. The idea that a drink or swim in its magic waves could make you stay young and beautiful forever, but sensed it would be much more complicated than that. Much darker.

"Maybe, but it's a dangerous game. All magic comes at a cost. If I'd been a moment later, that dark pool would have claimed your shadow too. Would that ever be worth the risk?" He shook his head. "Be careful what you wish for, you might pay for it with a piece of your soul."

I closed my eyes, turning away from him as a cold shiver spread higher.

The water had turned black... so did I just lose a piece of myself to the shadows?

51

WILLOW

I could barely lift my head, searching the blur around me.

"Zager?" My voice scratched the air. "What happened?"

I was meant to follow his lead, he promised to take me back, so where was I? I studied the door, confused by the bars. It looked like a prison cell.

I sat up quickly, back pressed against the wall as I took in the room more fully. I was still stuck in the other world, the magic world that didn't like humans. They must have discovered the sick girl trespassing through their forest.

Zager and Nazurin had been fighting. My fingers pressed into my temples, trying to remember. Fighting about Sam. My eyes flashed to the window, remembering how I'd just broken Nazurin's heart, lived through the pain of losing Sam all over again. This world was dangerous. I didn't belong here. Zager was supposed to keep me safe, but I was so sick! Trying to break free of the never ending pain! I only needed a moment of space, just a few breaths to compose myself... and then everything went dark.

My hands fell to the floor, silently pushing myself straighter against the stone wall, afraid to make a sound, afraid of who would come.

There was no way out, and I was too weak to fight, too weak to hold on. I didn't belong in this world, and it made it clear that it didn't want me in it. The magic had already rejected my blood, still pinching each breath. A curse spreading through my flesh from the inside out, all because of the metal in my leg. I was as caged by the metal inside as the metal bars in front of me, and together they would insure that I die on that grimy floor, stuck waiting on the inevitable with my long list of regrets.

Poor mom. I would have followed through on my promise, I'd finally been ready to commit. She would be so mad that I didn't show up, that I never called her back. Instead I pretended to be Sam, and now I'd disappeared completely. Now she'd lost us both.

If only I could go back. Go to the simple doctor appointment, visit the man so eager to step up and help me fight my battle. I just wanted to go back and live one more normal day, even if it was a sad normal. A fragile human normal.

My Sam charade landed me in a huge mess. I was never meant to be Sam. I wasn't fooling anyone. Not really. Two entire worlds rejected me, but this world would have loved her as much as ours did. It would have gladly offered her a full future if she chose it. But would she have chosen it?

Had a part of her already? Before?

An echo squeaked down the hall, interrupting my pity party as a door swung open. Were they coming to finish me off? My heart pounded as the footsteps grew closer, more than one set, sliding something along to ground.

"What do you want from me?" a girl demanded. "Why was he looking for me? What is the third piece? Piece of what!" The more she yelled, the more I recognized her voice, but it couldn't be—

Sage.

One guard shoved her against the door, while the other grabbed the key. Our eyes met through the bars and she froze, all demands gone silent.

"Recognize her, do we?" The man at her back was mocking. The second guard swung open the door and they tossed her in. She landed on her hands and knees, face up to hold my gaze, clearly trying to understand.

"Willow?"

My heart sank. She was asking. She had to think about it. Did her heart still see Sam when it looked into my eyes? Still holding onto the impossible in this other world? Begging for that second chance with a ghost?

"Hey Sage," I answered, watching as her tears flooded over.

She crawled over next to me and wrapped me in a hug, crying into my shoulder. I wasn't sure how she'd gotten wrapped up in this world with me, but we were together now.

"Good luck with that," the guard scoffed as they turned to leave. "She won't even survive the next moon." The truth in his words squeezed my heart tighter. He was right, I could feel myself fading.

"What is this place? Where are we?" Sage was frantic, each word a desperate cry at my neck. "Did the hunters bring you here because of me? I don't know what they want from me, I swear! I'm so sorry."

'Well I don't know anything about a hunter, and I have no idea why we're here... but I think I know the where. We're across the lines where magics mix."

She pulled her head back, looking in my eyes.

346

"What, like in Sam's poem?"

My lips pressed tighter with a grim nod. "Exactly like in Sam's poem." I started to cough, letting go of her to dry heave in the other direction.

"Willow?" Her voice was quiet with concern, pressing a supportive hand on my back.

"It's this world," I explained. "The magic... it rejects the metal plate in my leg. It's escalating my symptoms, trying to drive me out."

"How can I—" She stopped when I shook my head.

"You can't." The silence consumed me as I waited for her to understand. "There's nothing either of us can do. This world. It's killing me."

Her stare went blank, brows furrowing, like the words didn't connect. Like they couldn't be right.

"What? No! No, you can't just die—"

"I was already dy—"

"No! You're not just giving up! You're not allowed! That's not how this works!" Her tone became furious, demanding that I listen. "This is not the end, Willow. We're going to get you out of here."

Maybe she needed to tell herself that. To focus on saving me in order to save herself.

"Okay," I agreed, letting her win. I was too weak to fight it. Too weak to accept anything past each fading hour.

"Okay," she repeated, but her tone broke before leaning back into my shoulder, whispering it again to herself. "Okay."

She got up and moved to the front of the cell, grabbing the bars to shake, her eyes looking them up and down.

"They're spelled," she commented to herself, just loud enough for me to hear. "I feel it." She came back, practically falling into the spot next to me.

Her arm tucked in to hug my stomach, head on my shoulder. I wasn't a touchy-feely person by nature, but in that moment, I wasn't willing to give it up. I rested my head against her hair, soaking up the raw piece of friendship between us, a connection that I rarely let in, as two tears fell from my eyes to match hers.

She was so ready to protect me, to fight for my life. For a moment, I could give into her determination, could lean on it. For a moment, maybe I could dare to hope that somehow I might be saved too.

"Hey, Sage?"

"Yeah?" she whispered.

"I m sorry I didn't text you back."

The arm wrapped around me tightened for a split second, but then it relaxed. "I know."

STOLEN

52

AVA

My thumb trembled over the screen, staring at the phone number I'd typed in. What would I say? What would I ask? Would Mylo even be willing to talk to me? Was I even truly ready to talk to him?

The nightmare wasn't over yet. The edge of his small bite mark stuck out of my sleeve, reminding me of all the lies. The truth broke me out, but it never set me free. Somehow, I sensed he was still a part of this, a key that we needed.

My shaky thumb hit the call button, and I quickly cleared my throat, hoping it went to voicemail as I tried to pace off the empty feeling in my stomach.

"Hello?" His voice flooded me, warmth flushing my face. My heartbeat pounded against the silence. I let the word hang between us, like it could fill a void in my soul.

"Ava." He said it so calmly, the way he always spoke. He knew.

"Mylo." My mouth was dry, my brain stuck. I couldn't think of anything else to say.

"Are you okay?" he asked when I didn't offer more.

"Yeah, I'm... well." I sat on the log, leaning into myself. How did we move on? From the moment I woke up and the nightmare was him. From the sound of my voice ordering him to stay away from me.

"I made it back."

"Yes?" he gently prodded, always leaving it open for me to talk.

"But I'm sitting at... at *the line*," I admitted softly, eyes shifting through the trees to make sure I was alone.

"You should be far away from there," he warned, his voice deep, and stern.

"I know, but two of my friends... they're stuck in there. And another just went in to get them back... but I couldn't."

This time he was the one that went quiet. I didn't want the quiet, I wanted the sound of his voice to drive away my nerves. To tell me I was safe, that he was still there with me.

"I wondered... could you tell me more? About your world."

"I no longer belong to that world."

"But you did. Once." We both knew it was true.

"A long time ago," he countered. It was honest. He was giving me real answers now.

The plea trembled on my lips. "Please—" I thought of everything he'd done for me. A part of him still had to care. "As my friend?"

There seemed to be a wrestle behind the silence. He sighed. I could just imagine him sitting back in his chair as he gave in. "What is it you want to know?"

"That book," I started. "The one about the magic. It was about your world, wasn't it."

"A Hundred Tales of Magic."

"Yes." I thought of the pictures, trying to pick out something for him to talk about. "There was a castle in it. Was that your home?" I knew it wasn't. Somehow, through the magic, I'd seen his home. The memory of a little boy chasing his sisters through the twisted trees. A small cottage. The sound of his mother humming from the porch. That was his home... but I had to get him talking. I had to learn more.

"No," he answered. "Those grounds belonged to the shifters. A dear friend... in another life."

"Okay, well where do you fit into the story?" Nazurin told me Mylo might be a fae based on his gift, but I wanted to hear it from him. I thought of the story he told me, sleeping on his couch. The game of tag, the tawny fabric his mother hemmed all afternoon, the bright-eyed girl hiding behind the tree. What had become of that family? What happened to that little boy?

"I loved my life on the other side. I'd only left it a couple of times, and always hurried back. It was home."

"Why isn't it now?" I asked.

"Because I fell in love." My frame stiffened, head jerking back to frown at the phone. "I had everything there," he went on, "but I broke one simple rule, and for that, they took everything."

"What will happen to you if they close the gates?" I asked, dreading the answer, but I had to know. My question was met by silence. It seemed I'd caught him off guard.

"For years I've fed from the magic at the lines. The bits of that world that mix into this one. I crave it, and frankly, I wouldn't survive without it. I am not of this world. My magic was cut off, and the magic that keeps me here doesn't exist without those gates."

"So you would... die?" I stumbled over the word.

"Be careful," his tone lowered, making the hair rise on the back of my neck. "It would almost seem you care."

Ouch. His words were so serious, so unforgiving. "We

353

were friends once," I reminded him. "Even if it was short-lived."

"Yeah," he answered, but he didn't sound convinced. "Don't worry about me, Ava. They won't be able to close those gates. They've tried for a thousand years, let them try for a thousand more."

"Let them? Mylo—"

"I don't care what happens to that world. Not anymore."

"How can you not worry about it? They only need one p—"

Nazurin tumbled over the stones, rolling into the brush in front of me. He held his gut, a fresh cut under his lightly swelling eye.

"What happened!" I hung up and fell to my knees next to him.

"I couldn't..." he started to answer.

"You couldn't find her?"

"Pirates—" He could only get one or two words out between each heavy breath. "They—"

I straightened back on my knee. "Pirates? Where are my friends?" I waited, but he didn't answer. "You have to help me get them back!" He shut his eyes, turning his face away in defeat.

"What!" I demanded. "What are you hiding!" I shoved at his arm. He rolled, coughing into the dirt as he tried to push himself up.

"They took it," he dryly spat out.

"What? They took what?"

He gave in, looking into my eyes, and realization struck.

"The mirror," I answered for him, and he didn't correct me. "No!" I refused to believe it was gone. "No, you just went in there! We have to go get it back, they can't be far!"

"I was in there longer than that." He shook his head. "Time passes differently on that side of the line. And we are outnumbered."

I wanted to fight harder, but I couldn't figure out how. I fell back on my pockets, hugging my knees to my chest as I tried to process. "They have the last piece. They can close the gates now."

He sat up too, leaning against the trunk behind him. So many people that I cared about had just been jeopardized.

"My friends are still in there," I worried out loud, not mentioning anything about Mylo. "How long do they have?"

"The full moon," he answered. "If he truly has everything, there's no stopping it now. If they're not out by then, they'll be stuck in there forever."

53

HARPER

The forest was all starting to look the same to me. We could have been walking in circles for all I knew, but Rogue moved steadily along, calm and sure in his path. He glanced back, rolling his eyes at the fox trailing behind me.

"What!" I followed his gaze. "Oh, come on, how can you turn this away!" I picked it up, as if the cuteness would explain itself. "I didn't ask it to follow me."

"The breadcrumbs you dropped sure did," he countered turning ahead again.

My chin tucked in, trying to hide the laugh. "He wasn't supposed to see that," I whispered between two pointy red ears, petting the fox before setting it back on its feet.

Rogue slowed against a tree, scoping out the path ahead. As I caught up, I saw the shaded stone wall, covered in thick moss. He pressed a finger to his lips, and I nodded.

No more games, it was time to be serious.

We skirted the edge of the wall until Rogue found a laddering path of holes in the stone, sliding his fingers inside to start the climb. Had he done this before?

I stared at the top of the wall, wondering what waited for us on the other side. My fingers gripped the smooth handle, wishing it was deeper as I watched Rogue's boots climbing effortlessly above me. I'd made it this far, no turning back now.

My stomach twisted as I followed him up, the same sensation I got climbing a ladder to hang Christmas lights, but we had to keep moving.

Rogue practically merged with the shadows, making it hard to follow him in and out of hallways and paths. Every move he made so stealthily, I dreaded the moment I got us caught.

I kept checking the halls around me, making sure nobody followed. Not being able to hear was causing paranoia. Someone could turn a corner at any time and I would never see it coming. If only we had a map, but all I had was Rogue, and I'd put my life in his hands. All I could do was trust him to get me there.

Someone squeezed my arm, yanking me back. My hand flew to my chest with a gasp. I glared at the guard's face, questioning me with words I couldn't hear.

"—shouldn't be here, how did you get in?" he asked.

My mouth opened to answer, but I didn't know what to say.

His eyes shifted over my shoulder as another hand grabbed my other arm. My head tilted back at an angle to see Rogue standing behind me, calmly speaking to the guard.

I couldn't read his lips from that angle, turning back towards the guard.

He smirked. "Is that so? I'm sure Echo will be thrilled to learn that you've brought him his witch. Let's go find him, shall we?" I couldn't hear his tone, but there was a challenge in his expression.

I tried to resist, pulling my arm back, but the guard refused to let go, yanking me toward a tall arching door. Rogue held the other side more gently, slowly letting go as he shifted behind me.

The guard walked forward to lean into the door, when something shattered against the back of his head. His body fell limp to the stone floor, surrounded by the same broken shards of glass now caught in my hair.

Rogue didn't hesitate, reaching to squeeze my hand before pulling me down another hall.

He scanned each opening and window as we passed, keeping our pace swift until he reached the final door. He looked through it, then back at me, when he noticed the glass fragments still stuck in my tangled hair. He quickly brushed them off, before pushing my hair behind my shoulder.

"Come on," he said, turning back towards the open door. "They'll be holding her this way."

We moved together quickly, until he saw the cells, and held up a hand to stop me.

"Wait here," he mouthed.

I peeked around the corner just enough to watch him sneak through the shadows toward two more guards. Rogue yanked the first guard off his feet as I startled back behind the corner to stay hidden, waiting a few seconds before I leaned around again to peek. Rogue lowered the second guard's head to the floor, then searched his pocket for the key.

He tipped his head up to find me, waving me closer. I walked quickly, joining him in front of a barred door, veering straight for it. My face pressed impatiently into the bars, searching for my friends.

Two girls sat huddled together in the corner. My mouth opened to talk, but Rogue quickly caught my shoulder, pulling me back. I spun around as he gave me a wide-eyed look, holding a finger to his lips. I nodded, shifting out of the way so he could unlock the door.

I leaned in closer. "It's Sage!" I quietly insisted, trembling impatiently as he twisted the key. Sage sat on the floor, huddled over another person at her side.

"Sage!" I whispered, pushing through when he got the door open.

Sage's head jerked back, finding my eyes as water pooled in hers across the room, heavy circles below them. Her hand covered her mouth, as the other braced the floor so she could stand up.

Then I saw the weak face leaning against the wall behind her, and I froze.

Sam? My heart squeezed. The thought alone hurt too much. Sage threw her arms around me as I stared at the face behind her. Why couldn't my brain just accept that Sam was gone, and leave it in the past? This girl couldn't be Sam. It had to be—

"Willow?"

I pulled back, looking into Sage's eyes. Her silent sobs and quivering chin broke my heart.

"We're going to take you home," I swore.

Her hand let go and flew to her face, half covering it as she cried her next words. I softly grabbed her wrist and pulled it down.

"I can't hear you," I explained. She looked at my ears and nodded her understanding. "It's going to be okay, though. Rogue is going to get us out of here. I never would have found you without him."

I stepped out of the way as she looked past me to Rogue, but she didn't seem surprised to see him.

"And you?" Sage stood in place, tilting her head back a bit. "Do you have something to say?"

My eyes flew to Rogue, wanting to see what he answered.

"What do you want me to say?"

My eyes bounced back to Sage again.

"I don't know," she shrugged. "Maybe I told you so." He was silent, staring at her from across the cell.

"I told myself that when I found you, I'd rope your wrist to mine." My eyes widened at the threat behind his words, but he didn't move an inch. "Now I'm afraid if I get any closer, you'll disappear again."

My eyes flickered between the two of them, wondering what all had happened before.

"I'm sorry," she answered. She stepped closer to him. "I shouldn't have run."

He nodded, accepting her apology.

She was trying to hold strong, but her expression got sadder as she started to tremble.

"I knew you would come for me." She nearly crumbled into him as Rogue caught her, holding her up on her feet against him. He seemed to be processing it before pressing his cheek to her hair. Sage shook against him, breaking down completely.

I moved toward Willow, falling to my knees to pull her closer. Her response was weak, brows furrowing as she looked into my face. I wanted to squeeze her tight, this run over version of my dead best friend.

"Harper?" Her eyes were only half-open, and my arms strained with worry.

Rogue met my eyes from across the room, like it were hitting us both that we still had a long way to go. Then his eyes shifted to Willow. He frowned when he saw her, almost like he was surprised, giving her face some extra study behind the dirt. Had they met before?

Sage turned her face out to look too, her sad eyes falling to the floor when she saw Willow.

"She won't make it much longer."

"What's wrong with her?" I asked, grateful when Sage shifted closer, Rogue right behind her.

He was still studying Willow's face, hesitant, before reaching out to cup her cheek. His eyes shut to focus, using his gift to see her soul more clearly. When he let go, his head shook defeatedly.

"What is it?"

He gave me a grave expression. "Dead blood."

My brows drew together, looking from him, to Sage, to Willow. "What does that mean?"

"She won't make it." He always tried to meet my eyes when he spoke, but this time he avoided them, ready to turn away. "I can't help her."

"No," I argued. "We're not going without her."

Willow weakly squeezed my hand in her lap. I searched her face, so thinned and pale. "You have to leave me." She paused to swallow. "I'm already dying."

"No," I fought. "You're not dead yet."

I looked at Rogue, Sage leaning in at his shoulder. My eyes met hers, and she nodded, her expression as resolute as mine.

"We all go," she declared, and I'd never been more

proud of three little words. I wiped away the tear threatening to fall down my cheek, ready to be just as stubborn.

"Or we don't go," I agreed.

Rogue looked Willow over again before his face fell to the floor. His eyes shut tight, like he was trying to think it through. Once again my life was in his hands, all of our lives, because none of us were getting out of there without him.

"I was prepared to rescue one," he commented, shaking his head in frustration. "Now there are three."

I reached for his hand and squeezed. "You've gotten us this far."

"I work alone," he fought.

"You used to work alone," I corrected. "Now you have us... and your new friends really need your help."

He looked from me to Sage, losing himself in her eyes. She softly dropped her forehead into his cheek, and his jaw clenched beneath it. He let out a sigh, sending me a side eye, and a subtle nod.

"Okay, let's go."

54

HARPER

The journey out was much slower moving than the trip in. Rogue's patience was being tried as Willow wrapped one arm over him, and the other over me. All three of us girls stumbled to keep up, tucking nervously down behind trees when Rogue motioned to hide.

The dim evening sky hid us enough to move through more crowded paths, shuffling through the other faces unseen. They didn't notice us, but it was hard not to stare at them. The creatures of this world were so different than at home.

We turned a corner, when Rogue jerked us back, searching the path we'd just stepped out of.

"What is it?" I asked.

Rogue shook his head, turning back down the side street. "Nothing. I thought I saw someone. A hunter I used to train. He... disappeared."

"Well he's probably pretty good at that if you trained him," I answered, trying to ease his mind. Isn't that what the great rogue hunter specializes in?

The blanket of shading branches welcomed us back as we traded the kingdom for the forest. I'd never been so grateful to get lost in the trees.

"Will we climb back up the rocks?" I asked.

"No," Rogue answered. "Not like this, we won't make the trek over. We'll have to go around."

Rogue kept us on course for another hour before he let up, taking the first of many short breaks. The three of us girls were depending on him fully. Nobody talked, our only goal to escape and make it home. We moved slowly until the sun rose, then pushed with everything we had until it sank again, keeping our breaks minimal. Nobody argued when Rogue gave us the go-ahead, trying to find a balance between running and hiding.

Rogue threw a hand up, and the three of us froze behind him. He didn't move, waiting to see what happened when I noticed the guard shifting through the brush ahead. Rogue turned just enough to hold a finger to his lips.

"Stay here," he mouthed. Sage and I both nodded at him as we held Willow between us.

Rogue crept off to the side, low and calm, until both men were out of sight. Time seemed frozen, the three of us locked in place. Sage jumped, her head snapping to the path behind us, eyes wide. I followed her gaze, spotting the second guard combing through the forest.

Sage looked at me, and we both nodded, before pulling Willow to her feet and pushing deeper into the trees. Sage led the way, zigzagging through the trees and brush as we sank lower down a hill. I nervously searched behind us, unable to hear if he followed, when Sage tugged my arm.

She pulled out a small pouch, pouring some sand into her hand, then threw it at my forehead.

"Hey!" I grumbled, when she scolded me with a glare,

her eyes flashing angrily behind me. "Sorry," I mouthed. She dumped out more sand and threw it at Willow. The last of it went into her hair, when she let go, looking me in the eyes.

"Spin," she mouthed, then she quickly turned in a circle and disappeared.

My mouth dropped, fingers squeezing Willow tighter as we waited to understand. Then a hand I couldn't see grabbed my arm and pulled me up, forcing me to turn too. I looked down at my body, still completely visible, when the guard stepped across my view and I crouched back down.

The guard slowed, but as he scanned the forest, his gaze glazed right past us. A hand still held my arm tight as we waited, though I wasn't sure if it was Sage or Willow. My body sank as he slipped away, leaving us alone again.

None of us moved, waiting for something, anything that told us what to do next. I pulled a loose paper from my backpack and wrote a note.

> *Rogue told us to wait there. Shouldn't we go back?*

I set the pen and paper down, waiting for one of them to answer.

> *We'd just get more lost. It's Rogue. If we stay put, he'll find us.*

I stared at Sage's response, letting out a sigh. She was right. I'd watched him track her down before, he would do it again.

The fingers that held my arm squeezed tighter, pulling me back a bit. It was frustrating not being able to see them on top of not being able to hear. I searched the trees, trying to figure out what the person next to me was reacting too.

Something dark crept low through the brush, studying the ground. They inched closer until they were a few feet away, and stood up. Rogue searched the trail in front of us, and the arm holding mine let go. He stumbled back a step, dropping his bow as something dove into him, hugging the girl he couldn't see.

"Sage," he said. His hand cupped the back of her head to his chest, just as the dark brown strands started to show again. Her arms wrapped around him tight as she grew visible. Willow let her head fall into my shoulder as we came back too.

"That was too close," Rogue muttered. "I led them away, but we need to move."

My feet rubbed raw against my shoes when Rogue finally called it quits, picking our spot to camp for the night. Willow let go to sit on a log, as I fell against a tree and sighed, relieved for the break. I made my way over, sandwiching Willow between myself and Sage as Rogue set down the two small rodents he'd caught, and made a fire.

"He never stops," I joked, grateful to be back with friends. Who would have thought one week could feel so long. "Just a few days ago we were sitting on the couch eating popcorn."

"Take me back," Willow grumbled. "Is anyone going to find us here?"

Rogue shook his head. "Not here. I know every path through this forest. We'll be safe here."

I studied Sage, sitting there so silently. Her face covered

in dirt, and pain. She stared at the ground ahead, looking so lost.

Willow leaned back, reaching into the bush behind us. She plucked something off, spinning forward to get a better look at the deep red berry.

I smacked it out of her hand. "Don't eat that," I ordered, remembering what Rogue taught me.

He watched from across the lightly smoking pit, looking a bit caught off guard when he gave me a nod, and a hint of pride shined through. I laughed at myself for acting up so strongly, letting my muscles relax a bit more.

"Here," I offered instead, digging into my bag for a protein bar. They'd always grossed me out, but it seemed like a smart thing to pack for a rescue mission.

Willow was quick to accept, tearing the wrapper in half. I smiled, glad to have helped, when I noticed Sage again, still staring blankly into the same spot, a haunted look in her eye.

"You know, on our way here, I made friends with a fox," I told them. Willow's eyes widened at me mid-bite.

"You held it?" she asked, holding a hand up to cover the food in her mouth.

I nodded, a polite smile plastered on my face to hide how concerned I was that an animal rescue story hadn't broken down Sage's wall.

"It was so cute. If it shows up again I told Rogue he has to let Sage keep it."

A forced breath shot through Sage's nose, her only response as her eyes dropped down into her lap, hugging her arms over her chest.

My eyes flickered to Rogue, who noticed it too, still sitting on the ground across from us. He shrugged at me, dropping the stick he'd been using to draw lines in the dirt, pulling himself up to take the spot next to her.

Pain strained her face the closer he got, like she couldn't hold her composure any longer. The moment he sat down she fell into him completely. He hesitated, staring down at her, then wrapped both arms around her, soaking in that moment. His hands were so gentle, his gaze on her like he was still processing it. Then he looked past Willow, content just eating her protein bar, to me.

He'd gone on this grand mission to save Sage, but she was still going to need him when this was over.

Sage remained tucked into Rogue's chest as he filled them in on why this was happening, the prophecy that had them hunting Sage's blood.

I didn't pay close attention, tired of reading people's lips. Rogue had already told me all about this world's history. As I sat in silence, admiring his world, that's when it hit me that it was Sage's world too. She was catching up on her own history. My best friend, the witch.

I focused on the sky, the moon so bright and full above us, barely a sliver left to fill. My gaze locked in on it, imagining the wolves Rogue mentioned before, the ones that used to howl through the night. I imagined the sound of it, like I could almost hear it somewhere out there, far away.

I love you, Sam. If only you were here.

If only I could see her ghost sitting next to me. She had to be watching over us. I'd never wanted to be haunted more.

I stared at the berry I'd knocked to the ground, that same déjà vu feeling creeping back in. Something nagged at my mind, it had been since I woke up from that strange dream. Josh's gold coin. I'd asked him about it, when the two of us sat alone, awkwardly on Benny's couch.

"Do you still keep it tucked in your wallet?"

He had a weird expression on his face when he looked at me. *"No, I, uh... I lost it a while back."*

I nodded, but wasn't so sure I believed him. That lucky coin was too important to him, too sentimental. Too safely tucked away. He hadn't lost it, he'd offered it with a piece of his heart. He'd come looking for me.

My eyes fell to the trees. We'd gotten pretty far, back on the border of fae territory. Back on the Mella Marsh that skirted between their lands. We'd followed it to the kingdom, traveling the edge of those haunted woods. Why were they so haunted again?

A lost prince. A castle burned to ash.

The shadows pulled me in, like a whisper, calling my name, begging me to come closer.

Come back.

A glimpse of a dream that I could only see pieces of. Something flashed through the dark brush ahead. A shadow. I could feel it, lurking beneath the darkness, watching me from afar. It wanted something, and my gut told me to listen.

Hadn't I chased after enough ghosts already?

I waited for the nagging to stop, the pull of something beyond my reach, but it dug deeper.

My heart pounded as I watched Willow find a spot on the ground to turn in. Sage was close behind her, whispering something to Rogue before she rested on her side. Rogue sat next to her, his fingers brushing the hair back from her face, when he looked up at me.

I wiped my hands against my pants before folding them over my stomach, rocking back and forth in my seat. He was on full watch mode now. He got Sage back and he wasn't going to let her out of his sight until she was safe across the line.

I waited for my opening, when he got up to stretch and feed the fire. As soon as he turned into the tree line, I adjusted his backpack and the thin blanket I'd packed to make it look like I was sleeping next to Willow, then slipped out of camp the opposite way.

Stepping deeper into the thick forest brush, I searched for the dog. I knew this ghost, we'd met before. It flashed across the trees, pausing only slightly to meet my eyes before it dashed ahead. Another layer of déjà vu hit me hard. I'd followed this dog before, this wolf.

I chased after it, eager to see where it led. It wasn't a trick. It couldn't be a trick. My soul could feel it calling, and I was meant to follow.

My skin stung as I stumbled forward, slamming into a thorn bush. My hands hesitated against the prickle, staring at the dark berries bunched together around them. Again, I knew I'd seen those berries before, even before meeting Rogue. I wasn't meant to eat them. Someone got mad. A fallen pot of soil, smashed against the floor.

I stood back up, wiping the dirt off my pants as I searched the forest ahead. Something was waiting for me. I wasn't giving up.

The thick tree line broke, blocked by a wall of stone. I circled it slowly, trying to remember how I knew it, how I could already sense what waited on the other side... because I'd been there before.

The stone wall ended, replaced by towering metal bars. My fingers wrapped around them, my face leaning into the cold fence as the familiar view opened up in front of me.

Shane's Manor.

55

SAGE

Y ou'd think after being woken up for a prison break, and hiking through the forest for hours since, I'd pass out, but my mind was racing. The hurricane of emotions that had ripped through me left me empty. The anger, the panic, the pain. I'd been drowning in it, and a big part of me had shut down completely.

It was easier to pretend I was sleeping and process alone. Too much had happened. I'd been kidnapped and dragged into a nightmare. What was with this world and the strange people in it? Witches and fae? Illusions, spells, birds that attacked if you ran? Berries that gave you nightmares? A shadow pool that could steal half your soul?

No, thank you. This world could keep its prophecy and count me out. I didn't want any part in it. I couldn't wait to pack up my life and hide far from the lines on the other side. Not that there was much of a life to go back to.

And then there was Rogue, going against everything to save me. I should have listened to him. I was so sure he was the hunter Nina warned me about, and maybe he was.

Maybe she didn't know. But all he'd done was try to help, and I'd just made things harder.

Every time I dozed off to sleep, fear startled me out of it. Worries about what was next, worries about the creatures that might come looking for me again. My head jerked off the ground, searching the camp until I found Rogue. He shifted the wood in the fire before coming to sit next to me on the dirt. His fingers softly brushed my hair back. I reached for his hand, pulling it in front of my face, squeezing both hands around it like I could hide in it forever, curled up tightly on the ground.

Teeth softly chattered behind me. Willow was shivering in her sleep.

I sighed softly, meeting Rogue's eyes above me. Neither of us smiled, a sense of understanding between us before he let go. I stiffly spun over to face Willow, wrapping my arm around her, grateful Rogue's leg remained pressed along my back. A simple touch worth so much comfort.

Willow put a hand over mine in silent thanks. I wished I could do more. I was supposed to be a witch, but what good was that if I couldn't help a friend? I'd never had magic. I tried to sense something deep inside, to pull at whatever energy was there, but I just couldn't find it.

"You okay?" I asked her, resorting to friendship.

"I should have never walked away," her voice filled with regret. "If I'd stayed with Zager... he would have had me home by now. I'm just slowing the rest of you down."

"Yeah, but this way you give me something to fight for."

"I'm not worth the effort," she said through a shiver. "I'll die before we get there."

"Willow!" My head jerked off the ground, frowning at her from behind. "Of course you're worth it. You're our friend!"

"I'm not," she argued. "Not really."

I pushed up onto my elbow, pulling her shoulder softly to face me. "Sam wasn't the only thing that connected us. You know that right?" I should have said it months before, made sure she understood.

There was a raw pain in her eyes, different from all the physical pain she'd endured.

"You're a part of our group too, Willow. Our family. You always were. I'd stand by you as much now as I would have a year ago. Sick in a hospital bed, or in the dirty prison of another world, we're a team."

She nodded, accepting my rant. "Okay," she agreed.

I snuggled back in, pulling at the edge of Harper's blanket. "We'll get home, you'll see. We escaped that prison, and we're not going back."

"Never," she weakly agreed.

Rogue's leg tensed behind me. "Where's Harper?" He stood up quickly, pulling the thin blanket out of his way.

He cursed under his breath, spinning to search the trees around us. Willow and I sat up to see too, when he tossed the blanket back down to me. "Don't move!" he ordered, running into the woods.

I pulled up the blanket, readjusting it nervously as my last thread of comfort disappeared.

"We escaped that prison," croak.

I froze, staring at the talking blanket, then to Willow, who was just as stunned. Its voice sounded just like mine. I shook the blanket out as a toad fell into my lap, two eyes staring at us from both sides of its face.

"And we're never going back."

Our blood-curdling screams blended harshly through the air as we threw everything off and climbed over the fallen log behind us, wiping frantically at our clothes. The toad hopped off in the corner of my eye, camouflaging through the leaves as Rogue barreled back in.

"What!" he demanded, scanning the small camp. "What is it!"

I pointed at the ground. "There!" I insisted. "A toad! It was talking!" I shook out my hands as Willow's full body braced against a tree from falling.

"Dizzy?" I reached for her shoulder as she nodded, taking even breaths.

"Where did it go?" Rogue asked.

"Somewhere over there." I pointed again, but couldn't see it. "I think it's gone now, but it went that way."

"An echo toad. They live all the way up and down the Melle Marsh. They'll repeat anything you tell them."

"It sounded just like me!"

"It was just an echo," he assured me. "What did it say?"

"It repeated what I told Willow... about escaping and never going back."

Rogue rubbed the back of his neck, then looked up at the sky. "Someone will have heard that scream. We don't have time."

My shoulders sank. "I'm so sorry."

"We need to go," he said, picking up the things we'd thrown. He looked around, checking mental boxes.

"What about Harper?" I asked.

He didn't meet my eyes, holding them low.

"Where would she go?" Willow asked, her face still half-planted against the tree trunk.

I shook my head, a sinking feeling pulling me down as I watched Rogue's frustration grow. He was the calm collected one... if he was losing it, we were really in trouble.

"So much for working together," his husky voice growled, kicking a rock across the dirt. I was desperate to help, desperate to give him some kind of answer, but I didn't know what to say. He started searching the ground around our camp, focusing on tracks.

"Here," he commented, pointing through the trees.

"She was so off in her own head all night," I commented, trying to think back. It seemed out of character for Harper, but then again, she usually had her hearing aids. "While you were talking about the prophecy, she was busy staring at the moon."

His eyes shot to the moon before falling to the thick shadowed trees ahead of him.

"The Haunted Woods," he commented, like something had clicked inside his head. "When I touched her, I saw wolves."

"You think she went in there alone? But why would she?"

"We were playing cards. She told me pieces of a story, said she was lost in a dream. A burned castle. A wolf. An hourglass." His head shook. "I didn't think anything of it at the time, but now? It can't be."

"What?"

"Elijah," he coarsely answered. "The lost prince. I think she's gone after him." He kicked dirt into the fire, starting to put it out. "I told her not to wander!"

"I thought the shifters were all dead."

"Well either she's found him, or someone's messing with her."

"We have to go find her."

"We have to get you out of here!" he argued.

"I can't leave," I spat out in a panic. It was a lie, the first thing that came to mind, but I was desperate for him to listen.

"What do you mean?" he demanded.

"Until the full moon. I'm bound to this world. I can't leave." He had to save Harper, I wasn't going back without her.

"Why didn't you tell me that before?"

"I thought by the time we got to the line it would be close enough."

"Sage!"

"We still have time, promise me you'll help Harper too! I'm begging you, I won't leave her behind."

His eyes darkened, taking in my pleas. "I don't need to promise you, I've already sworn it to Ava, and Harper... and myself."

My bones chilled as he spoke, knowing without a shadow of doubt I could trust this man with everything I had.

"You should leave me," Willow coughed out.

"No," Rogue answered. "We'll get you to the line—"

"No," Willow forced out with a pained sigh. "It's too important. You can't waste any time. Go find her before it's too late. I'll stay hidden, just bring her back."

Rogue caved, unwilling to waste another moment. "I might know a spot, and it's on the way." He paced toward her, cradling Willow into his arms, then gave me a stern look before moving on.

I held up a hand in surrender, remembering his threats about roping our wrists together. "Consider me bound at your side."

Whether it was good enough or not, it was all he had to go on. He nodded, shifting toward the dark shadowed trees, and I reached for the back of his shirt, squeezing a handful of the fabric. Whatever came next, I wasn't letting go.

BROKEN

56

AVA

He lost the third mirror. The gates were closing.

Shock disconnected me from my body. I stared numbly into the distance, trying to make sense of it all. My friends were stuck in there, I was going to lose them forever. I was going to lose Mylo!

I stood, turning slowly as my phone screen lit up from the leaves, the familiar unsaved number written across it.

How could I answer it? How could I face him? A thousand years, and it ended with me.

"How could I be so stupid?" I whispered, breaking free from the silence that closed me in. Nazurin stared at me, still kneeling on the ground, equally lost.

I pointed a finger at him, ready to ram it into his chest. "You delivered the last piece right to them! My friends!" Then I crumbled. "And I let you go, because I was scared."

"It's not your—"

"Don't!" I ordered, my resolve growing stronger again. "Don't you dare do that. It is my fault. Sage is going to die! And Willow! Harper will be trapped in there alone!" I turned to face the circle of stones, determined to make it right.

"I'm going in."

"Ava!" Nazurin pushed to his feet. "Stop! Think about this! You can't just run in there blind without a plan."

"How can you stand there and say that?" I countered. "I have no time! I won't wait around, not anymore. This has already gotten too messy. I've crossed the lines before."

"And you came back a different person." The words were dry and harsh. "You just risk getting yourself stuck too."

I sent him an even stare. "I'd rather be stuck in there with the three of them for trying, than stuck out here without them because I didn't."

His jaw shut tight, the fight over. He nodded. "Okay."

"Okay?"

"Yes. But you still need a plan."

My breath held, brows raising. "You'll help me?" In the corner of my eye my phone went dark against the leaves. I gave in and picked it up, adding up the times Mylo had tried to call me back after I hung up on him. The phone started to vibrate again and I sighed. There were still a few more things I needed to ask.

"Ava," Mylo said as soon as I accepted. "What happened?"

"The last mirror." I wanted to keep cool, but the words spilled out. "They have it! They took the third piece! They're going to kill my friend! I have to help, but what can I do? You have to tell me how to—"

"Ava, slow down, you're not going back in there—"

"Yes I am," I sternly fought.

"They won't be able to close the gates."

"Didn't you hear me? They have the third piece!"

"They can't!" he shouted back. He always remained so calm that it caught me off guard.

"What do you mean?" I asked evenly, barely holding myself together. The call died in my ear.

"They don't have the last piece," Mylo answered. I spun around, finding him through the trees. He held up a small, silver-cased mirror to show me. "They can't... because it's right here."

"Mylo— How are you— What—"

"I just had to see that you made it home." His eyes flickered briefly over my shirt, a subtle curve in his lip. My cheeks warmed, realizing that after telling him I never wanted to see him again, I'd just been caught wearing his sweater.

My hands rubbed together reflexively pulling the sleeves tighter again. I frowned, head flinching when I turned toward Nazurin.

"You—" I was pointing again, blaming him for this mess. "You lied?"

"No," he stuttered. "No, well, I—"

"What did you do?" I demanded. "You said they had the other two."

Mylo walked up behind me, Nazurin cowering back a step when their eyes met over my shoulder.

"Okay, yes," he confessed. "They had two."

"Two of three," I confirmed.

His eyes flickered to Mylo with a gulp, his hands flying up to brace the sides of his head. "I broke it!" he blurted out. "My brother's piece, I broke it! A long time ago. I created a fourth piece."

"You what?" My voice rose higher, leaning back. "Why? You hate their world! Why didn't you just say that!"

"I—" His shoulders sank. "My home... my brother. I

couldn't lose him forever..." He swallowed again, choking on the words. "And Sam... I could never live there again, not without her... but I never wanted to lose the bits of her that I feel there."

"That explains the other portal," Mylo interrupted. "The fourth line in Alaska. I sensed its magic, but I never understood the connection. It was never one of the three. One of the originals. That's how you stumbled in through one and out of another so close, but so far away from home." Mylo shook his head. "Nobody else knows it's there. I'll admit I rather enjoyed the quiet."

"A fourth piece," I repeated, still watching Nazurin as I absorbed his secrets. My head shook. "But Echo doesn't know that. He'll still kill Sage, he thinks he has the last piece!"

"He'll only be madder," Nazurin agreed in a hushed tone.

I looked back at Mylo. "My friends are all in there." I spun around to face him fully, still holding the mirror at his side. Who was this man?

"Gifts given with a truce," I commented, admiring the smooth silver frame. But how did he have it? "You said you were cut off for falling in love," I went on. "You're him. You're the fae king. The one that created the truce and split the portal. The one that fell in love with the witch."

A consuming silence sat between us, the truth reflecting in his eyes.

"You had the last piece all along."

"The first piece," he countered quietly. "I created the mirrors."

"I have to go in there," I whispered, knowing he wanted me to stay away.

"I know," Mylo answered, taking a step back. "You're

not the type to sit back and wait. right? Not even when you forgot who you were. You had to act. It's who you are."

I couldn't speak, consumed by the raw truth in his words.

"I won't stop you." He held the mirror up between us. "It will portal you closer to the slab. Maybe it's just the bargaining chip you need."

"No," I refused, pushing his hand down. "It's the only thing that guarantees the lines stay drawn! You can't risk your lif—"

"I risk nothing!" His tone made me jump, mouth snapping shut. "I should have died a long time ago," he argued, his voice still firm. "So many years I waited for the end. I've already lived my lifetimes, Ava. You've only just started yours."

"But I only just met you," I softly whined.

"I know," he answered more gently, his half-smile inching empathetically into his cheek. His spare hand softly grabbed my wrist, twisting it up as he transferred the mirror into my palm. He cubbed both hands beneath mine before curling his fingers over to close mine around the cool metal.

"But you need them more," he finished.

He let go and I pulled the mirror in, close to my heart, knowing he gave up everything trusting me with it.

"I can't go with you, but Oculo will guide you home," he hesitated. "She's been my only companion for a long time now. Look after her, won't you?" There was a painful permanence behind his words, squeezing at my heart. He gave her to me in hopes she could help, but also in case the gates closed and he wouldn't survive.

He slid a vial of crimson liquid from his pocket. "If you truly need me, my blood will link us. Until the gates close."

"I'm not going to let that happen," I answered stubbornly.

"I know," he said, but there was a sad note in his voice.

"Kia," I started. "After she burned down the castle, she went into hiding—"

"Burned down?" His forehead strained. "That wasn't her. She loved the shifters, she would never have... she was the one who spelled their prince! Saved their bloodline!"

"Saved them... then who?" I asked, eyes bouncing between him and Nazurin to see what I'd missed.

Nazurin seemed just as confused, hanging onto every word. "How can you be so sure?"

Mylo shook his head. "I was not there, but Oco has remained a loyal friend."

"Your eyes," I clarified.

He nodded. "It was Cosimo that burned down those castle walls. It wasn't the first time he'd killed." His jaw flexed, voice lowering in anger. "He was always jealous, runner up in a long-lived line. I led the kingdom, Shane led the packs, and Kia led the covens. Things shifted when we created that truce, and he was eager to find the cracks, to fight his way to power. First he took my sister, fallen for the shifter prince."

"Beau," Nazurin commented. "Shane's oldest son. I read about him." Something seemed to click inside his mind. "And Briell."

"Brie," Mylo corrected. "A marriage to Beau would have put them both next in line after I was gone." His expression softened, eyes haunted by pain. "Two lives lost. Killed over a love so deep. You know the stories the way they wanted you to know them." Mylo's eyes flashed to Nazurin, uncovering more truth.

"Kia fled, but not before she went back to say goodbye.

Shane was a dear friend of ours. But she was too late. The castle had burned. His unconscious son lay in the field, all that was left of their pack. She tied him to both worlds, binding him and his moon to those grounds where they couldn't be touched until it was time."

"The witch, the prince, the banished king," Nazurin commented in a mused tone. "Out of the shadows. A crown of blood and ash returned. A grave of secrets disturbed. Sealed by shattered glass. Her prophecy, her warning to the new king."

"Not a warning," Mylo corrected. "A promise."

"If the gates close—"

"It would cut off the connection," Mylo finished for him. "It would kill the lost prince."

"This was never about walling apart two worlds," Nazurin said. "It's about claiming his throne once and for all. Banishing you? Killing the Thost witch? Cutting off the last shifter? All to remove those who still stand to take their power back!"

"Any truce we had before, dies with those gates," Mylo confirmed. "The prophecy expires. It's the only thing that stands against him. If he seals the glass, he seals his fate."

"We have to go." Nazurin stood eagerly, facing the line, but I looked back up into Mylo's eyes.

"Did she ever find you?" I asked. "Kia." Had his story truly ended in tragedy? Or had he gotten back a piece of that happily ever after?

His gaze fell to the ground. "No. Our tie was cut off. Her magic could never have reached me, and if she had..." his nose scrunched to the side in disgust. "She had to accept it and move on."

"I'm sorry you never got to be with her." He'd lost everything for her, and in the end, he lost her too.

"Me too."

"Heartbreak is a love story," I commented, repeating what he'd told me in his office. Pain shined in his eyes as he bowed his head in agreement.

Oco let out a low croak from the branches behind me. I turned to face the circle of stones, preparing to return to the world I was so eager to leave behind.

I squeezed the small vial of Mylo's blood in one hand, the mirror in the other.

"Just remember, his promise is his oath," Mylo said. "I hope to hear from you again... Ava."

I took a deep breath, glancing at him over my shoulder. He was letting me go, but all I wanted to do was hold on. He'd saved me again, and for a moment, all I could feel was the risk of losing him, of being stuck in a world where he couldn't exist.

I spun around, tossing myself into him, hugging my arms over his shoulders as I pulled him closer. His arms wrapped around my waist, pulling me tight. My face nuzzled into his neck, nose brushing against his skin as I breathed him in, a heated breath chasing out the cold between us.

My head leaned back just enough to kiss his cheek. "Just in case," I whispered toward the base of his ear. He slowly let me pull back, resistant to letting go, and a part of me wanted him to hold on forever.

"Thanks for being my friend," I told him as my feet planted back down. I slid his blood into my pocket as I turned toward the line, this time approaching it all the way. He was trusting me with his entire life, his whole future, but I refused to believe this was goodbye.

Naz waited at the side of the circle, one last respectful low nod to Mylo before meeting my eyes.

386

"Ready?" he asked.

"Ready," I answered, stepping up to him. I held the mirror between us, and he cupped his hand behind mine.

Oco dropped down from her perch, diving through with us as we took our first step across the line.

57

HARPER

I circled to the center of the gate, lost admiring the grounds that stretched beyond them, the house. I knew it. I could see the wishing well, the stream, the greenhouse. The stable of horses. The journal. The wolf.

My fingers traced a metal bar. Rogue told me that metal in their world was a mark of the witches, their magic influence left behind, still living inside it. Were those bars meant to block danger out? Or to lock someone in? Maybe I could convince Sage to learn spells like that someday.

A soft eerie fog swept across the field, hiding what lived beyond. I reached through the bars, twisting my fingers through the white haze, my brows drawn together. Someone was stuck in there. A ghost. I had to find him. I had to get him out.

I leaned against the gate, ready to push. They were always locked, I knew that, but this time... it had to be different. I was pulled there for a reason. I looked up at the moon, begging for its help. This time they would be open.

In the corner of my eye, a tall man with bright emerald

eyes and ginger hair stepped into the moonlight. I spun around, holding tight to the bars behind me like a lifeline.

"Interesting," he commented, looking me over. "Nobody's tried to open these gates in years. I wonder what draws you here."

"Just hoping to visit with a ghost," I countered defensively, rubbing a hand on my jeans. "I heard these woods were haunted."

"Ah," he answered, taking a step closer.

All I could think of was the wolves in my dream, the wild pack that roamed the forest around me. The promise that they couldn't reach beyond those walls into *his* territory. These men weren't wolves, but they felt just as dangerous.

I backed up into the gate, turning to shove my full weight against it. Just as it inched forward, one of the men grabbed me from behind, lifting me off my feet to carry away.

"No! Let go of me!"

"I'm afraid I can't do that." The ginger-haired man said as we passed by. I barely read the words on his lips between thrashing.

"Get off me!" I demanded as he carried me back through the shadows. "No," I begged, my fight turning to tears. "I was so close."

"You can join the spirits that lurk inside this forest soon enough," he finished, the threat behind it clear.

They tossed me into the same cell we'd broken Sage out of. The leader smiled at me through the bars, a prideful gleam in his bright green eyes.

"They're long gone," I told him. "You're going to lose."

"You mortals are all so pathetic," he answered with a smirk. "They'll come back *for you*." He stepped to the side, his easy gaze turning to scrutiny. "But I am curious. Nobody goes inside those gates." His tone grew suspicious. "They're spelled shut." His head tilted, brows drawing together. "So who are you?"

He'd seen the gate inch forward too.

I didn't answer, I'd already said too much, and he didn't push. He left, leaving two guards posted with their backs toward me, ready to prevent any more escapes. I noted the fresh cut on one's cheek, wondering how badly he'd been chewed out after Rogue got past him.

Sage, Willow, and Rogue would know I was gone by now. I was so foolish going off on my own. Number one priority was to get Sage safe, to prevent that ancient prophecy. Rogue warned me not to wander off. She had to get out of this world! But would anybody come back for me?

I sank back against the wall, pulling my backpack to my lap. I zipped it open, looking through the few things I had left. The worn journal still stuck out, like something that didn't belong. I pulled it free and set it against my legs, rubbing my fingers over the cover.

"Where did you come from?" I whispered. I'd woken up with it, with no explanation, no time to sit down and figure it out. I couldn't find the connection, yet there was this strange attachment, the urge to protect it, to keep it close. I opened to the first page.

The fire took my home. I'm trapped behind these broken walls of terror, and I cannot break free. The moon watches me from her sky above, but even her light cannot brighten the darkness inside me. I fear the forever that

lurks ahead, as nightmares of ash consume my
every breath, and I suffocate to their demands.

My breath caught. It was so raw, so cruel. So cursed. I traced the letters, wondering who wrote them. I turned the page to a list of names. *A list of victims.* Then I turned another, and I knew the handwriting all too well, for it was mine.

I stepped into a dream. I had to know the
world inside these gates. I had to see the
fields and flowers, even as they no longer lived
where I walked. It pulled me inside. I was
running, and it gave me somewhere to hide.
Hide from the joy that died, the dreams that
Sam took to her grave. I ran away, and I got
lost.

It never changed me though. The greenhouse,
the wishing well, the story that still lives with
each brick of these stone walls. In some way,
it felt like home, but I gave up every piece of
home that I had to meet it. To know it.

Each word was like a distant memory. I could see the horses lining the stables, the soil spilling out of a shattered pot. This was my story, my dream, and its was real.

I'll own who I am til the day I die,

whether it's tomorrow, or it's a thousand years away. My soul is my own. It's the one thing I can claim forever, and it will never die. I'll haunt these beautiful walls of ash forever.

I stepped into a dream, and it shifted into a nightmare. But not because of him. It was his nightmare too.

Fate turned into a horror story. I was warned, but I didn't listen. But I refuse to believe that the magic that I saw in this world was meant for terror. There is life still left in the soil across these grounds, and it is magical... it is good. And as I look into the starry night above me, I know everything is going to be okay.

I stared out through the small window of night beyond my prison walls, wondering if I could find that same strength. Had I gone too far this time? Gotten too lost?

I wish I could go back to where it all started. For this nightmare to be a distant dream. I'll step through those gates again and be reunited with the family that's waiting on me. My soul will always be tethered to my home. Even when I'm gone. Even after I'm free.

I'd written that. It was as vague a memory as my dream. I read the last lines over again, stating that I got out. I'd found my home. The last moments of a nightmare before I'd woken up. It was as if I'd written myself free with my words, but as I read my own story, my heart looked at it the other way around.

Some deep piece of me suddenly felt that that castle of ash was my home. I could step through those gates again, return to the world I belonged in, tethered to my soul forever, even after.

I pulled out a pen, imagining what it would have been like when that gate opened and I stepped inside. The man from my dream. The curse broken. He'd been lost in there too, he deserved home as much as I did. All I wanted to do was help him. I had to make sure he knew he wasn't forgotten, let him know that I knew he was real.

The distant dream became a memory. I was sitting in the darkness, my fear consuming me. A match struck against the black air around me, lighting the candle as it shined into his face.

"Elijah." My breath steamed with the whisper between us as the candle blew out. A flash of lightning struck down the gravel path ahead, lighting the silhouette of the castle walls, the wolf on its doorstep. The cursed wolf.

My wolf.

I stared at the page in my lap. "I wish," I read out loud. I'd wished myself out. This journal had listened to me before, like an answer to a prayer. All I could do was pray that it listened again.

He was real. Elijah.

"Elijah," I repeated in a whisper. My eyes flashed past the guards to the moon shining out over the trees. The years of suffering I'd seen in his forsaken eyes, the loneliness in his cursed heart. Could it hear me? Could it help?

I wished myself free, but I left him behind.

> We're connected, I can feel it in my soul. He is the family that waits on me, and I need him to wake up from this nightmare. I wish for him to be released beneath this moonlit night. To find me. To take me home.
> Let the hourglass tide break loose of this curse. Let the wild wolf run free.

"Flease help him," I softly begged the moon. "Let him free. I need him."

58

SAGE

Leave it to the rogue hunter to have every nook and cranny of this magic forest memorized. He led straight to a hollow tree, gently tucking Willow inside. It would have to do while we went after Harper. Lucky we had such an experienced hunter on our team.

Rogue followed Harper's trail to the front of a large gate, but the forest around us was empty, and hers weren't the only tracks left behind.

"She should have been here," Rogue growled in his raspy voice, raking his fingers through his hair. He paced back and forth in front of a gate that refused to open. I stared at the large, overgrown field. The burned edges of a stone mansion that used to be sat in the center, reminding the world around it of its emptiness. It was no wonder they said its woods were haunted.

"Who lived here?" I asked. "Before."

"The shifter pack. It's been far too long now, but these grounds did live happily once." He reached for the bars again, his boots bracing the ground as he shoved his weight against them. "It's spelled."

"You knew it? As it was?"

"I did." He pushed off the gate with another huff of frustration. "They were good people."

"If only they were here to help us stop this madness," I commented.

"But they're not, and Harper isn't either." He threw out his hand toward the gates in frustration. "These grounds do us no good now."

"Maybe I can track her," I offered, trying to find some optimism. "I'm supposed to be a witch, aren't I? Can't witches do locating spells or something?"

He didn't answer, gaze on the ground, pacing back and forth across the gates, thumb rubbing at his lip.

I tried to ignore him losing his cool, shaking my hands out to loosen the building stress. I took a deep breath, looking towards the trees instead. My eyes softly shut, searching for some kind of energy, anything that told me I wasn't crazy. Where did we go from there?

"Sage?"

I spun around, staring at the face of a ghost.

"Willow?" No, not Willow. I would never forget the bright light in her emerald eyes, the long auburn hair that curled over her shoulders. She waited for me to say the word. So many times I'd seen Willow, and wished it could be her *Impossible*.

"Sam."

Her smile dimpled into her freckled, rosy cheeks. The energy around her was so happy and warm, but she wasn't there. She couldn't be.

I looked back at Rogue, unsure what to think, but he remained still, his gaze fixed on her.

"Sage," she cried, stepping forward to throw her arms

around me. "I missed you so much," she whispered in my ear.

"What? But how?" I searched the trees as we spun one step to the side, my chin on her shoulder. The haunted woods. She was a ghost. She had to be.

"Where is everyone?" she asked, pulling back, but her fingers still softly squeezed my arms.

"They're," I searched her eyes, caught speechless. She wasn't there, but she felt so real, the sound of her voice, the touch of her fingers. "They're in trouble."

Her brows drew together. "They're here? In this world?"

I nodded, swallowing back my confusion. "We're going to help them." I looked back at Rogue, watching us cautiously from behind, slowly pacing around with his golden eyes focused on her.

"We have to help them," she answered. "Come on!"

"We can't," I answered, then cleared my throat. I searched her eyes, trying to make sense of it. "You can't. You're not real."

"I'm right here!" she argued. "You don't remember? I told you in my poem. My clue, you figured it out!"

"Where the magics mix."

"You'll always find me there," she confirmed, her smile beaming brighter. "Come on, let's go. I know the way."

I gave Rogue a longing look, desperate to believe it was real, half shrugging as Sam's hugging arm ushered me forward.

"The way to where?" Rogue's raspy voice questioned, taking a protective step forward to follow.

I looked at her, repeating his question when she didn't answer. "Where are we going?"

She rolled her eyes. "To save our friends of course."

"Harper," I corrected. "Right now we have to save Harper."

"Yes," she agreed, smiling a little too happily for a rescue mission, some kind of disconnect in her emotions. I bit my lip, sending Rogue a nervous side-eyed glance behind her. He followed closely, reaching forward to feel her shoulder.

Sam whipped around, yanking me in front of her. One arm caged mine across my stomach, as the other squeezed my neck. I froze, eyes locked in on Rogue as my friend choked the air to my lungs from behind.

"Let her go," Rogue growled in a low threat.

"I'm doing my job." I knew his voice, I'd been caught by his lies before, and I'd fallen for his tricks again. *Kett.*

"So loyal to a monster," I commented, but his grip made me wince.

"This is a much bigger game than you and I," Rogue warned, taking a sideways step to circle around us. Kett followed his lead, spinning us slowly in place so that I stayed between them.

"It's big alright," Kett answered. "Let the best hunter win... and I will."

"Let her go!" Rogue fumed.

"You're weak!" Kett mocked. "After all these years, what has your love for the witch gained you? Decades of failing at one, single mission. You're foolish, coming back here for her. They'll never let you live."

"I was never going to live past that full moon and you know that." My eyes widened at his words, hit by the truth. When I died, it would have taken Rogue's life with me. Keeping our bloodline alive kept him alive.

Kett's arms readjusted tighter. "Bigger game. Better players."

My eyes remained locked in Rogue's, unable to look anywhere else. I was desperate for a miracle, begging for some sign that he had this under control. That he could save me again, the same way he always did. He had to know that this time, I wasn't running. This time I chose him.

He met my eyes, gaze flashing to the forest floor behind me for only a split second. He saw something. Something he wasn't saying.

Kett's arms yanked me back, his steps shuffling to recover when something pulled him down, dragging me with him. My knees hit the rocks, gravel scraping my palms, when Kett choked me back in front of him as a shield. I stilled, eyes going flat as I sat face to face with a hunched, snarling wolf.

"Impossible," Kett mused angrily behind me. "It can't be, the wolves are all dead!"

"Elijah," Rogue offered in soft low awe. *The lost prince.*

The wolf lunged toward my face, locking its teeth into the hand at my neck. I fell to the side, fingers half-clawing into Rogue's arms as he pulled me to stand out of the way. He squeezed me to his chest, hiding my face as the wolf tore Kett apart.

We didn't move until the cries faded and the fight died.

"It's over," Rogue said, patiently holding me until I peeked through. I barely saw the pile of blood and flesh before he pulled my jaw back toward him, turning it up to look in my eyes. Concern shined in his expression, searching to make sure I was alright. His warm fingers pressed softly beneath my jaw, before falling away.

"He's gone?" I whispered. "Gone for real?" Each breath shook through me. "No more tricks?"

"He's gone," Rogue confirmed.

"And the wolf?"

"He's gone too. Ran into the trees."

"But what does that mean?" I asked.

"Means he's free." I turned around slowly, following his gaze into the trees. "The lost prince is free."

59

ZAGER

The full moon had everyone on edge. Change was coming, you could feel it in the air. Echo and his witch were busy getting things in order for the gates to close, and they'd been so close, until their witch escaped.

The Thost witch. A witch of legend. A part of me had started to question whether they would ever track her bloodline down. Now they had to find her again, with only the word of a distant scream to lead their search.

I didn't care about the witch though. I had to find Willow. I'd given her my word, and I was bound by it. At least with the Thost witch gone, I had more time. More windows amidst the chaos to slip away.

I'd proven my loyalty again, briefed my king from his towers in center sun, when Echo finally dismissed me, or more dismissed himself.

I turned toward the door, when I heard the faintest voice below the ledge. I hesitated, leaning over to look, but I saw no one. I couldn't sense anyone either. A ghost.

"We got out of that prison, and we're never going back."

A girl's voice, young. My heart squeezed, wishing it were Willow, but the optimistic determination in that voice belonged to someone else.

"We got out." Was this the witch? Hiding right below our noses? I subtly straightened back up, peeking to make sure Echo's guards hadn't heard from the room behind me. That witch had bought me time to help Willow, I wasn't going to turn her in now.

"How did the Thost witch escape?" I asked, ignoring the locks I got as I eyed Echo's witch. "Surely she didn't do it alone."

"The rogue hunter," Clover answered dryly, standing up taller as she waved her hair back behind her shoulder.

I'd heard of him. They said he was a shadow. His one mission was to hunt the Thost witch, and he'd been on her trail for decades. The only one with the ability to pick her out, but he'd gone rogue.

"Thanks to her sick friend, they won't make it far," Clover assured me, a cocky note in her voice.

I stilled, my eyes snapping more intently to hers. "Sick?"

Clover scoffed, grinning over the towering wall toward the center slab. The most central spot in our world, where the truce was formed and the mirror was split. I followed her gaze, heart thumping in my chest. Something was wrong. Something was off.

I slowly stepped around her, focusing my magic on Echo's witch. I'd never been able to dig very deep, though that wasn't uncommon with witches. They were guarded. Their magic naturally protected that, allowed it, but this was something different. Something I sensed in her had always bothered me.

Her bloodline confused me. She was a descendant of

Cosimo's witch, Ivy. A loyal witch, and he'd been fond of her until the end. Ivy disappeared, spewing rumors of black magic that went too far, of the shadow pool. Our world believed her dead for years, when Clover showed up one day with no explanation, ready to do Echo's bidding.

My eyes shut, concentrating harder, letting my magic seep inside. Who was this woman I'd handed my blind trust to for so many years? The king I'd loyally followed? They stood together side by side.

Darkness filled her veins, mixing through her blood, consuming her soul.

I'd never felt anything so dark. My eyes flashed to her feet, no shadow stretching out from beneath them. She wasn't just missing a shadow though... she was the shadow.

Her gaze snapped to mine, black as the waves of a forest pool, cutting off my magic touch. I'd dug too deep and finally found it, the secret she'd buried all these years.

"You're not Clover," I stated, realizing just how fooled I'd been. My head shook. "You're Ivy." She'd never died. She was there all along, serving her king.

"The shadow still lives," I whispered. "All those rumors of eternal life, the pool that would let you live forever... but if you're her shadow, then where is her body?"

She leaned in a step, face strained with rage. "Get out," a demonic voice demanded, echoing through my skull.

"You never died... you're still here... still looking for power."

Her eyes snapped back to normal, smile lifting. I looked back at the guards, but they were frozen, oblivious. They didn't see the monster standing on their throne.

"You shouldn't have said that," she warned.

She flicked her wrist up, but I lunged from the ledge,

diving into the trees before my wings spread out to catch my fall, feet slamming against the marsh soil.

"We're never going back," the voice echoed again at my feet. I snatched the toad up, squeezing it tight with one last look at the castle walls above me. That toad crossed paths with the Thost witch somewhere down the marsh, and I was going to find her now too.

I looked into its beady eyes. "The witch ran for the river," I lied, taking any opportunity to buy more time. If I had to help the Thost witch in the meantime, so be it.

I tossed the toad and spun around, freezing as two eyes met mine from beneath the trees. A wolf. I didn't move, waiting for him to go first. I recognized the power I sensed in him immediately, someone I should have been loyal to all along.

"You're Elijah," I commented, realizing how much of a war I'd stepped into. How could it be? Where had he been all these years?

"The lost prince still lives," I added in a whisper. So many lies, so much deceit. This was bigger than the lines. A grave of secrets. This was about the prophecy.

He held his gaze on mine, a low growl in his throat. I bowed my head, showing him the respect he'd deserved all along.

"We fight the same war now, prince," I told him. "I know what I must do. I hope to see you on the other side."

The wolf lunged back into the forest, disappearing with the silent shadows. My shoulders eased with a breath of relief, and I took one last look at the towering castle, realizing I'd be loyal to that prince until the day I died.

60

WILLOW

Everything felt like a dream, dancing on a thin line of consciousness.

Someone set me down, tucked me in.

"We'll hurry," Sage promised.

My life was in her hunter's hands. All I could do was wait.

What did they hurry for? My time was up.

Something flapped through the air. A breeze brushed my forehead. Footsteps. I wanted to look, but my eyes shut tighter with a scratchy, wheezing breath.

"Willow?"

I could only exchange another labored breath with the dream, nothing left in me to offer.

"Willow, I can feel you out there. Where are you?"

Zager? His magic could sense me?

"Zager?" I coughed out. My eyes slit open, searching the shadow that closed in on my hideout.

"How—" I couldn't find the strength to finish my words.

He reached inside, his arms cradling me weakly into him. I couldn't have fought against it if I'd wanted to.

"I'm not... doing so good," I whispered.

"I'm going to get you out of here," he stated. I was sure I'd become delirious.

Either way. "Thanks... for coming back," I said, grateful this illusion could accompany my last moments.

"I promised," he answered.

"Did you know... you have wings?" I asked, confident I was dreaming as my head rolled limply over his arm. There was a hint of laughter in his chest, but it couldn't break through the heavy air.

"Sleep." I let myself lull deeper into the darkness. *"Good girl,"* his voice echoed, the low hum of it rolling through me. I relaxed into the shuffle of each step, going back to the night we met, him carrying me off into a dream. Then the weight lifted, and breathing didn't hurt so bad anymore.

Zager stopped walking. *"What are you doing here?"* he asked from somewhere outside the dream.

"Waiting." I didn't know the other voice, but Zager went quiet. A shuffle of steps drawing closer in the leaves.

"The witch, the prince, the banished king... you're him," Zager commented, breaking the silence between them. Cold fingers brushed against my forehead.

"Dead blood," the voice stated dryly. *"Where will you take her?"*

"The hospital."

"They won't be able to—"

"I'll not give up!"

"Zager—" I tried to argue, but coughed instead, waking up from the daydream.

"No!" he fought. "I'm not losing you. I'll make them cut the metal out. We'll go back across! We'll be together. There's always a way, you just need to rest!"

I gave into the plea in his voice. He had to do this, had to try. Maybe he was right, but my fight was over. His could keep going until my heart stopped beating.

At least, in the end, I was truly loved. Surrounded by a family of friends that saw me for me. Once I was gone, they could let go of Sam and I completely. They could move on. I let myself fall back into the darkness.

Zager shifted forward, but hesitated. "Ivy," he warned in a low voice. "She lives. It's her shadow, I saw it in her eyes."

The stranger was quiet for a moment before answering. "The shadow pool."

"Is it true?" Zager asked. "The old rumors of black magic and eternal life?" My eyes strained open, searching Zager's face above my own before my head rolled forward to study the stranger.

Everything about him was dark and cold, what might be a handsome smile seeming lost forever. His serious eyes made me shiver. Who was he to answer such a question?

"Ivy is dead," he started. "There is only one way. Either she gave her body to the pool completely... or someone else made the choice for her."

"After all this time," Zager's disgust rang clear. "Someone had to have known."

The stranger's face held firm and unchanging, unwilling to say the word.

"Cosimo," Zager answered for them both.

The man's gaze fell to the forest behind us. "Her soul is lost to the shadow pool forever. Now her shadow must drown there to find it."

SPILLED

61

HARPER

S omething snapped in my ear like thunder, only it was wilder, like a sharp bite. The thrashing of a beast consumed my head from the inside out as it tore through the hallway, ripping apart the guards.

I covered my ears, as if I could block out the terror surrounding me, afraid of what came through the shadows, for I was sure to be next.

The deafening screams silenced back into the nothing I'd heard for days as I shakily peeked out from my cage.

A still wolf stood at the bars, staring straight at me. My back hit the stone wall behind me with a jolt, when I took a closer look.

His eyes were familiar, I knew them... from a dream.

"Elijah?"

The wolf howled, a roaring contrast to the silent days behind me. I covered my ears against it, but tears of shock pooled in my eyes.

Somehow the silence was gone. I could hear... *through* him.

"I hear you," I whispered, all of my fears forgotten. I

half-crawled to the bars, crumbling to my knees in front of him. For the first time, I could hear him! I could feel the connection between us, the way my mind linked to his.

"I can hear you!" I cried again louder, a miracle in the darkest corner.

But it was still dark. This wasn't over.

"It's okay," I assured him, feeling the rage that bubbled through him. The urge to fight, to destroy, to tear down their world from top to bottom.

"I'm okay," I promised. "They won't hurt me. He's after my friend." I searched his eyes, hoping he understood. So much had happened, but he wasn't just some ghost trapped behind those gates anymore. He wasn't a distant forgotten dream that I was still trying to grab hold of. He was real, and he was standing right in front of me.

"You have to help her, my friend! She's the Thost witch. He's going to kill her! Please don't let him get away with it, don't let him hurt my friends!"

"You're my forever," the deep words rolled through me, as if he couldn't hold them in. He had to state it, to get it out.

The declaration made me shiver, but I could feel it in my blood, in the promise of the moon behind him, in the link between our minds. I fought my tears, overwhelmed with emotions. I was meant to find him, he was my forever too. My fated mate.

I nodded at him. "Forever," I agreed. "Now go."

"I'll find you again," his voice swore inside my mind.

"I know," I whispered.

He lunged down the hallway, leaving me alone once again. I sank against the bars as the tears pooled over. I could hear everything through him, as if his mind had been unlocked and it wasn't ever going to close. The sound of his deep howl, threatening the air around him, his claws scratching the stone as he ran further away.

"I'll be waiting," I softly cried, reaching for the journal. I wiped dirt from the cover, then hugged it tight, turning to look at a distant moon that had never felt so close.

"Thank you."

62

SAGE

"Come on," Rogue said, supporting my elbow as I climbed a sharp rock. "The center slab is through here."

"What is the center slab?"

"It was the first portal, the original. One smooth, round bowl of water on a stone slab. Three faces looked into its reflection below a full moon, casting their uniting spell. The water froze to glass, and the fae king shattered it. Three pieces, for three lines."

"The lines where magics mix," I inserted.

"Each corner of our world claimed a piece of it. The pieces were spelled, disguised all this time, but when pulled free, they'll fit together in the slab. They complete the circle. They can unite the portal once more. It's the center of our world. The point where the three territories meet, where three rivers come together to join as one. He'll be across the bridge, only there can it be reforged. It's where they created the truce, where the three chose to live in peace."

"My great, great, whatever, grandmother." I tried to

imagine it, my ancestor, standing in the forest with some fae king and a werewolf.

"The Thost witch," he added.

"Did you know her?"

"Not well," he admitted. It was strange to hear confirmation that he was there all those years before.

My head was spinning. "It just doesn't seem real, all the magic."

"You'll find it," he reassured me.

My eyes fell to the rocks at my feet as I climbed up the last step of a hill. I hadn't been talking about my magic, I just meant the magic of this other world. His world. It still didn't feel like it was mine. Not yet.

But what if a part of me didn't want to accept it?

He reached an arm toward me, but I shifted forward, changing the subject. "Do you think that fox will ever show up again?" I asked, scanning the trees around us.

"I hope not," he grumbled, then hesitated. "Do you want it to?"

"I don't know. I just wish Nina was here. She always knew what to say to make things make sense. To make me feel better."

"She was one of a kind," Rogue agreed. I spun around to face him. He'd never mentioned my grandmother to me before.

"You knew her?"

He sighed, his eyes drifting across the sky in thought. "I'd been hunting your bloodline for years. Even when I didn't want to anymore. Eventually we would cross paths again."

"And you crossed paths with her? With my grandma?"

He smiled. "She made me see everything differently.

Changed my whole view. Maybe, in a way, she even saved me."

"She warned me about you. About the arrowhead on your arm." I turned his hand to study the dark lines above his wrist, my finger lightly tracing over it.

"The mark of the hunter," he explained before his hand slid over mine, turning it over. "And the mark of the Thost witch," he added, brushing a thumb over my birth mark. "The ones before you all had this birthmark. Much more discrete than mine," he added with a half-smile.

"Did you ever try to bring her here? My Nina?"

"She gave me a friendship that I'd never known before. I wish it had been enough." He looked away. "I was done. I wanted this life of hunting to be over."

I stumbled back, pulling my hand free. He hadn't denied it.

"She was there," he went on calmly. "Sila. Kneeling in her garden. I asked her why she never moved away, why she didn't hide from me. She'd never been afraid. She was so free." His head shook. "I just wanted to be free too. When I grabbed her—"

"What did you—"

"She spun around so fast." His head fell back, staring at the stars again. "Stabbed me straight through the heart."

"She?" *Stabbed?* That didn't sound like Nina.

"She stabbed you because she knew... you were going to turn her in?" I couldn't believe it. "No wonder she warned me to stay away from you." He'd come so far to save me, yet a part of me still wanted to defend my Nina for what he'd done before.

Rogue stared at me. "I barely saw the little brown-haired girl run across the grass, dancing in the breeze, begging her to join as I fell to the dirt." He reached

416

forward, his finger lightly waving down a loose strand of my hair.

I could remember it just as he said it, trying to test how my dress would fly when I twirled around, the bright purple ribbon dangling down with my long, tangled hair. I begged Nina to come hold my hands and spin with me. She always came, but that day she hesitated from her spot across the garden.

"I remember."

"Be there in a minute, sugar," Nina called across the grass.

"But before, you said she saved you." I shook off the memory, trying to understand. "How did you survive?"

"I didn't." The words stopped my heart. "That's when I discovered the blood bounty."

Something snapped in the brush. Rogue reflexively spun around to shield me behind him.

"Elijah," he greeted, still tensely blocking me as I hid at his back. I slowly peeked around his arm, taking in the familiar wolf.

"He came back for us," I commented.

"He found us," Rogue corrected.

"But why?" We watched the wolf, unsure of the answer. "Harper told me about him, you know. About the cursed man in her dream. You were right, she had to have gone after him, and now he's here."

"But she isn't," Rogue added.

I cautiously stepped out from behind Rogue's back, searching the wolf's eyes. "She's in trouble, isn't she. I can feel it in my gut. We should have found her by now."

"He knows where she is," Rogue cut off, his gaze still locked in the wolf's. "He's here as an ally." The wolf's neck snapped back with a deep howl toward the sky.

"What do we do?" I asked, still nervous with the unsettling memory of that wolf snapping its jaws toward my face, even if it was to save me.

Rogue sent the wolf a subtle nod. "Lead the way."

63

SAGE

It felt like we'd leveled up, following the wolf prince. I stared at the full moon through the treetops, in awe that there was a creature so connected to it here on the ground. "A shifter, a fae, and a witch, hiking through the forest together. Who would have guessed."

"I'm not a fae," Rogue corrected. "Not anymore."

I rolled my eyes. "Whatever. Don't steal my fun."

His gaze flashed questioningly back on mine, nearly stumbling as he tried to understand my humor. "Wouldn't dream of it."

The sincerity in it made me laugh under my breath, reaching forward to grab his hand. Rogue accepted the touch with a soft squeeze, silently securing the embrace. It was the most reassuring touch I'd felt in days, the first time something had made me smile, but as my wall cracked, some of the pain seeped back in. I leaned my face against the back of his bicep, wishing I could hide away.

We hiked behind the wolf in silence as more questions nagged at my mind.

"Did you ever consider turning me in?"

He didn't stop hiking, but there was reluctance in his voice. "No. But I did desperately want to know you. To see who you'd grown into. The bounty pushes that urge deeper, makes it instinctive to seek you out. I didn't want to help them anymore. I didn't want to find you, because I didn't want to risk leading them to you. Sila... she was my friend, for a while. She did trust me once. In another lifetime. At least, I thought she did. I know I trusted her. I cared more than I should have. It made me weak. It's why I lost."

"You never lost," I argued. He remained silent. "Not for loving her. That's what saved you."

"You have her strength, you know."

My steps caught mid-stride, studying the side of his face through the shadows.

"Really?"

"I felt it. The moment I first touched you. All I ever wanted was to keep you safe. I'm a prisoner to this bounty, but I'd choose my sentence again and again to know you. To let you live."

His words went deeper than I could grasp. I so badly wanted him to go on, but the wolf cut us off.

I stepped between the two, staring at the opening through the trees ahead. Three slow-moving rivers drifted out from separate ends of the trees, mixing together in a clockwise current. A platform rose above the pool, held up by a bridge from three sides. The three territories. This was it.

The low rumbling growl of the wolf startled me, making Rogue's hand squeeze tighter.

"They have her," he warned. I searched the platform until a dark figure stepped aside and I saw Harper waiting on her knees.

"No." I fell to my knees too. "Rogue."

"I know."

I turned my head slowly, realizing I was once again face to face with the wolf.

"Elijah," I whispered, staring into his bright blue eyes. "I'm so sorry. This is all my fault, I'm the one they want."

There was another low growl.

"We'll get her back," Rogue cut off, refocusing us on the task ahead.

Harper cried out as a woman yanked her to her feet, cowering from the hand at her neck.

"I can sense you, *witch*," Echo spat into the distance. "Come out now, or she dies."

Rogue squeezed my arm as I stood, tightening it as a silent order to stay. I pulled his hand up to cup my cheek instead, shutting my eyes to his warm touch.

"You have to let me do this," I whispered.

"You're not going up there. I never should have brought you."

"I have to save her." I studied his golden eyes, trying to memorize each vivid fleck of light. "This was my fate. You knew that all along."

His jaw set stubbornly. "He's not killing you today."

I gave a small smile, nodding against the denial. He had to believe it to let me walk away. I closed my eyes, pretending that moment could belong to us two alone, but Echo's distant threats tugged at the threads of my heart.

"Where will we go when this is over?" I asked, soaking up his touch for one last breath. My hand squeezed over his, pulling it back down.

"I'll follow you anywhere," he whispered, an ache for the future stinging his voice.

"You promise?" My eyes opened as I took the first step.

He hesitated to let my hand slide free. "Forever," he

agreed as I fell out of reach, stepping backward into the unknown.

I held onto that promise, that one small word, as I turned to face my fate.

Echo's wicked smile twisted higher when he saw me, shoving my mind back into that dirty prison cell he'd tossed me in before. My eyes shifted to Harper, focusing on her instead. This could be the day I died, but Harper was going to get out alive. It was me, and me alone he wanted. No one else had to be lost. She stepped into this world to save me. I was going to make sure she stepped back out. She would live, and Rogue would be freed.

I glared at Echo's victorious expression with a new sense of fight. It was time to be strong.

"So good to see you again," he mocked.

"If I step up there, you'll let my friend go."

He glanced back at his witch, his smile smug. "Of course."

I stepped onto the bridge, crossing toward the round, stone platform. The slab sat in the center between us. I glared across it, refusing to take another step until they held up their end of the deal.

"Let her go."

"Sage—"

The witch threw Harper down to release her, her tear-streaked face lifting to look at me.

"Just go," I softly pleaded, cocking my head back at the trees.

She looked past me, when a glimmer of light sparked in her eyes. I fought the urge to look myself, refusing to give anything away. She stumbled off the platform, bracing against the side, the fight still in her eyes as they matched mine. The urge to be stubborn, to stand by me until we were both out of this mess, but she listened.

My shoulders eased with a deep breath, knowing Elijah and Rogue would be there waiting for her. They would make sure she got out of this mess safe.

A guard grabbed my arms from behind, forcing me forward. Echo pulled out three round metal lockets and set them along the edge of the stone. Two matched, while the third sat more worn and bent. He lifted the first one, whispering a spell as he grabbed at the edge, before a long shard of glass slid free.

My mouth parted in awe, mesmerized by the impossible. The magic. *Spelled.*

He did the same with the second mirror, then the third, setting each broken shard of glass in a line on the edge of the stone, then pulled out a small vial of soot. The ash of the shifters.

Echo stared at the moon, taking in a deep breath.

"It's time," his witch said.

His gaze dropped back down on the slab, picking up the vial first. He sprinkled it evenly over the flat bowl in the center as a breeze picked up around us. "To bury the fallen pack," he stated, before grabbing a shard of glass. He set the larger two down neatly over the ash and stone, a small crack left between them.

"As the rivers run together," he said quietly as he set the last piece down. His smile fell short, mouth falling slightly open as his brows drew together.

I studied the shards of glass. A broken mirror, left incomplete. It was missing a piece.

Echo stood still, stunned, his mind racing. His gaze flickered over the glass, the three round metal lockets, then up to my eyes across the slab, going over each step, searching for answers that I didn't hold.

"You did something," he accused. "You broke the third piece, you tricky little *witch*!"

"No! I—" I tried to take a step back, but my feet were frozen in place, the guard still at my back. My eyes flashed to Echo's witch, smiling knowingly from behind her king as she locked me in place.

"What did you do!" Echo demanded. He closed his eyes and took a deep breath, as if to sense the world around him. "It's here. I can feel it." His eyes opened on me, glaring daggers. "You have it!"

"I never touched them—"

"I'll kill that friend of yours, I'll kill all of them if you don't give me what I want!"

64

AVA

"Come on," Nazurin prodded, nervously looking at the moon. "There's no more time." A nervous energy built in the breeze that picked up around us. We hadn't stopped moving since we crossed the line, and we weren't stopping now.

"Is that you?" I asked him, watching the swaying branches around us. How big of a storm could his emotions actually stir up under all this pressure?

He didn't answer, but he didn't have to. I pushed on faster, hoping he knew what he was doing.

"Hey, Naz?"

"What?"

"What did you mean before? When you said it's lucky I wasn't marked?"

"For knowing too much. We keep our world a secret. Sure, there's stories on your side, pieces of the truth, but it's labeled as fiction. People want to believe it, but their minds tell them they can't. Not completely. The mortals who really believe, who see past the glamor, the ones that threaten our peace with true exposure, they're marked. The magic of our world hunts them down, eliminates the opportunity."

"That's awful," I choked, when distant voices cut us off. Nazurin held up a hand to stop me, focused on the sounds ahead.

"The ceremony," Nazurin said. "He's already started it."

"He won't be able to finish it," I commented, terrified of what Echo was about to do to my friend.

"I'll talk to him," Nazurin insisted. "I'll make him see the other side of what he's doing. He doesn't have to close the gates."

"It s not about the gates!"

"I know, but there has to be another way. I have to try."

"You did this!" a distant voice growled. "I'll kill all of them if you don't give me what I want!"

"Stop!" Naz broke through into the clearing, a sudden rain sprinkling my face, growing heavier with each step he took. I stared up at the new gray clouds, blocking out the sky. Had Nazurin meant to unleash a storm, or was he losing it all together?

Echo laughed from his stage. "You might be able to block the moon's light, but you'll never stop its power," he challenged.

"I would never wish to," Nazurin countered. His shoulders slumped back, and he let out a long breath, the rain softening with it.

"I never thought I'd see you on this side of the line again, no matter how hard your brother fought for it."

"Then why send him on such a useless mission?"

"Don't flatter yourself," Echo said. "It was never about you."

"Only your precious mirrors."

"I'm putting things back to how they should have been all along. You knew that and you still chose getting cut off with the mortals over life in our world."

"Cut off? From what? I never truly lived until I stepped across those lines."

"You're a fool."

"This world is magic," Nazurin said. "It's bright, it's alive!" His hand rose to the trees around him, and I could have sworn the few stars I saw between the clouds twinkled brighter as it waved over them. Then it fell to his side.

"But there's magic there too. The humans? They're imaginative, creative, inventive. It's surreal. It's beautiful. It's imperfectly perfect. Their world won't hurt us. We can coexist, and we should! We don't have to close the lines! There has to be another way."

Echo smirked. "You're as foolish as your brother if you still think I care about those gates. When my blood seals these cracks, this kingdom will be mine." Just as Mylo called it. Nazurin wanted to believe it wasn't real, that we could change his mind, but this was so much bigger. I stared at Mylo's vial of blood, desperate for his help, but our time was up.

"The mirrors were made in the truce," Naz commented.

"Back when three fools chose to share the power of one. Now I'll be the one to claim it all." He stared at Nazurin as if he could see right through him.

"I'll take back the bits of power that that halfwit king gave away. Now give me the final piece!"

Nazurin stood still, and silent, unsure of his next move. His speech had failed.

Echo moved around the slab, grabbing Sage by the neck. She rocked forward with force as he stood ready to stab her.

"Don't kill her!" I yelled, falling through the trees into the clearing. "Don't, don't kill her."

Echo's eyes passed Nazurin to scrutinize me. "Why should I listen to you?" he challenged.

I looked down at the mirror, hidden in my hand, facing my own reflection in the glass. "I'm so sorry, Mylo." My hand trembled as I held it up for Echo to see.

"Because he doesn't have it," I answered. "I do." I stared at Sage, ready to do whatever it took to get her out of there. "I'm here to make a trade. She doesn't have to die. You get your power, you can close those gates— with us on the other side."

"The mirror, for the Thost witch." His jaw set, stewing on it for a moment. "Very well, I should only need a few drops of blood."

"His promise is his oath." Mylo's warning ran through my mind. It wasn't a warning, it was a tool.

"You swear it?" I challenged, needing to know for sure.

"I'll swear nothing until I see it's the last piece." I let out a shaky breath, trying to find another way around it, but there wasn't one.

I walked across slowly, Oco gliding through the air above me with a low croak, staying with me as always.

I paced up the stone steps, circling around the slab. He had Sage hostage, ready to end it if I made a wrong move. Whether he was truly willing to risk losing his witch or not, I wasn't willing to lose my best friend. Another world knew my name. It knew all of our names now. There was no turning back, only moving forward.

"When you see that this is the last piece, promise me you won't hunt us down," I countered, hesitant to take the last few steps. "We'll be free."

Amusement sparked in his eyes. "I give you my word."

"His promise is his oath."

I held out the last mirror, and Echo snatched it fast, holding it up to examine. He grabbed at the side of it, whispering words I didn't understand before sliding out a large piece of glass that never should have fit inside the small silver frame. His smile deepened with victory.

In a split second, he grabbed Sage's hand and slashed her palm, still holding her hostage in front of him as he finished the ritual. He set the last bloodied piece down, completing the mirror, then shut his eyes with a deep breath.

"Be free," he whispered against the back of her ear as his fingers let go.

As soon as she stepped away, Echo spun toward her back. Someone shoved past me, knocking Sage to the ground. My head smacked the stone slab, barely catching myself as I pulled up against the side of it, my vision blurring around me.

The man that blocked Sage was still, gagging on his breath as a dagger stabbed through his chest.

I spun dizzily over the slab, bracing my weight against it so I wouldn't fall. I stared into the cracked mirrors, fighting a blurry daze. My fingers brushed over my head, feeling the warm wet liquid before it ran down my forehead.

"You're bleeding," Mylo's voice called from my memories.

I pulled up the hand still squeezing his vial of blood. Like a lifeline in my pocket, I couldn't let it go. I couldn't lose him. I popped it open, my mind going blank. The only piece of him that I had left. If I was dying there, I was dying with him in my head. I was soaking up any chance to stay connected to him before those walls closed up for good.

My weight slumped heavier against the slab, and I

weakly pulled it closer, my vision giving up the fight to clear. I stared at the cracked lines of glass in front of me, the completed mirror. The face I'd forgotten, and had to memorize all over again.

The cold vial pressed against my lips as I searched the brown eyes of two different people, Jane, and Ava, longing for the future they both could have lived, the life I was missing... and then I saw clearly what I had to do, so I dropped it.

I held those eyes in my reflection as the vial fell to the edge of the mirror, his blood spilling free, running down the cracks of glass like a river come to life just to claim them.

"I'm sorry, Mylo," I weakly cried, sagging into my arms, still holding me over the edge.

65

SAGE

Someone shoved me down. I braced against the ground, turning just enough to see a dagger stabbing through Rogue.

"No!" I cried, trying to support him as he slowly fell on top of me. He wasn't supposed to die. I got out from under him, kneeling at his side. "It was supposed to be me!"

"Go," he ordered, a glaze in his eyes as they stared at me. I wanted to deny it, the pain in his breath. This wasn't how it was supposed to happen. He was never meant to get hurt!

"Not yet," Echo cut off. He stepped toward us, when his gaze snapped to the side.

"What is this!" He lunged toward the slab, ripping Ava out of his way. "What have you done!"

Ava hit the ground hard without a flinch. I reached for her under Rogue's dead weight, but she was just out of reach. Echo was scrambling for something, trying to undo what had been done. He picked up the glass pieces, each still lined in blood as he hugged them to his chest, blood he never got the chance to spill.

His witch stood dumbfounded behind him, eyes wide. This hadn't been part of her vision. She searched the tree line, the sky, waiting on some impending pressure.

"As the rivers run together," I repeated. Someone's blood had bound the cracks, bound the magic, and it wasn't his.

A howl lit the air, echoing from within the trees. Echo's gaze snapped back in terror, searching the dark forest around us.

Something pulsed inside my blood, a jolt of energy. I gently let Rogue to the floor, shifting out from beneath him to stare at my hands. I could feel it in my soul, in my bones, the shift in power. Something in this world had been unlocked, a piece of me given back.

"It's too late," I told Echo with a small smile, a tear streaming down my cheek. I didn't know how, but I could feel it. He'd lost. The mirror was bound, and I had my power.

He spun around, a sword stabbing toward me. I focused on the blade, the handle, a new energy vibrating through my skin.

Echo dropped the sword with a scream, bracing his palm in his gut. "You burned me!"

I thought of the witch magic, the spelled iron, the power living in his sword. Somehow I'd instinctively taken the magic back out.

"You have no power here," I warned, reaching down to grab the sword for myself.

"Neither do you," he spat back.

"But I do."

A man stood across the platform, his livid expression focused on Echo. I hadn't seen him before, but I could feel the power in my blood. Instinctively, I knew him. He was the true king. His blood had sealed the cracks. But how?

"Mylus," Echo stated dryly. "Still alive?"

"Eternally," the man growled, his tone dark and threatening. "But you already knew that."

He slowly circled the slab to stand behind me, stopping when he reached Ava, though his gaze still held Echo's.

Echo's witch looked just as lost behind him, staring at a ghost.

The true king's hand lifted, wrist snapping toward the enemy. Echo fell to his knees, screaming against the air.

The witch jumped forward reflexively, hands raising at Mylus in return, when something lunged toward her feet. She slammed against the stone as a wolf bit into her leg. His teeth ripped through her, clenched tightly inside her flesh. She cried out, stilling as Elijah's eyes locked on hers, daring her to move before looking past her to the king.

"It's her shadow," Mylus warned. "Her soul already drowned in the black pool, her shadow must drown there too."

The wolf's teeth dug in deeper, new screams scratching the air as she thrashed, desperate, clawing at the stones as the wolf dragged her down each step.

Mylus shifted his attention back to Echo, his face pressed to the ground with strained whimpers of agony.

"It's like shards of glass, racing through your veins," Mylus cooly stated. He was so calm as he slowly stepped around Echo's vulnerable body. "Your own world. Rejecting you."

"No," Echo fought out. "Please."

"Why should I show you any mercy?" Mylus challenged, clearly drawing out the suffering.

"Mylus," Echo whined, dragging himself off the ground to his knees.

The king knelt to brush his fingers over the fallen mirror shards, as if he were studying his reflection inside them, not worried about the enemy at his back.

"I wouldn't do that to the mortals," he mused, thinking over his options. He grabbed a long piece, looking it over, then turned to stab it through Echo's heart.

"Die," he ordered. Still holding the dagger between them. "And don't come back."

Echo's body fell back, a shard of glass sticking up from his chest as the returning king turned toward Ava and me.

"Sage Thost," he greeted, but his attention went straight for my fallen friend.

"I think she hit her head," I told him. He put his hand over her eyes and closed his own.

"You can heal her."

"I can't—" I stared at my hands, remembering that I'd felt the change. "I can feel it," I gave in. "What do I do?"

"Grab her hand," he instructed. I listened, picking it up off the stone. "Close your eyes, and focus on her pain." I tried to relax, doing as he told me to. I could feel the pulse of pain that pounded with her weak heartbeat.

"I see it."

"Wish it away," he said. I focused on the pain, like a red burn that needed to be soothed. I wanted to cool it, to take the burden off her heart.

"It's working," he said as Harper ran up behind us. "She'll be okay."

I let go, watching Mylus take over, carefully adjusting her neck.

Mylus.

"You're her Mylo," I said as the truth sank in. I'd heard a

bit about her amnesia trip. Now she had a dangerously cute king tending to her wounds?

He lightly bowed.

And he had good manners.

I turned, finding the other fallen body behind me. I crawled for Rogue, grabbing his hand and closing my eyes. I searched for his pain, denial tightening my face as I dug deeper, fighting back my tears when I couldn't find it. I couldn't find anything.

I was too late.

"Grim," I cried, my head falling against his chest. He was gone. He'd sacrificed himself to save me.

"Leave him," Mylo instructed. I glared up at him, but his expression was empathetic. "Willow is in the hospital. Go now, you might not get another chance—"

Ava weakly stirred, her eyes fluttering open as Mylo knelt supportingly at her side.

"I can heal her," I insisted. My hands shook, I kept losing people over and over again. I had to do something to stop it.

"You can't heal dead blood," Mylo argued.

"This world should have helped her! Instead it brought death closer!"

"This world can't fix dead blood. Our magic can only slow it down, give her body a chance at more time."

"No. No more people are dying." My hand squeezed Rogue's tight, not ready to let him go. We were supposed to stick together forever. Tears fell from my eyes as I pressed my head to his chest one last time. "There has to be another way."

"A curse," Ava weakly offered, her head leaning back to look at Mylo. "Like you."

"She's human," he argued. "It's not the same."

"Put her in-between worlds," I countered, head shooting back up. "Like Elijah."

"She'd be living on frozen time," Harper answered, her eyes sad as she came closer, a soft hand at my back. "Stuck on a lonely, eternal loop."

"I have to do something!" I cried.

"Go now," Mylo insisted again. "I'll make sure he's taken care of." I searched his eyes, the restored king. This was his world now, and I knew I could trust him.

"And Ava?" I asked, his eyes falling to hers. Her head rolled against his chest, answering for us both.

He nodded at me, and I knew he'd get her home safe.

"I'm coming back," I told him.

"I know."

AFTER

66

HARPER

Who would have thought going back to her normal sick could be an improvement. Willow was worn out, but she was steady. Somehow we'd bought her a little bit more time to sort things out.

Life seemed so normal not that long before, but that one week had destroyed her. It almost destroyed all of us, but she was barely hanging on. I had to believe she would heal.

The waiting room was crowded. So many faces without words to say, minds that hadn't processed everything we'd been through.

Elijah sat at my side, holding my hand the way he'd held it since he found me again. I'd just gotten to the hospital with Sage when he'd stormed through the doors to hunt me down, to claim my heart, and I never wanted him to let go. I leaned into his shoulder, squeezing his fingers tightly in mine as I listened to the world through him, and this time his soul knew such a new sense of peace.

"The shift happened too quickly," he told me, going over that last night in my dream. *"The hunt. I fought so hard, but*

the curse held no mercy. Then the door opened, and you were gone. You were safe."

"And you were alone again."

"Yes, but you were safe." He pressed something into my hand. *"That's all I truly wanted."*

"What's this?" I looked down at the clear glass bottle, holding several ounces of what looked like water.

"It's from the hourglass. It's portal water. Before they created the lines and split the portal, the witches used to use it in their spells. A powerful ingredient. The curse that held this water is broken, but the magic still holds. It's part of our story. I wanted you to have it."

My fingers slid over the glass in admiration, remembering the way the water slowly dripped down the hourglass, ticking away Elijah's eternal torment.

Zager was restless, only ever able to sit a moment before he'd stand back up to pace the walkway. Guilt shined in his eyes, holding the floor in front of each step as if he'd walked Willow right up to the edge of her mortality himself.

Sage was equally on edge, brainstorming any loophole around the magic.

I still couldn't figure out how we'd ended up tangled in this other world all at once. If only Sam could be there with us to see the world of her dreams. Amidst all the questions still lingering, the haunted nightmare, the ghosts, the curse, as I looked at the moon through the window, I felt peace.

Sage stood from her chair. "I'll spell the metal in her leg." I sat up, listening closely through Elijah's ears. Zager froze, staring into her eyes.

"I took the magic from Echo's iron. I could put that same kind of magic into Willow."

"The world wouldn't reject her body anymore," I agreed in a rush of hope, realizing Sage might actually be onto something. "Could it work?" My gaze flickered from Elijah to Zager.

"I don't see any other options," Zager answered.

"And your home is still in-between," I added, looking back at Elijah. "It's free now, she could be connected to both worlds. Live on your time, in a place where our world can still reach her."

The broken home he'd walked away from flashed through my mind. The burned walls, the overgrown fields. The skeletons of horses that had walked with him for so many hollow years. Even the greenhouse lost its magic when I broke the curse.

"In the truce, the witch blessed our soil to live as long as our pack," he mentally explained *"The pack died the day of the fire. The curse that kept it alive is broken."* I could feel the pain squeezing his heart, everything that kept him going for so long through his imprisonment was taken. *"It died. Left as it would have been without the magic."*

It was exactly as the fire left it. Broken.

"But it's still home," I corrected. *"It brought me you. It will always be ours."*

I thought of the wishing well, the silver roses, the orchards, and towering stone walls. We could fix it, restore the beauty those grounds once knew.

He looked at me, seeing the optimism in my thoughts, the hope for a new future.

"We'll rebuild it," I told him sternly. "You and me."

I looked back to Zager, still frozen in deep contemplation.

"You're sure you can do it?" he asked Sage.

She nodded confidently. "I can do it."

67

WILLOW

The blankets draping over my body weighed me down. A corpse in a coffin, lying in a grave, that's all it could have been.

I opened my eyes slowly, the blurry silhouette of wings shadowing out the light.

An angel?

"Willow?" Zager's voice broke through the fog as he leaned in at my side. My eyes opened slowly, searching for focus as I looked into his face. My hand pulled free of the heavy blankets to reach for his cheek.

"Zager?"

He grabbed my hand supportingly, and his face fell into it, taking a moment.

"I thought I died."

"Not yet," he answered, pulling my hand with him as he sat back up with a teary-eyed smile. "Not yet."

I searched his face, still trying to remember.

"We're at the shifter castle, between your world and mine." My attention shifted to the big open room around us, the stone walls nothing like a hospital room would be.

"The metal—"

"A certain witch spelled it," he explained. "The magic won't reject you anymore." My eyes bounced back and forth between his, trying to keep up.

"You mean I can stay?" I asked, processing what it all meant. *Stay where? Stay with him?*

"You can stay," he answered.

"I can't believe it," I admitted, blinking back my surprise.

Nazurin stood from the corner behind his brother.

My brows rose, swallowing back my surprise. "You're here."

He smiled warmly. "So are you." He reached for the door. "I'll just go tell the girls."

"The girls?" I asked hopefully, scrunching back on my elbows to lean up against the headboard. "My friends are here?" *My* friends. That was the first time I'd claimed them as my own, instead of Sam's.

Zager nodded with a smile. "They're here," he confirmed, softly supporting me as I sat up.

"Hey Naz?" I asked before he stepped all the way out. He paused to look back at me. All that pain between us hadn't been resolved. Not for me. Words I hadn't had the chance to say.

"I'm so sorry you never got to meet her."

"She was special. That's what drew me to her. She had all the magic of my world, with nothing but herself."

I nodded, a tear falling from my eye. Sam was exactly that. "Thank you," I whispered, and he stepped out completely.

I relaxed into the pillow. "It was like the strangest dream," I told Zager.

"Tell me about it."

I muffled a laugh. "Well. I could have sworn you had wings."

He looked down with a smile. "Uh oh. You might be starting to see past the glamor," he mocked. My jaw dropped. "My fae magic hides them. Sure makes walking around your world unnoticed a lot easier."

"Unnoticed?" Of course he had more fae tricks. "Your magic is why I thought I saw Nazurin that night we met, isn't it."

"I wanted you to see Nazurin. If I found someone who knew him, then I found him too."

And I'd led him right where he wanted. "It also explains why those boys at the party didn't see you kidnapping me after."

"Hey, I carried you home." His smile stretched wider, unashamed. "I took you, and you're stuck with me now. In my world."

"Sam's world," I countered, wishing she could have seen it.

"Our world," he corrected.

I shifted forward, leaning into him. "You saved me," I whispered.

The door bounced open as Sage burst through, Ava and Harper on her tail.

"You're awake!" Ava called.

"Finally!" Harper agreed. "How do you feel?"

"Honestly? For once I feel kind of... normal." I laughed. "I feel good." My gaze landed on Sage, pulling up a timid seat next to me, reaching for my hands. "Thanks to you."

Her cheeks warmed as she returned the smile.

"Has it really only been a couple of weeks?" I asked them, looking from face to face. So much could happen in such little time. "Longest days of my life."

"Worst ever," Ava grumbled sarcastically.

Everybody laughed, as Harper shrugged. "But weren't they also kind of amazing?" she asked.

The laughter softened into teary smiles as we soaked up this little taste of happy.

68

SAGE

The air around me was drowning in joy, but it still couldn't patch the fresh hole in my heart.

Two weeks before, my only worry was getting through one last year of high school. I was a different person now. Everything had changed. The life I'd known before was gone. I'd ventured deep into the unknown and became something new.

I'd lost everything along the way. And then I lost him.

I fidgeted with the wrap on my hand, covering the gash Echo made in my palm. Harper squeezed my elbow, sitting next to me at the edge of Willow's bed. Her head rested knowingly on my shoulder, like she could see my pain.

It should have been a happy moment, and a part of it was, but I wasn't happy.

I was an orphan. It didn't feel like I had much of a home to go back to, because how could that house ever feel like home again? I couldn't tell which world held my future, and I couldn't face those questions just yet. The person I was counting on to be there at the end, that while everything fell apart around me, still found a way to make me feel safe, that I wanted to run into the future with, was gone.

I barely registered the low hum of an engine until it echoed closer, up the long gravel driveway.

My muscles stilled, listening closer, waiting to hear what came next. I knew that sound, I wanted to know that sound, but it had to be a trick. My mind fought to deny my heart belief in the impossible, because it couldn't be... the engine cut.

I ran for the empty hall, peeking through windows, but moving too quickly to get a solid look until I reached the last one.

He swung off the side of his bike, straightening the bottom of his black shirt back down. He slid the dark helmet from his head as he turned, looking straight up at me, as if he sensed me there waiting on him.

I ran for the door, racing down the porch to find him as he slid his backpack to the side and pulled out the round silver mirror.

"I think you forgot this—"

"Rogue!" I dove into him, crying against his neck, my composure cracking as his arms wrapped tightly around my waist. "Don't ever let me wake up."

"You're not dreaming," he assured me in that gravelly tone I'd missed so much.

"But you were dead." I pulled away, ignoring the tears falling down my cheeks as I framed my hands around his face, studying every inch of it.

"I was dead," he agreed. "But not forever."

I searched his eyes, trying to understand. Then I remembered his story. "Nina stabbed you through the heart." He'd died before. "The blood bounty," I commented, filtering through my memories, realizing he'd never truly explained what that meant.

"The blood bounty," he confirmed. "Echo's father, Cosimo, he knew my gift was the one he needed in order to track down your bloodline. He wasn't willing to lose me... so he tied me to it. Before Sila, I thought I just had to complete the mission to be free. When I realized I live and die with it, it changed everything. I knew I was being used, I did, but realizing how deep it went made me stubborn. I fought against it so hard."

"That's when you went rogue," I commented.

"If you die, we both die. If I die, we live."

"I thought... the mirrors, Mylo, everything was broken."

"The spell was never completed," Rogue explained. "He did all the steps, but he never said the words. There's a lot to figure out, but me and you? I've been hunting your ancestors for years, Sage. I'm tethered to you. As long as your blood lives, so does my hunt."

"And now that you've caught me?" I whispered just between us. "What will you do next?"

His head dropped, mouth quirking into a faint smile as he softly nodded, eyes peeking up at me. "I already told you, we should stick together."

I smiled. "Stick with you? A stranger?"

"What, are you going to run away again?" he challenged.

My forehead fell against his shoulder, leaning on him with all the stress and heartache I'd endured. "Only if you promise to chase me."

"I'm still tempted to tie you to my side," his gruff voice muttered, one arm reaching up to rub over my back. "I heard you have your magic now," he added, leaning back only long enough to pull something from his pocket and lift it between us. He unwrapped a smooth stone from a dirty, wrinkled blue ribbon.

"Is that my ribbon?"

"Finders keepers," he said, handing me the stone, twisting the ribbon back up in his hand. "It's mine now." My fingers brushed over the gift in silence.

"It's a dragon scale," he explained, still looking at his hand as he fidgeted with the blue fabric.

"Wow, a dragon scale?" I repeated. "It's beautiful!"

"They react to witch magic. Maybe you can learn some tricks with it."

"Thank you." I held it in one hand as he set the silver mirror in the other.

"King Mylus said that belonged to you."

I thought again of my ancestor, Kia. A woman Mylo still loved and honored after so many years of pain. She must have been so strong. I opened it up, finding the beautiful stretch of forest that mirrored back.

"After Kett stole this, he could have just used it to take me back, but he dragged me all the way to that line instead."

"Each mirror connects to a specific line," Rogue commented. "He must not have wanted to go where this one led."

I was still trying to process that there was an entire territory of witches once led by my far-back grandmother. One day I would have to learn that land, meet that corner of another world, but not yet. First I wanted to know myself.

"What, are you going to start wearing ribbons now?" I asked as I snapped it shut, nodding my head toward the blue fabric.

"Just the one," he countered, starting to wrap it over his wrist.

"Here," I offered, grabbing the ends to double around

again before tying a knot, my fingers hesitating to let go. "Where will we go?" I asked, finally letting my hands fall to my sides.

His head was down, but he peeked up at me. "Anywhere you want."

I hugged my arms around him, and he only hesitated a moment before softening into it.

"Somewhere nobody can find us?" I asked.

"You want to disappear?"

"You think you could make that happen?"

"Of course I can. Nobody goes Rogue like me."

"The rogue witch," I commented, letting my chin rest against the front of his shoulder, memorizing the feathering of the arrows sticking out behind him. Hunter arrows. I loved the idea of it. Disappearing. It was so tempting. I'd lost so much and I wasn't ready to face what came next. I wanted to run away instead, to be free, to heal, and he was everything that I wanted to take with me.

"Yeah," he agreed. "Has a nice ring to it."

69

AVA

I sat by Willow on the couch as Zager got up to find her a glass of water. She looked so different, so much more alive. So much healthier than the unconscious girl Zager smuggled out of a hospital room under fae glamor a few days before. She was finally awake, as if she'd been cursed all along and she could finally breathe.

Sam would have been so happy to see her like this. To see a little spark of hope shining in her eyes again. She still had to face doctors, tests, and a search for answers, but now she had a safe place to slow down while she waited. Zager was so loyal to her, diligent about filling every need, eager to keep a touch of magic at her side.

We'd spent days cleaning out the shifter castle, the starting steps of a rebuild. Elijah's love for his home was tangible, there was a certain element of respect that I'd never felt before. So many had fallen within those grounds.

"I want to bring out the beauty still hiding in these walls," Harper told everyone, giving us jobs to do. Elijah was more than content letting her lead, as if he trusted that she knew it well enough to balance what was, with what would be.

"I still can't believe he hired you to help fix this place up," Ben commented, eyeing the world around him cautiously as if something was going to attack from the shadows. His nervous energy made me laugh, same person he'd always been.

"Yeah," she answered. "I guess when he saw me hanging out at the gates so much he felt like I cared about it as much as he did." Harper shrugged. "What can I say, it just kept pulling me in." Her eyes flashed to Elijah for a split second, who gave her a knowing smile. I guess she wasn't going to stick to her light-hearted rom-coms after all.

Josh was quieter than I remembered, awkwardly following Ben around. Harper seemed to sense it too as Elijah stepped in around them to kiss her forehead.

Ben shook his head as Elijah walked past. "So weird," he commented quietly.

"Well at least we're neighbors now," she added, free living while she worked there being part of the story. "I won't even make you climb the fence to come visit," she mocked. Josh's eyes widened at her.

"The fight's not over yet," she joked, reaching forward to shove his arm. Then she handed him something, it looked like a gold coin. He stared at it, his finger rubbing the edge as he flipped it over in his palm.

"To replace the one you lost," she explained.

He smiled as he took a step back, sliding it into his pocket as Ben turned to follow.

"Can't complain about the distance," Ben agreed. "Come get your hot cocoa fix anytime."

"Deal," she said, looking so purely happy as she watched them leave.

"So this is the game night you speak so highly of," Rogue commented later that evening, looking at Harper across a small table of cards. He was the perfect rival to her competitive streak, taking their round of poker equally serious.

Sage laughed under her breath, leaning into his side. She'd been quieter since coming back, different, but how could she not be after all that she'd gone through? All that had happened to her? All that she'd learned?

We'd all left her, and Rogue was the one who stepped in to fix it. I didn't miss the way her cheeks flushed when he caught her staring. Something deep had rooted between them, some connection I couldn't explain. She was as attached to his side as he to hers, ready to guard her against the world, both worlds, and a person like that is all I could have wanted for her.

Come find me where the magic's mix.

I scanned the faces around me, the people that had come together from two separate worlds and become a family. The magic had mixed, and it was beautiful.

I cuddled in closer to Willow.

"I think we found her," I told her, imagining Sam's spirit there with us. Harper stared at me intently from across the table. For a moment, she seemed lost, until Rogue put a card down and she jumped back into the game with a smile.

"I think you're right," Willow agreed. "It feels like we all found ourselves too." Her fingers played in the hair at my back. "What about you?"

"Me?" My smile fell.

I'd tried not to think of Mylo. He'd gone from being stuck in my world, to ruling the world I wanted no part of. Where did that leave our twisted friendship? I wasn't sure.

"What about me?" I countered, pulling the long black sleeves tighter over my hands.

"What will you do?" she asked.

I sighed. "I'm going to go home and carry on with life the way I always planned to." I was always going to help my dad work, I needed to stay productive, it's who I was.

I didn't belong in that other world, and Mylo did. He was the king of it. My spot remained as it always was, normal and mundane. It was the life I was born with, and the life I knew.

"Okay," she answered, letting the conversation fall. "But you should still say goodbye."

70

AVA

I'd never been so nervous, stepping up to the familiar circle of rocks, but it was silly. I knew what was on the other side, I knew he would find me. Maybe that's what scared me so deeply.

The raven dropped through between the branches, making me jump. I softly laughed at myself for being so ridiculous.

"Hello, Oco," I greeted.

"I wondered if you would ever come back."

I spun around, startled by the man in the shadows.

"Mylo."

He walked closer, staring deep into my eyes, and somehow everything that had happened between us was all right there out in the open.

"I didn't realize you were waiting," I answered.

"Yeah, well, it's just that there's this one thing I never did get to find out about you," he commented. "Something I've been dying to know."

"What's that?"

"You never told me your favorite book."

I smiled, remembering the answer I'd given people for years, ever since my friends started writing.

"My favorite book is the one I haven't read yet," I told him. "The one that hasn't been written." I looked forward to reading every word Harper published, always excited for what would come next.

He smiled, accepting it for what it was. My heart squeezed, knowing this moment was fleeting.

"So you're a king," I commented. It was hard to imagine that small boy from his little cottage all those years before, chasing his sisters through the trees, only to grow up to rule a kingdom. I'd skipped some chapters, and there was so much more to the story than I'd ever have time to learn.

"Thanks to you."

He was only a couple of steps away when I couldn't hold back anymore, rushing forward to lean into his hold. There was no fear now, no worry about his control. No question whether he would hurt me.

"How are you?" he asked.

"Alive," I answered. "Because of you." It was the only word I could think of, but it felt like the most important one.

"Me too," he answered. "You freed me."

I stepped back from the hug, eager to push away the praise before he said more.

"How about you?" I asked him. "How are you?"

"Free." His smile stretched wider, repeating that one, perfect word.

"Are you going to erase the lines between our worlds?" I asked before I could stop myself, surprised by how afraid I felt of the answer. He had all the power to do it now.

"Do you want me to?"

I didn't know how to answer. "I want to live in my

world," I admitted, avoiding the big, lingering question between us. It's all I did know.

"I know."

"And you belong in yours."

His gaze dropped between us. "I do," he agreed. "It was never about cutting off the magic. It was always about cutting out me. Cutting out Elijah. Taking out the witch. If Echo had closed the gates, the three of us would be lost forever. Our fates sealed. He would never have to worry about us finding our way back."

"No," I finally whispered. "I don't want you to take the lines away. I might live here, but I don't want to be cut off for good."

"Then I won't," he answered, pulling me back in.

He pushed something into my arms. I leaned back to look at it, the old, worn-out, handwritten book about his world.

"I want you to have it," he told me. "Keep it on that special shelf of first editions."

"Are you sure?"

"It's an only edition. The stories I've kept to myself for all these years. They're yours now."

I opened up the first page, where a new piece of paper waited with a list of titles neatly written down it, books under different pen names. Stories that had been popular, others not. Ones I'd read at the library and loved completely. Some of the sad, black-covered books that lined his office shelf.

"What are these— These are your—" I could hardly say the words. His books. He'd written them. I thought of all the times he sat in his office, typing away. How he never actually had anybody there for psychiatry sessions. The perfect job for someone who lived forever, changing their name every few years for the next book.

"The accounts have all been transferred into your name. I was never truly meant to be a part of your world, but you are. Whatever I made of my life there, I leave to you."

My jaw dropped, staring at the list of titles and pen names. I adjusted the page with my thumb, barely noticing the bank statements behind it.

"Every penny of it is yours," he added, answering more unasked questions. "It's all there, completely taken care of. Check it when you're ready."

"But... Why?"

"In all my years on your side of the line, you were the only thing I found that ever mattered to me. You broke my mind from the mundane prison it was caged in. I was asleep, and you woke me up. You saved me, Ava. You gave me everything. I could never leave you in a world where you know need."

I closed the book and hugged it tight, a new sort of tears pooling into my eyes. He'd given me everything, including the journal of all his secrets. Secrets of another world that still knew my name. That fact had haunted me, and I still worried what would come next.

"Nazurin told me some souls in my world are marked for knowing too much of yours... that the magic hunts them down." I stared into his eyes. "Will that ever happen to me?"

His jaw flexed, contemplating for a moment, before he lifted his hand, and softly bit his wrist. He wiped his thumb across the cut before sliding down the collar over my chest to press it above my heart.

I stared at his eyes as he held it there, waiting to understand why.

"My blood," he explained. "From now on, you have my mark. My world will recognize you as my own. You're under my protection and the magic will honor that." He pulled his thumb back, fixing the collar of my shirt back into place.

"I'll burn any world that would dare come after you, mine or yours. You'll live a safe life."

Safe. But so alone. Why did everyone have to feel so far away?

"But what if I still need *you?*" I asked, desperate for that moment to never end. There would never be normal again after knowing him.

He leaned in, kissing my forehead.

"Then you know right where to find me." He stepped up to the stone circle with one last look of goodbye. "And, for the record, Ava... I'll always be waiting."

71

WILLOW

I couldn't sleep, stepping down the cold steps toward the kitchen. The light was already on, the sound of papers being shuffled around as I turned the corner.

"Harper?" I asked. A mess of pages sat out on the counter as she scribbled down a note, drawing a line to connect it to something else.

"What are you doing?"

She stood straighter, her smile wide. "I'm solving her puzzle!" she answered. "Sam's puzzle."

"What puzzle? What are you talking about?"

"She left us a puzzle! It's like a treasure hunt, Willow! How did we miss it?"

"Harper—"

"Don't," she argued, cutting off my doubt.

"She wrote it herself," Harper went on. "Her poem! It was a message! She knew about their world! She left us a clue, don't you see it?"

I stepped around the counter slowly, scanning over the pages. One highlighted line caught my eye, just as Harper picked up the paper, holding it between us to point it out.

"It's just like Ava was saying before, we can still find her! Come find me where the magics mix!" Harper said, excitedly. "It was right here all along!"

"What are you trying to say?" I asked, chocking back the unexpected surge of emotions. "Sam died right in front of me. I saw her face. She wouldn't disappear like that, leave us like that! If that were true, she would have gone with Nazurin!"

"There had to be a reason for it," Harper agreed, nodding her head before her eyes snapped back to mine. My mouth gaped as I watched her, speechless.

"She's out there somewhere," Harper insisted, unwilling to see it any other way. "She's out there, and I'm going to find her."

DEAD

EARLIER THAT YEAR

"You were there. In my dream. How— I don't understand any of this, you get that right? How insane this is?"

"I get it."

"But it's real." I took a deep breath, there wasn't time to debate.

"It's real," he confirmed.

"Did you—"

"Yes. I've already planted the story. What's done is done. It's time." He shook his head disapprovingly, leaning slightly closer. "You shouldn't have written it that way. Someone is going to look."

He meant my poem. I rewrote the last line. If that was all I could leave behind, I was doing it. They had to know a small piece of me still lived. The magic could still live.

A ghost.

I looked back at Willow's room. When she woke up, I would be dead. I wasn't going to be there to help her anymore, to make sure she got better, to be her friend, to make her smile.

Either way, I wasn't going to be there.

Every relationship I had was over.

Every dream I'd dreamt was lost.

"Dead man walking," I whispered, turning toward the only future I had left.

"Dead man walking," he confirmed, pulling the door wide as I stepped through it, before following me out.

~

For updates on Book Two

AFTER MAGICS MIX

Follow Author V. T. Wren
on Facebook/Instagram/Tiktok

Learn more at:

thestoriesofscheetz.com

~

www.ingramcontent.com/pod-product-compliance
Lightning Source LLC
Chambersburg PA
CBHW051533250626
4715CB00001B/36